Benedict Canyon

Also by Laura Van Wormer

RIVERSIDE DRIVE

WEST END

LAURA VAN WORMER

Benedict Canyon

CROWN PUBLISHERS, INC.

New York

Grateful acknowledgment is made to Ann Hampton Callaway for permission to reprint an excerpt of lyrics from "How Can I Trust my Heart?" Copyright © 1991 by Ann Hampton Callaway.

Published by Crown Publishers, Inc., 201 East 50th Street, New York, New York 10022. Member of the Crown Publishing Group.

CROWN is a trademark of Crown Publishers, Inc.

Manufactured in the United States of America

Library of Congress Cataloging-in-Publication Data
Van Wormer, Laura
Benedict Canyon / Laura Van Wormer.—1st. ed.
p. cm.
I. Title
PS3572.A42285B46   1992
813'.54—dc20   91-33188
CIP

ISBN 0-517-58402-6

10 9 8 7 6 5 4 3 2 1

First Edition

For

Donna Mills

whose wisdom, talent, and beauty
inspired the idea for this story

With love and heartfelt thanks to

my miracle-working agent
Loretta A. Barrett

my wonderful attorney
Susan A. Grode

and my brilliant editor
Betty A. Prashker

who have a lot in common besides A as a middle initial
—like warmth, humor, and indefatigable esprit—

and

Nancy Evans

whose generosity as a friend
has changed everything in my life for the better

C O N T E N T S

C O N T E N T S

P R O L O G U E

Kate tried to listen to the conversation with detachment, like an out-sider holding no previous opinion.

"I don't care what the hell it is," Mr. Rushman said, "but we have to have something between two covers with Lydia Southland's name on it for the fall."

Oh, dear. Even an outsider would know that this was no way for a reputable book publisher to be talking.

"Do you hear that, Kate?" Rebecca de Loup said. "No la-di-da editorial aspirations—just get something out of her that resembles English."

Kate blinked. At thirty-three, she was an executive editor of the publishing house of Bennett, Fitzallen & Coe, and yet, until this mo-ment, she had failed to appreciate just how horrendous things had gotten. She glanced over at Mark—Mark Fiducia, the senior editor whose office was next to hers—and wondered if, listening to this, he felt as ill as she did.

Bennett, Fitzallen & Coe had entered the 1980s a distinguished inde-pendent giant of book publishing and had emerged from the decade a minor subsidiary of an international partnership formed by an Italian movie studio, a Japanese computer manufacturer, and a German print-ing operation, which, on this side of the Atlantic, was called Heartland Communications America.

As often happens to newcomers to American trade book publishing (that is, companies who sell fiction and nonfiction to the general "trade" public, as opposed to textbooks), after the new parent corpora-tion had streamlined the publishing house "to make it run like a proper business," Bennett, Fitzallen & Coe went from making a little profit to making no profit at all—and alienating many of its leading authors in the process.

Executives came, executives went; publishers were told to fire, pub-lishers were told to hire; every publisher was told to fire half of what they had hired and then the publishers themselves were fired and a new publisher was hired; and on and on and on it went, around and around, a merry madhouse of literary mayhem.

And still, Bennett, Fitzallen & Coe did not make a profit.

Last year, fed up with this unprofitable venture in "illogical" American trade book publishing, Heartland Communications America brought in yet one more publisher to run Bennett, Fitzallen & Coe, this time an executive from a subsidiary of theirs in Chicago. Andrew Rushman—or *Mr.* Rushman, as he preferred to be called—was not from the world of publishing. Mr. Rushman was from the toy business, where, evidently, he was quite famous for having revolutionized the distribution discount system of something called The Klicky Kart® Toy Collection.

The book industry in general did not react well to Mr. Rushman's appointment. But, as is true with all things, bad times for some made good times for others, and Kate Weston's career at Bennett, Fitzallen & Coe had blossomed as a result. She had always been known as a gifted editor in the industry—one for whom agents clamored to have take over on their client's book, often a client whose editor had been fired or driven from the house—but perhaps just as importantly in these short-tempered times, Kate Weston was known for great manners, warmth, and tact. As a matter of fact, many said it was her capability as a kind of gracious editorial lion tamer that was her key to success.

Kate also possessed a working knowledge of Bennett, Fitzallen & Coe that people found extraordinary, although she didn't find it so amazing. From the day she had arrived as secretary to the publisher almost twelve years before, she had made it her business to learn as much about the company as she could. She read the publisher's important files while doing the filing during her first year there; she made time to read through tedious contract files; she made friends in the copyediting, sales, sub rights, royalty, marketing, art, production, and business departments, asking endless questions about what it was they did; and in later years she traveled to company warehouses, visited major retail accounts, and combed the company's historical archives (now disintegrating unattended in some warehouse), because Kate Weston, from day one, had fully intended to become publisher of Bennett, Fitzallen & Coe herself. And last year, when Mr. Rushman promoted her to executive editor, Kate thought she was well on her way.

There seemed to be the distinct possibility of late, however, that there might not be a publishing house left to be publisher of, not if Mr. Rushman continued in his obsession for short-term profit at the expense of any long-range planning. And chief among Mr. Rushman's supporters in doing business this way was Rebecca de Loup, the marketing person he had brought in as an associate publisher less than a year ago.

Rebecca was extremely bright, but not so bright that Kate couldn't see how she was endearing herself to Mr. Rushman while also encouraging him to do himself in, and, at the same time, setting herself up with the parent corporation as indispensable. She had convinced Mr. Rushman to fire the fifty-six-year-old editor in chief and then had assigned his list of books to herself. Voilà! Rebecca was suddenly the editor of some of the house's bestselling writers without ever having spent a single day as an editor before.

The first trick for a noneditor like Rebecca was to take over on bestselling writers who either no longer needed to be edited or refused to be edited, and who were therefore primarily interested in how their books were marketed—which, in this case, was an area where Rebecca had both the clout and the experience to deliver. The second trick was to pass off books that needed to be edited to other editors, but in such a way so as to make it look like professional generosity instead of editorial incompetence. Rebecca executed both of these tricks beautifully and, the next thing everyone knew, Rebecca *was* the editor in chief, which, understandably, made Kate's back go up for more reasons than one.

Rebecca of course despised Kate. It was not hard to see why. Where Rebecca bluffed, Kate called her on it; where Rebecca bullied, Kate ran interference; when Rebecca got angry, Kate got more pleasant than pleasant; and when Rebecca complained to Mr. Rushman about Kate's "attitude," Kate explained to Mr. Rushman that she thought Rebecca resented her close working relationship with him.

Mr. Rushman would then smile fondly at Kate—he really did like her, she knew, and a lot more than simple office relations would dictate (which was why she avoided him late at night at sales conferences, Christmas parties, and the like, because he got *that* look in his eye after a couple of drinks and Kate had had bosses like that before)—and he would say something like, "Just try to stay out of her way, Kate. It's hard for her to have another dynamo down the hall, but for it to be such a terrific-looking woman to boot . . ."

The most troubled book project currently at Bennett, Fitzallen & Coe also happened to be the book the company most desperately needed to publish: the autobiography of Lydia Southland, the knockout gorgeous TV actress made internationally famous by "Cassandra's World," the hour-long fantasy/adventure costume drama in which she played Cassandra Hale, a history professor who each week found herself in the shoes of some famous woman in history. Mata Hari, Isadora Duncan, Cleopatra, Susan B. Anthony, Catherine the Great, Amelia Earhart—she had played them all, with "Ms. Southland bending history," as *TV Guide* said, "in *all* the right places."

"Cassandra's World" was currently being aired in sixty-seven countries around the world, illegally circulating in videocassette form in another nineteen, and was rating number-three in America in the Nielsen's. The show was actually pretty good, and Kate herself rather liked it; and while the story lines were always implausibly romantic—honestly, Susan B. Anthony as a femme fatale?—Cassandra was also a wickedly bright female lead who broke with TV tradition in a refreshing way.

The history of Ms. Southland's autobiography, however, was as complicated and troubled as that of her publishing house. In the last three years she had hired and fired three writers to work with her and had gone through no less than four Bennett, Fitzallen & Coe editors: the editor who had originally signed up Ms. Southland had been fired by the house, admittedly; but then Ruthie Renquist had been called a "she-beast" by Ms. Southland and was escorted from the premises by the Beverly Hills police; Ayres Hasnack had been sent home under the threat of a sexual harassment suit; and then the last "editor," none other than Rebecca de Loup herself, had been banished for the simple reason that Ms. Southland said she hated her. ("Intimidated, I think," Rebecca had sniffed in the editorial meeting. "She's not a very secure lady.")

And so now the Southland mess, as it was called within the company, had been assigned to Kate.

"Understand?" Rebecca was saying now to Kate. "Just bring back something we can publish. It doesn't have to win the Pulitzer Prize."

Kate nodded. "I'll do my best."

"Good," Mr. Rushman said, leaning forward on his desk. "Now, Rebecca's set everything up—be at Southland's tomorrow by one."

"You have the plane tickets?" Rebecca asked her.

"They came by messenger this morning," Kate said.

Rebecca glanced at Mr. Rushman and then back to Kate, raising an eyebrow. "The travel agent said you changed your hotel. He said you're going to stay in Santa Monica. Near the beach."

"It's less expensive than where you stayed," Kate said, "by about a hundred twenty dollars a night." *Ha, ha, Rebecca,* she thought.

"Good girl," Mr. Rushman said. He turned to Mark. "And you'll stay on top of things in Kate's office, right? This could take a while."

"No sweat," Mark said, smiling.

It would be a sweat, Kate knew. They were down to a skeletal staff in the company, and her office, like Mark's and everybody else's (except Rebecca's, of course) was overwhelmed with inherited books from editors who had been fired. But if Mark had to stay until three every morning to keep an eye on her office, Kate knew he would. He was, after all, her best friend at work. Quite probably in life, too.

Mr. Rushman turned to Kate. "Rebecca picked out something for you to give Southland—as a peace offering." Rushman brought up a large square box, elegantly wrapped, from behind his desk.

"What is it?" Kate said.

"A vase," Rebecca said. "It cost a fortune, so don't break it."

Now how am I supposed to carry this thing across the country? Kate wondered, taking the box from Rushman. *As if it couldn't be shipped.* This last thought made Kate think she had better open it to make sure there wasn't a bomb inside.

The meeting over, Kate and Mark walked down the hall to their offices. Mark was thinking, absently rubbing his beard. Not for the first time Kate thought how cute he was with this new addition to his face. And his glasses. His ex-wife's leaving had at least freed him to look the way he wanted to.

"Something's not right," Mark said. "Rebecca's being too helpful."

"I know," Kate said, "believe me, I know."

"And if I were you," he added, nodding to the box in her hands, "I'd open that thing to make sure it's not a bomb."

Kate laughed, thinking how it was true: great minds did think alike.

ONE

Editor and Actress

"Yes, hello?" the voice through the box outside the gate said.

"Hi, it's Kate Weston to see Lydia Southland," Kate said to the box from her car.

"One moment, please," the voice said. It was a lady's voice, Hispanic. She sounded very nice.

It was a lovely day in Beverly Hills and Kate, being from New York, still hadn't gotten over how wonderful it was to be driving around during the first week of April with the top down on the convertible LeBaron she had rented at the airport. Sitting here, perched at the foot of the Southland driveway, Kate looked around at all the greenery, not believing how lush and full everything was out here already.

No wonder people move to L.A., she thought.

The gate before her was about seven feet high, a solid blockade of wood and steel. Kate was curious about what she'd find on the other side of it. She had once worked on the memoirs of an MGM movie star and wondered how the taste of a television actress in Beverly Hills would rack up against that of the Old Guard in nearby Bel Air.

"Hello?" the Hispanic lady's voice said through the box.

"Hi," Kate said.

"Señora Southland would like to know—" the lady started to say.

There was a hum over the intercom and then Kate heard someone hiss, "Say it!"

Pause.

"The señora," the lady said through the box, "would like to know if you are from that idiot publishing house in New York."

Kate looked at the box.

"Well, yes," she admitted after a moment, pushing her sunglasses higher on her nose. "I came straight from the airport—I was told that Ms. Southland would be expecting me."

"Oh, señora, don't—" Kate heard the lady say.

Suddenly there was a great deal of barking. And then, a moment later, there were two loud *thunks* against the inside of the gate and a pair of German shepherds appeared over the top, baring their fangs at Kate. They disappeared and then—snarling, barking, clawing at the inside of the gate—their heads reappeared over the top again; and then they disappeared, reappeared, and disappeared, again and again and again, bobbing up and down over the gate like two crazed targets in a carnival booth.

"Do not be alarmed, they cannot get out!" the Hispanic lady was shouting through the box.

"If you say so," Kate said, sitting in the open convertible, putting it in reverse just in case.

"But maybe they can!" another woman's voice said, laughing. *"Maybe* they can get out and get you! Maybe you should just get out of here!"

Kate's head snapped around to look at the box. Now *that* was a familiar voice. It was Lydia Southland's.

Bark, bark, bark! Snarl, grrrrrr, bark! the dogs were saying.

Kate cleared her throat. "I take it Ms. Southland is still a bit upset with Bennett, Fitzallen & Coe."

"I'll say!" that familiar voice shouted. "Get out of here!"

"Yes," the Hispanic lady said, "I am afraid that she is."

The box went silent then.

"Well," Kate said after a moment, "I guess that's it, then. If you won't let me in I can't very well help her finish her book."

Silence.

"Hello?" Kate said to the box.

There was a click. "Yes, I am very sorry," the Hispanic lady said, "but I am afraid that is it." Pause. Click. "I cannot let you in. The señora will not let me. I am sorry. Good-bye."

"Okay," Kate said, "but please tell Ms. Southland that I really wanted to work on her book with her. That I didn't have to—that I *wanted* to. I'm a big fan of hers and I felt sure I could help her."

Bark, bark, bark! Snarl, grrrrrr, bark! said the dogs.

"I know the house has messed up things very badly," Kate said, raising her voice, "and normally I wouldn't ask to be assigned to a project with such a troubled history, but I know Ms. Southland's book could be as brilliant as she is as an actress, and I would love to be the editor who could make it happen. And believe it or not—I think Bennett, Fitzallen & Coe would be the ideal publisher for her. We're desperate for a blockbuster this fall and her book would have been the one."

Pause. "I am very sorry," the Hispanic lady said through the box.

A flash of anger swept through Kate. "Please wish Ms. Southland the best of luck for me then," Kate said. "And tell her she can reach me through my office at Bennett, Fitzallen & Coe in New York."

Bark, bark, bark! Snarl, grrrrrr, bark! the dogs said, up and down over the top of the gate.

Kate eased off the brake and backed down onto the road. *I'll strangle Rebecca,* she thought, slamming the car into drive and stepping on the accelerator. She'd been set up. No wonder Rebecca had given her trip to Los Angeles such a big buildup! She knew Southland was through with the house and that Kate would waste considerable time, energy, and money before finding that out. "Why, I have no idea why she wouldn't see you," Kate imagined Rebecca saying to her with a straight face. "Mr. Rushman," Rebecca would say then, turning to him, "as far as I knew, Kate was going to come back with the book. Look, I even saved a two-page spread in the catalog. Why would I do that if I thought she would fail?"

By the time Kate had swerved and curved two miles down Benedict Canyon Drive, she knew her anger and her driving habits were only going to get her lost with great conviction. She pulled off into a driveway, slammed the transmission into park, and yanked a map of Los Angeles out of the side pocket of her briefcase. *Okay, cool it,* she thought, *no need to tear the map apart.*

She took off her sunglasses and pressed the bridge of her nose for a moment, composing herself. A breath. *Okay.* She looked at the map again and saw that Benedict Canyon Drive wound down a couple miles more to meet Sunset Boulevard. Right, she remembered that. The Beverly Hills Hotel was right there, at that corner. Okay, right. She knew where she was.

She'd be damned if she would come home empty-handed. She took a file out of her briefcase and pulled out a sheet of paper upon which her assistant had photocopied a number of her office Rolodex cards. She was looking for Esther and Richard Shapiro Entertainment. *Here they are. North Maple Drive.* Kate checked the map, memorized the turns, and put the map away. Fine. If Southland wouldn't see her, then Kate would see if she couldn't at long last talk the Shapiros into writing a novel. And then there was the rumor to follow up on that Janet Leigh was writing a novel. And then there was young Lisa Hilboldt, the actress, and her novel, the one Kate had heard about through CAA.

Kate felt a little bit better. She wouldn't waste this trip. She'd just be home a heck of a lot sooner.

She carefully backed out of the driveway and continued down the road. Soon she reached the lower portion of Benedict Canyon Drive. The road straightened and then widened, easing to a gentle slope where—in contrast to the winding wilderness of trees, shrubs, fences, and gates above—houses and yards began openly appearing on either side of the road. As she was passing Ambassador Avenue, Kate glanced in the rearview mirror to see a Watson Security patrol car swing out on the road behind her, lights flashing.

"Uh-oh," she said. This wouldn't be the first time she had been stopped for speeding.

Kate pulled over and so did the patrol car. While Kate reached for her purse to find her license and the papers for the car, two uniformed patrolmen got out and walked up to her car. The first patrolman, walking up on Kate's side, smiled and took off his hat. "Kate Weston?" he said.

Kate blinked. "Yes?"

"Mrs. Southland would like you to come back up to the house."

"What?" Kate said, taking off her sunglasses.

"Mrs. Southland would like you to come back up to the house," the patrolman repeated.

Kate looked at him. "You've got to be kidding."

"No," he assured her. "She'd really like you to come back—now, if you please."

Kate burst out laughing and let her head fall back against the head-rest.

The second patrolman laughed, too, resting his hands on the passenger-side door of the car and saying to his partner, "She's got a sense of humor—that's good."

Kate looked at him.

"You must be here about the book," the first patrolman said.

Kate looked back to him.

"We've spent a lot of time chasing people who've worked on it," explained the second.

Kate looked back over at the second patrolman, and then back up at the first again. "You gentlemen are kidding, right?"

"Not really," he said, smiling and showing excellent teeth.

He was handsome, Kate thought. Probably an aspiring actor.

"So you're a writer?" he asked Kate.

Kate shook her head. "No, an editor."

"Oh, an editor," he said, nodding. Pause. He looked at his partner. "Wasn't the one who hit the tree that night an editor?"

"I think so," the second patrolman said. He looked at Kate. "Did you know a Charlene?"

"Turner, sure," Kate said. "But she got fired."

The second patrolman nodded. "Yeah, well, I guess she would have. Drank too much. Lost her license while she was here."

"Lucky that was all she lost," commented the first.

"Mr. Steiner tried to help her," the second one continued. "But it didn't work."

"He works with Mrs. Southland at the studio," the first patrolman added. "He's always around, you'll meet him. Drives a red Porsche."

A beeping noise came from the patrol car. "Excuse me," the second patrolman said, jogging back to it.

"So if you're working on the book, I guess we'll be seeing you around," the first patrolman said.

Kate smiled. "Thanks for the vote of confidence."

"Jeff," the second patrolman called, standing outside their car. "Mrs. Southland wants her up there—now. She just called again."

Jeff smiled at Kate. "You heard the man. You will go up now, won't you?"

"Sure, why not?" Kate said, putting her sunglasses back on. "She only sicced killer dogs on me the first time."

"Hey, listen," Jeff said, bending closer to Kate, "give the lady a break. She may surprise you."

Kate looked at him, taking off her sunglasses again. "How so?"

He smiled and shook his head, backing away from the car. "Just keep an open mind, that's my advice. She's not what you think."

"Okay, if you say so," Kate said, shrugging and putting her sunglasses back on. She started the car.

"Oh—and Ms. Weston?" Jeff called, standing at the door of his patrol car.

She turned around. "Yes?"

"Slow down," he said.

"Slow down," Kate repeated, nodding. "Okay," she said.

— 2 —

Kate turned around on Chevy Chase Drive and headed back up Benedict Canyon—up and up and up and around, winding left, winding right, up and up and up, left and right, left and right—to arrive, once again, at Lydia Southland's gate. The dogs were there again, too, within moments, jumping up and down over the top of the gate, barking their heads off.

"Okay," Kate said, "let's try this again, gang," and she pushed the button on the intercom.

"Hello?" the Hispanic lady's voice said through the box.

"Hi, it's Kate Weston," Kate said. "I'm here to see Lydia Southland."

Bark, bark, bark, grrrrrr, bark, said the dogs.

"One moment, please," the Hispanic lady said.

"Cookie!" Kate heard a woman cry from somewhere behind the gate. "Cupcake!"

Instantly the dogs stopped barking. In a second they disappeared.

Cookie and Cupcake?

A few moments later, the Hispanic lady said through the box, "The señora is most pleased you have come. Please drive through the gate and park near the garage." There was a heavy clinking sound and then the gate slowly swung open. Kate drove in, looking about for her canine pals. They were nowhere to be seen.

She followed the driveway up through a woodsy glen and drove past the house to park in an area set off by a three-car garage. A blue BMW convertible and a white Toyota were already parked there. Kate turned off the engine, untied the scarf that was holding back her hair, tossed her sunglasses on the passenger seat, and got out. She brushed back her hair with both hands twice, reached down into the backseat to get her briefcase, and then straightened up.

It was very quiet up here. Beautiful and quiet.

She walked to the house, high heels crunching over crushed gravel. The house was very Old East looking. The two-story center portion of it, in fact, looked an awful lot like a three-hundred-year-old English colonial house—which, of course, was impossible in Southern California. And yet the house looked authentic to Kate. It had white shingles and windows with antique (that is, warped, vaguely purple) panes of glass, and nifty dark green wood shutters with a little imprint of an urn cut out of them. Ivy ran up the stone chimney in the front; there was even a white picket fence.

Hmmm.

She walked through the gate and up the walk to stand at the front door. It was painted dark green also. She rang the doorbell. Chimes played the first bar of the theme song to "Cassandra's World."

The door opened and there stood a very pleasant-looking Hispanic woman of about sixty. She was a bit on the heavy side and her black hair—with a few flecks of gray—was up in a bun. She was wearing an electric blue warm-up suit with flashy red piping and white high-top Adidas. "Hello, Señora Weston," she said, extending her hand, "I am Gracia Rodriguez, the señora's housekeeper."

Kate didn't think she had ever seen a housekeeper dressed in an electric blue warm-up suit with flashy red piping and high-top Adidas before.

She smiled and reached to take the woman's hand. "It's very nice to meet you," she said, "but please, it's Kate—call me Kate."

"Oh, I am afraid I could not do that," Gracia said, smiling and shaking Kate's hand. "The señora wishes for us to maintain a sense of decorum in the only way we have ever managed to have one."

Kate laughed. "Well, in that case, I better tell you up front—I'm not actually a señora."

"Oh, but a *very* experienced señorita I bet," a voice said.

Lydia Southland's face appeared over Gracia's shoulder in the doorway. Her long blond hair was drawn back up off her face in a ponytail, her makeup was minimal (a trace of eyeliner, a trace of mascara, a trace of blush, a trace of lipstick), and her physical beauty was considerable. Enough so, at any rate, that Kate was taken aback.

Southland's almost luminous skin, seemingly without pores, would have been awe-inspiring on any woman in her thirties, but it was absolutely extraordinary on this thirty-nine-year-old who was more than likely really forty-three. And Southland's mouth, in real life as on small screen, was extraordinary, too, in that it was both voluptuously seductive and somehow still exquisitely ladylike. As for her trademark, those world-famous blue eyes—*the Southland eyes*—they were, at this moment, giving Kate the once-over, and in a moment they came up to connect.

"So this is you," Southland said.

"This is me," Kate said. Pause. "I like your doorbell."

"If anyone asks," Southland said, "we pay royalties."

"There is a little counter attached to it," Gracia explained. "A man comes to read it every six months."

"Oh," Kate said.

The two were looking at Kate; Kate was looking at the two of them.

"You're very pretty," Southland said.

"Thank you," Kate said. Kate had been blessed with wonderful hazel eyes that people loved to look into, a ready smile that was most often real, and longish light brown hair that was a bit on the unmanageable side but which tended to draw all the more compliments the more unmanageable it got. Kate's health was good, too, and her constitution strong; she was five feet seven, had long arms and legs, and could pretty much eat what she wanted and still remain slim. She had breasts that didn't seem remarkable to her but which men had always seemed to appreciate (Kate noticed a great deal out of the corner of her eye, which said a lot about the way Kate preferred to examine what was going on in the world—on the sly, while no one knew she was looking).

"Pretty in a *Town and Country* kind of way," Southland added.

Kate felt her face flush. It was true. Like a lot of women who had grown up in Windy Hills, Connecticut, she did look a little like something out of *Town and Country.* As her first boss in New York always used to say, "You can take the girl out of Fairfield County but you can't take the Fairfield County out of the girl."

Kate gestured with her hand. "I love your house. It reminds me of New England."

"Thank you," Southland said, "but you probably won't like the back then."

"Why," Kate asked, confused, "what's in the back?"

"Another house," Southland told her. "But it's all one house now. Different architecture in the back. Modern. Very California."

"Oh," Kate said, looking around at the front of the house again. "But where did this come from? It looks authentic."

"It is," Southland said. "It's from Massachusetts. Some poor shipping tycoon moved it here because his wife was homesick." Pause. "She left him anyway."

Kate looked at her. "To go back to Massachusetts?"

"To go to Brentwood," Southland said. "She ran away with a composer from up the road."

"We still get mail for them," Gracia sighed. "After all these years."

Kate couldn't help but smile. These two ladies were really something. "And how many years has that been? That you've been here?"

"The señora has lived here for six years," Gracia said, "and I have been with the señora for over five."

Southland was frowning now, squinting at Kate.

"What's the matter?" Kate asked her.

"I can't read you," Southland said, as if Kate were a book she had only just discovered was in a foreign language. "I know what I'm supposed to see, but I know there's more back there. I just know it."

Pause. "Excuse me?" Kate said.

"Right now," Southland said, snapping her fingers in Kate's face, peering at her, "tell me what you're thinking—right now, this split second, looking at me—what are you thinking?"

"I'm thinking," Kate said, "that this is the first time I've ever met an actress who's every bit as beautiful off camera as she is on."

"Oh, señora, you see?" Gracia said, clasping her hands in delight. "I just knew this one would be different. I could tell by the way she spoke at the gate."

But Southland was still squinting at Kate, as much as to say, *Ha! You don't fool me.* "Well," she finally said, "you do handle yourself well, I'll give you that. I didn't realize editors came with acting skills these days."

Kate smiled. Southland was bright. And right. Kate was a bit of an actress. She had to be these days. "In my line of work," Kate said, "we don't call it acting skills—it's more like a divine sense of manipulation for the good of literary posterity."

Southland looked at her a moment and then burst out laughing. Kate laughed, too.

There. It was done. The ice was broken. They knew each other. They liked each other. This book could be fun.

"Call me Lydia," she said to Kate, extending her hand.

"Lydia," Kate said, shaking her hand.

"I called your office, you know—after you came up to the gate. Your assistant's good. Sarah—I liked her. She put me through to Mark. He told me you're the best editor in the business."

"Mark?" Kate said, surprised. "You talked to Mark Fiducia?"

"I told Sarah I needed to talk to someone who knew you, someone other than horrible Rebecca."

Kate smiled. "Oh—you don't like Rebecca?"

Lydia narrowed her eyes. "I *hate* Rebecca."

"Good," Kate said, "because so do I."

"Good," Lydia said. And then, clapping her hands and startling Kate, she said, "Okay! Show Kate into the living room, Gracia, and then please find Noél. We need to get this show on the road."

"Very good, señora," Gracia said.

"Oh, and Kate—" Lydia came back to the door. "Do you have your bags with you?"

Kate nodded. "I came straight from the airport."

"Good," Lydia said, disappearing down the hall, "because we'll be leaving in a couple of hours."

Kate looked at Gracia. "Leaving?" she said.

"This way, Señorita Weston," Gracia said, holding the door for her.

"Gracia, leaving for where?" she whispered.

But Gracia only smiled. Evidently she did not discuss things her employer had already announced as fact.

— *3* —

The inside of Lydia Southland's home was glorious. Everything that could possibly be made of natural materials was, from polished dark wood floors to dark wood beams in the ceiling, from lovely linen wallpapers to intricate woodwork trims, from beautiful cascades of chintz to exquisite Persian rugs. Old paintings were softly lit from below by small brass lamps. The furniture, Kate knew at a glance, was collector caliber.

She couldn't imagine the kind of money that had gone into this house.

Gracia led Kate through a foyer, a living room, a sitting room, down a hall, down a short flight of stairs, and then—suddenly—the whole house changed. Still there were dark wood floors, but the ceilings vaulted high and every part of the house that could be opened to natural light was. Skylights were everywhere. There were soft beige fabric wall covers, occasional brick-mosaic inlays, and plants and flowers everywhere. And light—light was everywhere as well. And where natural light was not streaming in, a tract of light was beaming down from somewhere in the ceiling, usually drawing the eye to some demurely extraordinary thing in the process: a painting, a sculpture, a piece of ceramic.

When Gracia led Kate down some open stairs into the living room, Kate gasped. The room was enormous, first of all, with a cathedral ceiling, and the far wall was made of nothing but wood and glass panes, looking out over Benedict Canyon. While the main part of the house was built on top of the ridge, Kate realized, the rest of it—this part back here—was literally built down into the side of the hill. There was a patio out back and then, down a few stairs, a terrace and swimming pool and a pool house, and behind that, a tier of terraced trees dropped down to somewhere out of sight.

Lydia was standing by a set of french doors in the wall of glass, looking out, one hand resting on her hip. Kate realized that she had probably come in first so that she could pose herself this way for effect. It was very dramatic. At five eight, dressed in a white loose-fitting silk blouse and trousers, barefoot yet, she looked as though she were some kind of heavenly angel assigned to protect the canyon.

"Like it?" Lydia asked her without turning around.

"Love it," Kate said, stepping down into the center of the living room and putting her briefcase down. As she straightened up she saw through the side window, behind some fir trees outside, the green-gray windscreens of a tennis court. And here, just inside the window, in the corner of the room, was a gleaming black grand piano, top down, with an enormous vase of spring flowers on top of it. Kate turned to Lydia. "Do you play?"

"Tennis, yes," Lydia said, stepping away from the french doors, "piano, no—games, only sometimes." She looked down at her feet, pointed her right toe, and then suddenly swung her leg back to hold her body in an arabesque.

Forty-three and a body like that! Kate thought, watching her. Of course she didn't know for sure if Lydia Southland was forty-three. She claimed she was thirty-nine. It was just the almanac, Lydia's first agent, and *People* magazine that said she was forty-three.

"Tell me what you know about my book," Lydia said, holding the arabesque with amazing control. Behind her, outside by the pool, Kate could see a young woman with red hair rummaging around in the bushes. It wouldn't have struck Kate so odd if the woman wasn't wearing what looked to be an Adolfo suit and high heels. It wasn't what Kate would wear for such an activity.

Kate returned her attention to Lydia and rattled off the writers and editors she knew Lydia had worked with thus far; she outlined some of the problems in the manuscript (the ones she was sure Lydia would agree with); she assured Lydia she understood the frustrations she must feel from working with a publishing house in transition—

"Oh, is that what you call it," Lydia smirked, lowering her right leg and raising the left into another arabesque.

Behind her, the redheaded woman was going into the pool house. "Well, whatever shape the house is in," Kate said, "I suggest we use the situation to our advantage and make your book the blockbuster bestseller of the year."

Lydia laughed, sending waves down through her arabesque. She turned her head to look at Kate. "Boy, you *are* good."

"Excuse me, señora," Gracia said coming down the stairs behind Kate, "but I cannot find the little señora. Her car is here, but she is not in the office or in her room."

"Does she have red hair?" Kate asked Gracia.

"Oh, no," Lydia said, "don't tell me you know her." She lowered her leg and stood up straight. "Good God, that's all we'd need—some old friend of Noél's here."

"No," Kate said quickly, "I don't know her. It's just that I keep seeing a redhead walking around outside." Said redhead was now coming out of the pool house, dragging a large green plastic lawn bag behind her. "There," Kate said, pointing, "there she is."

Lydia turned around to look. "Oh, yes, that's Noél—but what on earth is that?"

Gracia, by this time, had crossed the living room and was opening one of the french doors. "Little señora," she said, "the señora would like to see you."

"Okay," the woman said, leaving the bag where it was and skipping up the stairs in her heels. "I knew it, Lydia," she announced as she came in, "I told Philippe's nephew what you said—to stop dumping weeds by the tennis court—so now he's hiding them in the pool house."

"Oh, wonderful," Lydia said. "Gracia, call Philippe and tell him we're sorry but his nephew has flunked his tryout again."

"But make sure to tell him that he didn't steal anything," Noél said to Gracia, "because that was Philippe's worry—that he'd commit armed robbery again or something."

Lydia turned around to look at her. "You didn't mention it was *armed* robbery, Noél—not when you recommended I give him a chance."

Noél swallowed. "I didn't?"

She was a genuine redhead, Kate could tell, with faint freckles under her tan. She was twenty-eight or -nine and very attractive in an all-American way. She had the greenest eyes—really lovely—and a body kept thin, Kate guessed, from a high metabolism. She teemed with energy; you could feel it when she came in.

"Noél," Lydia said, "*you* call Philippe and tell him his nephew has flunked his tryout for the last time."

"Okay," Noél said. She glanced over at Kate and then glanced back again—and her eyes stayed. "Well hel-*lo.*"

Kate hoped she didn't look as startled as she felt. Noél was looking at her in a rather strange way.

"This is my new editor," Lydia said, "Kate Weston. Kate, this is Noél Shaunnessy, my personal assistant."

Noél walked over to shake her hand. "And from what publishing house are you?"

"Bennett, Fitzallen & Coe," Kate said.

"Well-well-well," Noél said, smiling, shaking Kate's hand, "you must be as wonderful as you look. Last I heard, Lydia was suing you guys."

Kate smiled.

Noél smiled.

"That's enough, Noél," Lydia said.

Noél looked at her. "Well, you were."

"I meant," Lydia said, "that you can let go of Kate's hand now."

Kate blushed scarlet and Noél laughed, letting go.

"Do not mind the little señora," Gracia said to Kate, coming over to take Noél by the arm and pull her a little farther away from Kate. "She is in very high spirits today."

"Of the kind which will cease at this moment, please," Lydia said. "Noél—" She raised her eyebrows, waiting for Noél to look at her. "This is the last go-round on the book. We've all got to try."

"Okay," Noél said. She looked at Kate. "No playing around, Kate," she told her, eyes dancing in merry deceit.

Kate was so thrown she couldn't think what to say.

Noél turned back to Lydia. "Listen, since we didn't have any warning, I'm going to need some time to get things ready for you guys—unpack the manuscript, get all your notes out, get things organized."

"When we get back," Lydia told her. "Right now I want you to see if you can get Kate on our flight."

Noél's eyebrows went up. She looked at Kate again. "My, *my* but you seem to have made an impression around here."

"Excuse me," Kate said, turning to Lydia, "but what's this about not having any warning that I was coming?"

"We didn't know you were coming," Noél said.

Kate glanced over at Noél and then back to Lydia. "But didn't Rebecca call you?"

"No," Lydia said. "Unless," she said, looking at Noél, "there was a message I didn't know about."

Noél shook her head. "No." She looked to Gracia. "Unless there was a message I didn't know about."

"No, there was no message I knew about," Gracia said.

"But we did get that letter, Lydia," Noél reminded her employer.

"Oh, right," Lydia said, "but that was about the lawyer."

"It didn't actually say it would be a lawyer," Noél said. She looked at Kate. "But it certainly gave the impression that it would be a lawyer—somebody who was going to stop by this ˜week to settle everything about the book, once and for all."

"And that's what it said, didn't it?" Lydia said. "Settle everything once and for all. The nerve—as if *I* had done something."

Pause. "Are you sure it just said *somebody?*" Kate asked. "Not me? My name?"

"No," Noél said, shaking her head, "it didn't. I'll show it to you."

"And it didn't say when either," Lydia said, "what day. I was hoping to sneak out of town before whoever it was got here."

"I don't believe this," Kate said, rubbing her eyes. She sighed and dropped her hand. "I was told Rebecca had set everything up and that you were expecting me."

Silence.

"That's some company you work for," Lydia finally observed.

"No," Noél murmured, "it certainly doesn't sound good—does it?"

"What doesn't?" Kate asked her.

"Not to be rude, Kate—" Lydia said.

Kate turned to look at her.

"But are you going to last? The last thing I want to do is get involved with this book again if you're not going to be around to see it through."

"I'm not going to leave," Kate said. "I've been there twelve years—I'm not going to leave now."

Lydia and Noél exchanged looks. Then Noél shrugged, as if she didn't have an answer to the question Lydia was asking her. Lydia looked at Kate. "Give me your word you won't quit until we're finished?"

Kate raised her hand. "I swear."

Lydia smiled. "Okay, it's a deal—you won't quit and the book's back on."

"Let me get on the phone," Noél said, leaving the room, "I need to call the airline and hotel."

"I'm very pleased, Kate," Lydia said, opening one of the french doors. "It's not my style to leave something unfinished. Gracia—see if Kate would like anything before we leave. I'll be back in a minute." She slipped outside and disappeared around the side of the house.

As soon as Gracia was sure Lydia was safely out of earshot, she whirled around to Kate, whispering, "Oh, Señorita Weston, I am so glad you have come! The señora has been working on the book for such a long time and it has made her so very unhappy. She is not used to working on something that no one sees—but this book, she writes and writes and writes and no one ever sees anything and she gets so upset!"

Kate smiled, helping herself to a seat in a chair. "I can see how it could be pretty discouraging," she said, crossing her legs. "This book's had a rough time."

"Gary—Señor Steiner," Gracia continued, stepping closer, "has known the señora a great many years. He wants to help the señora and I think you should talk to him because he is a writer. He writes the señora's show and is very talented. I wrote down his name and telephone number for you." She glanced over her shoulder, pulled out a slip of paper from her pocket, and handed it to her.

"Thank you," Kate said, accepting it, "this is very helpful. And what about Noél? Can she help, do you think?"

"The little señora helps with many things," Gracia said, "but with the book"—she shrugged—"I am not sure. The señora writes things down one way and the little señora tells her to write it another way—a way that has perhaps a bit more of the truth in it—but you cannot tell the señora what to do because it only makes her do whatever it is you do not want her to do and so the little señora starts arguing with the señora—" Gracia threw her arms up and let them drop. "And since the little señora lives here they can argue all day and all night, and many, many times, Señorita Weston, believe me, they argue all day and all night about this book." A sigh. "The only peace we have is when it is packed away."

Kate spotted Lydia coming around the house. "Here she comes," she said.

"I will make you some fresh orange juice and a sandwich," Gracia said, backing away, "and then I will show you where you can freshen up for your trip."

"My trip," Kate repeated. Lydia opened the door and in the next instant the guard dogs were bounding in and across the room at Kate.

"I hope big dogs don't scare you," Lydia said cheerfully as the dogs stopped just short of Kate, plunked themselves down to sit, and panted, tongues hanging out, sharp white teeth gleaming, dark eyes shining.

Kate resumed breathing. "Hi," she said to them. They were gorgeous German shepherds, but big. Really big.

"Cookie, Cupcake," Lydia said, "say how-dee-do to Kate."

Cookie and Cupcake both offered Kate a paw.

Kate hesitated.

"You can shake their paws," Lydia said.

"Uh, hi Cookie," Kate said, gently shaking one dog's massive paw.

"That's Cupcake," Lydia told her.

"Oh, sorry, Cupcake," Kate said. "How-dee-do."

Cupcake barked, making Kate jump.

"He likes you," Lydia said. "Cookie—Cookie, now be sweet to Kate. Show Kate how sweet you are."

Cookie promptly rolled over onto her side on Kate's foot, waiting for her stomach to be rubbed. Somewhere in the house a telephone was ringing.

Kate rubbed Cookie's stomach. "Oh, yes, you are a nice girl," Kate said.

Cupcake barked again, making Kate jump again.

"He's jealous," Lydia explained.

Jealous German shepherds, housekeepers in flashy warm-up suits, gardeners committing armed robbery, personal assistants making passes at her, going on a trip to God knows where—it was beginning to dawn on Kate just how complicated editing Lydia Southland might be.

Now Cupcake was lying on his back, wanting his stomach rubbed.

Kate laughed quietly, more relaxed now, and she got down on her knees on the floor to rub both the dogs' stomachs. "You are little puppies at heart, aren't you?" she said to them.

"Trained attack dogs, that's what they are," Lydia said, correcting her. "You can touch them, but *always* be careful how you touch me. They see what they think is a wrong move and they'll be on you in a second."

Kate smiled nervously, wondering if the dogs could feel her anxiety. There was nothing worse to Kate than imagining the worst—like if the dogs just started to tear her apart right now, what it would feel like, what her blood would look like on this off-white rug.

"Okay, everything's set," Noël announced from the far doorway, holding a clipboard in front of her. "Kate's on the flight, Kate's got a hotel room, and the car will be here in fifty-five minutes."

"What about Dee?" Lydia said.

"She'll be in the car with the new script," Noël said.

"Good," Lydia said.

"And Lydia," Noël said, "the FBI called—they want to know if they can take a deposition from you next week."

"Sure. Tell them I'll be their defrauded poster girl if it'll help."

"Fine," Noël said, making a note.

Lydia looked outside for a moment. The dogs, sensing something not right, trotted over to stand on either side of their mistress. Lydia sighed then, bending to pat them. "My business manager has absconded to South America," she said to Kate.

"What?" Kate said, getting back up to sit in her chair. "You're kidding. Did he—"

"Steal all my money?" Lydia said, turning. "Fortunately no, he only got about three million. I never gave him check-signing privileges, thank God."

He only got about three million, Kate reran in her head. How much money did she make anyway?

"Do you know Kenny?" Lydia asked her. "The guy who plays my father on 'Cassandra's World'?"

"I know of him," Kate said.

"He was supposed to retire this year," Lydia said, "but he lost everything to Fanning. He was his business manager, too. Everything—can you imagine? He'll have to work until he's a hundred and ten now."

"Excuse me, señora," Gracia said, coming in, wiping her hands on a dish towel, "but do you know if Señor Fanning paid the electric bill before he left for South America?" She took one look at Lydia's expression and went back to the kitchen.

"Lydia," Noél said, holding up her clipboard, "I need answers on this other stuff for Diane, okay? She's going to do some calls and correspondence tomorrow."

"Okay," Lydia said, bending to pet the dogs.

"Will you or won't you be a judge for next year's Miss America pageant?" Noél said, reading from her clipboard.

"No," Lydia said, kissing Cupcake on the nose and then letting Cookie kiss her on the side of the face.

Scribble. "Do you want to go to the next Willie Nelson IRS concert?" Noél asked next.

"No," Lydia said, straightening up, still scratching the dogs behind the ears, "but buy ten tickets and give them to people who would."

Noél scribbled a note. "Okay," she said, "what about the premiere of the Schwarzenegger movie?"

"How many murders in this one?"

"Lots."

"My regrets," Lydia said.

Scribble. "Okay. Now, let's see . . . oh, right—*Lear's* would like to use you on their November cover."

"No way," Lydia said quickly. "I'm not old enough."

Noél looked at her.

"Noél!" Lydia said.

"Okay, okay," Noél said, smiling, making a note, "don't kill the messenger."

Kate suppressed a smile and pulled a legal pad and pen out of the side of her briefcase.

"Next," Noél said, "do you want to go to a party for Cecil Barker?"

"Never heard of him," Lydia said.

"Well, then, I guess you're not going," Noél said. Scribble. "Okay, next—a reception celebrating the art of Hillie Stratford."

"You mean Hillie Scribble-Scrabble," Lydia said.

Noél looked at her. "Does that mean yes or no?"

"No," Lydia said.

"Okay," Noél said, making a note. "Oh, this one's important, Lydia," she said, looking up, "have you decided which you're going to do, the cancer or the AIDS research fund-raiser?"

Lydia hesitated. "Can't I do both?"

"They both say no—they want an exclusive."

"That's ridiculous," Lydia said.

"I know," Noél said, "but it's kind of political."

"Then tell them both no and let's do something for the Los Angeles Center for Living," Lydia said.

Noël paused. "Are you serious?"

"Of course I'm serious," Lydia said. "I'm sick of this political mumbo jumbo. If people are ill, it hardly matters if they're Republican or Democrat—so if they won't let me do both fund-raisers then tell them both no and let's do something for the center—and Project Angel Food. Call Project Angel Food and see if there's something I can do." Lydia noticed that Kate was writing on her pad. "What are you doing?"

"Making a note," Kate said, glancing up. "What's Project Angel Food?"

"They deliver meals to housebound AIDS patients," Noël explained.

"And the Center for Living?" Kate asked.

"It's a support group and counseling and learning center for people with life-challenging illnesses," Noël said.

"Illnesses other than AIDS?" Kate said.

"Oh, yes," Noël said. "All ages, all illnesses. Kids to old age. Cancer's a big one."

"And why," Lydia asked Kate, "may I ask, are you writing this down?"

"Just making notes on things I need to ask you about later," Kate said without looking up. "You should have a section in your book on the charity work you do."

Lydia considered this a moment and then returned her attention to Noël. "Anything else?"

"The University of Southern Florida would like to give you an honorary doctorate," Noël told her.

"Why?" Lydia asked her. "To make up for cutting off my scholarship during my sophomore year?"

"Oh," Noël said. She looked down at her notes. "Seems they neglected to mention that part."

Lydia waved it off. "Tell them thanks, but no thanks." She bent over to ask the dogs, "Do you guys want to go out? Yes? Can you wag those tails any harder? You can? You can?"

"Oh, here's a goodie," Noël said, smiling at her clipboard. "A real blow-out global affair."

"What's that?" Lydia said, leading the dogs to the french doors.

"Speaking at the eighth-grade commencement exercises at the Saint

Matthias Middle School in San Francisco," Noél said. Pause. Lydia was letting the dogs out. Noél looked over at Kate, winked, and continued. "Teresa—their student council president—says if you'll come they'll sell tickets and give the money to the shelter at their church."

"What kind of shelter?" Lydia asked, closing the door.

"For women and children," Noél said. "There's a soup kitchen too, apparently, but that's for everybody, men and women."

"Okay," Lydia said, turning around, "if I can do it, schedule it."

Noél blinked. "Really?"

"Really," Lydia said.

Noél looked at Kate. "She always gets me on the curveball."

A very loud buzzer sounded in the kitchen. Lydia looked in that direction and frowned, waiting. After about a minute, Gracia came out. "Oh, señora," she said, fretting, "I do not even know how to tell you this."

"Why, what is it?" Lydia said.

Gracia grimaced and said, "Mr. Mortimer Pallsner is at the gate."

"Mort?" Noél exclaimed. "Mort's *here?*"

Lydia's expression was unreadable. "Guess he got my letter," she said calmly.

"He says it is an emergency, señora. He says he must see you before you leave."

"An emergency," Lydia repeated.

"Yes, señora."

Lydia turned to Noél. "Noél," she said, "you are to take Kate upstairs and you are not—under any circumstances—to come back down until he leaves. Do you understand me?"

Noél nodded. "Yeah, okay."

"Kate," Lydia said, turning to her.

Kate stood up.

"You are to go upstairs with Noél—and under no circumstances are you to allow her to come downstairs until he's gone. Do you understand?"

"Not in the least," Kate said, "but I'll do it."

"Oh, baby," Noél said, smiling, walking over and picking up Kate's briefcase for her, "but do you ever learn fast."

— 4 —

This was a most peculiar house—to say nothing of household—Kate decided, ascending the stairs behind Noél. The upstairs was split-level too and seemingly went on for miles—and not in a particularly straight line.

At the top of the stairs, Noél put Kate's briefcase down and turned to her. "How about a tour?" she whispered. "I can give you a really good one while she's busy with Mort."

Kate hesitated.

Noél laughed. "Oh, don't worry," she said, "I know you're straight. I just go into that shtick to make myself feel more significant than I am. Let me tell you, I am so well behaved these days it's sickening."

The way Noél said this—sort of, "By the way, just between us, I feel terribly insignificant"—for some reason charmed Kate.

"So actually I guess I owe you an apology," Noél said, eyes serious. "I won't do it anymore."

The doorbell rang, the first bar of "Cassandra's World" chiming through the upstairs.

"Whoops," Noél said, taking Kate's elbow and steering her down the hall, "Lydia'll kill me if I let him see me."

"Who is he, anyway?" Kate whispered.

"The president of Bestar Studios," Noél whispered. "He's also executive producer of 'Cassandra's World.'"

Kate stopped in her tracks. "And why can't he see you?"

Noél smiled. "I don't mind invading Lydia's privacy," she whispered, "but I do mind invading mine. Come on, while we've got a chance." She led Kate over the lush carpeting past two doorways to the very end of the hall. There was a tall, wide, solid oak door. "Okay," Noél whispered, "this is it—the inner sanctum, where the queen sleeps."

Lydia's bedroom was very large and had a four-poster bed and yards and yards of blue-and-white chintz. There were floor-to-ceiling windows overlooking the canyon, lovely lace curtains cascading down, a fireplace, and a—

And a—

Kate walked over to get a closer look.

"Yep," Noél said, "it's real."

It was a Monet. Lydia had a Monet in her bedroom.

"How much does she make, anyway?" Kate whispered, staring at the painting.

"On the series, I think it's a hundred twenty an episode now."

Kate did some math in her head. Twenty-two episodes a year—that was two million six hundred forty thousand a year.

"That doesn't include residuals, though," Noél said. "After worldwide distribution she gets about another eight hundred thousand on each."

Dumbfounded, Kate turned to look at her. "She makes a million dollars on each episode?"

"Yeah, but it takes like ten years or something for all the money to come in." Noél smiled. "I know, Kate, but out here you get used to figures like that. Come on, this way."

Off of Lydia's bedroom was a sitting room with french doors leading out to a balcony. There were bookcases full of books but Kate was too preoccupied with figuring out how much money Lydia made on "Cassandra's World" to check out any of the titles.

Six years times twenty-two is one hundred thirty-two—times one million . . .

"You mean she'll make over a hundred thirty million dollars on the past six years' work?" Kate said as they went into the bathroom.

"She hasn't always made that kind of money," Noél said. "The first two years, I think, she only made something like fifty an episode."

"Only," Kate repeated, looking about, taking in the bathroom for the first time.

Some bathroom! There was a sunken bathtub set in a gorgeous tile mosaic; a huge dressing table circled in lights, with a ton of cosmetics and makeup brushes on it; a marble basin; two vases of fresh-cut flowers; and, in the corner, on a shelf, a TV set. All that was missing was the toilet. As if reading Kate's thoughts, Noél pointed to a door. "In there."

Kate peeked inside. A toilet and a bidet. Huh. Like a water closet.

Kate closed the door and went back to the dressing table. "What kind of makeup does she use?" she asked, looking around at bottles and tubes in the white wicker baskets there.

"Her own, of course."

"No," Kate said.

"Yes," Noél said, walking over and pulling a tube out.

Sure enough, it was moisturizer from a line of cosmetics called Love of Lydia—products people could buy even in Kmart.

Kate squinted at Noél. "I don't believe she uses that."

"Well," Noél said, tossing it back in the basket, "maybe not, but she does use her own cosmetics." She pulled open a drawer to reveal dozens of unmarked plastic bottles, tubes, and compacts. "A chemist makes them up for her."

"Huh," Kate said. "And what does she make on the Love of Lydia line?"

"A million a year plus royalties—it came to about four million last year, I think."

Kate whistled.

"You know, Kate," Noél said, leading her out of the bathroom, "or rather, you should know, if you're going to work on the book," she added, stopping at the doorway of yet another room and turning around, "that Lydia is very generous. She spends a lot of money on appearances, her lifestyle, but she has to—that's part of being a big star. You *have* to live a certain way out here to be perceived by the industry as big—to get paid big—and certainly the press requires it."

"Oh, you bad little señora!" suddenly came from behind them. It was Gracia, shaking her finger at Noél.

"Oh, come on, Gracia, Kate'd see this sooner or later," Noél said.

"Achee," Gracia said, throwing her hands up in the air and turning around. "I do not see you, I do not know what you are doing. There is lunch for you in the guest room." And she was gone.

Kate turned to Noél. "I'm not going to get you in trouble, am I?"

"That's my confirmation name, don't worry about it," Noél said, waving for her to follow.

The next room had three walls of mirrored closet doors—one, two, three, four, five, six, seven, eight, nine, ten, eleven in all—four on the sides, three on the far end. Noél opened a few so Kate could see long dresses in one, short dresses in another, blouses in another, suits in—

"Wait," Kate said, reaching past Noél to touch the sleeve of a pale blue jacket. There was a skirt that matched. "What are these tags? What do they mean?" Almost every piece of clothing had a white tag with numbers and letters on it.

"Oh," Noél said, pointing for Kate to see, "this is the date Lydia last wore this suit—three twenty-five, that's March twenty-fifth—and this is the code for where she wore it. Gracia knows the code, I don't really, but—let's see, B-L, M of D." She thought a second. "Oh, I know," Noél said. "Benefit luncheon, March of Dimes."

"And what's this S-P-H at the bottom?" Kate said.

"That means there are shoes and a purse and a hat that go with it."

"Unbelievable," Kate murmured, shaking her head.

"Now watch this," Noél said, closing the closet door and walking back to the doorway. "I love this part." She opened a little panel in the wall, fiddled with something, and the room went pitch black for a moment. And then there was a faint glow of light, now a little brighter, and the mirrored room got brighter and brighter until after several moments, Kate had to shield her eyes against what felt like direct sunlight overhead. "From zero light to candlelight to direct sunlight," Noél explained, turning the lights back to normal. "So she can see how the whole thing will look. There's even a setting for 'In the shade, sunny day.' "

"Little señora," Gracia whispered from the doorway, "I am a nervous wreck. You know how the señora is about her privacy."

"Let me just show her the lingerie closet," Noél said.

"No!" Gracia whispered. She pointed to the bedroom. "Now, while we are still lucky. You do not want her to send Señorita Weston away."

Noél reluctantly led Kate out of Lydia's suite of rooms. They walked down the hall, jogging left, jogging right—what a crazy house this was—to the guest room. It was a large room, but cozy, with a double bed, desk, couch and, by the window, a little tea table for two. On it Gracia had set two places for lunch: cold cucumber soup, tuna fish sandwiches, and fresh-squeezed orange juice. The food was delicious.

"Am I imagining it or was the air in Lydia's room different?" Kate said halfway through their meal.

Noél shook her head, swallowing a bite of her sandwich. "No, you're not imagining it—she's got climate control in there. She keeps it cool but pretty humid."

"For the Monet?" Kate said.

"For her face," Noél said.

Since she was on such a roll with Noél, Kate took the opportunity to grill her about the maintenance of Lydia's looks: Did Lydia have a special diet? No, according to Noél, Lydia had a basic food plan she followed. What did that mean? It meant that a lot of things simply did not exist in Lydia's world, that wherever she was, she always made sure the foods she ate were there for her to eat when she was hungry. Like? Vegetables, fish, pasta, fruit, honey, some poultry, and once in a while lean beef. What didn't exist in Lydia's world? Junk food, soda pop, caffeine, white sugar, stuff like that. You could wave a candy bar in her face and she just wouldn't see it.

How much did Lydia sleep? On her own, at least eight hours. When she was working, sometimes as little as four.

Had Lydia ever had plastic surgery? Was the pope Catholic? Noël wanted to know.

What kind of plastic surgery had Lydia had done? Where did she have it done? How?

"Tacky, tacky, Ms. Weston," Noël scolded her. "One would think sneaking around in Lydia's bathroom quite enough for any intruder."

Did Lydia color her hair?

A few highlights, but basically, no.

Really?

Really.

Did Lydia work out?

Did she? Noël jumped up from the table and took Kate by the arm down the hall, at the opposite end from Lydia's suite, and opened the door. Inside was a tremendous exercise room with just about every machine Kate had ever seen: a StairMaster, stationary bike, Nautilus, rowing machine, NordicTrack, treadmill, Gravitron. One wall had mirrors and a ballet bar; there were mats on the floor with strip-on weights lined up neatly along the side; there was a bench press with barbells. There was also a sound system, a stack of towels, and a small refrigerator set up in the corner.

"She works out at least an hour every day," Noël said, "most often two, sometimes even three. She does most of her reading on the StairMaster," she said, pointing to the reading rack on it, "but lately she's into floor exercises with weights. Says it increases bone mass or something."

Kate looked at her. "Does she have a trainer?"

"Once a week—every day if she's working and is all distracted—"

They heard the man downstairs yell something.

"They're in the office," Noël said matter-of-factly. "Right under us." She looked at her watch. "They're probably wrapping now."

"Wrapping what?" Kate said.

Noël smiled. "Sorry. It's not for me to tell—not yet, anyway." She led Kate out of the exercise room and down the hall. As they neared the front staircase, Noél stopped suddenly, cocking her head to the side and holding her hand back for Kate to stop.

For a moment, Kate couldn't hear anything. And then, practically right underneath them in the front hall, she heard Lydia say, "Mort, the door is this way."

"You are the most fucking selfish bitch I've ever worked with," the man said. "You don't give a goddamn shit about anybody but yourself."

"Now that sounds like the Mortimer I know," Lydia said. "And I appreciate your expressing your true feelings before you go."

"A whore, Lydia, that's what you are," he said. "Paid to perform—a whore who performs because it's the only thing she can do!"

Kate's mouth fell open. She was in a state of shock. This was the president of Bestar Studios? Talking to Lydia Southland like this?

But downstairs Lydia was laughing and Kate heard the sound of the front door being opened. "Come on, don't be such a spoilsport," she said, "you've made plenty on me, you know you have."

"You're nothing without me, *nothing!*" he spat. "You're a fucking worthless piece of shit! You don't have any friends, Lydia, you don't have any family, you don't have a husband, you don't have anything without me—you're just another aging cunt nobody wants!"

"My God," Kate murmured.

Noél turned, holding her finger to her mouth.

"Out, Mort," Lydia said downstairs, "my patience is wearing thin and I've got to work this evening, remember?"

"You don't even have a kid to visit you in your old age," he said. "You'll just be a lonely old bag who *used* to be somebody, Lydia—all alone, except for what money can buy. Maybe you can buy a beach boy, Lydia—maybe if you buy a beach boy you can have somebody in your life."

They heard a loud *smack.*

"Ohmigod, she hit him!" Noél whispered with glee, covering her mouth so as not to laugh.

"Thanks again for stopping by, Mort," Lydia said. And then she slammed the front door so hard Kate could feel the floor shake.

— 5 —

Mark Fiducia couldn't believe it Tuesday afternoon when Sarah had run into his office to say that Lydia Southland was on the phone, demanding to talk to someone other than Rebecca about Kate Weston.

"Why?" he had asked.

"Who knows?" Sarah had said. "But now and pronto next door— the lady means business." Kate's assistant, Sarah Steadwell, was almost always very calm, so for her to come running in here meant that, indeed, Ms. Southland must mean business.

And so Mark had gone next door into Kate's office and picked up the phone. "Hello, Ms. Southland?"

"Is this Mark Faith and Trust?" she had said.

"Excuse me?" Mark said.

"That's what Fiducia means, doesn't it? In Italian?" she said. "I played Queen Isabella in an episode last year and Columbus, I think, said something to me about not betraying my fiducia."

He laughed. "Yes, yes it does."

"Okay," she said then, "enough chitchat," adding under her breath, "God forbid they send me someone whose name at least sounds like he might be sincere."

"But Kate Weston is the absolute best, Ms. Southland," Mark was quick to say. "I'd choose Kate over any editor in town and I swear to God I'm not just saying that."

"So she's an editor?" Southland asked.

"Yes," Mark said, "an executive editor."

"Not a lawyer," Southland said.

"No," Mark said with a laugh.

He heard her say to someone, "Call security and tell them to get her back up here—we may have made a mistake." She came back to the phone. "We sent her away," she explained.

"But now you've stopped yourself from making a terrible mistake," Mark said.

Silence.

"Ms. Southland," Mark said, "Kate knows how badly the house has messed up with you—that's why she's out there."

Lydia Southland laughed. "I like you, Mr. Faith and Trust," she said. "Thank you and good-bye." And then she had hung up.

[35]

Kate had only been gone a day and the office was already boring as hell. There was no one to overhear on the phone next door saying, "You may speak to me that way, but you are never, *ever* to speak to a publicity assistant or any assistant or any secretary or any receptionist of this company in that tone of voice again. Do you hear me? They work hard and for next to nothing and all to see that you get properly published—so pick on someone your own size!" (There would be a silence and astonished people up and down the hall would stop to listen.) And then there would be a burst of laughter from Kate and something like, "Exactly! *I* don't want her job, *you* don't want her job, so please, don't convince her that *she* doesn't want it either—somebody has to answer the phone in publicity!" A breath and then, "Now, about your brilliant book . . ."

Oh, Kate, Mark thought, *where are you? We need you.*

With Kate gone, there was no one to be shamelessly happy, skipping up and down the halls singing about good reviews of any book published by Bennett, Fitzallen & Coe; there was no one to tell Rushman when to throw a party for morale before everyone was so low a dog could kick them (or there was no one left working at B, F & C but dogs); there was no one to express admiration at the editorial meeting for jobs well done; and last, but not least, with Kate away, there was no one to come into Mark's office, close the door, and collapse on the floor, declaring that her love life would kill her for sure, that she couldn't marry Harris and become one of the silently despairing masses, and that Mark, poor lamb, if she did or if she did not, was still going to have to listen to every sordid detail as she sank—alas—in the sea of life.

Mark, aforementioned poor lamb, loved it when Kate lay across his carpet. Mark loved it because it was the only time he could see that Kate was less than the perfect person he otherwise thought she was. Take Harris—the guy she lived with—and her struggle about whether or not to marry him. The complaints she made about him were almost identical to the ones Kate made about her father, and it seemed incredible to Mark that she never saw the correlation between the two.

"This morning," she would say, lying on the floor of Mark's office, "Harris told me that if I played squash regularly I wouldn't need a therapist." She would roll her head to the side to look at Mark. "He says he works his problems out on the squash court. He says he doesn't need a therapist." Pause. "I asked him, 'Oh, so you mean if I played squash, I wouldn't feel any emotions either?' " A wince. "He said," she said, dropping her voice in imitation, " 'Kate, you have to learn how to shut certain things out. You can't waste all this time and energy thinking and talking about things that don't matter.' 'Oh, things that don't matter—like how I feel,' " Kate said in imitation of herself, tears hinting. Long pause. "Oh, Mark," Kate would say quietly, lying there on the floor, eyes now on the ceiling, blinking rapidly, "what is the matter with me? Why can't I be like other people?"

Of course, Mark was hardly in a position to judge the way Kate conducted her love life. His own wife had left him last year, for a Wall Street whiz kid of all things. But then, depression about their personal lives for the past four years was a big part of what had drawn Mark and Kate so close. That and the fact that they were two talented editors working at a company that seemed to be falling down around their ears.

"But you're an executive editor now," Mark would occasionally point out.

"But you're a senior editor," Kate would point out.

"But you're an *executive* editor," he would say again.

"But with no executive powers whatsoever," she would say. "Mark," she'd sigh, "let's face it, I'm the executive in charge of ladylike demeanor around here."

They would laugh but Mark knew, in a weird way, that Kate was right. That it wasn't her editorial skills so much as her looks, grace, and charm that endeared her to Rushman. And her background. It was said there was no class system in America and yet when the Rushman-Weston relationship was seen in action around Bennett, Fitzallen & Coe, it became embarrassingly obvious, at least to Mark, why such a class system might exist if there was one. The merchandiser-turned-book-publisher had some manners but no class at all, and Kate had quite a bit of both, and so it was rather peculiar to see the two of them on the same side in the same meeting in the same place. It didn't seem fitting somehow.

It also made Mark nervous for Kate.

But when Mark caught himself thinking these kinds of thoughts he got annoyed with himself. He was second-generation Italian-American on one side and third-generation Italian on the other, so if he went about making judgment calls on guys like Rushman, that meant other people must make judgments about why he was friends with Kate, too. Where Kate was all old-line American WASP and looked the part,

Mark, at almost five nine, had all his life suffered nicknames like "Mr. Mafia." Yes, he had grown up in Westchester; yes, he had dual degrees in English and history from Georgetown; but still, he wondered if people thought it appropriate for a son of a delicatessen owner to be friends with Kate Weston as opposed to, say, Sylvie Botnik down the hall, whose grandparents, she had once told him, had made their money with a hot food stand at Coney Island.

No, no, no! Mark would think, *I loved and married Carla for the same reasons I like Kate—Carla was smart, funny, and sexier than hell.* And in the next moment he would think, *But she wasn't warm and caring like Kate. Carla pretended to be but she wasn't. Ever. So if being warm and caring are old-line WASP characteristics, then, okay, I'm as bad as Rushman—I love Kate for her old-line WASP characteristics.*

Once, early on in their friendship, when Mark one night served as Kate's escort to a black-tie dinner for the National Book Awards, he made some comment about his background, about how did Kate feel being escorted to this dinner by a guy whose college roommates had called him Don Marco? Kate had turned to him and said, "That's the first stupid thing I've ever heard you say. And I hope it's the last," and then she had started talking about something else.

The one drawback to their friendship had become rather painfully clear since Rebecca de Loup had arrived at B, F & C. Both Mark and Kate knew they should be making motions to leave Bennett, Fitzallen & Coe for healthier houses, but neither, at this point, could imagine working without the other. They were a formidable editorial team, and by default of a lasting administration they had become almost a small publishing company unto themselves, constantly going to bat for each other's books and supporting each other's offices completely.

Besides, Kate's assistant, Sarah (a wonderful young black woman out of Goucher College in Baltimore), got along famously with Mark's assistant, Dale Reilly (a bright but spacey aspiring writer out of Boston College), and so the four of them would have an early morning breakfast together once a month as a kind of private state-of-the-nation editorial meeting; a drink after work once a month, too, but just to gossip; and then, about once every six months, the four of them would do something fun and silly like organize a bowling tournament or a pinball machine play-off for anyone at Bennett, Fitzallen & Coe who cared to join them—and people from all over the company would.

But none of these things meant anything to Mark in comparison to what Kate had done for him after Carla left. He had been a mess. A total mess. He had cried, he had raged, he had shaken and threatened and walked the streets of New York at night praying for someone to kill him. No one did, though, and he suffered through it and got through it, but only because of Kate. She called every night for two months to make sure Mark ate. She called many mornings to tell him to make up his bed and clean up any dishes in the kitchen before coming in to work ("You have to act as if somebody lives there whom you care about—namely you," she would say). She took him, that second month, literally by the hand to her own therapist. And there were two—no, three—times he had called her at Harris's at around three in the morning, feeling suicidal, and Harris—well trained by Kate—had always sounded as though they had been up and expecting his call.

Three months after Carla's departure Kate announced it was time that Mark started looking like himself. When he asked her what that was supposed to mean, she reminded him that his contact lenses were a constant irritation to him, that he was always saying he thought he looked like a banker in his suits ("Watch it, hotshot," Kate would say when he said that, "I may be about to marry one,"), and he was always going on and on about being sick of having to shave twice a day.

"Yeah, so?" he had said, standing there in her office.

"So now you're free to be who you are," Kate had said. "You don't have to dress to please anyone but yourself anymore."

She was too tactful to say it outright. That he had always made himself look the way Carla wanted him to look because—well, because he knew what Carla wanted in a man. (Now, why he thought a book editor dressed like Wall Street would satisfy her craving for wealth was beyond him. The marriage was doomed from the beginning.)

And so Mark stopped shaving twice a day and grew a beard. ("Good grief, Fiducia," Kate had said, stroking it once with her hand to feel it, "four days and look at you." Smile. "I love it!") He also put his contact lenses away and had himself fitted for the kind of horn-rimmed glasses he had preferred to wear until he had gotten married. And then he left the suits Carla had liked in the closet and went with Kate to scout thrift shops in Fairfield County.

At Tots 'N' Teens in Darien they struck it rich. A lovely woman named Marjorie clapped her hands with glee when Kate told her what they were looking for and took them to the back of the store to show them three gorgeous tweed jackets, all the same size, which had come in on consignment only the day before. And so while Mark tried on these barely worn Ralph Laurens, Marjorie and Kate oohed and ahed, remarking on how minor the alterations would have to be.

"And my dear," Marjorie said to Kate, "do you have any idea what those would cost new?" "Oh, I know," Kate said, and Mark smiled to himself, noting how absolutely at home Kate was out here in affluent suburbia. "And Mark," Marjorie added, turning to him, blue eyes twinkling in delight—for it had become apparent that this really was the "heaps of fun" for her that she said it was, helping him pick out new clothes—"you look sensational. It's as though they were made for you!"

Mark was going to buy two, but Kate made him buy all three plus two spring jackets, three pairs of pants, and three ties, "Because," she said, "not only do you need them, but the shop's for the benefit of Planned Parenthood and Marjorie and these women are all volunteers." (Leave it to Kate, Mark thought, to raise money for Planned Parenthood while pushing him back into the world of dating.)

And so, one day last fall, Mark had shown up at work as his complete new old self. "Oh, it's true!" Kate cried when she saw him in one of his new jackets. "You're a hunk, Mark! You are"—she had paused, straightening his tie a little, brushing a little imaginary lint off his shoulder, and then giving him a kiss on the cheek—"a woman's dream of romance. And I'm proud of you. We're going to have to take a picture and send it back to Tots 'N' Teens."

Of course Rebecca had to make a couple of cracks in the editorial meeting like, "Where's Mark and who are you?" and, "Assuming that Mark's brain has not changed along with the rest of him, perhaps he'll read this proposal," snicker, snicker—but the other women in the office all complimented him. And they looked at Mark now. *Really* looked. And he felt great for the first time in years.

Of course, it didn't last. As the divorce proceeded, the old sick self-torment about Carla returned, the sleepless nights, the crying, the rage and anger, the replaying of every scene between them, saying something new, something different, something that might have made things come out differently . . .

And then, miraculously, it stopped. It had been around Thanksgiving. Instead of it being a nightmare without Carla, it turned out to be a release. He had spent it at Kate's—rather, Harris's. Kate's father and stepmother were in Portugal on holiday, so she was off the hook with the Windy Hills contingent, and Harris had his kids for the holiday, and so Kate begged Mark to come, if only because there was no one else who knew how to cook a real Thanksgiving dinner.

"And I refuse," Kate proclaimed, "to have Thanksgiving dinner catered like Harris wants. I mean really, I said to Harris, I think we'd be missing the spirit of things, don't you? I'm not sure the idea was for the Pilgrims and the Indians to go out and hire a caterer."

Mark gave Kate a shopping list and came over early Thanksgiving morning to help. He was, admittedly, a terrific cook—but then, when one's parents owned a delicatessen one learned young, and things like turkeys, chickens, and roasts were basics. As the morning proceeded, however, Mark began to catch on that Kate was not nearly so helpless in the kitchen as she had led him to believe (to which she responded, when he said something about it—after he noticed that she had gone ahead and stuffed and closed the turkey, forgetting to ask him how to do it—"If you breathe a word to Harris I'll never talk to you again. I can't be a good editor and have dinner ready every night—which is exactly what he'll want"), and they made a feast to be proud of: turkey and stuffing, real mashed potatoes, creamed onions, turnips, string beans, gravy of course, a molded salad, hot rolls, and an endive salad to start.

Sarah Steadwell came to dinner too, with a new beau, Will, a trainee at DBS News; some banking friend of Harris's named John Halifent, whose awful wife, Ramona, never stopped picking on him the entire time they were there; Harris's two rather sulky children from his previous marriage—Harris, Jr., and Juliet—neither of whom ever left the TV, not even to eat (causing an argument between Kate and Harris, which everyone overheard, about whether the children should join them at the table, as Kate maintained—prompting said children to screw up their faces at the prospect—or, as Harris maintained, to be left to eat in front of the TV because all they would do was crank and fidget at the table—thus winning quiet hoorays from his off-spring); and a blind date for Mark, a writer friend of Kate's from college named Loraine, nicknamed Miss Loola, who lived and worked in Australia.

They ate too much, talked too much, and Mark, after a couple of glasses of wine, unwisely disagreed with his host about why, exactly, the Indians had taught the Pilgrims to use a raw fish as fertilizer when planting corn. Harris insisted on the good neighbor version, that it was the first and best example of true diplomacy between two peoples in this land (*He's probably related to half the Pilgrims,* Mark thought; *no wonder he's so adamant*), while Mark explained that they had done so to make sure that animals would smell the fish and dig up the corn and wreck the crops so the invaders wouldn't have anything to eat and would go away. The nothing-to-eat part did happen the following year, but the invaders did not go away—although many did die of starvation, so, in a way, the plan had worked, but not in the way the Indians had intended.

Harris, tired of the discussion (he had drunk a lot of wine, Mark had noticed), finished his side of it by saying to Mark, "I never thought of you as a racist before."

Stunned silence at the table, forks halted in midair over pumpkin pie.

"The truth may not always be nice, I agree," Sarah said quietly, "but presented in the proper context I don't think it's racist."

Well, that was that. Harris Pondfield was not the kind of man to pick an argument about racism with a black woman at his dinner table.

And the end of the day—oh boy, the end of that day! Miss Loola was taking off for Australia the next day and she decided that more than anything else she wanted to make love to a good ol' fashion American man again before she left—namely Mark. "Has Kate ever seen you naked?" she said to him later, lying in bed at the St. Moritz.

"What?" he said, propping himself up on one elbow to look at her.

"Did she know—well, how well endowed you are?" she asked, smiling, touching his beard.

He was embarrassed and showed it; not knowing what to say, he simply made a growling sound and buried his face in her neck.

"I just wondered," Miss Loola said, "because she knows how I am."

He had raised his head to look at her again, this time somewhat shocked. *Did women talk like this with each other?* "Are we talking about Kate?"

Then Miss Loola had laughed, reaching down to pull him close. Pull him close down there, against her. "Oh, you're right," she said, "Kate's funny about these things. She listens but she doesn't talk." Pause. Smile. "But she must have had a hunch what you'd be like."

Mark smiled, realizing then that he knew Kate better than she did. "You mean," he told her, kissing her once, briefly, on the nose, "she had a hunch what you might be like for me."

Life changed after that night. Miss Loola went back to Australia, but Miss Loola had not been it. It hadn't been *her* that had made the night so special; it hadn't been the sex either (although, wow, what a welcome respite if only to know that everything still worked); what had made the evening so special was the absence of Carla's presence. And he had not missed her.

"Excuse me—Mark?"

He looked up to see Sarah standing in his doorway. He looked at his watch. "You should get going," he said. "Kate wouldn't like it if she knew you were here after seven." (Kate was concerned about the safety of the assistants and their potential for burnout, but she also, Mark knew, liked to end her office day undisturbed. Even after going out to meet an agent or author for a drink, Kate almost always came back to the office to wrap her day from seven to eight. Mark had learned to do the same.)

"I'm going in a few minutes," Sarah said, "but I just talked to Kate and I thought you'd like to know that everything's going really well with Lydia Southland now."

"Great," he said.

"So well, in fact," Sarah said, "she's going to Tucson, Arizona, with her as we speak."

— 6 —

When Kate called Sarah she left out the parts about Cookie and Cupcake attacking her at the gate; the security guys coming after her to bring her back; Lydia's female assistant making a pass at her; and the president of Bestar Studios yelling at Lydia Southland that she was a whore. Kate didn't mention these things because, judging from Lydia's behavior, none of it had happened—or if it had, it was irrelevant and certainly not worth discussing. Kate also didn't tell Sarah about how Lydia, bundled up in a trench coat, dark glasses, and a scarf over her head in eighty-five-degree weather, had only minutes before been pulled aside by LAX airport security at the checkpoint because she looked so strange.

"I thought you called ahead," Lydia had said to Noél, yanking her arm away from the woman guard and taking off her sunglasses.

"Jesus, it's Lydia Southland," the male security guard said.

"Oh, Miss Southland, I'm sorry," the woman guard said. "I didn't recognize you."

"You're not *supposed* to recognize me," Lydia said, putting her sunglasses back on.

"Hey, Cassandra," a man behind her, also wearing dark glasses indoors—and a black sweatshirt with the sleeves torn off—said, "heh-heh-heh, how 'bout a kiss?"

Lydia looked at him. "You're going to be kissing the ground in a minute," she said with a withering delivery, and pushed her way on, Noël, Kate, and Lydia's acting coach, Dee Powers, hurrying down the corridor after her.

There was a small incident at the gate, too; apparently security had called ahead to say Lydia Southland was coming and the gate attendant told another attendant and some passengers overheard and so by the time they reached the gate there was a small mob scene waiting. Lydia simply stared straight ahead, looking neither right nor left, and plunged right through the crowd, thrusting her boarding pass into the hand of the attendant and disappearing through the gate.

There had been twelve minutes remaining before the flight departed, and that was when Kate dashed back to a phone to call her office. Heaven only knew the next chance she'd get.

"I won't fly anything but a commercial flight anymore," Lydia said, sitting side by side with Kate in first class. "After one of our directors died this year in a chartered plane, I thought, 'Lydia, this is how Ricky Nelson died—and Carole Lombard, too.'"

"And Buddy Holly," Kate said, "and John Tower, Reba McEntire's band—and Kirk Douglas nearly died in that helicopter—"

"Exactly," Lydia said. "So only commercial flights for me."

They were on their way to Tucson so Lydia could shoot a new version of the season cliff-hanger for "Cassandra's World." (One of the tabloids had gotten hold of their scripts and had exposed the ending the week before.) The rest of the cast and crew had already flown ahead on a private plane.

Kate looked at Lydia. "Are you a Carole Lombard fan?"

"And who, may I ask," Lydia said, "isn't? She was wonderful."

"No argument here," Kate said, scribbling a note on a legal pad in her lap. "*Nothing Sacred* was always my favorite, I think."

"What did you just write down?" Lydia asked her. Kate showed her the pad and Lydia read, out loud, "Idolizes Carole Lombard." She looked at Kate. "So what?"

"So that should be in your book," Kate said. "You say nothing about who your favorite actresses are—or were."

Lydia thought about this for a moment and then nodded. "Okay," she said. "But there are others, too."

"Katharine Hepburn, for one," Kate said.

Lydia smiled. "How did you know?"

"You 'do' Hepburn in some episodes."

Lydia's smile expanded. And then she looked a little puzzled, tilting her head to the side. "This is very strange, you know, this rapport of ours—why is it, do you suppose?"

"I don't know," Kate said, shrugging, "but since it's not broken, let's not try to fix it." Actually, she had a pretty good idea why they were hitting it off so well. The best editors were often like the best actors, changing themselves to fit whatever role was needed to complete the job. And, too, Kate had grown up in a rather temperamental household; she was accustomed to reading the wind for answers when normal people would be found bothersome by asking out loud what was going on.

"Tell me something about yourself," Lydia said.

"What would you like to know?"

"Where are you from?"

"Connecticut," Kate said, "Windy Hills."

"Hmmm, sounds WASPy."

"It is," Kate admitted.

*

"Oh, no," Kate's roommate at college, Sherry Berman, had groaned that first night. "You're from Windy Hills?" Sherry had buried her head under her pillow.

"What? What?" Kate would say again and again to Sherry that first fall, angry and not really knowing why except that she knew she was being linked with something awful and Kate—even then—couldn't stand for people to think ill of her, particularly when it wasn't true.

"Weston, get it through your head," Sherry would say, "you don't order *salmon* for breakfast. Lox, *lox!* That's what normal people in the real world call it—lox!"

*

"Where's your father from originally?" Lydia asked her.

"Connecticut."

"Hmmm, sounds WASPy," Lydia said again.

"He is," Kate admitted.

"Weston . . . any connection to Weston, Connecticut?"

"Yes."

"Oh." Blink. "And where's your mother from?"

"Cosgrove Springs, Texas."

"Texas?" Lydia said. "Now that sounds promising. Is she nice?"

"She was," Kate said. "She passed away a long time ago."

"How long ago?"

"Uh—twenty-two years ago."

Squint. "And how old are you?"

"Thirty-three."

Pause. "So you were eleven."

"Uh-huh."

"And did she work? Your mother?"

"Outside of the house, no," Kate said.

*

In the Windy Hills Kate grew up in, fathers drove foreign cars to the railroad station and took trains into New York City to work, and mothers drove station wagons, raised children, and aspired to the presidency of the Junior League in between chauffeuring their young lot around to piano lessons, dancing lessons, swimming lessons, tennis lessons, riding lessons, and sailing lessons, to say nothing of baseball practice, choir practice, or any of the other practice-for-life sessions that went on in Windy Hills ad infinitum.

It was often said there was no such thing as a homely girl from Windy Hills. This was true. A girl was either good-looking by grace like Kate was, or she was made good-looking on sheer maternal will-power, involving endless trips to orthodontists and dermatologists, secret escapades in plastic surgery, covert vacations at fat farms, and the frantic calling-in of favors to get in to see one of *the* hairdressers in the city so that something could be done about daughter's awful hair. And if for some strange reason a girl from Windy Hills still somehow managed to grow up homely, then she never *left* Windy Hills, but stayed on to do something constructive like raise purebred huskies in her parents' backyard.

The boys, on the other hand, were all pretty much deemed attractive the way they were: bright, prone to smiling, addicted to athletics, acceptable at any height so long as never fat. The real wringer for the boys was the issue of brains, and so there had always been a most lively tutor trade in town, thus helping to significantly raise the standard of living for many of the town's teachers.

*

"And your father," Lydia said, "what kind of work does he do?"

"He's a surgeon. Orthopedic. He's still affiliated with Vanheusen Hospital in New York," Kate said, "but he's largely retired now."

"A surgeon," Lydia murmured. "And how old is he?"

"Almost eighty," Kate said.

*

Arthur Adams Weston, Jr., M.D., chose not to take a wife until he was thirty-five, and people who knew him found the way he did rather shocking. He met Elizabeth Gates in Austin, Texas, while attending a medical seminar at the university. She was a sparkling beauty of eighteen, a freshman at the university, working her way through as a waitress. She happened to wait on Dr. Weston. Dr. Weston, in turn, returned two times more to Austin and married the girl essentially the third time he saw her, whisking her out of Texas and plunking her down in Windy Hills to live as a housewife.

Only years later, looking back, could Kate see how out of place her mother must have felt. The front line of wives in Windy Hills tended to be women who had brought money with them into marriage, and those who hadn't usually brought class and breeding, often including a Smith or Radcliffe or Wellesley degree. Whenever she thought of her mother—so young, without benefit of higher education, never having ever been out of the state of Texas before—trying to make friends in such a community, Kate would wince, hurting inside, wondering how her mother had lasted as long as she had.

*

"Do you have any brothers or sisters, Kate?"

"Yes, one of each—they're twins, actually."

"Older or younger?"

"Older," Kate said. "Eight years older."

*

Elizabeth delivered to her husband Matt and Sissy—alias Matthew Adams and Cecilia Kindricks—right off the bat, and then, as a kind of wild afterthought, gave birth eight years later to her "baby," Kate, otherwise known as Katherine Gates Weston.

Kate grew up in a five-bedroom house with four acres of lawn and woods around it. The silver, the china, the paintings, much of the furniture, and many of the carpets handed down through the Weston family were considered irreplaceable. That's why, Kate's mother would say, it was so impossible to live there, that if she had any sense she'd pack up the children and take them to Texas and let Mr. Big Shot Surgeon take care of this museum himself.

But Kate's mother did not leave Windy Hills. Kate's mother had stayed on. The twins had gone to boarding school and then on to college and Kate was largely brought up as an only child—and largely as an only child with only one parent, because, after a while, Dr. Weston stopped coming home.

He came back, though, after Kate's mother died.

*

Lydia was studying her. "Why do I suspect there's a lot more to this story than you're going to tell me?"

A smile. "Because I'm not writing my autobiography—you are."

Lydia laughed. And then she looked across the aisle at Dee. The drama coach was studying a script. Noél was sitting next to her, curled up against the side of the plane, her eyes closed. "Dee," Lydia said, "are you ready?"

She looked up from the script. "Anytime."

"Would you mind changing seats now?" Lydia said to Kate. "I really need to start on—"

"Excuse me, Miss Southland?" a woman said, interrupting, appearing at Lydia's side in the aisle. "I hate to trouble you, but could I have your autograph?"

Kate thought Lydia was amazingly good-natured about giving her autograph to the woman, particularly since what she had been handed to do it with was an air sickness bag and half of a green crayon.

"Why does Gracia call you little señora?" Kate asked Noél after moving across the aisle.

"Because I used to be married," Noél said.

Kate's eyebrows went up.

Noél smiled. "Guess he didn't keep me sufficiently occupied, did he?"

"I'm sorry," Kate said, quickly, "I didn't mean anything by that."

"Of course you did," Noél said, laughing. Then she glanced over at Lydia—who was quietly reading from the script to Dee—and back to Kate. "I must say," she whispered, "you sure have come out here at an interesting time. Lots is going on."

"Tell me more about this Mortimer Pallsner," Kate said in a low voice. "You said he runs Bestar."

"Yes," Noél said.

"But isn't that unusual?" Kate said. "For an executive producer to also be president of the studio?"

"He wasn't always," Noél said, reaching forward for the flight magazine. "There was another president before—Ivan Kleindorf." She opened the magazine and started flicking through it. "He started Bestar with Mort in 'eighty-one, back when there were only two shows."

"Oh," Kate said. "And what happened to him?"

"Ivan?" Noél said, glancing up from her magazine. "He killed himself. Hung himself from a Calder sculpture in his front yard."

Kate stared at her. "What?" she finally said.

"He did," Noél said, returning to the magazine, flipping pages, "and it cost a fortune to keep it quiet."

"God almighty," Kate said, stunned, falling back in her seat. She turned her head to look at Noél again. "Does anyone know why?"

"Why?" Noél said. She shrugged, still looking at the magazine. "Because Mort wanted to be president, I guess."

Kate swallowed and looked straight ahead, wondering what, in Sam Hill, she had gotten herself into.

$$- \ 7 \ -$$

The heat hit Kate at the airplane door. She saw it, too, the distortions of the air being drawn sideways in it, the mountains in the horizon rippled by it.

Heat. Heat. Arizona dry heat. Six-thirty and it was, Kate thought, exactly like opening an oven door.

"Phew!" Lydia said in front of her, heels plunking down the stairs. "Now I know why they wanted to shoot the exteriors first. Another week and forget Calamity Jane, I'd be Miss Baked Potato of 1870." She had her trench coat and scarf and sunglasses back on and Kate thought she looked absolutely ridiculous. This was a way of not calling attention to herself? Walking around like Claude Rains in *The Invisible Man* when it was over one hundred degrees?

"There should be a driver here to meet us," Noél said from behind Kate. "He'll be holding up my name."

The terminal was mercifully well air-conditioned and Lydia headed straight for the driver holding a sign saying SHAUNNESSY. "Hello,"

Lydia said, handing her carry-on bag to him and turning for Kate's.

"Hello, ma'am," the driver said, tipping his cowboy hat with his free hand. He was in blue jeans, cowboy boots, a work shirt, and Texas string tie with a turquoise clip, and didn't seem fazed in the least by Lydia's getup. As a matter of fact, to Kate's astonishment, as they walked through the terminal, no one else seemed to pay the slightest bit of attention to Lydia's getup either.

"Oh, they see her," Noél explained. "But they figure she's a drug dealer or a terrorist and get the hell out of her way."

As they exited the front entrance of the terminal, Kate's attention was caught by a girl of fourteen or so trailing along beside them, eyes on Lydia. As they waited to cross the lanes of traffic to where the limo was parked, it was clear the girl was agonized over whether to say anything or not. Lydia noticed her too and, as they followed the driver across to a traffic island, she waved for the girl to follow.

"It *is* you!" the girl said, running over.

"Shhh-sh-sh-sh," Lydia said warningly, looking around. Back to the girl: "Now you are going to let me get out of here unrecognized, aren't you?"

"Yes, ma'am, of course," the girl whispered obediently.

"Good." Lydia slipped her glasses down just enough so the girl could see her eyes. "Your name?"

"Hazel Pralinski," the girl said. "Oh Miss Southland, you're the greatest! And once you gave your autograph to my grandmother in New York when you were on 'Parson's Crossing.' She framed it and everything and showed it to everyone, but then after she died Aunt Ruth took it—but I just can't believe it! Here you are!"

"I've got to go, Hazel," Lydia said, pushing her glasses back up on her nose and reaching inside her coat pocket, "but listen—" She took a card out of her pocket and pressed it into the girl's hand. "I want you to write me at this post office box in Hollywood and I'll send you an autographed picture that will make Aunt Ruth sick with envy."

"Gosh, thanks, Ms. Southland!" she said.

"Bye-bye, Hazel," Lydia said, giving the girl a warm handshake and smile before continuing to the car.

"Put the word *Cupcake* on the outside of the envelope," Noél instructed Hazel. "Then she'll be sure to open it right away."

"Great, thanks," Hazel said.

Kate couldn't help it. She looked at the girl. "How on earth did you know it was she?"

"I don't know, I just knew," Hazel said, shrugging. "Her aura, I guess."

Kate nodded, thinking she should make a note. Lydia's aura.

The car drove them straight to Old Tucson Studios. It was here, Lydia explained in the car, over the next two days they would reshoot scenes for a new ending to the Calamity Jane episode, the season cliffhanger.

"Ever see a picture of Calamity Jane?" Lydia asked Kate. She had taken off her disguise now and looked like herself. She leaned across the back of the limo to hand a photo to her. "They say Wild Bill Hickock gave her a tumble, but I don't know—I think she looks like Gertrude Stein on Slim-Fast."

Kate looked at the picture and smiled. Lydia was right.

"Let me see that," Noél said, taking it from her. She took one look at it, made a face, and tossed it back to Lydia. "She'd have to be straight—only a man would sleep with that." They all laughed.

Old Tucson was an amusement park as well as an "Old West" locale and so their car drove around to a back entrance of the studio. Originally, Lydia told Kate, the "town" had been built to shoot the movie *Arizona* in 1939, expanded to become the most convenient Old West locale to L.A. for movies—*McClintock, Rio Bravo, Rio Lobo*—and, after 1970, television: "Bonanza," "Gunsmoke," "Death Valley Days," "How the West Was Won," "Little House on the Prairie," and "The Young Riders" had all made use of the facility.

They stopped in front of a large trailer and a good-looking man in his early forties came out to meet them. "There's Gary," Noél said and Lydia looked and smiled.

"Hi," she said when he opened the door for her.

"Hi, Lyddie." He kissed her on the cheek as she got out. "Max and Skip are inside." He said hello to Dee when she got out on her side of the car, kissed Noél as she got out behind Lydia, and then looked a bit startled when Kate got out behind Noél.

"My new editor," Lydia said, "Kate Weston. Kate, this is Gary Steiner, head writer and story editor of 'Cassandra.'"

Ah-ha. The man Gracia had urged Kate to contact about Lydia's book.

"Kate, it's wonderful to meet you," he said, shaking her hand. He had warm brown eyes and wavy brown hair with a smattering of gray. He was about five ten, perhaps a little taller, dressed in jeans, cowboy boots, a striped cotton shirt, and a blazer that had to be stifling out here.

"Very nice to meet you too," she said to him. And then, as they followed the others, she added, under her breath, "Gracia said you might be interested in helping on the book."

"Somebody better," he whispered. "It's awful."

Kate laughed out loud.

"What are you two whispering about?" Lydia said, standing on the front step of the trailer, holding her hand over her eyes to get a better look at them. She turned her attention to Gary. "You can't be making a pass at her already."

"You'll have to excuse Lydia," Gary said to Kate. "She thinks I have no greater interests in life than women."

"Well, you don't," Lydia said, turning around and going into the trailer.

"I *am* a writer," he called after her, "and Kate *is* an editor."

"Lydia, Lydia, darling Lydia!" a deep male voice was saying from within.

The inside of the trailer was a makeshift conference center, complete with TV screen, bar, and kitchenette. Kate was introduced to Max Zacharius, the senior producer, a very large, bearish-looking man with a kind face, and then to a cute short guy named Skip Morris, who was some kind of producer.

"This is my new book editor," Lydia announced, "Kate Weston."

Max got a worried look. "Oh, no, it's on again?"

"It's on again," Lydia confirmed, moving on to the refrigerator and opening it. "Kate? Dee? Noél? How about some Perrier?"

They all said yes and Lydia went about setting four small bottles on the counter.

"Mort won't be pleased about this," Max said. "Not on top of everything else."

"Who cares?" Lydia said, opening the bottles with an opener.

"Lydia," Max sighed, "we have to work together."

"So we work together—" she said, looking around.

"Straws are on top of the fridge," Skip said.

Lydia reached for them.

"He's coming, Lyddie, to Tucson," Gary said. "He'll be on the set tomorrow."

Lydia shrugged, putting one staw in each bottle. "Then we'll just make sure Noél isn't."

"I can take care of myself, Lydia," Noél said, walking over and taking two of the Perriers, handing one to Kate and then one to Dee.

"I'm sure you can," Lydia said, "but on my time I'll call the shots, thank you." She looked at Max. "Why is he coming here?"

"He's bringing investors with him," Max said.

"So that's why he was so crazy this afternoon," she said, smiling to herself. She looked at Max. "Investors from where?" she asked, taking a quick sip of her Perrier, "Alcatraz School of Finance?"

"I can see this is going to be quite a shoot," Skip sighed.

Lydia looked at Kate. "Among the many favors our beloved executive producer has done for us all, Kate, Mr. Mortimer Pallsner was also kind enough to recommend my business manager to me—Mr. Fanning, the one who has run away to South America. Good friend of his, he told me, trustworthy."

Silence.

"And I find it so interesting," Lydia said, looking around the room, "that no one else seems to think it odd that the year poor Kenny wanted to retire from the show is the year Mort's friend ran off with all his money."

Silence.

Kate realized, in a split second, that everyone in that room was scared of Mortimer Pallsner. Everyone, that is, except Lydia—and maybe Noél. But then, why wouldn't they be after everything Kate had seen and heard so far?

Skip looked at his watch. "We should be thinking about getting you over to Aaron, Lydia."

"Yeah," Max said, coming back to life. "If you're up to it, he wants to walk through the street scene with you tonight."

"Sure," Lydia said, walking toward the door, sipping from her straw. "Oh, Gary—Dee and I have some line changes to go over with you."

"Why don't you go to wardrobe?" Skip said to Gary. "I'll be bringing Lydia there next."

"Fine," Gary said.

"And Noél," Lydia said, turning around, "will you get things squared away at the hotel? And then bring the car back?"

"Yessum, boss," Noél said.

"And Kate," Lydia said, "you come with me—but no talk, okay? You watch, you listen, but otherwise you don't exist. Got it?"

Kate nodded. She got it.

*

"Sorry about the heat wave, Lydia," Aaron Platz, the director, said. He was in a short-sleeved shirt, shorts, loafers with no socks on, and was wearing a safari hat. He was only about five feet four.

"Only directors who think they're God apologize for the weather, Platzer-puss," Lydia said, giving him a playful punch on the arm. "How are you?"

"Wish we could wrap this," he sighed. "My kid's graduating day after tomorrow in Pennsylvania and I'd like to be there."

"You'll be there," Lydia assured him. "I have a book to write."

"Oh, no," he said, wincing. "Mort's not going to like that."

Skip leaned to whisper in Kate's ear, "In case you haven't noticed, we all tend to be a bit vulnerable to Mr. Pallsner's moods." They were standing in the shade of the saloon on something called Kansas Street. Around them people were working on the Old West town, putting up signs, laying out electrical cables, measuring things.

"Can you at least wait to tell him about it until I'm out of here?" Aaron was saying to Lydia in front of the saloon.

Lydia only laughed.

Aaron and Skip then took Lydia down to the end of the street, about a hundred yards away, and stood there awhile, talking. Then, with Aaron walking backward in front of her and Skip to the side, Lydia slowly came down the street, mimicking the rhythm of horseback. She pulled up to the front of the saloon, got off her imaginary horse, tied it to the railing, and went up to the swinging doors. Again she and Aaron and Skip talked awhile.

Skip motioned for Kate to back away some—which she did—and Aaron took Lydia in through the swinging doors. In a moment, Lydia came bursting out; she walked down the steps to the street and then, slowly, turned around and made a motion as if she were pulling out a gun. She aimed it at the door and Aaron said, "Door first," and she said, "Bang"; Aaron said, "Then the upstairs windows, first left and then right," and Lydia aimed up there, "Bang," and then, "Bang"; "Whirl to your left and hit your knee, aim at the water trough," and slowly she turned, sinking to one knee (but not all the way) and aiming, "Bang"; "Then you're hit in the shoulder," and she clutched her left shoulder; "You turn around, shocked to see who it is," which she did, slowly, clutching her shoulder, eyes widening in disbelief; "And then he finishes you off—three bullets—leg, gut—you fall—and then one in the back," and Lydia bent suddenly, as if shot in the leg, then doubled over as if shot in the stomach, then twisted, starting to fall, but, instead of falling, she jumped up and cried, "Oh, poor Cassandra!" and everyone on Kansas Street burst out laughing.

*

As Lydia was being wrapped in soft leather, she said, "There izn't nuthin' a woman can't do if only she wants to try, so you tell Hickock from me that there izn't nuthin' Martha Jane Cannary can't do—" She broke off and groaned. "Oh, Gary, this is all gobbledy-gook—who can say this?"

"You're right," he said, jumping up from his stool and taking her script. With a pencil he sat down and scribbled away, conferred with Dee, raised his head, and read, "There isn't nuthin' Martha Jane Cannary can't do—*includin'* blow off that funny-lookin' little tie of Hickock's if he don't get out here and talk to me!"

"Better," Lydia said, turning so she could see in the mirrors how the pants fit in the back.

They fit unbelievably. But then they weren't really pants. They were two pieces of leather that were *stretched* around Lydia and hooked together. They were only for scenes where Lydia was standing, because she couldn't sit in them. "Perfect. Very perfect, Mrs. Southland," the seamstress said, running a hand down the side of Lydia's leg, smoothing imaginary wrinkles.

"I want to see these with the chaps over them though," Lydia said, turning around to view her rear end in the mirrors again. "Something looked funny to me in the rushes from last time."

The seamstress dutifully went off and returned with a pair of rough leather chaps and Lydia put them on. "Yep," she said, "there—look there, on the right—" She was pointing to her right buttock. "Something happens if I turn this way, it buckles or something."

"We'll fix it," the seamstress promised, fussing with the material over Lydia's derriere.

"Ready?" Dee said. Lydia nodded and Dee read, "There ain't nuthin' Martha Jane Cannary can't do—*includin'* blowin' off that funny-lookin' little tie of Hickok's if he don't get out here and talk to me!"

Without missing a beat, Lydia said, "Look here, mister, there isn't nuthin' Martha Jane Cannary can't do—includin' blowin' off that funny-lookin' little tie of Hickock's if he don't get his rear end out here and talk to me—*now!*"

"Good, good," Gary said, scribbling madly—as was Dee. "I like that 'look here, mister' and 'rear end' bit."

Lydia looked at him. "You sure?"

"No, it's good, Lyddie," he said, looking up. "And it's better that you don't say 'ain't.' "

Lydia looked at Kate. "Cassandra may wound," she said, "but Cassandra never kills. And that, in my book, includes the English language."

*

Kate was starting to fade until they had a dinner break at nine-thirty—in which, she noticed, Lydia didn't really partake. Kate's eyes traveled from Lydia's plate, which had a little tossed salad on it, back to her own, which in comparison was heaped with food. She looked up and found Lydia smiling at her. "I don't like to eat after six-thirty," she said.

"Why not?" Kate said.

"I'm never sure if I'll be up late enough to burn it off," Lydia explained.

Oh. Another reason Lydia looked the way she did. Kate made a note of it.

*

Ten o'clock. Kate and Noël and Skip stood outside the horse corral, watching.

Lydia was in blue jeans and cowboy boots, talking with the trainer. The corral—part of a studio area called High Chaparral, after the TV series—was lit like a night baseball game. A beautiful palomino was waiting nearby, saddled, ready to go. "Is this the horse Stella's using?" Lydia was asking.

"Who's Stella?" Kate whispered.

"Her double," Noël whispered back.

"No, ma'am," the trainer said, "but she's a close match."

"What's the matter with the horse Stella used?" Lydia said, patting the horse and taking the reins in her left hand.

"The insurers had a problem with her," he said, offering Lydia a boost.

She smiled, shook her head no, put a left boot into the stirrup and effortlessly swung her right leg over to sit on the horse. She allowed the trainer to adjust the stirrups. "I'm glad we decided to try this tonight, Alec," she said to him, settling in the saddle, standing in the stirrups and then sitting again. "I don't know why, but with these long stirrups, even galloping sidesaddle in a medieval costume seems more natural."

"You understand there's no posting, don't you, Mrs. Southland?" Alec said.

"Yes," she said, giving the horse a little kick to move, which he did. Instinctively Lydia tried to post anyway, was frustrated in the attempt and—bumping around the corral in the saddle—said to Alec, "If I can't *po-* ost, *wha-* at *am* I *sup-* posed *to* do?"

"Stand up in the stirrups," he called. "Just stand up and get your balance."

Lydia tried it, gave a laugh, and said, "Oh, that's right—giddap, my friend!" and a second later she was gently cantering around the corral.

"If you don't mind me saying so," Alec said, standing in the middle of the corral, hands on his hips, turning to watch Lydia as she went around and around, "I think maybe you were born to this."

Lydia only laughed.

*

"So how do you like being an actress?" Lydia asked Kate around midnight, yawning, pulling off her cowboy boots in the back of the car.

"I don't know how you do it," Kate said.

"I am paid very well to be able to do it," Lydia admitted.

"But none of this is in the manuscript," Kate said. "You say next to nothing about what your work is like."

"The only thing anyone has ever cared about," Noél said, "is who has Lydia slept with and who's on drugs, who's a pervert, who stole from whom—you know, the usual."

Kate looked at Lydia. "Is that true?"

Lydia nodded. "If not, very close to it. And I haven't even really gotten into the subject of Mr. Mortimer Pallsner yet, have I, Noél?"

"But do you want to write about your work?" Kate asked her.

"Of course I want to write about my work," Lydia said, sounding exasperated, "but I've had all those nincompoops to deal with and we never got anywhere."

"Oh, Lydia," Noél assured her employer, "you got somewhere— you've still managed to trash everybody in town." Noél turned to Kate. "And she thinks she's going to walk on two legs after the book comes out."

"I wanted to ask you about that," Kate said.

"About what?" Lydia said.

"About how you'll be able to work with people—like Mortimer Pallsner—after all the things you plan to write about him."

"If the book comes out in October," Lydia said, "I'll only have to work with him for about five months more. And after seven years, what's that? Nothing. Besides—Mort wouldn't dare do anything until the final episodes are in."

Pause. "Final episodes?" Kate said.

Lydia nodded. "This fall will be my last season—and then I retire."

Pause. "From the show?" Kate said.

"From everything," Lydia said. "Good-bye public life," she sighed, "and good riddance, I say."

Kate looked to Noél.

"Yeah, I know," Noél sighed. "Bummer, isn't it? But if it's any consolation, Kate, Mort didn't like the news much either."

$$- \ 8 \ -$$

"I don't know what to think," Kate said into the telephone a little before seven the next morning. She was sitting in her bed at her hotel, the Tucson *Daily Star* spread out before her, room-service coffee on the nightstand.

"Maybe room and board's part of her salary," Mark Fiducia suggested on his end. He was in his office at Bennett, Fitzallen & Coe.

"Beats me," Kate said. "I've known them—what? Less than eighteen hours and I've never been so confused in my life. Lydia says she wants to write the book, Lydia says she never wanted to write the book, Lydia says she loves acting, Lydia says she hates acting, she's leaving the show, she's leaving her life—she's married, not married, been married, Noél's married, Noél's gay, Noél lives with Lydia, their last boss hung himself in his front yard—I don't know what to make of it!"

Mark was laughing and Kate knew exactly how he looked: hair a little messy, tie loose already, jacket tossed on the windowsill, feet up on the typewriter stand, eyes looking out the window at Central Park, a mug of piping hot coffee (black, no sugar) that said SPORTS ILLUS-TRATED on it in his hand. Every time he took a sip, his glasses would fog.

Kate smiled at the image. She missed him.

"Leave it to you," Mark said, "to find out the siren of the century's got a live-in girlfriend. Now *that's* a publicity handle, Weston. If she won't promote the paperback, just drop that little bombshell to the press and the book'll promote itself."

"Oh, stop it, Mark," Kate said. "I have to protect her—if that's the case."

"There's also the little matter of you protecting yourself," Mark reminded her. "Rebecca's selling the book around here as if it's a fait accompli."

Yes. She would. So that if Kate failed to bring the book back it would be a complete unmitigated disaster for the publishing house and, not inconsequentially, for Kate. The time she had spent thus far with Lydia had done much to teach Kate about why Rebecca had been so eager to assign the book to her. The chances of getting everything sorted out with Lydia and the manuscript revised, rewritten, and edited in time were not terribly good.

"I've got a call in to Rushman," Kate said. "I've got to tell him about Lydia's plans to retire."

"You know what he'll tell you," Mark said. "As long as she's around to promote our edition, he won't care."

"We can't *not* tell the paperback house that she's not going to be on the air *or* be available to promote their edition," Kate said. "Mark, they're paying us a lot of money."

"That's why he won't care," Mark said.

The other line on her phone was ringing. She put Mark on hold to answer it.

"Hi, honey, how's the wild wild west?" Harris said. Kate could visualize how Harris would look this morning, too. Gray suit, pale blue shirt, blue-and-gray tie. As he talked to her on his speaker phone, he would be taking off his jacket and hanging it on the back of his office door. The office itself was a corner one, two walls of glass overlooking New York Harbor. Outside his office, Patty Ann, his secretary, would be making a fresh pot of decaf, and other employees, junior investors, would be lining up in the hall to see him.

"Hi," Kate said. "Honey, listen, can I call you back? I've got to finish some stuff here and I'd like to be able to talk for a bit."

"I beat Johnson in squash last night, that's the big news," Harris reported. "I'll be here in the office—call before lunch if you can."

"Will do," she said, thinking how much she hated his speaker phone.

"I miss you," he said, his voice sounding distant. "It was lonely in bed last night."

"I miss you too," she said, wondering if the line of junior investors outside his door was listening to this.

"Love you," he said, his voice coming closer again.

"Love you," she said.

*

Kate was a woman who had lived in New York City long enough so that every cab ride she took was haunted. No matter what part of the city she was riding in, at some point she could look out the window and feel her heart sink, a terrible loneliness coming over her, an unresolved grief.

Midtown made her think of Tom, of how whenever they had met, in those first two years out of college, Tom insisted on meeting somewhere like under the clock at the Biltmore for a drink and then having dinner somewhere like the Top of the Sixes, just as Tom's father had done with his wife-to-be in the 1950s.

That was the only time in her life, Kate thought, that she really might have been ready to get married, before she had known anything more about life. After Tom's mother had died—the circumstances of which had not been terribly different from those of Kate's mother—Kate had felt closer to Tom than to any other human being in her life before. Perhaps since, too. But then Tom had started drinking a lot and there had been episodes that had scared Kate, and so Kate had not married him.

To this day, Gramercy Park made Kate feel anxious. The three years she had spent in an affair with Lawrence—the older, powerful newspaper executive who had been free but who had not wanted her (he had never been faithful)—made Kate realize just how close to the rails she had been riding from age twenty-five to twenty-eight and how fortunate she was to have escaped that relationship.

The South End, near the World Trade Center, had been Alan, the state prosecutor, a dashing, really wonderful man whose only sin had been to be far too understanding of Kate's ongoing obsession with Lawrence after she had left him. Hating herself, she could not think highly of a man who said he could love her like this. She tried, she had tried (for Kate knew Alan would make a terrific husband and father), but in the end she succeeded only in driving him away.

SoHo—oh, God—was a tangled, tortured memory of Kate's brief romantic venture into the arts. Patrick the actor. The affair had been mercifully short but devastating and Kate vowed never to go near another "creative" type again.

The Upper West Side north of 110th Street was no longer a source of complete blinding pain, but it did still cause Kate to feel the low-ache echo of utter loss and failure every time she went near it. It was here, at Columbia University, that she had spent another two years of her life in a very complex affair with a dean of students. Kate had been madly in love with him, but he had still been madly in love with his ex-wife.

At age thirty, then, Kate's heart had ventured to Greenwich Village, where, for the first time in years, she got involved with a man her own age. He, like Kate, had been a book editor. And he—Sam—had been very smart, stable, good-looking, reliable, fun in bed, and—

And Kate, after six months, knew she had to leave Sam because he was in love with her in a way she knew she would never be in love with him—and should have been. And so there went all of Greenwich Village, wrapped in the painful memory of having met the right person, finally, but of having herself been the wrong person, as always. Or so it had always seemed.

Kate, age thirty-one. Location: the East Side. Enter the Doctor. A brilliant man who had offered to write the introduction to a book by a colleague of his, and who had come into Bennett, Fitzallen & Coe to deliver it to Kate and with whom Kate had fallen in love on the spot. Only she had not known it right then. All she had known was that she thought he was the most wonderful man she had ever met in her life and that although he was married and had children—both facts he brought up very quickly—Kate thought she would do anything if only just to know him. She asked him if they could have lunch sometime, to talk about the possibility of his writing a book, and they had had three such lunches on the East Side before the doctor told Kate that he was sorry, but he could not see her again. It was too dangerous, he said.

Yes. Right. Of course he was right. Of course.

Kate was not that kind of woman.

No, she wasn't.

So Kate had run into the open arms of Roger, a nightclub comedian she met at a publishing party, a month-long fling so disastrous that for several months afterward Kate considered herself extremely lucky if only to be left alone for the rest of her life.

Then, when she was thirty-two, Harris Pondfield entered her life. At forty-two, Harris was a private investment banker, former big-time corporate banker, and adviser to the Reagan Administration on debt.

They met at a party and he called her and called her and the next thing she knew, she was thirty-three and living with Harris on Central Park West, postponing acceptance of his proposal for marriage, wondering how on earth she was ever going to get to work if they broke up since she worked on Central Park West now, too—Central Park West, about the only neighborhood left in Manhattan that didn't break her heart.

"I'm beginning to think you're a woman who falls in love with people's apartments," Sherry Berman Meyer, Kate's former roommate at Saint Lawrence, said to her recently on one of her jaunts into the city.

"Don't start," Kate said to her.

They were in Harris's apartment. Dinner and dessert were long over. The foursome had stayed on at the dining room table, the men at one end and the women at the other, drinking wine, talking.

"I don't know, Kate," Sherry said, "I guess I would just feel better if we ever had dinner with you at the same apartment with the same man for two years in a row."

"Me too," Kate sighed.

"Or if we ever went to your place," she added. "I mean, it's very peculiar, Kate, to have an apartment for ten years that no one's ever seen."

It was true. Kate had an apartment on the Upper West Side, in the eighties, and she never invited anyone—not even Harris—to come over. Kate didn't know why she was like this, really, except that all her life she had needed a place to go where she knew she could shut out the world and be left alone when she needed to be.

"Why don't you marry Harris?" Sherry said, glancing down the table at him. At the moment he was deep in discussion with Jonathan, Sherry's husband. "He's stable, secure, and seems to love you," she said, turning back to look at Kate, "which I'd say is a vast improvement over that married doctor you used to go on and on about."

"There was nothing between me and that married doctor," Kate said.

"That's what worries me," Sherry said. "He's the only guy I've seen you fall in love with for years."

"That's not true," Kate said.

"It is true," Sherry said.

Kate put her glass down and looked at her friend, which she found a little unnerving, actually, because every time Kate did she remem-

bered they were no longer eighteen and college roommates, but fast
approaching thirty-four; and Sherry not only had a husband of eight
years, but two children, a house in Greenwich, two black labs—Zingo
and Zango—a cat called Kitty-Puss, a bunny named Twinks, and a
fully remodeled kitchen with two complete ovens and a built-in microwave, and Kate didn't.

Sherry glanced at Harris again and said, "They seem a little alike,
Harris and your father."

"A little," Kate said, drinking more wine.

"And I suppose he cares about his kids about as much as your father
cared about you," Sherry sighed.

"Sherry!" Kate said, putting her glass down hard enough so that a
little wine sloshed over the side.

The men stopped talking and looked up the table at the women.

Harris smiled. At forty-three, he was very attractive. A little short
on hair, but very long on charm, height, brains, and blue eyes. He had
a fairly wonderful body under those meticulous suits, too.

Kate smiled at him. "Sherry's giving me a hard time."

"Don't give Kate a hard time," Jonathan said to his wife, smiling.

"Okay," Sherry said.

When the men resumed talking, Sherry said in a low voice, "It's not
that I think anything's wrong with Harris—I like Harris."

Kate reached for her glass and finished drinking the wine in it,
thinking how Sherry was right, there wasn't anything wrong with
Harris—but thinking also there might be something wrong with their
relationship, namely that Kate was in it.

"He certainly does well," Sherry said, looking around the dining
room. "And at a time when I thought bankers were not supposed to
be doing very well." She turned to Kate. "Where did you say his
ex-wife and kids are? New Jersey?"

Kate only looked at her.

"Wish he didn't have those kids," Sherry continued. "But then
again," she sighed, shrugging, picking up her glass, "he's probably the
only eligible WASP left in all of New York." She took a sip of wine
and swallowed. "So if you're ever going to get married, I guess it's
going to have to be him or some young boy-child from Montana who's
gotten lost on a field trip."

"Oh, for God's sake, Sherry!" Kate said, thumping her elbow down
on the table and clamping her hand over her eyes.

There had been silence between the two women; there was the

murmur of the men talking at the other end of the table. After a minute, Sherry took Kate's hand away from her face and held it. "Kate," she whispered, "I'm sorry. I didn't mean to hurt you. But I worry about you, *bubeleh*. I want you to have something real in your life." Pause. "And so if Harris can be there for you, then, I say, okay, so be it—Harris it is."

*

Kate tried to clear her mind, returning to the other line on the hotel phone, back to Mark. "Sorry."

"Who was that?" Mark asked.

"Oh, nobody," Kate said.

"Oh, it was Harris," Mark said.

Pause. "Don't," Kate said.

"I didn't say anything," Mark said.

"But I can hear what you're thinking."

"I'm not thinking anything."

"That's right, you don't think, Mark," Kate said, "you just make silent little editorial comments about the content of my life."

"Kate, you're the one who makes silent little editorial comments on herself, not me. You've got the voices confused."

"Yeah-yeah."

"I love it when you're like this," Mark said. "You're always telling me about learned optimism and listening only to the supportive voices in my head. When the hell are you going to take some of your own advice?"

"Yeah-yeah," Kate said again, knowing what he said was true. She never had trouble consoling other people, but when it came to consoling herself she was still a no-show. Why, she had no idea. Or maybe she did and was too scared of the shake-up that might happen in her life if she recognized it.

He laughed. "Listen, just keep me posted on what goes on out there, okay?"

She smiled. "Of course I will. Oh!—and Mark, listen, could you check on the Quigley manuscript for me in copyediting? They swore they'd get it to us today and poor Sarah—"

The other line was ringing again. "Uh-oh—gotta go, Mark."

"I'll talk with copyediting," he promised. "Have a good one."

"You too." Click, click. "Hello?"

"Kate?"

"Yes?"

"Please hold the line for Mr. Rushman."

She did, sipping a little coffee to prepare her voice.

"Kate—how's it going?" Rushman said.

"Fine," she said. "I'm in Tucson—we're shooting a new cliffhanger ending. I wish you were here, Mr. Rushman, you'd like her a lot. You'd like the operation down here." Lies, lies, lies, but they always worked with him.

"Will you get the book?"

"I hope to. I think I've found someone to help—a friend of hers, a writer who's out here. We're supposed to go back to L.A. tomorrow, but she has to shoot some more scenes at Bestar on Thursday and Friday, so we won't really get started, I don't think, until Saturday."

"And how long after that?"

"At least two weeks—more than likely three. But I don't think we should count on a finished manuscript before mid-June."

"Can't you just finish it while you're out there?" he said.

Inwardly Kate groaned. What a pain it was to work for a toy salesman! Had he read *any* of the manuscript to see what a mess it was? How did he think she could write a book in two weeks?

"No," Kate said. "There are too many legal problems with the content of the manuscript," she added, knowing that this would at least register with Rushman. Maybe he didn't care if the book was in English or made any sense or had any redeeming value whatsoever, but he did care about lawsuits.

"I don't care what you have to do to get that book, Kate," Rushman said. "Stay until May if you have to, but we've got to have it."

"Even if it isn't finished until June," she said, "production says we can still make October on a crash schedule."

"Rebecca says we have to have the manuscript in May."

"It would be nice," Kate agreed, "but if you want me to have better luck with Lydia than Rebecca did, I wouldn't count on the finished manuscript being in until June fifteenth."

He sighed. "We have no choice then."

"No," Kate said. "And Mr. Rushman, I'm afraid we have a major snag on the paperback. After this next season, the one that begins this fall, Lydia told me she's retiring—leaving the show, leaving acting."

"So?" he said.

"So that means she'll be around to promote our book this fall, but won't be around the following fall to promote the paperback."

"So?" he said.

"So I think we better check with sub rights about the contract—about the guarantees that Lydia would promote the paperback."

Pause. "How much are they paying?"

"Minimum six hundred thousand—as high as one million four with escalators tied to hardcover performance."

"And how much have they paid so far?" Rushman said.

"They paid two hundred on signing," Kate said. "And then they pay another two on hardcover publication."

"Fine," Rushman said. "We wait for payment on our hardcover publication and then we tell them."

Kate swallowed. First he'd take their money, then he'd fight with the paperback publisher. "But . . ." Kate said, letting her voice trail off.

"I will apprise Rebecca of the situation, but I do not want you discussing this with *anyone*—do you understand, Kate?"

"I understand," she said, wishing that she didn't.

Someone was knocking on her door. She yelled, "Just a minute!" and then came back to the phone to get rid of Rushman. After hanging up, she went to the door and looked out the peephole. It was Noél. She opened the door, saying good morning.

"Wow, is my timing great," Noél said, openly admiring Kate's robe and nightie. "Anyway," she said a second later, clearing the air with her hand and walking in, throwing herself down in a chair, "Lydia wants to know if you'd like to join her at the studio."

"Sure," Kate said, sitting down on the corner of the bed. "What time is she going over?"

"Oh, she's been there for hours," Noél said.

"What?" Kate looked at the clock on her nightstand.

"She had a five-thirty call for rehearsal." Noél saw her expression and smiled. "It's not all fun, you know—she does work awfully hard."

"No, I knew that," Kate said.

Noél shook her head. "No you didn't. No one ever does, not until they have to keep the pace themselves—and find out why the stars of TV series want out after a while." She looked at her watch and stood up. "I'll take you over in about an hour, okay?"

Kate hesitated.

"What's the matter?" Noél said. "You need more time?"

"No, no—that's not it," Kate said, getting up. She hesitated again and said, "Well, to be honest, I thought Lydia said you weren't supposed to go near the set today. Because that man Pallsner would be there."

"My, my, Ms. Weston," Noél said, walking over to the door, "but you certainly do assume responsibility for other people fast, don't you?" She turned around, hand on the door, smiling. "Amazing," she said, shaking her head, "Lydia's got you so well trained already."

"Noél," Kate said, "you could at least tell me why she doesn't want you on the set with him."

"If you really want to know," Noél said, arching her eyebrows, "then I suggest you get dressed and come with me to find out."

— 9 —

At the studio, Noél led Kate into an enormous hangarlike building, a soundstage with four sets in it, each an angle of an Old West saloon. Lights and cameras and microphone booms and a camera crane were set up around the main saloon scene, a set of swinging doors and a long, long bar. About forty people—actors, technicians, crew (Kate spotted Dee, Gary Steiner, Skip Morris, and Max Zacharius)—were milling around, waiting. Lydia, in her skintight leather pants and chaps, blond hair under a wig, sporting a gun belt, guns, spurs, and a hat riding back on her shoulders held by a string around her neck, was standing by the swinging doors, looking—what? Bored? Impatient? Spaced out?

In any event, Lydia was just standing there, watching the director, Aaron Platz, talk to an older man dressed as a cowboy. Behind them were maybe ten other "cowboys" at the bar, a bartender, two dance hall girls; and, sitting in a chair in the corner, dressed in a black suit and black hat, with a funny little mustache and beard, Kate recognized Hal Lasher from the old TV series "Bolton, Private Eye."

"I'm going to leave you here," Noél whispered.

Kate looked at her.

Noél nodded across the soundstage. Three men in suits were coming in through a sliding door. "There's Mort," she whispered, "the one leading the way. See you," she said, and she was gone, slipping out the way they had come in.

Mortimer Pallsner did not look like a big-time TV studio president to Kate. Nor did he look like someone who could be responsible for his business partner's hanging himself from a Calder sculpture in his front yard. Quite simply, he didn't look important enough—or crude enough, for that matter—to say the things Kate had overheard him say to Lydia at her home. In fact, although he was wearing an elegant Armani suit, Kate thought Mortimer Pallsner looked like an aging tie salesman who had won the lottery or something. He was five feet nine, a little heavy, with brown eyes—a little like a basset hound after an eye job, maybe?—a dark tan, teeth too perfect to be real, and a brown-and-gray toupee that was pretty good. Was he fifty? Sixty? Kate didn't know, but she thought maybe closer to fifty since his eyes were so keenly alert, at this moment darting around the soundstage, taking inventory.

His eyes, in the course of his inspection, landed on Kate. He said something to the men with him and then walked over to Max Zacharius. He whispered something to Max and Max turned around, saw that it was Kate, smiled (a little nervously, Kate thought), and brought Pallsner over to introduce her. Max then excused himself, indicating there was a problem on the set he needed to watch.

"So you're Lydia's editor," Mortimer Pallsner said quietly to Kate, shaking her hand. "I was under the impression the book was off."

Kate was surprised at how firm and dry his handshake was. And how smoothly he spoke. (This guy was trouble.) "The old version is off," Kate said, "and we're hoping the new one will make you very proud. Certainly Lydia is very proud of what you've accomplished with 'Cassandra's World.' We were just talking about it—about how much Bestar has done to change the face of television. For the better, she thinks."

Pallsner looked at her and, for the first time, Kate noticed that he was chewing gum. For some strange reason she also noticed how good he smelled and wondered what it was he had on.

"I asked Lydia if she thought you might consider writing a book yourself one day," Kate added, smiling. "She said she didn't know, but that I should ask you."

Pallsner stopped chewing. "Lydia said that," he said.

"No, Mr. Pallsner." Kate laughed, touching his arm. "You're supposed to say, 'Me? Write a book? Gosh, I'd love to explore the idea!' "

There was a moment of hesitation and Kate wondered if she had been too obvious in her attempt to win him over. But no, she hadn't been, because now Pallsner had his hand over hers and was patting it softly, smiling. "Maybe we can explore it," he said. "How long are you out here for?"

His touch was not unpleasing. A shocker, but true. There was something perversely attractive about the man . . . She withdrew her hand, wondering if it was power. Sometimes that got to Kate. Power. When someone had it, earned it, exuded it. And even if Mortimer Pallsner was a glorified gangster of some kind, like the most successful people in any field, that meant he had worked harder at being a glorified gangster of some kind than most everybody else. Maybe he should write a book.

Wait—*what* was she thinking?

"Two or three weeks," she told him.

"And where can I reach you?" he asked, gazing into her eyes.

"Um, well," Kate said, "at Lydia's, I guess—"

"And at night?" he said softly.

"Uh, the Shangri-La Hotel in Santa Monica," she said.

"I know it," he told her.

"You do?" she said.

"I know everything," he said, winking and giving her hand a quick squeeze as he turned around toward the set.

It happened so fast Kate wasn't sure at first if he had really squeezed her hand. But he had. And as if to complete the illusion that it had not happened, he asked her, eyes on the set now, "How long have they all been standing around, Kate, do you know?"

"I just got here," Kate said. "I'm afraid I don't know what's going on."

"I bet I know," Pallsner said. "Lydia insisted we give that old coot Benneger a guest shot before he starved to death and now he can't remember his lines." He sighed in disgust. "I told her I'd pay him *not* to come."

Charles Benneger? Kate thought. Sure enough, it was Charles Benneger, the great swashbuckler of the forties, on the set. But old. Really old now.

Pallsner gave a low whistle and hissed, "Max!" Max came quickly. "How long and how much are we gonna pay to support this exercise in Alzheimer's disease?" Mort demanded. He pointed to the men who had come with him. "Mr. Viellas and Mr. Cord are not impressed."

"If you'd let Lydia—" Max started.

"Fine, I hereby let Lydia," Pallsner snapped. "Get this vehicle on the road, Max—now." He turned to Kate. "Excuse me, but I have business to attend to." And then he smiled, lowering his voice. "I look forward to seeing you again, Kate—when we can have a chance to talk. Properly. Dinner, perhaps."

E-gad! Kate thought as he walked away. *Now what have I done? The guy runs the studio, Lydia's at war with him and he's probably murdered somebody, and I told him where to find me at night?* With a creeping sense of anxiety, Kate tried to return her attention to the set.

Max was across the soundstage talking to Lydia. In a few moments Lydia nodded and went over to Charles Benneger. Aaron, the director, retreated to the sidelines. Heads close together, Lydia and Benneger talked. Then Lydia took a few steps back and murmured something; Charles Benneger took a step forward, said something, and nodded. They did it again.

Gary Steiner appeared at Kate's side. "There's an ironclad rule at Bestar about stars not directing," he whispered. "Not that Lydia wants to—but people respond to her in a way they never do with Aaron."

"Then why is Aaron the director?" Kate whispered.

"Because he's Mort's cousin, mostly," he said. "But he's not so bad."

On the set, Lydia gave a pat to Benneger's back, waved to Max and Aaron, and returned to her position by the door.

"Okay, let's have quiet," Aaron said. "We're going to try it again."

"Okay, everyone in position, we're going to try it again!" Skip yelled across the soundstage. "Let's go people, we're going to do it this time!"

There were murmurs as people climbed back up ladders, cowboys sat down to play poker again, the bartender returned to tending bar. A piano started playing somewhere and the dance hall girls sashayed in once more and stopped on their marks.

"Okay, quiet, quiet on the set!" Skip barked.

In a moment, things were indeed quiet. Aaron looked around the set and then nodded. "Roll 'em!" A young man scampered out onto the set with a clapper board. "Scene seventeen, take nine!" he said, clacking the board shut.

"Okay, action!" Aaron said.

The cowboys were fraternizing when suddenly the swinging doors burst open and there was Lydia, looking pretty sexy and mean and tough. Kate tried to remember what Noél had told her to keep in mind—that Lydia was not playing Calamity Jane, but playing a modern-day history professor who was pretending to be Calamity Jane.

The bar went silent, the piano stopped, everyone looked at her.

"No women allowed in here," the bartender growled.

"That's not just a woman," Charles Benneger said, thunking down his glass, "by golly, that's Calamity Jane!"

"Calamity Jane!" the crowd murmured.

"God almighty, Deadwood'll never be the same," Charles Benneger said.

Lydia threw her head back and roared in a deep, sexy laugh. And then she looked at them all. "If there are no women allowed," she said, striding in, "then what are those ladies doing here?"

The bartender said, "Whoring," and the men broke up.

"You—" Charles Benneger started to say—but stopped.

Uh-oh, Kate thought, *he's forgotten his lines again.*

Lydia had pulled out her gun and was now walking over to the bartender—slowly, spurs jingling. Boy, did those pants fit! "He was going to say," Lydia said, kicking her head in Charles Benneger's direction, "that you shouldn't have said that—because *I* once worked in a saloon." She leaned against the bar and stroked the bartender's throat with the barrel of her gun. "I think you made a mistake, mister," she told him. "I think women are allowed in this saloon and I think you owe those ladies an apology."

Silence.

Lydia cocked her gun. "What do you say?"

The bartender swallowed. "I—I'm sorry."

"Louder, please—and look at them while you say you're sorry."

The bartender looked at the women. "I'm sorry."

Lydia lowered her gun.

"Hello, Calamity," Hal Lasher said from the corner.

Lydia smiled, swinging her hip out as she put her gun back. "Well, hello, Wild Bill. Some people are looking for you, I hear."

"Ohhh, here it comes!" Charles Benneger cried, falling back from the bar. "Ain't no good gonna come out of Calamity and Hickock together—I'm getting out of here!" He hurried out the door and there was the sound of a gunshot "outside."

Hal Lasher stood up and put on his black hat. "Sounds like people have come a' callin' on us, Jane."

"Cut!" Aaron cried.

"Yes!" Max cried.

Charles Benneger came back to stand in the swinging doors. He looked old and small and sheepish. Lydia went over and kissed him on the cheek.

"Excuse me, Miss Weston?" a woman said to Kate. She was young-ish, but dressed very efficiently in a business suit. "I'm Mr. Pallsner's secretary, Helena Carbonelli."

"Call me Kate," Kate said, shaking her hand.

"Mr. Pallsner wanted to know if you would like to join him for dinner this evening," she said.

"Tell Mr. Pallsner that Kate has plans for dinner," Noél said, appearing out of nowhere. "She's eating with Lydia."

Helena's eyes had gotten quite large. "Noél," she said, sounding surprised.

"Nice to see you too, Helena," Noél said.

"I mean," Helena stammered, "you look so different—so wonderful!"

"Thank you," Noél said. "You look good, too—you've lost weight."

"I'm on Jenny Craig now," Helena said.

"Did you bring a lunch?" Noél asked her. "We're eating in Max's trailer—you could heat it up or boil it or whatever you have to do to it."

Helena looked surprised for a second time. "You mean, for me to come eat with you?"

"Sure," Noél said, "why not?"

"Well, Mr. Pallsner is going into town, so maybe," Helena said, looking a little apprehensive. "But I thought . . ."

Noél smiled. "You never did anything, Helena. Lydia knows that. Besides, she likes you. So do Gary and Max and everybody. I'll tell them you're coming."

Helena went off and Noél led Kate out of the soundstage. "So," Noél said, after they had walked awhile, "old Mort's hit on you already." She laughed to herself, shaking her head. "I had a feeling he might go for you—if not for your looks, then to get a spy on Lydia's book."

"Yeah, great," Kate sighed. "So now what do I do?"

"Hide behind Lydia," Noél advised her. "Whatever he asks you, say you can't because you're with Lydia."

Kate felt some of her anxiety dissipate. "Okay, I will."

"And don't feel bad," Noél said. "Everybody hides behind Lydia when it comes to Mort."

Kate looked at her. "And you?"

"I have," Noél said. "Actually," she added after a few steps, "I had to. I don't know what would have happened to me if it hadn't been for Lydia."

"Why, Noél?" Kate said gently.

Noél looked at Kate. And then she smiled. "Because I used to be Mort's mistress," she said.

— *10* —

For a girl from Hingham, Massachusetts, who was supposed to have the perfect life, Noél Shaunnessy had certainly screwed hers up with some of the choices she had made. Her choice of friends at boarding school, with whom she drank and smoked pot almost every night; her choice of boyfriend at Brown, who talked her into trying cocaine; her choice of husband, that is, her preppy drug dealer, Kevin Arsford; her choice of a best friend when they landed in Los Angeles, a woman who promptly seduced her; her choice of lover she left her husband, that is, her drug dealer, for, Hesta Logan; and then Noél's choice of lifestyle after she met Mortimer Pallsner, executive producer of "Cassandra's World": to accept a production job from him, later to accept cocaine from him, and, finally, to accept Mort himself sexually too.

It had come as as much of a surprise to Noél as to everyone else that she had been his mistress. She had never once thought of it in those terms while it was happening. In fact, until three weeks into treatment at the Betty Ford Center, she had not believed there had been anything between her and Mort that could have been construed as any kind of relationship. "How could I have been his mistress if I think I'm gay?" she had asked her group, who in turn had broken up with laughter.

In the past year and a half, however, it had become painfully clear to Noél that if the world had ever even heard of Noél Shaunnessy from Hingham, Massachusetts, it had only been in the context of her being Mortimer Pallsner's young and pretty and sort of crazy redheaded mistress.

Yes, *that* Pallsner, the man whose name came up at the very end of the credit rolls of no less than three prime time TV series as executive producer. Yes, that Pallsner, the fifty-five-year-old with the toupee who recently graced the cover of *Emmy* magazine.

On one hand, however, Noél's time at "Cassandra's World" had been a success. She had learned a lot and, indeed, had learned how to be a first-rate production assistant. Only at the end did she have to have drugs to function, so only at the end had there been the more awful humiliations: the trysts Pallsner had demanded in the little room behind his office; the blowjobs he had wanted in the backseat of his limo (and under the table once in a restaurant); and the flaunting of Noél and his other drug-abusing mistresses (for he had quite a collection, at least for show) in front of his creepy friends. But therein lay the benefit of having been an alcoholic and drug addict—Noél had to experience those humiliations only after the fact, really, because at the time she had been too out of it to care.

But her past had caught up with her. She had not had a drink or a drug in over eighteen months, but she was still hearing things about herself. Stories. About things she had done. And Noél had started to remember a lot, too. About her past. About things she had done. And so Noél was still prone to crying late at night. About her past. About things she had done.

Still, though, there was a sickly kind of rush from having been associated with someone that anyone in Hollywood with a brain in their head was terrified of. Lydia had asked Noél early on if the stories were true, that Pallsner was tied to organized crime. Noél told her of course he was—where did Lydia think the "investment capital" in Bestar Studios from South America had come from anyway, coffee bean growers? Criminy, Mort *was* organized crime. It was cocaine cartel money behind Bestar Studios, everybody knew that. Mort and Ivan Kleindorf had agreed to launder the cartel's money in exchange for a chance to produce television shows.

What was so funny—and people had to hand it to Mort, Noél thought—was that nobody had expected Bestar to produce some *hit* TV series as well as eighty cents clean on every dirty drug-profit dollar. So old Mort—in his own thoroughly debased way—had made a goodly fortune by ostensibly honest means. He had put a lot of it to good use, too. He built a new lab for a cancer research hospital, a screening room for a major university, provided seed money for a program to assimilate minorities into TV production, and, by 1988, had become the fourth-largest fund-raiser for the Republican party in the state of California. All of this, needless to say, had helped his social standing immeasurably.

Noél had run into the second Mrs. Pallsner in Palm Springs only two weeks ago, at a celebrity-professional tennis tournament Lydia had been playing in. Beatrice Pallsner was probably the only person who hadn't known about Noél's role in her husband's life, but even if she had, she never would have acknowledged it. Too much depended on her not doing so. Pallsner had rescued her from a New York millionaire who used to beat her, had vowed to kill her, and, at the very least, was determined to get his kids back from her. (That's what Mort said, anyway—but then, who knew? Studying his picture in *Business Week,* Noél hadn't thought Beatrice's first husband looked like a wife beater. But then—again—who ever knew?)

"Noél, my dear, how are you?" Mrs. Pallsner had said, kissing the air on both sides of Noél's cheeks.

Noél had always liked her. As "Mr. Pallsner's special assistant" at Bestar Studios, Noél—coked higher than a kite—used to help her with studio-connected fund-raisers all the time. But then, after one of them, held outside on the Pallsner estate, Mrs. Pallsner had taken Noél into the pool cabana and kissed her longingly on the mouth. After that Noél had taken great care not to be lured into being Mort's wife's mistress too (particularly since Mrs. Pallsner was on the executive committee of the Hollywood "Just Say No" campaign).

In any event, while Noél's mental, physical, and spiritual self had been busy deteriorating on the cocaine Mort's associates supplied her with, she had managed—to this day, she didn't know how, except that she must have been acting very normal at the time, that is, had enough coke and alcohol balanced in her to be somewhat stable—to start an affair with the supporting actress of "Cassandra's World," Holly Montvale. In the beginning, Holly thought she could pull Noél out of the downward spiral she was in. After several months, however, she panicked that Noél was going to pull her down with her and so— terrified for Noél, terrified of Pallsner, terrified for her own career— Holly had gone to her friend at the show, Gary Steiner, himself a recovering alcoholic, and pleaded for his help and advice about what to do.

Gary had then gone to the only person on the production who could interfere with one of Pallsner's drug-addicted mistresses without getting fired. Namely Lydia, the star of the show; namely Lydia, Gary's longtime friend from their New York days working on a daytime soap.

And Lydia, not even knowing Noél except by sight, had gone up against the executive producer of "Cassandra's World" to demand that his "special assistant" at Bestar Studios, namely Noél, be put in a rehab for her drug and alcohol abuse before she died. Though Pallsner had not taken this edict well, nonetheless Noél had been sent away—but then Noél checked herself out and went straight back to Pallsner and the house he kept her in *and* back to the drugs and the drinking. Two months later she was vomiting blood at the studio and the next thing she knew she was in Cedars Sinai Hospital; two weeks later, in the Betty Ford Center in Rancho Mirage; and six weeks later, Gary Steiner was driving her back to Los Angeles, informing her that she was going to live at Lydia's and work as her personal assistant until she got back on her feet.

That had been sixteen months ago. Where Noél would go from here, she still didn't know. Her life "out there" was still uncertain. Her own brain, she thought, was still uncertain. Lydia had made it clear to her that she was welcome to stay as long as she liked—the only two rules being that she regularly attend both AA and Cocaine Anonymous meetings and that she would never, ever be alone with Mortimer Pallsner again.

— *11* —

Kate was still trying to digest the implications of what Noél had just told her. That she had been Mortimer Pallsner's mistress, but with the added revelation that she was now—and had been, since she had left him—a recovering drug addict and alcoholic. Kate assumed this disclosure was offered as an explanation of how she could have gotten herself into such a situation.

It still didn't explain much to Kate about Noél's relationship with Lydia, though. Did this mean she had gone from being Pallsner's mistress to *hers?*

No, no, that can't be it, Kate thought, following Noél into the trailer.

The conference table had a spread of catered food and Max, Skip, Charles Benneger, Hal Lasher, Aaron, Gary, Lydia and a few others were gathered around, eating from a very expensive version of paper plates. Lydia was sitting with Gary, still in makeup, dressed in a robe, eating pasta salad. Looking up, she did a double take at Noél. "What are you doing here?" she asked her.

"Don't worry," Noél said, "I've been incognito all day."

Lydia looked at her a moment, and then looked at Kate. She started to say something, but then stopped. She stood up, put her plate down on her seat, and said, "Excuse me, but I need to make a phone call. I'll be right back."

— *12* —

The intercom on Mark Fiducia's office phone buzzed, startling him. He was filling out the financial sheets on a book he wanted to buy. The straight numbers didn't work and so he was employing some numerical sleight-of-hand in an attempt to get the proposal past the anal, arithmetic-fixated mind of associate publisher Dick Skolchak and approved by Rushman when it seemed that no acquisitions were being approved under any circumstances. He picked up the receiver. "Yes?"

"Ooo-la-la, vive la Hollywood," Dale said. "Lydia Southland's calling!"

"Huh," Mark said. He punched the phone line button. "Ms. Southland, hello," he said. "How are you?"

"In desperate need of information," she said. "And so I'm hoping you will be a reliable source"—pause—"Mr. Faith and Trust."

He grinned. "Well, I hope so. What's up?"

"Wait, hold on a sec," she said. Then he heard her say, "No, that's not the right color—I was wearing a pale pink blouse in that scene." Pause, a murmur from someone. "Then don't believe me—go check the continuity sheet. Go! And close the door behind you, please." A squeal and thunk. "Sorry about that," she said.

"That's okay," he said. "You're in Tucson, aren't you?"

"Yes," she sighed. "Trying to do fifty million things in two days. Anyway . . ."

"What would you like to know?" Mark asked her.

"Well, first off," she said, "you can tell me if Kate's straight."

Mark hesitated, blinking rapidly. "I'm sorry, what?"

"Is she straight or gay or what?" Lydia said. "I don't have much time, so—"

"I don't see what it would matter *what* she is," he said. "It would never have the slightest bearing on the job she did on your book."

"So she's straight," Lydia said, giving the impression that she might be writing this information down.

"I didn't say that," he said.

"Come on, I live in La La Land," she said. "Yes, you did."

"Now wait a minute," Mark said.

"No, you wait a minute," she said. "Do you or don't you want Kate to finish my book?"

"Not if it takes snooping around in her personal life," he said.

"And *what*, for crying out loud," she said, "do you think she's doing out here with mine? I'm trying to shoot an episode while Miss Smoothie Weston is out here sneaking around with my staff—probably trying to find out who *I'm* sleeping with."

Mark started to smile. Miss Smoothie Weston. Yep. A good name for an editor with powers of somewhat divine manipulation. "Ms. Southland, I can't imagine Kate ever asking a question like that."

"Listen, this is important," she said, "because before I take her home I have to know who and what she is. After all, you were the people who sent me that pervert Ayres Hasnack."

Mark couldn't help but laugh. Ayres was pretty awful. "Ms. Southland, let me assure you, you have no worries with Kate on that score."

She sighed. "I don't like making this phone call, you know. And I could care less what her sexual persuasion is—but if she had a thing for parrots, Mark, and I knew I had a parrot living in my house, a *lonely* parrot, then I should know beforehand, shouldn't I? Just so I know what we might be getting into?"

He was smiling. "Yes, I understand." He cleared his throat and said, "Well, listen, Kate lives with a guy. She'll probably marry him. His name's Harris Pondfield."

"You don't sound very enthusiastic," she said.

"I'm not," he admitted.

"Why?" she said.

"Well, you know, Kate's a friend, and you never think anyone's good enough for your friend."

"And he's not?"

"I don't think so, no," he said.

Pause.

"More a bastard or a buffoon?" she asked next.

"Sorry?"

"Is her live-in more of a bastard or a buffoon?" she said. "With her temperament, it's one or the other I'd imagine."

He hesitated and then said, "Uh, buffoon."

"Uh-huh," Lydia said. Again Mark imagined she was taking notes. "Okay," she said a moment later. "Now, are you married?"

Mark laughed. *Well, why not? She's only one of the most beautiful women in the world and, as Kate always says, you never know.* "Was. I'm divorced now."

"Me too," she said.

Mark smiled.

"And how old are you?" she asked next.

Mark's forehead wrinkled. "I'm sorry, but what does—"

"Have a little faith and trust," she told him. "How old are you?"

"Thirty-two."

"You weren't born in July, were you?"

Mark was really thrown now. "Yes, I was. July fifth."

"Right," Southland said. "My secretary's astrologer says that Cancer would be a strong sign with Kate. I'm a Cancer too."

Mark couldn't believe this conversation. But then, Lydia Southland did live in California.

"Well now," Lydia said then, "this is all very helpful." Pause. "Mark, I don't think we need to mention this call to Kate, do you? Then, you see, we could keep our line of communication open for the next couple of weeks while she's out here."

He cleared his throat and touched at his glasses. "I'm sorry, I don't understand."

"You know, if I have any more questions," she said, "or if you do."

"If I have questions about what?" he asked her.

"About Kate," she said.

Pause.

"I'm sorry," Mark said, "I still don't understand."

"Oh, but I think you do," she said in a decidedly inflected tone.

He really didn't understand, and yet a thrill ran through him.

"You don't think she should marry the buffoon, do you?"

"Well, it's not really any of my business," he said.

"But maybe it should be," she said. Pause. "I've only been with her a day and I know all about you and she's never even mentioned him."

Swallow. Careful. "I'm her colleague. It would be natural for her to talk about me."

"How ever makes you most comfortable to think about it," she said. And then, softly, "Mark."

"Yes?"

"Why not let our line of communication stay open," she said. "What harm could it do?"

A lot, he thought.

"Will you give me your home phone number?" she said.

He gave it to her.

And when he got off, he remained in his chair, staring at the phone. Shaken. Really shaken. It wasn't sickly fear but the thrilling kind—the kind that makes one feel scared to feel what one's feeling because one knows it's irrational and yet, with a kind of sixth sense, one thinks maybe there's good reason to think what one is thinking because it might be true; and, if it is true, then what one is feeling is not only a good thing, but maybe the start on a road to a dream coming true.

She knows, he thought, *somehow she knows.*

How, in a few hours, could Lydia Southland have come to know what had taken him months and months and months to know for himself? That he was so very much in love with Kate?

— *13* —

Lydia was in much better humor when she returned to the trailer after making her phone call. She came straight over to Kate to ask if she had gotten enough to eat, and had she gotten something to drink; and then, as she walked back to her seat, she touched Noél's shoulder in a way that Kate knew was a sign that all was well with her.

"What happened to Lydia's last husband?" Kate asked Noél, watching Lydia sit with Gary Steiner again.

"Oh, she got rid of him," Noél said matter-of-factly. "But that was a while ago."

"Bill Lakersdale, right?" Kate said. "He's in the manuscript. And her first husband was Chuck somebody, right? When she was very young?"

Noél swallowed a piece of her salad. "There was another one, you know, in between those two—now whether she'll admit to him or not on paper is another question. John. She really doesn't like him."

Kate looked at her and Noél shrugged. "You'll have to discuss it with her—and for Pete's sake, don't tell her I told you about him. Say you read it in some magazine or something. Helena," she called to Pallsner's secretary, who had come in, "come sit next to me and tell me how you are." Helena sat down on the other side of Noél, balancing what looked like a frozen dinner on her lap. "Are you still married to that handsome man?" Noél asked her.

"Jerry has his own air-refrigeration company now," Helena reported.

"Kate," Lydia called across the trailer, waving for her to come over.

Kate moved to the other side of the trailer, sat next to Lydia, and discussed the scene she had watched being filmed, and then the work Lydia had to do in the afternoon and evening. They had already filmed the shoot-out sequence in the street at six this morning, because the early morning light was similar to the light during the evening, when the shoot-out was supposed to occur, and they needed this evening's light to film the sequence of her riding into town, which also was supposed to occur in the evening. Kate laughed and asked if all these scenes were supposed to make a story somehow and Lydia explained that nothing ever made any sense while shooting; everything was shot in order of production needs, and only later, after everything was edited into sequence, did the story make any sense.

"And not always then," Gary added.

"I didn't realize writers worked so closely with actors," Kate said to him.

"Well, they don't usually," Lydia said. "It's just that Gary and I have worked together for a million years."

"I used to write for 'Parson's Crossing' in New York," Gary explained.

"And made me a daytime star," Lydia added, looking at him with obvious affection.

"And you've worked together all these years?" Kate said.

Both Lydia and Gary smiled. "No, not all," he said. "I came out the second year of 'Cassandra.' "

"Lydia?" Skip said from the trailer door.

She was on her feet immediately, excusing herself to get ready for the next scene. Gary also excused himself, saying he needed to find the rewrite person. Kate went back to sit with Noél and listened to her chat with Helena. Noél, Kate knew, was not just having a friendly little lunch with Helena. Noél, Kate knew, was working, hunting for clues about what was going on in Pallsner's office these days. Sarah did the same thing for Kate at Bennett, Fitzallen & Coe.

After Helena left, Noél got them each a cup of decaf, settled back in her chair, and said to Kate, "Do you want to know how cheap Mort is?"

"How cheap?" Kate said, sipping her coffee.

"Picture this," Noél said. "The star of the show flies down to Tucson at the request of the producer to reshoot an episode she has already finished. Given the fact that she's supposed to be on hiatus and wants to work on her book, said star decides to bring her book editor with her."

"Right," Kate said.

"Executive producer meets said editor on soundstage and hits on her," Noël said.

"Right," Kate said, wincing slightly.

"And then he turns right around and tells his secretary to find out who's paying for the editor's airplane ticket and hotel room, that it better not be his studio."

Blink. "You're right," Kate said, "he is cheap."

"Lydia's paying for them, by the way," Noël said. "That's the way she is—she doesn't stick it to the studio like everyone else does."

"We should put that in the book," Kate said. After a moment, she turned to Noël. "I didn't know Lydia and Gary worked together in New York. She doesn't say a word about him in the manuscript."

"Well," Noël said, "I guess some things in the past are better left unsaid."

Kate was confused. "Why?"

Noël looked at her expression and laughed. "Gosh, for an editor you sure miss a lot of the story line around here, don't you?"

Kate shook her head. "I'm sorry, I don't understand."

"Can't you tell?" Noël said. "Most people can after being around them."

"Tell what?" Kate said.

"That Lydia and Gary used to be lovers."

— *14* —

While Lydia filmed her riding scene that evening, Gary had a chance to talk to Kate Weston about the book. Kate, he quickly realized, was on Lydia's side and, thank God, thought the working manuscript was as awful and detrimental to Lydia as he did. She asked him a lot of questions about how he worked on scripts, was very interested to learn that he kept a journal—writing maybe three or four thousand words of narrative each night on his computer—and that his background was in English.

She liked him, Gary knew, and he knew she liked the idea of working with him over hiatus to salvage Lyddie's book. But would Lydia like the idea? That was the question.

"Why would she object?" Kate asked him.

"Because she's had all these jackass writers and editors telling her how wonderful the manuscript is," he said. "Remember, Kate, she's been working on it for three years and that manuscript is all she's got to show for it. Under those circumstances, you tend to get a little attached to whatever progress you've made."

They looked at each other and burst out laughing.

Yes, it was going to be a good fit, Gary knew, the two of them.

When Gary had graduated from Columbia University in 1970—cum laude—he had looked for a job related to writing and, after extensive research, interviews and follow-ups, had narrowed his search to three incredible opportunities: to enter the prestigious training program at Doubleday & Company for six thousand a year; to enter the prestigious internship program at the *Paris Review* for nothing a year; or, to write a script on spec and, if they liked it, join the writing team of "Parson's Crossing" for fifty thousand a year—which is exactly what he had done. But then he had been both exceptionally lucky and exceptionally talented, two attributes graduates of Ivy League colleges in those days had rarely directed toward the perpetuation of TV soap operas.

Ah, New York. Good ol' New York . . . Had Gary become elitist by moving to L.A.? he wondered. His neighborhood wasn't all white or anything, far from it—but his neighbors were very well off and anyone who wasn't was stopped by the police within minutes and questioned. So yes, he thought; the answer was yes, he had become elitist. He had come to feel more at home in a city where the east side and the west side were sixty miles apart—and might as well be entire worlds apart.

In New York Gary had lived on the West Side of Manhattan, not far from where "Parson's Crossing" was taped near Lincoln Center. His neighbors had been a mix of friendly middle-class and upper-middle-class people, a rainbow of age, race, religion, and income; but then things had started to change. Rapidly. His neighbors started getting really, really rich or really, really poor; some bought entire floors of the building to expand their residences while others were bought out or simply harassed out to make way for them. Street-death kind of drug dealing moved into the streets of Manhattan with crack, and street-death kind of poverty moved in as well with the dismantling of federal programs: the mentally ill were turned out of hospitals; convicted felons were turned out of prison by court order because of overcrowding; single-room-occupancy hotels were converted to condos and co-ops, pushing low-income people into the streets, too, with nowhere to go; and the otherwise usual bureaucratic nightmare that was New York City continued on, with organized crime, as tradition demanded, draining one-fifth of the city's treasury gross.

Drug-dealing school principals, billionaire crooks, desecrated temples and churches, gang rapes, gang murders, police hits, precinct scandals, premeditated murders, unpremeditated suicides, babies found in trash cans, babies having babies . . .

Suddenly Gary had hated Manhattan.

Hated it, hated it, hated it.

Of course, Gary had been slowly drinking himself to death at that time, so his outlook on life had not been the greatest. He could have resumed doing all the things he had always loved to do before, but had stopped: he could have gone to Mets games and Knicks games and Rangers games and cheered and booed; he could have gone to the most magnificent research library in all the world at Forty-second Street and Fifth Avenue; he could have played softball in Central Park and tennis on clay courts in Riverside Park; he could have coached a basketball team for the Police Athletic League; he could have wandered the food fairs and ethnic festivals with his wife, holding hands, sampling too much of everything; he could have gone to the museums he loved, or to Lincoln Center, or to the movies, or to the theater; or he could have gone bowling, played some pick-up basketball in the schoolyard, shot some pool, or taken a nighttime sail up the Hudson.

He could have kept up the mortgage payments on their Connecticut house, too; he could have refrained from totaling two cars, one on the West Side Highway, one on the Merritt Parkway; and certainly Gary could have tried to do something about his drinking. But he hadn't, and the drinking kept him in bars, in lots of dark places (particularly in his own head); and the drinking cost him his wife and very nearly his life in a number of ways and on a great many occasions.

But Gary Steiner was Jewish, and everybody knew Jews didn't drink. Right?

Yeah, right, Gary thought.

It was a long story, really, stemming back to when Gary had first met Lydia years ago in New York—he as a "Parson's Crossing" writer, she as a fledging actress landing her first big break, a role on the daytime soap. For nine years they worked together and then, in that last year, they had been lovers, too. Lydia's third marriage had failed; Gary's first had failed; they had been the walking wounded; they had turned to each other.

*

"Oh, no," Kate Weston groaned, holding her hand above her eyes, squinting up the "wild west" road, "they're going to make her do it again?"

Gary snapped out of his thoughts to look. Yep, they were going to make Lydia ride into town again. She had down it twice already. The first time, something had gone wrong with the principal camera; the second time, a lighting technician fell off his ladder into the reflector he had been holding and then down on top of Aaron.

It was hot as hell still, and dusty, too. Lydia had to be broiling in that outfit, but she didn't complain. She merely trotted back to the end of the street to try the scene again.

*

How could he not have fallen in love with Lydia in those days? She was so incredibly young and talented and beautiful—and vulnerable. And helpless. And depressed. And dependent. Those gorgeous big blue eyes always longing to be rescued. Just the kind of woman Gary liked in those days. But, as luck would have it, Gary had been married all of a month when he first met Lydia Southland. Still, had she done as much as crook her finger in his direction, even that first day, he knew he would have dumped Rachel in a second.

Lydia *needed* someone like him, he had thought at the time. He could help her with her career, and he could help her with her self-esteem; most of all, he could make love all day and all night to a woman who looked like that! Maybe she was a little weepy and flaky, and maybe she was terribly insecure and a little wishy-washy, too, forever changing her mind, not being able to make a decision . . .

Yes, Lydia Southland in her twenties had been very different from the woman she was today.

Within a week of her arrival on the set of "Parson's Crossing," Lydia's nightmare of a husband at the time became common knowledge. This was her second husband, John. Lydia was forever in tears over him, forever scurrying to the phone in between takes to try to find him, to try to check up on him.

He was a drunk, John was. A wealthy, drunken bully from West-

[85]

chester who one day actually came in and hit Lydia in the studio. In front of everyone.

And that did it. Finally. Young, weepy Lydia seemed to turn into a cool iron lady on the spot. She looked her husband straight in the eye and said, "It's over, John, that's it," and calmly walked to her dressing room while security ushered him off the premises. Lydia divorced him on the grounds of physical and mental cruelty, using, in fact, the incident at the studio as evidence. In that one regard Lydia had not changed much. If someone compromised her in the public eye, then that was that. They were gone. Banished. Even then Lydia wanted to be a great actress more than she wanted her neurotic love relationships.

Within a month of her divorce a Texas zillionaire named Bill Lakersdale appeared on her arm around town. It took a while for Bill to get his divorce finalized back in Houston, but when he did he and Lydia were married. It was a big deal. Outwardly Gary had been happy for Lydia. Inwardly Gary had been dying. No doubt about it. He loved her.

In the six years Lydia was married to Bill, Gary was promoted first to head writer and then to head writer/producer, and Lydia's popularity on "Parson's Crossing" soared, basically because Gary was so in love with her that he wrote every show *for* her. The other actors had gotten increasingly upset over this, but the breakthrough ratings on the strength of Lydia—year after year—made the creators and producers and network all very happy.

But Gary's drinking increased steadily. He fought with Rachel more and more, he started sleeping around, he started getting half-cocked at lunch, all the while watching Lydia, longing after Lydia, every day of his life wishing like hell she could somehow love him, too. Rachel left him finally. Rachel divorced him finally. He lived by himself with a constant stream of women.

And then cracks started appearing in Lydia's perfect marriage and Bill was around less and less, and then, not at all. Rumors started that he was in Houston dating a twenty-two-year-old socialite.

But Lydia was a full-fledged actress now, a huge soap star with five daytime Emmys to her credit, unable to go anywhere without fans besieging her. If there was trouble in her personal life, she no longer let it show. She simply carried on, her usual warm, endearing self, prying out of Gary yet another new sensational story line to make her even bigger.

And then it happened. Lydia came into Gary's office one afternoon, closed the door behind her, looked at him, and said, "Bill and I are getting a divorce. I think I would like to start a new relationship with someone—and I think that someone is you."

Gary had nearly fallen out of his chair. (He'd had two martinis and two glasses of white wine at lunch, so he might have anyway.) He managed to stand up and say, "When?" in a strangled voice, and Lydia had said, "Tonight? Could you come for dinner?" And then she had frowned and shaken her head. "No, not my place—I don't want the memories." She looked at him, big blue eyes pleading. "Your place? Could we go there?"

Of course they could. (Gary had to get on the phone and get his cleaning lady over there posthaste: "Get all that shit out of the closet in the bedroom." "Miss Berry's things?" the cleaning lady had asked. "*Any* woman's things," he said. "Merry Christmas, it's all yours, just get it *all* out of there!")

They left the studio together at seven and went to his apartment. The cleaning lady had done her job well. The apartment fit the story he had concocted for Lydia: that he was devastated when cruel Rachel had left him; that he did not know if he could ever love again. ("Of course you will, darling Gary," Lydia would say, squeezing his hand sympathetically, tears hinting in her eyes.)

In any event, from the assortment of delivery menus in Gary's never-used kitchen, they ordered food in. Mexican. They never ate it, though. Instead, it languished on the kitchen counter as they sat on the couch in the living room, talking—Gary drinking scotch, Lydia drinking white wine—about the show, about the story lines, about Lydia's strong points, about areas Gary thought she could work on. "Would you like to be my Svengali?" Lydia said to him, scooting over to lay her head gently on his shoulder.

"Yes," he said, kissing her ear lightly, "yes. I'll be anything you want." And he had put down his glass and taken her glass and put that down as well, and he had kissed her the way he had dreamed of kissing her for years. As he kissed her, though, as her mouth expertly eased open and her tongue so perfectly teased him, he had to wonder if she was really feeling anything. Or was she so used to all those clinches he wrote for her on television, week after week, that he was now simply getting back from his creation the choreography of his own fantasies?

It was indeed like a fantasy, and years later Gary realized that Lydia

was such a basket case after Bill left her that she had probably no more
made love to him emotionally that first night than the man on the
moon. She had been lonely and frightened, he could see in retrospect;
she had been searching for somewhere to go at night, somewhere
where someone might care for her. And she had known what to do
to please him; someone had taught her well. She knew how to kiss his
neck and ears, whisper in them, run her hands through his hair and
over his chest. She had known what blouse to wear and how to sit so
to let him slip his hands easily into her blouse to get at her amazing
breasts. And she knew—oh, she knew—how it would feel to him if she
suddenly kissed him hard, as if she could restrain herself no longer, and
reached down to feel him between his legs. And then, hands trembling,
a look of both desire and fear in her eyes—again, as if she could restrain
herself no longer—she fumbled to unzip his pants and touch him.

And touch him.

And touch him.

The way she touched him had been reverent. He did not think any
woman had touched him that way before. Not with such exquisite
care, not with such gentle purposefulness, not with such an unabashed
desire to excite him until he couldn't stand it any longer. Her hands,
her mouth, even her breasts—he had simply sat there, holding his
breath, wondering how long he could hold back.

His drinking had made him accustomed to slow and occasionally no
starts by that time, but with Lydia's touch that night and with Lydia's
mouth—oh, *God* . . . he didn't mean to, but . . . oh, *yeah*—he held her
head in his hands and came in her mouth. He couldn't help it. She
seemed not in the least disturbed by it—pleased, even—and she got
him a new glass of scotch and returned to the couch to cuddle with
him, talking, whispering, bare breasts rubbing against him, clothes bit
by bit coming off over the hour, slowly and exquisitely seducing him
all over again, working him up to such a state he ended up taking her
right there on the living room floor, unable to wait.

Had Lydia come for real that first night? He thought so. She had
cried afterward, lying there, asking him not to move, to stay right
there, on top of her, and he did. It was very beautiful and he would,
frankly, never forget it.

But that was the only good night they had. They tried, but it didn't
happen again. It was all arguments over his drinking, it was Lydia
getting hysterical over his drinking, it was Gary drinking even more
in spite; and it was, for the next month, very little sex, even if she

wanted to have it, because by the time they finished fighting and making up he was too drunk to get an erection. "You've got to stop," she would say. "You've got to stop being so fucking neurotic and making me drink," he would say.

And then something happened. What, exactly, Gary didn't know, because he was in a blackout when it occurred. All he knew was that when he woke up the next morning Lydia and her things were gone and when she came into work that afternoon, gingerly creeping in, it was with one broken rib and three cracked ones. She told everyone she slipped and fell on some stairs. Everyone told Lydia she was heroic to show up when she was in such pain.

They would not be lovers again. There were nasty phone calls instead, nasty scenes behind closed doors at work. Two months later Lydia abruptly gave notice to "Parson's Crossing" and disappeared. Really disappeared. No one knew where she was, not the press, not even her agent. And then, nearly a year later, she resurfaced in Los Angeles.

"I still care about you, Gary, but I need time," she said in their first telephone conversation. "Then we can try to be friends again."

"But I don't want to be friends, Lydia," he had said, pleading, "I love you! I want to marry you!"

"Gary," she had said (in a tone of voice he wished he could forget), "that's out of the question. You are a mess. An absolute mess. Your whole perception of life is screwed up; your self-esteem is nonexistent; you're always depressed. The drinking is just the overt suicidal part. I can maybe someday be your friend—but not in your personal life. I've been getting help, Gary, and I understand a lot of things about myself I didn't know before. I'll never be with an alcoholic again. Never."

"But you said you still cared about me," he said.

"I do," she said. "And that's why I hate you so much right now." Pause. Her voice breaking, she finished, "Leave me alone, Gary. I'll call you when I can be friends."

In between the time of that conversation and when Lydia called again, Gary had quit "Parson's Crossing" over artistic differences (which is to say he was fired, bought out of his contract) and he stayed home to write a novel. Which he didn't. For three months he did this—not writing a novel. But he did drink a lot. Lydia, on the other hand, was having incredible success in the lead of "Cassandra's World." That first season had been a bit shaky in the ratings, but the demographics were good, the critics sort of liked it, and the network renewed for another season. "Come talk to Mortimer Pallsner," Lydia said to Gary when she called again. "We need someone like you on the writing team. You know me, you know my strengths—Pallsner said he would see you, so come."

"And we'll be friends?" he asked, hoping maybe they could be more than that, but only having to look in the mirror to know that it would be impossible. He was a mess physically by then, too; really, a sad case, not even out of his thirties. The bloating, the skinny little legs. (*When did his happen?* he remembered thinking.)

"We can try to be friends, Gary," Lydia said, "but first you've got to clean up your act, and then let's try to get you employed."

And so Gary had taken a week to dry himself out, pull himself together, and he borrowed the money to fly out to L.A. to have dinner with Mortimer Pallsner, executive producer of "Cassandra's World." The dinner started out great, but then Gary had some wine and, later, at Pallsner's urging, hit the brandy. He had no memory of the evening after that, except that Pallsner's limo had driven him back to the hotel. The next day Pallsner called to say he could have a year's trial on "Cassandra's World"; who was his agent? And Gary, that afternoon, went out and got a new agent, since his last one had cut him loose.

He started work, desperately trying to keep his drinking under control. Lydia was friendly, but wary, making it clear he was not to cross the professional line. And so he did not. He worked—hard. And he contributed a lot to make the "Cassandra's World" scripts better.

And then he heard about the new Mortimer Pallsner series going into production, "Robbie's Gang," and Gary, outraged, had gone to see Pallsner, remarking on what a funny coincidence it was that his new show was about a team of private investigators working for a young paraplegic mastermind.

"Coincidence with what?" Pallsner said.

"With the concept I told you about at our first dinner," Gary said.

Without batting an eye, Pallsner said, "I don't know what you're talking about, Gary. You were drunk and anything you said—if I were you—I should hope is forgotten."

"And if it isn't?" Gary said.

Pallsner's demeanor had changed then. His eyes had narrowed and he had taken a step forward, saying, "It doesn't matter," giving him a little shove backward, "because you're a drunk, Steiner, a lousy, stinking drunk. Everybody knows what happened in New York and anyone who doesn't only has to ask anybody who's ever worked with you to find out what your problem is."

The next day Gary had received a one-hundred-thousand-dollar bonus from Mr. Pallsner. The check stub said it was for "Creative Consulting on 'Robbie's Gang.' " Gary had then gone out on a bender. He came out of it in a Santa Barbara detox ward.

"Golly," Lydia had said to him when he came to, "if this is what working with you is like, I can hardly wait to see what being friends with you is like." Yes, there was Lydia, sitting next to his bed in the detox ward, making the other guys who were shaking and retching and moaning in the ward think they were seeing things. Cassandra was here. From TV. Wow.

And she told him, as he lay there, what had happened. About how he had called her at her Malibu beach house (he remembered that); about how she had been having a party, and said that if he wanted, he was welcome to come (he remembered that); about how he had arrived a bit intoxicated (he remembered that); about how later he had jumped over the deck railing and run down to the beach (he did not remember this); about how he had run into the surf; about how Lydia and her boyfriend had plunged in after him, new dress and everything; about how they had hauled him out of the ocean and carried him up to the house, half-drowned; about how the ambulance had arrived and Gary had somehow disappeared (he remembered this; he remembered knocking some guy out of the way and running down the driveway through the parked cars); about how six hours later he had called Lydia from a phone booth in Santa Barbara, crying, "I'm going to kill myself, Lydia. Good-bye, I always loved you," and how Lydia promised that she would come, if only he would tell her exactly where he was. And so he told her where he was and Lydia had called the Santa Barbara police.

From the hospital in Santa Barbara Gary had entered the Betty Ford Center. He was ready. And it worked. And when he got out and returned to Los Angeles, he went to an AA meeting every single night even though he hated it. And then he came not to hate it. And then he came to feel better. And then time passed, a day at a time, and he used his one-hundred-thousand-dollar "bonus" to pay off some of his debts from New York—to the IRS, for one, before they sent him to prison—and he worked hard on "Cassandra's World" and the scripts got better and better and Gary got better and better and now, today, Gary Steiner was the story editor of a hit television series he loved, and he was healthy and good-looking and was, best yet, five years, three months, and two days sober.

Lydia had been unbelievable in his recovery. When he had come home from Betty Ford, she had been there, sitting on the front steps of his rented house with two guys, Sturgeon Fields, an actor from the series, and Skip Morris, the associate producer. "They thought you might like to know that you all have something in common," Lydia said, and that night Skip and Sturgeon took him to an AA meeting. Skip, in fact, soon became Gary's sponsor—and still was, to this day.

And Gary did not even remember how it happened, exactly, but after being invited over to breakfast at Lydia's a couple of times, he had also started to be invited for lunch on weekends, and then for dinner once in a while, and then he had been welcomed to just stop by and take a swim or hit a tennis ball or something after work, and then, pretty soon after that, it seemed, he was coming and going as he pleased as a friend—no, as family. And Gary didn't question it; he didn't analyze it; he didn't mess with it; he did as Skip strongly suggested that he do, which was simply to accept Lydia's offer of familial friendship as the gift it was—and take his neurotic romantic impulses elsewhere!

Lydia had seen him through a lot these past five years. And Gracia too, bless her. Drink signals, high anxiety, deadly depressions, failed romances, debts, insomnia, more failed romances, the death of his father, more debts after crazy spending sprees, run-ins over his perfectionism, court with the IRS! Gary couldn't imagine his life without Lydia and Gracia—and they generously said they couldn't imagine their lives without him. And then there had been the whole Noël bottoming-out escapade and, after she came to live with Lydia, the four of them—Lydia, Gary, Gracia, and Noël—had been bound into a kind of family relationship Gary prayed would never diminish.

They meant everything to him. Lydia especially.

Lydia. Always Lydia. Always Lydia.

T W O

Friends

— 15 —

Bestar Studios in Los Angeles was located in the old Metropolis Pictures studios near Burbank. There was no affiliation between companies, Noël told Kate as she drove her there; it was a straightforward rental agreement, so well negotiated by Ivan Kleindorf and Mortimer Pallsner that not one of the three subsequent owners of Metro had been able to get Bestar out. "They hate having the FBI watching the place all the time," Noël explained.

After being checked through the front gate by the guard they drove slowly down Main Street, turned left on Tom Sawyer Avenue (having to stop short to miss hitting some guy cutting across in a golf cart—the mode of transportation, Noël explained, in production areas), and then they turned right on Cassandra Boulevard, which, despite its impressive-sounding name, was merely a narrow asphalt access road through what looked suspiciously like army surplus housing to Kate, but which was, in fact, Noël said, the production offices of Bestar Studios.

They turned into the "Cassandra" parking lot and spotted Lydia's car immediately, the silver Rolls-Royce Corniche (Noël said Lydia always played the star bit to the hilt in the vicinity of the studio), and parked at the end of the first row in a space stenciled VISITOR 1 in white paint.

To Kate, the studio looked like Westchester Airport times five. There were no outdoor sets here, not like Universal or Old Tucson. Here it was one enormous hangarlike building after another. They reached a hangar that said CASSANDRA'S WORLD over the entrance, but Noël didn't go inside, pointing to the red light above. "They're filming—we have to wait. Hi, Alfred, how are you?" she said to the uniformed guard.

"Miss Shaunnessy," Alfred said, tipping his hat. "It's been a long time and may I say that time has treated you well."

Noël grinned. "Thanks. You too."

When the red light turned off, they went inside. Here, Noël explained, were the permanent sets for "Cassandra's World": Cassandra's office at the university where she taught; the podium of her lecture hall; the faculty lounge of the history department; the foyer, living room, kitchen, bedroom, bath, and "outside" patio of her home. (The establishing shots they used for the exteriors of the school were actually from the UCLA campus in Westwood, the exteriors of Cassandra's home were actually of a little old lady's house in Glendale, and the fictional town of Los Panos was actually Whittier.)

Lydia was on the set of Cassandra's living room/library. Her hair was up on the back of her head in a bun; she was dressed in a conservative cream-colored suit and wearing horned-rimmed glasses. This was her professor outfit. The concept of the show was that Cassandra had developed a psychic ability to transport herself through time—an ability that rendered her the best history teacher in the world. The problem was, however, that sometimes her concentration accidentally pulled her off into the past when she was quite unprepared to leave the present; and while she was gone, time stood still, so that many times when she returned to the present she would be acting very peculiarly.

The fun of the show was not only in the reenactments of historical events, but also in dramatizing the unsettling effect her historic adventures had on uptight Professor Cassandra Hale. Cassandra, in other words, was forever having inexplicable and horrendous mood changes in the present.

The scene they were currently shooting was set in the present. In Cassandra's living room, Cassandra (played by Lydia) and her boyfriend, Chase Draper (played by Wesley Hart), were being asked by Cassandra's friends and neighbors, Jane and Trainer Phelps (played by Holly Montvale and Sturgeon Fields) to baby-sit for their daughter, Faith (played by seven-year-old Sybil Montgomery).

They were all gorgeous, these actors. Wesley Hart was a so-so actor but a very handsome man with an on-screen warmth that had made him into a kind of matinee idol; shorter than Lydia, Holly Montvale was a voluptuous brunette, whose looks, Kate could tell, had been deliberately played down; Sturgeon Fields was very tall and almost bald, but with a very handsome, rugged-looking face; and the little girl, Sybil Montgomery, had brown hair and the most amazing big blue eyes.

Someone asked for quiet on the set. People were in place. The lights came on, brilliant. Silence. Roll it. Scene one, take two.

Lydia and Holly were talking over Sybil's head. Sturgeon spoke from where he stood in the doorway. Wesley was sitting on the couch, looking annoyed at the intrusion of the neighbors. Sybil took Lydia's hand and tugged on it, saying, "Please, please, please, Aunt Cassandra, can't you please baby-sit me?" And then something happened. The child was to run over to Wesley, but when she did she caught her foot on the coffee table leg and went down—hard—making everyone gasp.

Lydia was the first to reach her. The little girl was at first too surprised to do anything, but a moment later she started to howl. The "baby wrangler" came running onto the set and carried her off to the side. The child's howl turned to simple crying as she was comforted. A doctor arrived. The lights on the set were shut off while the cast and crew stood, waiting.

"She's absolutely fine," the doctor called across the soundstage.

The cast and crew cheered and the child tried to bolt from the doctor and the baby wrangler. The wrangler caught her by the hand and Sybil screamed, "Let go! I want my mother! I don't want you!" and the baby wrangler tried to calm her and the doctor tried to calm her, but Sybil kept screaming for her mother.

"For God's sake, someone get Sybbie's mother!" Lydia bellowed across the set.

All fell silent. Nobody moved.

Sybil succeeded in pulling away from the baby wrangler and she ran over to Lydia. "You'll take me to my mother," she said confidently, taking her hand.

Lydia hesitated, swallowed, and turned to Holly Montvale. "Would you take her, please?"

"No!" Sybil said, "I want you!"

"Come on, Syb," Holly Montvale said, holding out her hand, "don't hurt the feelings of your TV mom."

Sybil sighed and said okay, taking Holly's hand and walking off the set.

"Okay, everybody," Aaron yelled, "that's a wrap. We'll use the first take."

They started to strike the set. Lydia was walking toward Kate and Noël, but Kate stopped herself from greeting her when she realized Lydia was only on her way out. She looked pale beneath her makeup, shaken, and she walked right past Kate without seeing her.

"She'll be herself in a little while," Max whispered over Kate's shoulder. "She doesn't take well to being jolted out of concentration."

"Or to children being hurt on the set," Kate observed.

Max sighed. "I think what upsets Lydia is Sybbie's mother doesn't come with her anymore."

"Why not?" Kate asked, turning around.

Max shrugged. "I guess she thinks she has better things to do."

— 16 —

"Lydia, please," Kate was saying, "if we don't get the facts straight on your parents, how are we to get the facts straight on anything else about you?"

Silence.

They were sitting in the breakfast room of the Benedict Canyon house. Kate and Lydia faced each other across the table; in front of each lay a copy of the manuscript. Lydia was dressed in blue jeans, a white cotton shirt, and a Dodgers cap. Her hair was back in a ponytail, and she wore no makeup. Kate, on the other hand, had arrived in a pale yellow skirt and silk blouse, pearls, earrings, bracelets, and heels, bearing also typing paper, legal pads, and pencils. Noël, in a short blue jean skirt and tank top, sat at the end of the table, taking notes. Gracia, wearing a rose-colored warm-up suit, left a fresh pot of decaffeinated coffee on the table and disappeared through the swinging door into the kitchen.

It was Lydia's first day off, but any joy about it had disappeared with a phone call from the studio: they would need Lydia again at the end of the following week; the lab had somehow scratched the negative of a scene. Luckily it was one of the ones shot at Bestar.

Lydia was very tired, Noël knew, and Noël had tried to warn Kate about how much Lydia hated dividing her concentration on projects, that perhaps now wasn't the best time to start work on the book, not until she knew for sure she was finished with the studio. But Kate said she was sorry, there was no time left, they had to push ahead if there was ever to be a book.

"Excuse me, señora," Gracia said, opening the shutters of the service window into the kitchen. "What time would you like luncheon to be served?"

"One o'clock, please," Lydia said.

"Pasta with steamed vegetables?"

"And a salad," Lydia said. "And french bread." She glanced at Kate. "Anything else you'd like?"

Kate shook her head. "Sounds great."

"Thank you, Gracia," Lydia said.

Gracia closed the shutters of the window.

"So what's your problem again?" Lydia said to Kate, as if Kate were some bitchy neighbor complaining about a hedge or something.

"My problem is," Kate said, flicking through pages of the manuscript, "I want to know which name was really your mother's." Kate spoke not unkindly, but firmly. "She starts out as Lavenia and then turns into Lilliana on page two-thirteen."

"She changed her name after my father died—when we moved to Florida," Lydia said.

"But just her first name, right?" Kate said.

Lydia nodded.

"And she did this . . . ?" Kate said.

"To make a fresh start," Lydia said.

"Okay, great," Kate said, making a note. "Now, what about your father?"

"What about him?" Lydia sounded outright hostile now.

"Well," Kate said gently, "he starts out as Al, changes to Hal, and then—well, then he dies as Hank."

Noél bit her lip, trying not to laugh.

"I don't want to talk about my father this morning," Lydia said abruptly, reaching for the pot of coffee.

Pause. "Okay," Kate said, making a note. Another pause. She glanced over at Noél. "Maybe we should just skip around a little."

Noél nodded.

"Just skip around and touch on questions I have," Kate said, looking through her notes.

Pouring coffee into her mug, Lydia said, "Why don't you just tell me what you think's wrong with my book?"

Kate looked up and hesitated.

"I mean it," Lydia said, looking at her. "Just say what's wrong with the book. This is going so horribly this morning, what do we have to lose?"

"Look, Lydia," Kate said gently, "I don't want working on this book to be horrible for you."

"Just tell me," Lydia commanded her. She put the coffeepot down. "Tell me," she repeated.

"Well," Kate sighed, "okay." She took a moment to gather her thoughts. "The biggest drawback I see in the manuscript," she said, "is the absence of description of your friends, your family, your personal life—and of your day-to-day professional life."

In other words, Noél thought, *your whole life, Lydia. That's all that's missing from your autobiography.*

"These are big gaps we need to fill," Kate continued, "and need to fill with you. Who you *are,* Lydia."

"Well, you can forget that," Lydia said quickly, stirring skim milk into her coffee.

"I don't understand," Kate said. "Why?"

"It's no one's business who I am," she said simply.

Silence.

"Well, Lydia," Kate said carefully, smiling a little, "usually when one wants to write her autobiography . . ." She let her voice trail off on a hopeful note.

Silence. Lydia was reading her copy of the manuscript.

Noél suppressed a smile and sipped her coffee.

"Look, Lydia—" Kate said, a little more strongly.

"No, you look," Lydia said, looking up and then crossing her arms and leaning forward toward Kate, resting her elbows on the table. "I want to be as honest as I can be in this book—"

Noél choked on her coffee, spilling some on her notes.

Lydia looked down the table to frown at her.

"Sorry," Noél said, using her napkin to blot up the coffee.

Lydia turned back to Kate. "I'm not about to go out as anything different from the image my fans have of me—and that's final."

"But Lydia," Kate said, "this is your swan song. You really don't want people to know *anything* about the woman they love?"

"They *don't* love me," Lydia said, irritated, "they love the actress they watch."

"Don't be too sure about that," Kate said. "The best of ourselves always comes out in our work—and the worst."

Lydia looked at her for a moment. "Oh, bull," she said then, taking off her baseball cap and throwing it across the room.

"Okay, okay," Kate said, raising a hand. She sighed and dropped it. "But look, Lydia . . ."

"If you say 'Look, Lydia' one more time to me, I swear I'm going to scream," Lydia promised.

"Then I will simply say it," Kate said. She put her pencil down and folded her hands on the edge of the table.

This was not going to be good, Noél could tell.

"There are enormous inconsistencies throughout this manuscript," Kate said. "In fact, even the inconsistencies have inconsistencies with inconsistencies—and considering that you say next to nothing of any importance about yourself, that's quite an achievement for an autobiography."

Noél bowed her head, biting her lip again.

"Oh, really," Lydia said.

"Wait," Kate said, holding up a hand, "it's not a criticism—just an observation." She lowered her hand. "And my job, you know, is to protect you—and to make sure that you present yourself in book form to the public in the best light possible. And so I don't frankly care what other people who worked on this book did or didn't do, or said or didn't say. All I care about is publishing a book you will always be proud of—to say nothing of making a contribution to the history of popular culture." Pause, losing steam. "And to the history of women who made a difference."

No argument from Lydia on this.

"But," Kate said, "I can't do that unless we put *you* in the book—otherwise there *is* no book. A litany of grievances against the riffraff in Hollywood isn't an autobiography."

"You certainly seem very sure of yourself," Lydia said, meeting Kate's eyes directly.

"I've seen you work, Lydia—I've *seen* your finished work, Lydia—and how you could ever settle for something like this manuscript is not only out of character, but in direct opposition to your talent and professionalism."

After a long moment, Lydia sighed and lowered her eyes to the manuscript. "Then we're going to have to forget it," she said. "I can't write the book you want."

"I'm not talking secrets," Kate said, "I'm talking the essence of you, Lydia, your personality. Relate your past in a way that makes sense of who you are today, that marries yourself and your work into a full-fledged person people can relate to." Pause. "And if you're leaving acting, then for heaven's sake, think carefully about what you're doing. You owe it to your fans to give them at least a sense of who you are and why you need to lead another life now—and you need to tell aspiring actors what it takes to make it in television, and how to stay in one piece once you get there. Leave your profession as a role model, Lydia—leave as a mentor."

Silence.

Lydia was looking down again. She was upset, Noél could tell, but about what, she wasn't sure. Who ever knew with Lydia?

"There will always be 'Cassandra's World' on videotape," Kate said, "but there must be a written record of the woman who made it happen. You know you have to leave a legacy behind, Lydia—of your experience, your outlook, your philosophy of life."

Lydia suddenly slammed her fist down. "No!" She looked at Kate, her voice softening then. "I can't."

It sounded like a plea to Noél.

Kate evidently heard it the same way. "But you *can* do it, Lydia, I swear you can. But you can't do it working from this," and she swept her copy of the manuscript off the table. It went *thunk-splat* on the floor, paper sliding across the room. "We're going to start over," Kate announced, reaching across the table.

"What?" Lydia said.

"What?" Noél said.

"What?" Gracia said, head bursting through the shutters of the window.

"You heard me," Kate said, sweeping Lydia's copy of the manuscript to the floor too. *Thunk-splat*, it went, fanning out across the floor. "We're going to start over and this time it's going to be"—she pointed to Lydia—"*your* book."

It was one of the few times Noél had seen Lydia absolutely flabbergasted.

"So this is the deal, Lydia," Kate said. "Throw in with me and trust I can help you write a great book, or we forget the whole thing and I go home today."

Noél held her breath, waiting for Lydia's reaction. She was sitting rock-still, blue eyes blazing.

Gracia took one look at her employer and ducked back into the kitchen, closing the shutters behind her.

"Needless to say," Kate added, pulling her legal pad in front of her and picking up her pencil, "Bennett, Fitzallen & Coe would go insane if they knew what I'm suggesting." She looked at Lydia. "They don't care what they publish as long as it has your name on it." She ripped off the sheets on her pad she had written on this morning and threw those on the floor, too. "Now then," Kate said, pencil poised over paper, eyes on Lydia, "Gary Steiner's going to write the book with you."

Lydia's mouth parted.

"He's agreed to give his full time and concentration to the book over hiatus." Kate looked at Noél. "Which gives us . . . ?"

"Eleven weeks," Noél said. "But he's supposed to be going to Hawaii."

"Well he's not going now," Kate said. She nibbled on the end of her pencil for a moment, thinking. "Now, B, F & C has to have a finished manuscript by June fifteenth to make October—but I bet I could get another two weeks if we need to, move it to November."

"Gary is going to write my autobiography," Lydia said. Her face had turned scarlet.

"He didn't want to offer his help until he talked to me first," Kate said. She gestured to the kitchen. "Gracia suggested I talk to him—and I'm glad she did. I think he can do a fine job." She turned to Noél. "How is your interviewing and typing these days? We're going to have a hell of a lot of transcripts over the next couple of weeks."

"Fine," Noél said. "And we'll get a typist." Noél was excited. Kate made it sound as though it could really work this time. That Lydia would finally write the book they all knew she was dying to write but kept pretending she couldn't.

"I thought," Lydia said, turning to Noél, "Gary liked my book the way it was."

Noél hesitated, and then said, "He didn't want to discourage you."

Lydia's voluptuous mouth was disappearing into a very fine line.

"But it wasn't the work you did he didn't like," Noél hastened to add, "it was that he didn't think the book had much of the real you in it either. I told him I didn't think you *wanted* the real you in the book—"

"The real me," Lydia repeated. Her head snapped around to the kitchen. "Gracia!" she barked.

The shutters of the window opened. "Yes, señora?"

"Is it true that you told Kate to talk to Gary about my book?"

Gracia swallowed. "Yes, señora, I did." Pause. "And I'm glad I did!" she added defiantly. "You are a very wonderful person, señora, but that book is all this way and that way and not like you at all!" She pulled the shutters closed with a slam.

Wow, Noél thought, *something's happening around here.*

"Noél," Lydia said sharply, making her jump to attention. "What do you think? And I want the truth."

Noél's face flushed. "Well . . ."

"Well what?" Lydia snapped.

"Well," Noél said again, "I always did think the book sounded like a Connie Francis song gone wrong—that title, *Don't you wish you were nice to me now?*"

Lydia glared at her for a moment. "What else?" she said.

"I don't know, Lydia," Noél said, shrugging. "I guess it's just sort of—well—the whole thing's so bitchy."

"Bitchy, huh?" Lydia said. "Well then, that's exactly the way I'm going to get if that's what it takes to get a straight answer around here." She vaulted to her feet, chair skidding back into the wall behind her. "Do you mean to tell me you've all been skulking around, talking to each other about my book behind my back? That you never thought to talk to me about it?"

The shutters to the kitchen opened again. "Oh, señora," Gracia said, "we do not skulk. We love you. We care about you."

"Do you hear this?" Lydia demanded of Kate, gesturing to the shutters—which were closing again. "Do you have people working for you who talk to you like this?"

"I wish I did," Kate said truthfully.

"I wouldn't mind doing a little overtime with you, Kate," Noél said.

"Noél!" Lydia shouted.

"What?" Noél said.

"Be-have!" Lydia shouted.

"Yes, sir!" Noél said.

"Besides," Lydia added out of the corner of her mouth, dropping her voice and leaning on the table with both hands, "I checked—she's got a buffoon of a boyfriend named Harris."

Now Kate's mouth fell open.

"See?" Lydia said to Kate. "See how it feels? Knowing that people have been skulking around behind your back, sticking their noses into your private business?"

"How did you—?" Kate was stammering.

"I see my timing's perfect as usual," Gary said, walking in through the swinging door of the kitchen.

"You!" Lydia shouted, still standing, pointing across the breakfast room at Gary.

"Sounds like you've been discussing our plan with Lydia," he said, touching Kate's shoulder.

"How dare you talk about my book behind my back!" Lydia shouted.

"Somebody had to, Lydia," Gary said. He waved down the table. "Hi, babe."

"Hi, Gare," Noél said.

The shutters to the kitchen opened. "Herbal tea, Señor Steiner?"

"Yes, Gracia—please, thank you. That would be great." He walked around the table and reached for Lydia's hand. She snatched it away. He snatched it back, took it firmly in both of his, and brought it up to his mouth to kiss. "Lyddie, we love you," he said, lowering her hand. "We know you want to write your autobiography and we want to help you."

Lydia jerked her hand away and ran out of the room. They heard her running upstairs and then, a moment later, a door slam.

Gary sat down in Lydia's seat, looking down under the table at all the pages on the floor, moving them around a little with his boot. "Wow," he said, "did Lydia do this?"

"No," Noél said, "Kate did."

Gary chuckled, bending to pick up a few pages. "You catch on quick," he said, sitting back up in the chair and making himself comfortable. "Dramatics tend to work around here."

"You should have seen Lydia's face, Gary," Noél said.

He smiled, tapping pages in place on his knee. "I can imagine."

Silence.

Gary was reading and Noél was surveying the damage her coffee had done to her notes.

"Excuse me," Kate said after a moment, "but shouldn't somebody go up and talk to her?"

"Hmmm?" Gary said, eyes still on the page.

"Shouldn't one of us go talk to her?" Kate said. "She seems awfully upset."

"Oh, no," he said, glancing up and shaking his head, "she's fine."

Kate looked skeptical.

"She's not upset the way you think," Noél said. "She's just overwhelmed that everybody cares so much."

Kate looked to Gary.

He nodded. "Noél's right. She's happy—that's why she's crying."

"Oh—well, all this makes perfect sense," Kate said, tossing her pencil over her shoulder.

"Don't worry," Noél assured her, "you'll get used to it."

— *17* —

"What is this?" Kate asked the night auditor on duty at the desk when she returned to her hotel very late that night. He was smiling, pushing an ice bucket over the desk toward her. In it was a bottle of Dom Perignon on ice.

"There's a card," he said, pointing.

She opened it.

> A hard day's work by a very talented lady
> deserves refreshment
> at the pleasure of a very hard-working man.
>
> *Mortimer Pallsner*

"Oh, God!" Kate said, dropping the card as if it were on fire.

"What's the matter? Don't you drink?" the auditor asked.

— *18* —

Gary couldn't believe how much they accomplished with Lydia in the first week. Kate, it turned out, was part shrink and part mindreader, indefatigably cheerful about their task in a way that was contagious. It was simple, she kept telling them; they ask Lydia questions on tape, they have the tapes typed into transcripts overnight, and they file the transcripts in order of the date of the story being related in the transcript. From these, later, when they had enough, Gary would draft rough chapters. The more transcripts they had, the more questions they knew to ask Lydia; the more material they got from Lydia, the quicker the book would take form.

The trick, Kate taught them, was to let Lydia talk about whatever interested her at any given moment and gently lead her into full disclosure on that subject while paying close attention for leads to follow up on later. It was essential, therefore, that Lydia, Kate, Gary, and Noël all carried small tape recorders with them to capture Lydia's thoughts. Lydia of course hated this idea ("Do I look like Andy Warhol?"), but tried to cooperate—and Gary found that Kate was right, this strategy of talking about events in Lydia's life out of sequence was a way to get something that resembled the truth out of her.

Kate said she thought Lydia resisted chronological discussion of her life because she might have dropped a few years off her age and got confused and flustered—and then angry—trying to keep all the dates straight. (This was true, incidentally, the part about Lydia dropping a few years off her age. Gary could remember back in New York when Lydia had been twenty-eight and twenty-nine years old. It was a process that had taken from 1975 to 1980.)

Because it was such a gorgeous day, the four of them, Kate, Lydia, Gary, and Noël, decided to work outside on the terrace, at the big table, under the umbrella. Actually there were five of them, because Gracia was there, too, messing around with some potted plants. And then there were seven, because Imelda, the Filipino maid (named after Mrs. Marcos, whom she still idolized, shoes or no shoes), was putting cushions out on the lounge chairs around the pool and Philippe, the gardener, was clipping shrubbery.

The four were hard at work discussing the elements of what Lydia believed made a good actor, when she suddenly stopped and said, "There was another story in the *Times* this morning about how book publishers are in trouble. Is there even going to be a publisher left to publish my book?" Kate said, yes, of course there would be, and then tried to give a quick overview of how the trade book industry worked and some of the problems that were unique to it.

"But *why* are profit margins so small in comparison to the other communications industries?" Gary asked when she was finished.
"Books are expensive."
"Because some mass communications are a lot more mass than others," Kate said. "A smash hit for me in hardcover means maybe three hundred thousand buyers, and a smash hit for you means—?"
"About sixty million people," Lydia said.
"Exactly," Kate said. "Three hundred thousand for my audience, sixty million for you—plus we have all the problems attached to having all unsold books returned to us." She smiled. "No station sends your signal back to the network for a refund."
"And people don't know how to read anymore, do they?" Noël said.
Kate sighed, nodding. "It's a big problem, illiteracy."
"But aren't computers changing that?" Gary said. "Kids have to

know how to read in order to use them, right? And they all use them."

"But not necessarily to read," Lydia said. "Not unless Nintendo starts writing words into their programs."

"The games you play on the TV," Gracia suddenly added from under the portico, holding a potted plant in one hand while wiping a stray hair back off her forehead with the other. Her warm-up suit today was lavender and the stripe on her Tretorn sneakers matched exactly. "The señora bought my grandchildren one for Christmas," she explained to Kate. And then, with some concern in her voice, she quickly added, "But they read a lot, Señorita Weston, my Billy and Catalina. They love to read. They are allowed to play Nintendo only on Friday and Saturday nights and for one hour on Wednesday after they finish their homework."

Lydia looked at Kate. "Ever play Super Mario?"

"Who?" Kate said.

"My Billy says the señora is very good at Super Mario," Gracia reported.

"Well, of course I am, Gracia," Lydia said. "I only played it two hundred million times that night I was waiting to hear whether I was nominated for an Emmy or not."

"You play computer games?" Kate said.

Gary didn't know why Kate sounded so surprised. God knew, Lydia had everything under the sun down in the playroom. Windowless and below ground, it had previously been a cellar; Lydia had paneled the walls in barn siding, laid wall-to-wall carpeting, put in a fireplace, a bar, a pool table that could be covered for Ping-Pong, a pinball machine, jukebox, dart board, bongo board, American shuffleboard table, knock-hockey, fusböl, and an enormous TV, on top of which sat the Nintendo set.

"Occasionally, sure," Lydia said.

"By yourself?" Kate said.

"Yes, by myself," Lydia said, sounding impatient. "Sometimes."

Kate was smiling. She murmured, "So you still play by yourself."

"Excuse me?" Lydia said.

"Yesterday," Kate said, "when we were talking about your parents' motel in Wisconsin, you were telling us how important the playroom there was to you. Because you were an only child." Pause. "That you used to play there for hours by yourself, completely happy."

Lydia's expression was blank. She was dressed in shorts and a blouse, hair swept up in a blue baseball cap that said CASSANDRA'S WORLD on it in white letters. The blue matched her eyes exactly.

"And so now, as an adult," Kate continued, smiling as though this were the nicest thing she had ever heard, "once in a while, when you're nervous or upset, you play by yourself in the playroom to calm yourself down. Just like you did when you were a child."

Lydia was frowning. "We're not putting *that* in the book."

"Why not?" Kate said. "I think it'll help people to see what you're really like."

"How many times do I have to say it?" Lydia said, banging the table. "I don't *want* people to know what I'm really like! I'm an *actress*— people don't want to know what *I'm* like. They just want to be allowed to go on thinking that I'm exactly like whatever they *want* me to be like!"

Kate looked to Gary.

"I'm afraid I have to agree with her on that one," he said.

"Take my word for it," Lydia said, pointing her finger across the table at Kate, "no one, *no one*, besides you, Kate Weston, wants to visualize Lydia Southland playing Nintendo by herself in the basement. That's not the fantasy that made me a star."

Kate and Gary and Noél all burst out laughing.

"But could you not, señora," Gracia said from under the portico, where she was shifting another potted plant around, "maybe say in your book that you enjoy playing Nintendo with the children of your friends?" She straightened up, touching her back briefly as she did so. "I think people will i-dent-ti-fy with that." She wiped her forehead again with the back of her hand. It really was warm. "Imelda," she said, pointing, "that cushion is upside down."

"Sorry, Mrs. Rodriguez," Imelda said, moving immediately to the offending cushion.

"That's an excellent suggestion, Gracia, thank you," Kate said. "I think that's exactly what we'll do."

"Oh, great," Lydia muttered to Gary, "another editor. Just what we need."

He laughed, but made a note about Lydia and Nintendo on his legal pad all the same. Gracia was right. People should know that side of Lydia, the side that loved children.

"Kate," Noél said, "when we finish the manuscript, how long did you say it'll be before it comes out?"

"Well, this book is a special case," Kate said.

"I'll say," Lydia said, plunking her elbow down on the table and dropping her chin in her hand.

"Cheer up, kiddo," Gary said, tweaking the brim of Lydia's hat, "it's going to be great."

"Normally, the process of a book—from manuscript to publication day," Kate began, "takes about nine months."

"Like a baby," Imelda observed from down around the pool.

"Make that three editors," Lydia said to Gary. "Imelda's editing the book now too."

"Oh, excuse me, Señora Southland!" Imelda said, covering her mouth with her hand, "I'm so sorry."

"It's okay, Imelda," Lydia said, waving it off, "relax."

"But not too much, please," Gracia said. "You will remember that those tables need to be wiped down."

"Yes, Mrs. Rodriguez," Imelda said.

"But Imelda's right," Kate said, "a book is like a baby. And the editor is like a doctor, in a way, an obstetrician, helping the mother, that is, the writer, through the whole process, from conception through birth, or publication."

"Hear that, big Gare?" Noél said, elbowing him. "You're having a baby—with Lydia—the child you always wanted."

"Cut it out, Noél," Lydia snapped.

"My," Noél said, recoiling slightly, "aren't we a little touchy."

"Oh, you wish," Lydia muttered.

"Hey," Noél said.

"Sorry," Lydia said, reaching over to lay her hand on Noél's wrist for a second, "I didn't mean that. Sorry, I'm just nervous about all this."

"Excuse me—" a tentative voice said.

Gary, Lydia, Noél, Kate—and Gracia and Imelda—all turned to look.

It was Philippe, the gardener, standing there, holding his shears in one hand and his straw hat in the other, pressing it to his chest as though he were about to recite the Pledge of Allegiance.

"Yes, Philippe?" Lydia said.

"Who is the doctor?" he asked.

Gracia walked out from under the portico into the sunshine. "An editor is a doctor to a book like a doctor is to a baby," she said. "Like you are a doctor to the flowers, Philippe."

"Yes," Philippe said, nodding, "I am like a doctor too. Thank you." He put his hat back on and resumed clipping.

Everybody turned back around and then Lydia slumped down in her chair. "Oh, God," she said, "I'm so depressed suddenly."

"Why? What's the matter?" Gary said.

"I've been working on this book for three years and I don't have a manuscript to give a doctor *or* Philippe. I don't have anything to give anybody," she said, dropping her face into her hands. "We'll never get it done."

"I keep telling you, Lydia," Kate said, leaning forward, "forget the past—think *wonderful book* and it will be done before you know it."

The telephone started ringing. Noél reached back for the cordless on the little table.

"Oh, Gary," Lydia said, standing up and pushing her chair out behind her, "*you* do it before I know it. I'm going swimming."

"Lyddie," Gary said, catching her by the wrist, "one more hour and then you can go swimming."

Lydia made a face, looking not terribly unlike a cranky child needing a nap.

"It's Max," Noél said, holding the phone to her.

Lydia sighed, dropped back into her chair, and took the phone. "Hi, darling Max—miss me, do you?" She listened.

"I think it's important we highlight the charity work Lydia does," Gary said.

"Oh, Max," Lydia said, sounding not the least bit happy.

They all looked at her.

"All right," she said. She looked at Gary and rolled her eyes. "All right," she sighed. "Yes, Max, of course I will. Tomorrow. Yes, I'll be there. Yes, I'll know my lines. Yes, I still love you. Bye." She handed the phone to Noél.

"What's up?" Gary said.

"Aaron's back," Lydia said, "so they've moved the shoot up to tomorrow." She stood up. "Sorry, my friends, but the real me has to go inside now to become a real actress again."

"Excuse me, Mark?" Sarah Steadwell said from his office doorway.

He looked up from his desk, where he had been filling out production forms for an illustrated history of the Yankees. "Come in."

Sarah came over to stand in front of his desk. "Sorry to bother you," she said in a quiet voice, "but—well, I don't know what to do. It's Rebecca."

Oh, great, Mark thought, *trust Rebecca to start in on Sarah while Kate's away.*

"Sit down," Mark said. "What happened?"

Sarah sat down on the edge of a chair. She was the best of the editorial assistants. Like most, she was extremely bright and a burning overachiever, but there was also something about Sarah that was so inherently respectable and responsible that she seemed far older than twenty-four. Kate adored her, and for good reason.

But book publishing would no doubt lose Sarah. The problem was these damn salaries. Sarah had college loans to repay and living in Manhattan . . . well, everyone knew the story. Being black didn't make it any better or worse, only perhaps a bit lonelier. And her future in terms of promotion was not good. An editorial assistant getting promoted these days usually meant inheriting a fired senior editor's list, near-death from overwork, and, ultimately being fired later anyway.

No, it was not a good time to be at Bennett, Fitzallen & Coe. Not even for Sarah, the brightest and the most personable—and the prettiest, too, which never hurt anyone's career.

Today, though, Sarah looked upset.

"Rebecca walked past my desk this morning and saw a package from CAI." CAI was Communications Arts International, one of the most powerful entertainment and literary agencies in the country. "She asked me what it was and I told her that it was a novel Kate had been promised an exclusive on, the one she had been waiting for, the Seth Roberts."

"Right," Mark said. They had all been waiting for it. Thriller/ suspense writer Seth Roberts was looking for a new publisher and CAI, knowing how many authors Bennett, Fitzallen & Coe had lost in recent years, was no doubt acting on the likelihood B, F & C would be willing to overpay just to get the Roberts name on their list. Every house needed bestsellers to pull the rest of the list into the stores, but some needed them more than others. Like B, F & C. Like now. And Kate, CAI knew, was an editor who'd be good for Roberts. He was getting sloppy in his writing and needed someone to charm him into being edited.

"I told Rebecca I was about to Fed Ex it out to Kate," Sarah continued, glancing back over her shoulder and then looking back at Mark. "And then she took it—the manuscript. Picked it up and said, 'Don't worry about it, I'll call the agent and tell her I'm taking over. Kate's got enough to do right now.' "

"Uh-oh," Mark said.

"Right," Sarah said. "So I called Kate—"

"And she went berserk," Mark said.

"No," Sarah said, "actually, she didn't seem the least bit surprised—although that may have been just to calm me down." She paused and then admitted, "I was pretty upset."

Mark smiled. "If someone stole what could be next year's big book for the house from me, I'd hope Dale would get a little upset too."

Poor Sarah. It could be so awful apprenticing with an editor, stuck with zero money, all the paperwork, all the grief, all the phones—and caught, always, in the increasingly icky-sticky protocol between editors and management.

"So I don't know what happened," Sarah continued, her voice low, "but Rebecca just came by a minute ago and threw the manuscript on my desk and then stood there, glaring at me. And then she said, 'If you're looking for trouble, you should know that you just found it.' "

Mark got a chill. This wasn't good. Not good at all.

"So I Fed Exed the manuscript to Kate," Sarah said, "and"—she shrugged—"here I am. Alive for the moment." She offered a weak smile.

Mark sat back in his chair. "Does Weston know how to hire or what?" he said in admiration.

"Excuse me?" Sarah said.

"Sarah," Mark said, sitting forward, putting his hands on the desk in front of him, "*first* you sent the manuscript to Kate and *then* you came to tell me what happened?" He smiled. "No wonder Kate loves you so much. No wonder why I love you so much—you're incredible. If Rebecca said that to me, I think I'd be out having a whiskey neat."

Sarah smiled. But then her expression darkened and her shoulders sagged. "But what happens now?" She sighed. "You know what Rebecca's like."

Mark did know what Rebecca was like. She tortured people who crossed her and, if she couldn't get them fired, she drove them out. She had the mentality of a slum landlord, Kate always said, and Mark agreed with her.

"Don't worry," Mark said, "I'll run interference until Kate gets back. You steer clear of Rebecca and come to me about anything you need approved—okay?"

"Okay," Sarah said, getting up, "thanks." She hesitated and then gave a little shiver, holding her arms as if to warm herself. "She's so mad, though." She glanced back over her shoulder and then whispered, "And I'm terrified she's going to find that box in Kate's office."

Kate had opened Rebecca's present for Lydia Southland and groaned. "Unbelievable," she had said. "Only Rebecca would choose a vase with porcupines on it as a peace offering to an actress." And so, the present for Lydia Southland was still sitting in Kate's office behind her desk.

"It'll be okay, Sarah," Mark said, offering a reassuring smile. "I'll protect you—I promise. And I'll get that box out of there tonight."

Sarah smiled slightly. "Thanks."

Ten seconds after Sarah left his office, Rebecca appeared in Mark's doorway. "What was she doing in here?" she said.

"What was who doing in here?" Mark said, swiveling his chair toward his typewriter.

"Sarah," Rebecca said.

"Oh," Mark said nonchalantly, putting a piece of paper into the typewriter, "she was helping me with these production forms on the Yankee book. She's a whiz at design, you know." He turned around in his chair. "What's the matter?" he asked her, feigning concern. "What's happened?"

"Nothing," Rebecca said, leaving.

Mark whipped the phone to his ear, simultaneously punching in the numbers 4669 with his other hand.

"Kate Weston's office," Sarah's voice said.

"You helped me with some production forms on the Yankee book," he said. "About design."

"I'm sorry, but she's working out on the West Coast for a couple of weeks," Sarah said. "May I help you with something, or may I relay a message?" Pause. "Excuse me," Sarah said. "Hold on one moment, please."

But she didn't put Mark on hold and Mark could hear Sarah say, "He has to get the Yankee book into production. I was helping him with some of the forms. A special design request."

"If Mark needs help," he heard Rebecca snap, "then Mark should go to the managing editor. You are not the managing editor."

"I'll remember," he heard Sarah say. After a moment of silence, she came back onto the phone. "I'm sorry to keep you holding. Would you care to leave a message?"

"That fucking bitch," Mark said.

"Yes, okay, I'll tell her," Sarah said brightly. "Thank you so much for calling."

Oh, Kate, Mark thought, hanging up the phone, *come home. We need you.*

He sat back in his chair, looking out the window at Central Park. *I need you.*

— *20* —

Gary turned his red Porsche into the "Cassandra" parking lot and spotted Lydia's car immediately, not that it was easy to overlook a silver Rolls-Royce Corniche with a convertible white top. Then he spotted Noël and Kate walking from the direction of Lydia's trailer. He honked and waved; Noël spotted him, said something to Kate, and they both smiled and waved.

Gary parked his car in his spot (14 GARY STEINER the spray-paint stencil said) and met the women by Lydia's car.

"I just got the official go-ahead from Max," Kate said. "He says Lydia's all ours now."

"Great," Gary said, taking off his Ray-Bans. He looked at Noël. "How'd it go?"

"Okay," Noël said. "I think Lydia wanted to do it again because Sybil's still a little hyper, but"—she shrugged—"she let it go." Pause. "She's nervous around Sybil, have you noticed?"

"Little Sybbie?" Gary shook his head. "No, just—you know—last week, when she fell. Lyddie got a little rattled over that, but that's understandable."

"Take it from me," Noél said, "she was strange around the kid today."

"But if she is," Kate interjected, "it's probably because I've been grilling her all week about her childhood. It happens, you know—when someone's working on their autobiography, a lot of emotional stuff about their past tends to come up. They can feel pretty vulnerable."

"Then maybe we ought to lay off the childhood stuff for a while," Gary said.

"Agreed," Kate said.

"Here she comes," Noél said, waving down Cassandra Boulevard.

"Noél," Gary said, "have you seen Holly yet?"

"Not to talk to," Noél said.

"Well, you're about to," Gary said, looking past Noél.

Behind her, Holly Montvale was walking across the parking lot toward them.

"Oh, God," Noél said under her breath.

"Relax," Gary said out of the corner of his mouth, waving to her.

"Yeah, right," Noél said.

Kate was confused, Gary knew, but he wouldn't explain. It was no business of Kate's that Holly Montvale was Noél's ex-lover. To the outside world, to which Kate belonged, Holly was not only happily married, but devoted to her husband.

"I'm a free woman," Lydia announced, smiling radiantly.

"Lucky duck," Holly said, arriving at the same time.

"Holly, have you met my editor?" Lydia said. "This is Kate Weston—and Kate, this is Holly Montvale."

"It's a pleasure to meet you," Kate said, shaking hands with her. "I'm a great admirer of your work."

"Thank you," Holly said. "I hope to be of yours too, soon. I'm dying to read Lydia's book."

"Yeah, well, some people around here may be dying after it's finished," Noél said. "Max asked me again, Kate, if you couldn't get Lydia to lighten up a little on Mort."

Lydia rubbed her hands together, making a witchlike sound of glee.

Holly was looking at Noél. She touched her on the arm. "Hi," she said.

Noél looked at her, face taut. "Hi," she said, quickly looking away.

Was it going to take another year for Noël to face her? Gary wondered. The guilt Noël carried about Holly was incredible, and she had to come to terms with it, sooner or later. It had ended badly between them, very badly, when Noël had bottomed out.

"What are you doing over hiatus?" Kate asked Holly.

"Oh, no you don't," Lydia said quickly, "Holly is *not* working on the book." She turned to Holly. "No offense, Hol, but Kate's got the whole house working on it, Gracia, Imelda, the gardener, everybody."

They all laughed and Holly turned to Kate. "I start right in on a TV movie," she said. "It's good for me—gives me a chance to play something a little more dramatic."

"She means she gets a chance to be the star," Lydia said, putting her arm around Holly's shoulder and giving her a brief hug, "as she deserves to be. Okay," she said then, dropping her arm, "let's get this show on the road." She opened the door of the Rolls. "You want to ride with me, Kate?"

"Sure," she said.

Lydia looked at Gary. "And what about you? What are you up to?"

"I have a meeting with Mort."

Her eyebrows went up. "What for?"

"Don't know. He just asked me to come in."

Lydia got in the car and started it while Kate walked around and opened the passenger door. "Got your tape recorder, Kate?" Gary asked her, teasing. She had been on them again last night about not going anywhere without one.

"Of course," she said, holding up her hand. In it was a little microcassette recorder.

Lydia's window slid down. "Are you coming over later?" she asked Gary.

"In about two hours?" he said.

"Okay," she said. "As Calamity would say, see ya'll later." She backed the car out.

"Bye," Holly said.

"I've got to go too," Noël said as Lydia drove off.

Holly turned to her. "Maybe we could have tea or something."

"Not today," Noël said, "I can't."

"Well, call me," Holly said.

"Okay," Noël said.

Holly turned to Gary. "I wish you were working on my movie. I don't like a lot of what they've done in the script."

"Sorry, but I've got my hands full," he said.

"You both do," Holly said. She turned to Noél and quickly kissed her on the cheek. "You look wonderful, baby, I'm proud of you," she said. "See you, Gary," she said, giving him a quick kiss. "Bye, you guys."

"Bye," Gary and Noél said, watching as Holly went to her white Corvette.

After Holly drove out of the lot, giving a honk and a wave, the two of them, Gary and Noél, stood there awhile.

"Seems to me she'd be receptive to an amend," Gary finally said.

"You sound like Lydia," Noél said.

"Maybe because Lydia's right."

Noél looked at him. She had tears in her eyes. "You guys think it's so easy." She turned away.

Gary grabbed her arm and turned her back around. "No, hold on—you're not getting away with that one." He waited until Noél raised her eyes. "God knows, of all the people in the world, Noél, *we* know it's not easy." Pause. Gently: "And we know it's worth it."

He walked to the executive building, buttoning his blazer and straightening his tie, pausing for a moment to do a quick shine of his boots on the back of each leg of his blue jeans. It was beautiful out and he left his sunglasses in his breast pocket, determined to enjoy the true color of the sky. Blue. Really blue today. The wind had cleared away the smog. He loved L.A. on a day like today.

He walked through the smoked-glass doors of the Bestar executive building.

"Hi, Mr. Steiner," the guard at the desk said.

"Hi, Roy," he said, bending to sign the register. Security was extremely tight these days because of three incidents in the past six months: a former employee put what he said was a deadly virus *(it wasn't)* in the air-conditioning system of the executive building; some kook tried to run the studio gate in his pickup truck because, he said, he wanted to invite Lydia to a barbecue; and one of the tabloids had tried to sneak a transvestite into Wesley Hart's trailer for a picture for their next issue.

Popular opinion around the studio, however, held that these events had been staged to cover the real reason for triple security—pending new investigations by the FBI into the business dealings of Bestar Studios. Gary thought this was much more than likely. Lydia herself was in negotiation with the studio for what her former business manager and lawyer had estimated to be at least fifteen million dollars they owed her.

Lydia owned a piece of the net profits of "Cassandra's World" and found it odd that Bestar kept saying there weren't any net profits when the show was in the top ten in fifty markets around the world. This, however, was not uncommon in Hollywood. Profits were things that were taxed and so everybody hid as many profits as they could in their production "costs." A superstar could get a piece of "gross profits" and make millions—because gross meant the take before expenses were deducted—but Lydia had not been a superstar when she had first signed with the show and so she was merely one of the lowly who had a percentage of "net" profits, after expenses, which is to say, a percentage of nothing.

But Lydia was paid very, very well and her residuals from worldwide distribution would continue for years. And while many new millionaires went wild and woolly in the financially crazy eighties, Lydia had stayed very conservative in her investments and, despite the attempts of her runaway business manager, need never worry about money again. That's why she could afford to leave the show after next season.

But Gary couldn't imagine Lydia not acting. Worse yet, he couldn't imagine Lydia carrying out her long-threatened plans of moving to eastern Long Island and breeding horses. Long Island! Breeding horses! What kind of crazy idea was that? To leave Los Angeles? And more to the point, to leave him? And Gracia? And Noél? Her life here? *Why?*

But then, Lydia wouldn't be Lydia if anyone could make absolute sense out of the way she lived her life. To care about Lydia was to feel at home with open-ended questions.

"I'm going up to Pallsner's office," Gary said to Roy as he signed the log book. "He's expecting me."

"Just let me call up there," Roy said, picking up the phone. In a moment, he waved him through, slapping a sticker on Gary's breast pocket as he did so. Today's clearance sticker was a weird aqua square with the letters ssw on it.

Gary took the elevator up to four, the top floor, was waved through by the receptionist, waved through by the security guard standing at attention next to her, and wound his way through the carpeted, hushed halls of the Bestar executive suite. On the walls were blowups of the stars of all the Bestar shows, past and present. There were two different shots of Lydia in the hallway and then, hanging outside of Pallsner's offices, a horizontal one of her with the supporting cast of "Cassandra's World": Wesley Hart, Holly Montvale, Sturgeon Fields, and Sybil Montgomery. The show was the studio's blockbuster money-maker (even if it didn't make any profits after "expenses").

"Go right in, Mr. Steiner," Pallsner's outer-office secretary said.

"Go right in, Gary," Helena, his inner-office secretary, said.

The guard, standing behind Helena, nodded as well, indicating that to him Gary did not appear to be a psychopath or an FBI agent.

Pallsner's office was large and sunny, furnished with antique American furniture, comfortable overstuffed chairs, and very pretty, sedate carpeting and drapes. Behind his desk, however, was the outline of a locked door, which, according to Noël, led to an "icky" bedroom used for God-knew-what these days.

"Gary, how are you?" Pallsner said, striding across the office as if he hadn't seen Gary in a great many years.

He wanted something. That was clear.

"Good, very good," Gary said, allowing Pallsner to shake his hand with both of his.

"Sit, sit," Pallsner said. He was chewing gum, looking more than a little like a rabbit. Like so many around town, he had given up smoking only to become addicted to prescription nicotine gum.

"Look, Gary, I'm not going to mess around, I'll tell you straight out," Pallsner said, leaning forward from the couch where he was sitting. "We have *got* to get Lydia to re-sign for another two years."

Gary sighed. "I know. Max and I have been talking about it."

"You'd think she'd care about the people who made her a star," Pallsner said. "But now that she has what she wants, to hell with everybody else—she'll just take off and let us all be damned."

"It's not really like that, I don't think," Gary said.

"Oh?" Pallsner said. "What is it like, then?"

Gary didn't know what to say. He didn't think Lydia should leave the show either, but the way Mort made it sound . . . If she left after next season, she would have done the show for seven years, which was a lot, after all, and for a one-star vehicle: the mornings sometimes starting at five, the returns from the studio sometimes as late as midnight; the location shoots that meant whirlwind trips to anywhere from Yugoslavia to Stonehenge; the dramatic acting she had to do, the comedic acting she had to do, the singing, dancing, jumping, climbing, sword swinging and acrobatics on some shows she had to do; and always, *always*, that incredible, all-encompassing pressure about her appearance. Exercise, exercise, exercise, eat right, sleep where she could find it; exercise, exercise, exercise, eat right, sleep where she could find it, be beautiful, stay beautiful, be perfect Lydia Southland!

Oh, yes, there were good reasons why Lydia would want to leave the show after seven years. She had no life outside the series. Even when she was off she had to stay on. She was a star. A huge one. And she felt the pressure in everything she did. But then, she did her job so well and handled the pressures so well it seemed as if Lydia *had* to do the job—because who else could?

"And to top everything else off," Pallsner said, throwing his hands up in the air, "I hear *you're* writing her book."

Uh-oh. Gary didn't know how Mort knew about that, but since he did, he nodded. "Just getting it into shape—my name won't be on it or anything. She's been working on it for three years, you know." He said this because if it appeared he was helping Lydia to trash Pallsner, he knew he could be trashing his own future.

"And do you think this is a wise move on your part?" Pallsner asked him.

"But I'm not writing the book," Gary said again, "I'm just helping her get organized."

"I see," Pallsner said, standing up and moving over to the window. He leaned against the windowsill, looking out. "Get her to re-sign for another two years, Gary, and I'll triple your salary. I'll also throw in a producer's title, but you'll go on as you have been, heading up the writers, directing the story line with Max."

Gary cleared his throat. "That's a generous offer."

"So go ahead and work on the book," Pallsner said, coming over to stand in front of Gary, "but get her to re-sign—and soon. We need her commitment."

Gary took his cue that this was the end of the meeting, and stood up. "I can talk to her—but she's always had her own plan."

"Convince her," Pallsner said. After a moment he turned away, leading Gary to the door. "It's in her best interests, too, you know," he said, placing his hand on the doorknob and turning around. "Lydia'll go off her rocker not working. She's a born actress and she's got years and years to go."

"Yeah, I know," Gary sighed. Pallsner was right, although he could hear what Lydia would say in response if she were here: "Acting is *not* my life. It's what prevents me from having one!"

"By the way," Pallsner said, his voice changing slightly—a bit softer, Gary thought, "I heard Noél was here today. How's she doing?"

Gary blinked. He certainly seemed to hear a lot of things awfully fast. "Great," he said, "she's doing very well."

"Good, good, glad to hear it," Pallsner said, nodding. He hesitated and then said, "She's a smart girl, you know. Talented, good with people. I hope she's not going to stay at Lydia's forever. She should be back in production now that she's—now that she has things under control." He cleared his throat. "What I mean to say is—"

"She should be working in production again," Gary said for him. "And I agree." Pause. "Any chance there's a job for her here?"

"Of course there is," Pallsner said. "That is," he added, "if 'Cassandra's World' continues."

"We've still got a season to go," Gary pointed out.

"I'll talk to Max," Pallsner promised, opening the door.

"And I'll talk to Lydia," Gary promised, walking out. A job for Noél was as good as hers. Max always said they should just recruit from the Betty Ford Center alumni roster, that's where the best talent and most sincere efforts always seemed to come from.

"Oh, and Gary," Pallsner called after him.

Gary turned around.

Pallsner was gesturing him back. Gary dutifully returned and Pallsner pulled him inside, holding his elbow, and said, in a low voice, "What do you know about this Kate Weston?"

"She's smart, good, and Lydia likes her," Gary said. "Why?"

"She a tease or what?" Pallsner said.

Gary blinked. "Kate?"

Pallsner looked around, smiling slightly. "Yeah," he said out of the corner of his mouth.

Oh, brother, Gary thought. Noél was right. Pallsner would hit on Kate.

"God, I don't know, Mort," Gary whispered, hoping he sounded nervous. "I mean, I don't have anything to hide anymore, but I don't think I'd—not with the father. God only knows what the connection is."

Pallsner looked at him.

"He's old CIA," Gary said, making a mental note to tell Kate that her father was now old CIA even though she had said he was—what?—a doctor?

"No shit," Pallsner said, considering this news.

"I'm not sure," Gary said, "but I think so."

Pallsner gave him a pat on the arm. "Thanks," he said.

— *21* —

"Hang on a second," Kate said to Mark. She dropped the phone and hauled herself out of bed, walked over to the window, and pulled open the vertical blinds—and immediately blinded herself. Arm over her face against the brightness, she staggered back to the bed. Picking up the phone with one hand and shielding her eyes with the other, she climbed onto the bed and squinted at the window.

The sky was blue, the tops of the palm trees green along the Santa Monica promenade, the beaches in the distance spangly white, the Pacific beyond a glittering blue/gray. "Mark," she said, "I hate to tell you, but I'm never coming home. You wouldn't believe how gorgeous it is here this morning."

"I know," Mark said, "because I'm the one who told you about the Shangri-La, remember?"

Oh, right. Carla—Mark's ex-wife—used to stay here, at the Shangri-La in Santa Monica, on buying trips. She used to meet clothing manufacturers from Australia here. (That's what she said, anyway.) A white stucco, art deco apartment building from the thirties transformed into a hotel, it was situated on Ocean Avenue on the palisades overlooking the ocean. It took Kate a good half hour to get to Lydia's, but here she could have a bedroom *and* a kitchen *and* a living room in contrast to what she'd get in landlocked Beverly Hills, where a classy little single went for twice the money.

"So what's going on?" Kate said, falling back into the pillows. It was only six-fifteen here, nine-fifteen in New York. "How's Sarah holding up?"

"Let's just say," Mark said, "that you better come home with a *big* book."

"I think I just might," Kate said.

"That's good," Mark said, "because Rebecca's on your case big time. According to her, you're out there lying around the pool while letting your office fall apart."

"Yeah, right," Kate said, thinking of her living room here, a complete and utter mess with manuscripts and faxes all over the place. Last night she had been up until nearly one working on a manuscript; checking over catalog copy, clauses of a contract in negotiation, a rough sketch for an ad in the *New York Times Book Review;* and redoing financial figures on the Seth Roberts novel she wanted to buy from CAI. So many faxes were flying back and forth between Bennett, Fitzallen & Coe and the Shangri-La Hotel, in fact, that the front office manager, Dino, asked Kate if she knew about portable fax machines. Maybe her company should be looking into one?

"You spent more on faxes yesterday than on your room," he had said, showing her the entries on her bill.

"Yeah, I know," Kate had said, wincing, "but I needed to get the last three edited chapters of a book back so it could go into production."

"Hi, Ms. Weston, how's it going?" David, the desk assistant, had said, coming on duty. "I guess I should tell you, we all bought stock in the fax industry this morning."

"And that item in the *Post* yesterday didn't help much," Mark said.

"What item in the *Post?*" Kate said. The other line was ringing on her phone but she chose to ignore it. This early it had to be a New York call and she was not ready to face the world yet.

"The one that said you were seen wining and dining with Lydia and her pals at Le Dôme," Mark said.

"We had lunch," Kate said, "Lydia, Gary and Noél, that's it."

"It didn't say who her pals were," Gary said, "it just said that you were there and commented that New York literati must be going Hollywood."

"Oh, that's nice," Kate said.

"So this is Rebecca's new handle," Mark said, "that you're out there playing around, making a spectacle of yourself."

"I guess that's better than telling her I threw the whole book out and started over," Kate said.

Mark laughed.

"Oh, Mark," she sighed, "what am I going to do? I'm so behind, but I just can't leave yet. And I'm still not sure about the structure Gary's come up with—I think maybe I'm too close to it."

"Then let me help," he said.

"You'll read what we've got?" she said.

"Better than that," Mark said, "I'll fly out for the weekend and work on it with you. I've got a free ticket from United coming and it would be fun."

Silence. Kate was looking up at the ceiling, thinking she could not let Mark do this, there was too much time, money, and trouble involved. On the other hand, he'd be such a shot in the arm for the book—and for her.

"Kate?"

"I'm not saying anything," she said, "because I'm hoping that you'll just come, because no rational person would ever expect so much of a friend. It's just too much."

"I'm coming Friday, it's settled," he said.

"You have to let me pay for your hotel room. And I'll pick you up at the airport." Kate smiled. "Oh, Mark, I can't believe this—it would cheer me up so much, you have no idea."

"It'll cheer me up too," he said. "I miss you."

"I miss you too," she said.

As soon as Kate got off the phone with Mark, it rang again. It was the front desk. "Harris has called several times," the desk clerk said. "He'd like you to call him at the office. The number's—"

"I know the number, thank you," Kate said. She hung up and fell back against the pillows.

And sighed.

And rolled over on her side, scrunching herself up around a pillow, pulling the covers over her head.

She didn't want to call Harris.

No, she didn't.

Kate sighed and flung the covers back, wondering if Harris, by himself this morning, had gotten out of bed, saying, "Up and at it!" the way he always did when she was there. His energy early in the morning had always been somewhat horrifying to Kate.

She blinked, feeling a familiar heaviness settle in her chest.

Harris had a picture frame of what his life was supposed to look like and Kate had been trained to fit it. But the day was approaching, she knew, when she would be too tired to go on pretending. And the moment she stopped pretending to be the woman Harris had made up his mind she was, the woman he had decided fit his image of what his life should look like, was the moment, Kate was sure, the relationship would start to fall apart.

And after it fell apart—after Harris would say, over and over again, "What's gotten into you, Kate? Why are you acting this way?" and Kate would say back to him, over and over again, "I'm acting this way because this is who I am. You're in love with someone who doesn't exist!"—Harris would find a new woman to fit into his picture frame and he would quietly explain to her (with long, thoughtful, deeply drawn sighs) that his former love, Kate Weston, had had deep psychological problems that he simply could not help her with.

Oh, how tragedy would hang in the air as Harris related this tale of woe for the first time! That first time was always magical with Harris—it had worked on Kate, had it not? Hadn't she believed there had to be something very special about a man who understood that his beautiful first wife had suffered from deep psychological problems he simply could not help her with? Surely this was no ordinary banker! she had thought. Of course, at the time, it had not occurred to Kate that this meant, then, that Harris had left his children in the care of a woman with terrible psychological problems.

Kate, stop it! she thought, closing her eyes. *It wasn't like that!*

Oh, no?

After she and Harris broke up, it would never occur to Harris that anything was wrong with him, anything wrong with a man who fell for the outside package of a woman and then made up the interior of her so he could be "in love" with her without having to know her. Because if Harris really did know Kate, he would know that once, just once, when Kate asked him, "What's the matter? You seem a little down," he should say, "I'm feeling a little depressed," instead of, "I don't know—I must have the flu or something."

And if Harris really did know Kate, he would have sensed by now how much she had to keep from him and how hard it was for her to pretend she was fine when sometimes she felt as if she were dying inside, scared to say anything because his reaction would only make her feel worse.

Not everyone felt as deeply as Kate did, Harris would say—as an explanation of why he wished to discount Kate's feelings, Kate's fears, Kate's insecurities, Kate's whatever-it-was she experienced and apparently he did not. She shouldn't pay so much attention to feelings, he would tell her. She needed to take her mind off herself. A walk—didn't

Kate think she needed a walk? She had already taken one? Maybe she should talk to her doctor then; it could be hormonal, couldn't it? Kate should talk to her gynecologist . . . She had? But was he any good? Oh, a she? Was she any good? Was Kate sure?

Stop it! Kate thought. *You can't put it all on him, you just can't. The fact that he's there for you is probably the biggest problem! You know how you are!*

If Kate married Harris, she would receive some jewelry of her mother's, jewelry which she knew she'd probably never take out of the safety deposit box, but which she could always sell if she had to get herself and the children out of a bad situation. (*Great,* she thought, *I'm not even married and I'm already hocking the family jewels and fleeing with the children.*)

And, if Kate got married, she would receive an antique sterling silver service for eighteen, six sterling candlesticks, two candelabras, and a tea service; a set of crystal decanters and glasses set in silver latticework; a sideboard of hand-painted china; and a steamer trunk of Belgian linen and Irish lace.

And, if Kate got married, her brother, Matt, and his wife would have to turn over to her the walnut secretary in their living room and the brass-and-crystal chandelier in their dining room, while Kate's sister, Sissy, and her husband would have to hand over the satinwood, box-wood, white mahogany, and ebony cabinet in their living room, and also the sketch by Van Ruisdael that hung in their dining room.

And, finally, if Kate got married, she would receive a check for at least twenty-five thousand dollars from her father.

But if Kate did *not* get married, Matt and his wife would keep the secretary and the chandelier, and Sissy and her husband would keep the cabinet and the sketch; and all of Kate's mother's jewelry, all of the silver, all of the china, all of the linen, and all of the twenty-five thousand dollars would remain a part of her father's general estate until he died *and* Kate's stepmother died—at which time Kate would then inherit one-third of things material (that is, heirlooms, including only one-third of all the things she would have gotten already had she married), and one-sixth of things monetary, the Weston children and their stepsiblings, the Sorrels, evenly dividing.

And that was right, wasn't it? That Kate shouldn't get anything now—no money, no heirlooms—because she wasn't married? Because Matt and Sissy both had spouses and flesh-and-blood heirs while Kate had—well, at the moment Kate had a boyfriend named Harris who had two ill-behaving heirs of his own by an emotionally disturbed wife out in New Jersey?

Dr. Weston's logic was this: valuable family possessions should stay in the possession of the family, and if one child did not produce a family to inherit the valuable family possessions, then that child should not get nearly as much as those children who had produced a family in time to inherit the valuable family possessions.

Still, though, Kate wished she could muster up enough courage to question this doctrine of her father's. But she couldn't. Most days she considered herself lucky that her father even acknowledged that she was his child.

After all, Matt and Sissy *had* given Dr. Weston everything he had wanted from them, everything Kate had thus far failed to produce: a good marriage, nice children, a house located near his own. And, too, Matt and Sissy got along with their father in a way Kate never would. The twins were eight years older than Kate. The twins had gone away to school when they were young. The twins, in other words, had missed a lot.

Unlike Kate, the twins had never made any connection between the way their father was and the reasons why their mother had—

Well, done what she had.

But then, Matt and Sissy had never been very tuned-in to Kate either. They thought Kate was some kind of Don Juanita of the fast lane in New York. They thought Kate didn't get married because she was having too much fun.

Fun, yes.

Kate did, however, possess one significant Weston furnishing in her apartment in New York. It was an Empire sofa. She had very wisely whisked it off to Canton in her senior year because as soon as she had heard that Sissy and her husband were buying a five-bedroom house in Trumbull she knew Sissy would be on her way to Windy Hills to get it. And Kate loved that sofa, because when Kate was little and her mother had wanted her to come out and charm company in the living room, Mrs. Weston would coax her little buckaroo into exemplary behavior by telling Kate that if she sat on that sofa, "You'll be the queen of Egypt, little one, floating down the Nile on your barge. Show the people all the majesty and kindness that make them love you so."

The Westons had home movies of Kate sitting on the sofa in her little party dresses, little legs sticking out, herself uncharacteristically still, merely smiling and nodding into the camera as if she were, indeed, a queen—one not wishing to overturn the barge, as it were.

Kate flung herself onto her stomach on the bed and hid her face in a pillow. She couldn't think about this stuff without getting crazy.

And she was tired of making herself crazy.

But what am I going to do about Harris?

She didn't want to be alone, she didn't want to start over yet *again*, and she loved Harris, really she did, and she could trust Harris and, unlike almost everybody in her life before, she could count on Harris day in and day out. But there was no way Kate could think about being married to Harris without feeling a kind of panic inside, a panic that said that even if a marriage between them were to work and they were to have children, the instant one of those children expressed a desire for a set of golf clubs or an MBA Kate had a feeling she might—

Might—

Because, Kate would think, the way all of these people lived—these people who were Harris's friends, these people who were supposedly *normal*—was not a way of living that would keep Kate alive. She was sure of it. Yet the right money and the right social connection and the right stringing on one's squash racket seemed to be making these normal people happy—in between snip-snapping things out of magazines, things they were always telling Kate they had or wanted to buy, things they were always telling Kate they had or wanted to see, things they were always telling Kate they had or wanted to experience—and Kate, for the life of her, could not understand what was so wrong with her that she couldn't get the hang of it and make it a lifestyle that worked for her too. But she couldn't, and she didn't, and it didn't. She hated everything about her life outside of work. She hated entertaining Harris's friends, she hated going out with Harris's friends, she hated Harris's friends' parties; and she certainly hated all of Harris's stupid goddamn Wall Street dinners when all of Harris's normal friends would say to her, "Oh, and so do you read all day? Is that what editors do?" because to Harris's friends what Kate did for a living was okay for a trophy wife, but didn't compare with *real* life, where people made *real* money.

"Will you stop it!" Kate said aloud, sitting bolt upright in the bed and flinging a pillow across the room. "Stop it! Stop it! Stop it!"

And then she fell back on the bed, looking up at the ceiling, swallowing, breathing deeply, trying to compose herself.

How did she always get started on this downward spiral? One where she remembered nothing of Harris's strength and kindness, the love and gratitude that often shined in his eyes, his efforts to make her happy? This downward spiral allowed no memory of the laughs they had shared, the secrets, the late night discussions of their careers. And it never remembered the first time Harris had run out to Endicott Booksellers and then to Shakespeare & Company at night to buy one copy at each of a book Kate had edited, a book whose sales she had been agonized about.

Now was that a way to an editor's heart or what?

Kate smiled and the pang of guilt hit. Hard.

Yes. The guilt. Making her feel scared inside, cold, not just a little bit alone.

Mark was coming out for the weekend, because it was Mark she wanted to see. Harris, who repeatedly offered to fly out, was too much of an effort.

It would kill Harris if he knew this.

But sometimes, she thought, consoling herself, *you don't have anything to give when you're working hard. Sometimes,* she thought, *you can only have friends around.*

Yes. That was right. Sometimes one could only have friends around.

— 22 —

Kate changed into shorts and Top-Siders and a polo shirt, crossed Ocean Avenue, descended the cliffside path stairs, walked across the pedestrian bridge over Route 1, and went down the stairs to the acres and acres of gorgeous sandy expanse that was the Santa Monica beach.

Kate was not a runner. She was a walker. And she walked on the water's edge, briskly, heading north, away from the Santa Monica Pier.

There were a lot of joggers out on the hard-packed sand and Kate wondered why they looked so natural running, whereas in New York, the runners (Harris included) always looked so serious and strained about it. After a mile or so Kate decided that out here they ran like deer and gazelles; at home, Kate decided, they definitely ran like predators.

What is with you this morning? she asked herself.

A second later the answer came. *I like it here. I don't know why, but I like it out here. I feel good here.*

*

Gracia buzzed her through the gate and Kate saw that Gary was here already (the red Porsche), Gracia was here (the white Toyota), but Noél (the blue BMW) was out. Kate swung her car around the drive and parked by the garage. As she turned off the motor she waited a moment, thinking that she heard something.

Evidently Cookie and Cupcake heard something, too, because in the side yard they were barking their heads off and Kate could hear them hurling themselves against the chain-link fence of the kennel. She undid her seat belt and got out of the car, reached in the backseat for her briefcase, and walked quickly toward the house.

Yes, she had heard something all right. Someone yelling. Inside the house. And now, as she drew closer to the front door, Kate could make out that it was Lydia yelling—and Gary yelling. He was yelling something about Lydia throwing her life's work away; she was yelling something about how would he know, he threw *everything* away, people, places, *and* things!

Kate, not sure what to do (but knowing that she didn't particularly feel like walking into the middle of this), sat down on the front step, setting her briefcase beside her, hoping that maybe Gracia would come out and find her and tell her what was going on.

And then . . . silence. All was quiet in the house. The dogs stopped barking.

But then Lydia screamed and Kate jumped to her feet and the dogs went wild. Lydia started yelling again, so Kate at least knew she was alive ("How dare you! How dare you let that creep even say her name!"), and Kate sat back down on the step again, wondering if maybe she should leave. She felt as though she were listening in on something she shouldn't be hearing.

Now Gary was yelling and Kate could make out something about an associate producer, something about Bestar, and then, clear as a bell, she heard him say, "You can't keep Noél under lock and key forever, Lydia! You've got to let her go sometime!"

Ah-ha. They were fighting about Noél.

Oh, dear. This only brought up the question that Kate had failed to ask yet. What, exactly, was Lydia's relationship with Noél?

Bam! Slam! went the front door behind Kate and Gary came storming out of the house, nearly falling on top of her in the process.

"Sorry," Kate said, trying to move out of his way, dragging her briefcase with her.

"Stupid goddamn idiot!" Gary yelled. He looked at Kate, pointing to the house. "She thinks I'd hurt Noél—she thinks I'd hurt her!" He turned to the front door. "Stupid idiot!" he yelled into the house, and then stormed down the front walk.

Kate started breathing again.

"And you're a stupid jackass!" Lydia suddenly yelled from behind Kate, making her jump. "That sleazy son of a bitch doesn't care about you or Noél or anybody! All he wants is what he wants—don't be dumb! Don't let him use you!"

"He's not using me!" Gary yelled from the driveway, yanking open the door to his Porsche.

"Of course he is!" Lydia yelled, standing now on the front step. She was in tennis whites this morning, a little skirt and pretty blouse with a trace of color around the edges. "He's using you to get to me!"

"I only said I'd talk to you!" Gary yelled at Lydia over the roof of his car.

"Mortimer Pallsner?" Lydia yelled at Gary. "You would talk to *me* on behalf of Mortimer Pallsner? Are you sick or crazy or both?"

"Go ahead, throw it all away!" Gary yelled, getting into his car and slamming the door.

"Just you remember who you're talking to!" Lydia yelled, this time losing her balance on the step and half tripping down to the front walk to regain it. "Consider your track record!"

"Forget it! Just forget it!" Gary yelled through the open sunroof. He started the car, revving the engine.

"Fine, go ahead, run away!" Lydia yelled as the tires of Gary's car squealed into reverse. "Okay, act like a five-year-old!" she yelled, as he peeled out. "Go ahead, drive off a cliff again—see if I care!" she yelled as the Porsche disappeared down the hill. She sighed, letting her head and shoulders go slack, and then, slowly, dejectedly, turned around. She covered her face with her hands, sighed into them, and shook her head. "He has such an awful temper," she said. "You'd think he'd have it under control by now."

Kate couldn't help but smile.

"He gets these ideas," Lydia said into her hands. "He thinks a lifetime of damage can be reversed in five minutes. I don't know how he can think that way when he knows how long it takes to heal."

Kate's smile vanished. There was something in the tone of Lydia's voice that was deadly serious. Kate swallowed and said, gently, "You're upset, Lydia. Maybe this isn't something you want me to hear."

Lydia dropped her hands as though she were exhausted. "I suppose you're right," she sighed. She walked over and plunked herself down on the step next to Kate. She leaned forward then, resting her forehead on her knees, closing her eyes.

Kate placed her hand on Lydia's back and simply let it rest there.

"I have to control things," Lydia said. "I have to. I know I shouldn't, but sometimes I have to or it would all unravel." Pause. "I don't want to see people I care about be hurt." Pause. "Sometimes people have to be protected. Even if it's not what you want—you have to protect people sometimes—if you love them."

Kate had no idea what she was talking about.

After several moments, Lydia, still bent over, said, "My life has been such a mess, Kate." There was another sigh. "There's been so much hurt, so much pain. I don't want to write about it, but you should know that it's there."

Kate nodded, lightly rubbing Lydia's back. "You're a survivor," she said. "Someone who has overcome a great deal in her life—someone who's in the process of yet another resurrection of sorts." Pause. "That is what your retirement's about, isn't it? Another try? At living life differently?"

"I used to think so," Lydia said. "Now I'm not so sure." Pause. "I get confused sometimes—about if what I'm doing is right, or if I'm simply doing what I want to do for selfish reasons disguised as something else." A long sigh. "The older I get, the less I seem to know about anything."

Kate smiled and gave Lydia's back a final pat, withdrew her hand, and then locked her arms around her own legs. Looking up at the trees, which were blowing in the breeze, she said, "Your life certainly isn't messed up now."

"Oh, but it is," came the reply.

Kate realized that Lydia was crying.

"I've got a hole inside of me I'll never be able to fill," Lydia said.

They were silent for several moments, Kate looking up at the sky, Lydia with her head down. Finally Kate said, "Your life couldn't be that much of a mess. Not with what I see in the eyes of everyone around you."

Slowly Lydia's head came up. She sniffed, wiping tears away with the back of her hand, "Why, what do you see?"

"A lot of love," Kate said, reaching into the side pocket of her briefcase. "And gratitude, lots of gratitude." She handed Lydia a Kleenex.

Lydia smiled slightly. "The magic word—gratitude. Did Gary or Noél tell you that? Thank you, by the way," she added, holding up the Kleenex.

"Tell me what?" Kate said.

Lydia blew her nose and wiped it. "That the password around here is gratitude."

"What, to the gate?" Kate asked.

"Come here, little Slinky," Lydia said. She was talking to the alley cat she had rescued from the studio lot. Lydia said the cat had been emaciated, flea-bitten, and with one ear torn. It was certainly a very healthy-looking cat now—a tiger with a very nice white chest and feet—but her ear still had the tear. Lydia wanted to put a picture of her in the book. She said the cat had always wanted to be famous, that's why it had been hanging around the studio. "Come here, Slinky-Binky-Puss-Puss." (The cat's name had a habit of coming out a bit differently every time Lydia spoke to it, although it did have an official name, Miss Slinky St. Marie.)

The cat crept out of the bushes and over to rub against the legs of her mistress. Lydia picked her up and kissed her once on the head. "Hi, Slinky-Minky-Kitty-Katty."

"Lydia?"

"Hmmm?"

"Gratitude's the password for what?" Kate asked.

Lydia smiled, kissed the cat again, and put her down. "For the inner circle around here." When Kate looked puzzled, Lydia added, "I don't like people who don't have a sense of gratitude about things. Life is hard enough. You have a sense of gratitude—about life, I mean. That's why I like you."

Kate wasn't following any of this too well.

"But now," Lydia sighed, standing up and drawing her hands up to her hips, looking out to the driveway, "what am I going to do about Gary?"

Kate thought, *Now. Ask her.* "Lydia?" she said. "There's something I need to ask you about—and there's something I guess I should tell you I know."

Lydia turned around. "What is it you know?"

"That you and Gary were once involved."

"A hundred years ago," Lydia said, turning back toward the driveway. "It's not going in the book."

"Yes, I know," Kate said, her mind racing for a tactful way to put the next. "And we've talked a little about your marriages."

"Yes," Lydia sighed, "my marriages."

"But we haven't discussed what's going on now," Kate said.

Lydia turned around.

Kate hesitated and then said, "I'll protect your privacy, Lydia—I think you know that. But I can't do a good job of it unless I know what you might need to be protected against."

Now Lydia looked confused.

"Your private life," Kate said. "I want to know if there's anyone in your private life you prefer no one know about."

Lydia visibly paled. "I don't know what you mean," she said softly.

"I mean," Kate said, "like a lover."

Lydia relaxed then. She even smiled. "And what kind of lover are we talking about, may I ask? Or who? Surely you can't object to my going out occasionally with Steve Brannicker. He's a nice, honest guy. But we're not really a couple or anything."

Kate stood up. "Well, what I wanted to know was . . ."

"Was what, Kate?" Lydia said. "Come on, spit it out."

"I wanted to know if there was anything about Noél I should be aware of."

"Noél?" Lydia said.

"What her relationship is to you," Kate said.

Lydia looked blank for a moment and then she got it—and then she exploded with laughter, clasping a hand over her heart and staggering backward. "Noél!" she said, throwing her head back to the sky, laughing and laughing.

"Excuse me, señora," Gracia said, appearing in the doorway.

"Oh, Gracia," Lydia said, "you should have heard Kate!" She exploded into laughter again, expiring this time into a heap on the grass.

Well, Kate thought, *so much for Lydia and Noél.*

"Señora," Gracia said again, looking down at her employer, coming out onto the step to hold out Lydia's pocketbook and car keys. "Señora, please!"

Lydia was flat on her back now, arms out to the sides. "Me and Miss Shaunnessy!" she cried with glee, curling up into a ball and rolling over onto her side.

Gracia pushed the pocketbook and keys into Kate's hands. "Please tell the señora," she said, "that she should go after Señor Steiner."

"Oh, Gracia," Lydia said, looking up at her, laughter winding down, "I'm going to have to send you to Al-Anon."

"He is very upset," Gracia said.

"He's a baby," Lydia said, wiping her eyes.

"He is a very fine man," Gracia said.

"Then you go after him," Lydia suggested, sitting up.

"But *you* hurt his feelings, señora," Gracia said.

"And he hurt mine!" Lydia said.

"But not the same way, señora," Gracia said. "You know that. No one upsets Señor Steiner the way you do."

"Oh, Gracia," Lydia sighed, "all right." She got up off the grass, brushing her tennis clothes off. She took the pocketbook and keys from Kate. "I'll go."

"He was only trying to help you, señora," Gracia said, sounding like herself again. "He only wants what is best for you—and the little señora."

"Right," Lydia muttered, walking down the front walk. "Stick Noël's head back in the lion's mouth and make me work until I'm a hundred and nine." She turned around. "Come on, Kate. You don't need your briefcase—and *no* tape recorder." Kate left her briefcase and hurried to catch up.

"I will fix you a very nice luncheon," Gracia called after them.

"I wish I could remember exactly when it was that Gracia overthrew my household," Lydia said, leading the way to the garage.

"She loves you very much," Kate said.

"And I love her," Lydia said. She opened a little box on the side of the garage and punched in some numbers. "God knows, she's been mother, saint, and savior to me." The middle door of the garage went up. They were taking the dark green Mercedes 250 SL, leaving the Rolls and the Country Squire station wagon with wood paneling on the side.

"That's such an interesting car for you to have," Kate said, climbing into the Mercedes, "a station wagon."

"Well, sometimes I act like a real person," Lydia said, getting in the car and closing her door.

"And what do you do as a real person?" Kate asked.

"Go to a shopping mall," Lydia said, putting on her seat belt.

"Really?" Kate said.

"Sometimes. Incognito," Lydia said, turning to look at her. "You can't portray people if you don't know how people are. So I sit on a bench for a couple of hours, move around some, watching people—how they move—listen to how they talk, treat each other. This way," she added, reaching over to show Kate how to work the seat belt.

"Thanks."

"And I like going to tree nurseries and garden centers," she said, starting the car. "And it comes in handy when I have children around." She looked at Kate. "You can't imagine how hard it was for me to get a tailgate that goes down instead of one that swings out. You wonder what kind of childhoods the car designers of today had anyway."

"What children?" Kate said.

"Oh, I don't know, just children," Lydia said, shrugging, and turning around to back the car out. "I do a lot of fund-raising, as you know—but I like to spend some time with some of the children too. Get a sense of how the money can help them in their lives. So I take them to the zoo or the beach or something."

"I didn't know that," Kate said.

"You're not supposed to," Lydia said, pushing the garage remote control to bring the door back down.

"Why not?" Kate said.

Lydia glanced over at her before starting down the drive. "I'm just telling you this, Kate—like a friend. This isn't for public consumption."

"But why is it a secret?" Kate said.

Lydia stopped the car. "Look," she said, turning to Kate, "I don't do it for the children, I don't do it for the public—I do it for me. Okay? I do certain things because they make me feel good, make me feel like a worthwhile human being—and that has nothing to do with being an actress. Charities have my endorsements, charities have my appearances, my money, my support, but there are times and experiences that belong only to me."

"I understand," Kate said, although she didn't really. There were so many things that didn't quite add up with Lydia. Missing motives.

They drove down through the gate and instead of turning left to go down Benedict Canyon Drive into Beverly Hills, Lydia turned right, to wind her way up to Mulholland Drive. There were a couple of pin curves on the way and Kate did not look down.

When they reached the flat, open, four-lane intersection with Mulholland Drive, they turned right—and almost immediately Mulholland narrowed to two lanes, continuing its serpentine twists along the spine of the Santa Monica Mountains. To the left, some several thousands of feet below, lay the sprawl of "the Valley"—the San Fernando Valley—and to the right was the alternately woodsy and craggy (terrestrially complicated, at any rate) series of canyons that made up the northern border of Beverly Hills: Benedict, Peavine, Franklin, and Coldwater.

"Okay, there he is," Lydia said, pointing ahead, to the left. The Porsche was parked in what appeared to be some sort of scenic lookout.

They crossed the road and parked. Lydia undid her seat belt and looked at Kate. "Wait here, okay? And let me see what the whether's like—as in, whether or not Gary's up for company."

"Okay," Kate said.

Lydia climbed out of the car, closed the door, and walked to the edge of the lookout. She looked down. Evidently she saw him, down on the embankment to the right somewhere, because she slowly made her way over, and then, gingerly, down, disappearing out of sight.

Kate rolled down her window, thinking she could hardly wait to tell Mark about this latest innovation in the editorial process.

In a minute a car of Japanese tourists pulled in next to her, one woman and two men. Kate could tell they were tourists because they were looking at maps and snapping pictures. Kate ended up getting out of the car to take their picture—on two different cameras—while they stood in front of the sweeping view of the Valley.

"Kate," Lydia's voice was calling from down below somewhere.

The Japanese tourists looked at each other.

"Kate! Come on!"

Kate snapped the last picture and then, taking the camera straps off from around her neck—one by one, handing them to their owners—she nodded politely, wished them a pleasant visit, and walked over to the edge of the lookout.

Down a narrow path (with a sheer drop near it that Kate did not wish to consider for more than a split second—God, it looked like *miles* down to the bottom), sitting on a grassy ledge next to a boulder were Gary and Lydia, waving up to her. "Come down," Gary called.

"*Sow-lan!*" cried the woman from behind Kate. And then there was a flurry of excited chatter in Japanese.

Of course. They recognized Lydia. Lydia was very big in Japan.

Lydia ended up coming up the path to sign autographs. She refused to have her picture taken with them, however, explaining to Kate that weirdos tended to fabricate entire romances around such pictures and then sell them to the tabloids, so no, she never had her picture taken with strangers. Never. The tourists took it well, though, and left graciously, with little bows and nods of thanks.

Kate—willing herself not to look down—followed Lydia down the path. At one point Kate did look and promptly froze, but then Lydia, without comment, simply came back up and took her firmly by the hand to lead her down.

"Hi," Gary said, offering his hand to help Kate sit. Her knees weak, Kate took it and sat down.

Okay. This was not so bad. This ledge. She could handle this.

"Welcome to Gratitude Rock," Gary said.

"Whenever Gary gets crazy at my house," Lydia said, "which tends to be rather frequently, I'm afraid—he comes to Gratitude Rock to put life back into perspective."

"I fell behind this once," Gary said, patting the boulder behind him, "and my car fell down there." He pointed down the cliff. "So, as you can imagine, I have a great deal to be grateful for."

Kate followed the line of his finger and closed her eyes.

"I was drunk at the time," he said. Pause. "But I don't drink anymore. I haven't for over five years."

"That's wonderful," Kate said, opening her eyes. "How did you do it?"

"Betty Ford and then AA," he said. "I still go."

"That's great," Kate said.

"Gary's done incredibly well," Lydia added. "And he's helped an awful lot of people."

Gary shrugged, looking down at a blade of grass in his hands. "So have you, Lyddie."

Silence.

A bird started to sing.

"My mother was an alcoholic," Kate heard herself say while looking at the sky.

"Was?" Gary said.

"She died," Kate said.

"Cirrhosis?" Gary said.

"Suicide," Kate said.

*

The women in Kate's family had traditionally been a hardy lot, most often dealing with depression by simply pulling themselves up by their bootstraps and getting moving. All except Kate's mother that is, Elizabeth Gates Weston, who had, in fact, killed herself right after talking to Granny Gates in Texas on the telephone, Granny who had been telling her daughter that she simply had to pull herself up by her bootstraps and get moving.

So Kate was a woman who pretty much thought that if she was still moving, she was not—and would never be—depressed like her mother. And Kate's mother had even left instructions for Kate about how to avoid getting depressed like her, instructions that Kate had done her best to follow. Her mother had written them in the little red autographing book Kate had been given on her eighth birthday:

> *My littlest angel, my dearest Katherine,*
> *Remember always to be a very good girl*
> *and to get very good grades—*
> *because then you'll never end up*
> *like your poor old mother.*
> > *Love you, buckaroo,*
> > *Mom*

It was an odd sort of thing for a thirty-six-year-old woman to write to an eight-year-old child, but then it was the only written communique Kate had from her mother, and she cherished it. (She did have a hastily scribbled grocery list her mother had once written, which Kate had found in a cookbook years ago and had immediately hoarded away.) And Kate, as a part-time mischief-maker and a full-time over-achiever (student council president, homecoming queen, third in her class at Saint Lawrence, girl-wonder publishing success story, etc., etc., etc.), was the last person anyone would say was going to end up like her poor old mother, Elizabeth Gates Weston, the woman who had so tragically killed herself at age thirty-nine.

*

"I knew it," Lydia said.

Kate looked at her.

"I knew there was something," Lydia said. She looked at Gary. "Didn't I say so?" She looked at Kate again and smiled. Gently. "You get along too well with all of us to have had a normal life."

"Well," Kate started to say, "I did have a fairly normal—" She stopped when she saw their expressions. "I guess you're right," she said, correcting herself. "It wasn't a very normal childhood." Pause. "But we certainly *tried* to make it look normal."

They all laughed at this, evidently identifying with her.

"Kate thought Noél and I might be lovers," Lydia said to Gary. "She asked me about it because she wanted to protect me—isn't that sweet?"

"Don't feel bad, Kate," Gary told her, "a lot of people think that." Lydia's eyes got very large. "They *do?*"

"Yeah," he said, smiling. "I think Mort lent a hand with that one."

"Oh, that creeping crud," Lydia said. "It would be just like him to tell everyone that Noél's *my* mistress." Then she caught herself and looked a little guilty. "I didn't mean to imply . . . ," she said to Kate, clearly unsure of how to proceed.

"Don't worry, Noél told me about it," Kate said.

Lydia and Gary looked at each other, apparently surprised by this.

"And she told me she's in AA—and CA," Kate said. "But she didn't tell me about you, Gary." She turned to Lydia and smiled. "But you know what I'm going to ask you now—don't you? If you're in recovery too?"

Lydia shook her head. "No, I'm not an alcoholic."

"I know," Gary said to Kate, "with *her* temperament, I would have sworn she was one too."

"But my father was," Lydia added. "Not recovering—just an alcoholic."

Kate blinked. According to the book, Lydia's father had been an icon, tragically killed in a freak car accident at age forty-two. *But of course,* Kate thought, *a freak car accident. Mom used to have those all the time too.* "I'm so sorry," Kate said.

"And I'm sorry about your mother," Lydia said, standing up and brushing off her tennis skirt.

Gary was sitting there, dumbfounded. "Lydia Allyson Southland," he finally said, "I have known you for eighteen years and you have never, *ever,* said anything to me about your father being an alcoholic."

"So now you know," Lydia said, starting back up the path. She turned around. "Are you guys coming?"

— 23 —

He did not have a free ticket from United Airlines. He had, in fact, paid nearly eight hundred dollars for a round-trip ticket on such short notice. But Mark didn't care.

Kate and convertibles, Mark decided at LAX, went together like horse and carriage. Top down, sunglasses on, streaking up the San Diego Freeway early Friday afternoon to Lydia Southland's with Kate in the sunshine, Mark felt happier than he had been in years.

He felt free.

Lydia was, as he suspected she would be, overwhelming. Was this a beautiful woman or *what?* And the house! And the people—Gary, Noël, Gracia, Imelda—and the animals—Cookie, Cupcake, Slinky St. Something-or-Other—and Kate . . .

Yes, and Kate. There was Kate. Happy, laughing, looking better than she had in months. Clearly this was a change of pace that agreed with her.

He spent the afternoon helping Gary and some computer guy install a phone modem on the computer in the office. The idea was to be able to link it to Gary's computer at home in Pacific Palisades, the secretarial offices where transcripts were being typed every night and also to one of the IBM compatibles at Bennett, Fitzallen & Coe in New York. When Kate went home, the idea was she could work directly on the "manuscript," work on copy and transcripts with Gary and/or Lydia or Noël while talking to them on the phone and they would all be able to transmit and print out new pages as they were finished.

Saturday.

While Kate and Lydia and Gary and Noël worked in the office, Mark took what they had of the new manuscript outside to the hammock. Two hours later he came inside for the transcripts they had yet to incorporate, a legal pad, a pad of stick-em note paper, and a pencil. Two hours later he came back in announcing his verdict.

"It's terrific," he announced.

The little group cheered.

"But you've got a long way to go," he said.

The little group booed.

And he sat with them and went over his perspective on the material thus far and how he thought the book should take shape.

"I hate to tell you," Gary said when Mark was finished, "but what you're saying is very close to what Kate's been saying all along. I hope we didn't waste your time."

"It's no waste of time," Kate quickly assured him. "Believe me, when you've chucked out a bestseller and started from scratch again, there's no such thing as wasting time by asking another editor's opinion."

They worked all day and then, in the evening, Gracia and her grandchildren, Billy and Cathy, arrived to organize a cook-out out back. Mark marveled at how at home the kids were in Lydia's house; of course, he also marveled at Gracia's role. Kate was right. She was no housekeeper. She was resident mother.

Turning the food over on the grill outside with Gary—burgers, fish, chicken—Mark asked him what part of the book he thought was weakest.

"Oh, definitely the beginning, the middle, and the end," Gary said, laughing.

"I'm serious," Mark said, pushing his glasses up higher on his nose against the smoke. He hoped he was cooking this stuff okay. He had never cooked for an international superstar before.

"So am I," Gary said. "We're working around Lydia's sore spots—the years after her father died, her last years in New York before coming to California, what her plans are for the future. She won't talk about any of it." He sighed, holding a platter near as Mark picked up the fish with the spatula again. "Kate says we'll come up with something; we should just go on and finish the rest."

"Think that's done?" Mark asked him, putting the fish on the platter and poking it.

Gary squinted. "I don't know."

"My oh my, great cooks in action," Lydia said, coming over to them. She put her arm around Mark. "Doesn't it seem like he's always been here?" she asked Gary, giving Mark a squeeze.

Mark was in heaven. Lydia felt as wonderful as she looked.

"It's weird, isn't it?" Gary said. "And I feel like we've known Kate a million years."

"You're right," Kate said, driving back to Santa Monica. "But I think it's more than just painful memories."

"Like what?"

She shrugged, making a turn. "I don't know—it's just a feeling I have. And I think it might have to do with the fact that her father was an alcoholic. I think there's something specific he may have done that she's determined no one is to know."

"What, like incest?" Mark said.

"I don't know," Kate said, "but there's something."

They drove for a while.

"What about before she came out to California?" he asked her.

"Well," Kate said, "she was with Gary and he was an alcoholic too."

"He's a nice guy, I like him," Mark said.

"Yes, he is."

Mark looked at Kate. "Think he beat her up or anything?"

She shrugged again. "I don't know."

Mark sat in on Sunday's work session in the breakfast room, offering a bit of advice here and there. They broke for the day at five, everyone needing an evening off, and while Kate and Gary and Noël went to the office to put things away, Lydia stayed with Mark.

When she was sure they were gone, Lydia turned to him and said, "She adores you, that's obvious."

Mark felt his face burn. *Out of the blue she says this.*

"I know what you're going to say," she said, "that she doesn't adore you the way I make it sound."

He looked at her. Was she a mindreader as well?

Lydia smiled. "She doesn't know—but I do. I've been there." Pause. She touched the side of his face. Gently. "Be patient and don't give up," she told him.

Mark's eyes broke away. Kate was coming back.

Lydia dropped her hand and turned around. "I was just thanking Mark for coming all this way," she told Kate.

They ate dinner at Michael's in Santa Monica and walked under the palms on Ocean Avenue for a while, talking, as they always did, about all kinds of things: work, family, the S & L crisis, Zen Buddhism, *Kirkus Review*, world cup soccer, air bags in cars, whether or not Madonna would survive her celebrity (yes). They stopped for frozen yogurt, walked and talked some more—*Vanity Fair*, curfews in South

Africa, lost letters of Emily Dickinson, new lefty for the Yanks, Paul Newman's microwave popcorn, the palace at Versailles—and finally, near eleven, they walked back to the hotel.

"I wish you didn't have to go back in the morning," Kate said as he walked her to her room.

The Shangri-La was a wide **V** shape, facing the ocean, and the hallways were on the inside, in the open air, overlooking a large terrace and gardens. It was very quiet. Dim. Lovely.

He felt so strange. No. He knew what he felt. He felt in love with Kate. Hopelessly in love. And he didn't want to think what that meant. That when she came back to New York, when she came back to live with Harris, that she would be out of his reach in a way he knew would only be extremely painful from now on.

Oh, Kate, why don't you love me?

"I don't know how I'll ever be able to thank you," she said, slipping her key in the door. She turned around to look at him. Her eyes were sparkling. She was smiling—but now with a crease in her forehead. She touched his arm. "Are you okay?"

He shook his head. He looked around. "This place, I guess," he sighed.

Kate threw her arms around him and hugged him close. Holding him, she said, "I'm sorry, I should have thought of it before—what coming back here might mean to you." She released him and looked into his eyes. "You're free, Mark, remember that. Carla can't hurt you anymore."

Carla. Great. She thought he was upset about his ex-wife.

He kissed Kate on the cheek and said, "Good night," thinking that for someone so smart, Kate sure could be awfully dumb sometimes.

— *24* —

On her second-to-last morning in Los Angeles, Kate worked with Noël in the office at the big table, reviewing transcripts and flagging areas where she wished Noël could get Lydia to expound a little more. She also encouraged Noël to edit more. "You have such a feel for how Lydia talks."

"You mean I have a feel for how Lydia would like to be *heard,*" Noël said. "I'm doing a fair amount of editing as it is." She sifted through some pages and then stopped at one, pointing with her finger. "See this part?" Kate read:

I felt as though I had no one to turn to. The producers were only interested in the money the actors could generate with advertisers. They cared not at all about any one of us as people. But when Doris Bern was hired as the network executive in charge of "Parson's Crossing," all this changed.

"Yes," Kate said.

"What Lydia actually said was," Noël said, leaning forward to read from another piece of paper, " 'I felt like shooting those idiots with a machine gun. They didn't give a flying—f word—about any of the actors. They didn't give a flying—f word—about anything—nobody did, until Doris came. She kicked the living bejesus out of them and things finally got back on track.' "

Kate laughed, glancing up at the ceiling. For the last hour and a half Lydia had been thumping around overhead in the exercise room. Hers was quite a workout, involving floor exercises with weights, the Stair-Master, a stationary bicycle, a rowing machine, a treadmill, bar exercises, and plain old jumping jacks—which were, at the moment, thumping along as they spoke, signaling that Lydia was nearing the end of her regimen.

Kate looked at her watch. Almost ten—when Lydia and Gary were to join them. As if Lydia could hear Kate's thoughts, the thumping overhead stopped.

"Noël," Kate said, "I'm counting on you to get more out of Lydia about her romantic life."

Noël rolled her eyes.

"I'm serious," Kate said. "If anyone's going to get any more out of her, it's you."

"Wrong," Noël said. She pointed at Kate with her pencil. "You, Mademoiselle Editor. You're the one Lydia talks to."

Just then Lydia came waltzing into the office in a blue perspiration-soaked leotard. With her hair pulled back in a ponytail, she had a white terry cloth sweat band around her forehead and a white towel slung around her neck. She was holding a bottle of Pellegrino water with a glass over the top in one hand and a card of some sort in the other. "Morning," she said.

"Good morning," Kate said. For three and a half weeks she had been here and for three and a half weeks Lydia had come in soaking wet from her workout, perspiration dripping into her eyes, smelling of nothing but mineral water maybe.

"You're invited, if you'd like to come," Lydia said, tossing an engraved invitation down on the desk in front of Kate and Noél.

Mr. & Mrs. Mortimer G. Pallsner
Lydia Southland
the cast and crew of "Cassandra's World"
and Bestar Pictures Corporation, Inc.

would like you to join them in celebrating
the 7th Season of
"Cassandra's World"

Tuesday, September 24 8:00 P.M.
The Four Seasons Hotel
300 South Doheny Drive

Your attendance will mean a $500 donation from Bestar Studios
to the Children's Hospital Outpatient Program
for the Hospitals of Greater Los Angeles

"The invitations are done already?" Noél said to Lydia.

"It's only a prototype." She glanced at Kate. "I think Mort's trying to audition as a good guy for my book."

"Weird though," Noél murmured, "that he'd send it now—the thing's not until September."

Lydia looked at Kate. "What would you think if you were me?"

"Well," Kate said, "I'd think I was being reminded of all the good I can do while starring in a TV series—good works I couldn't do if I retired from public life."

Lydia looked at Kate for a moment longer, but didn't say anything.

"I like the type," Noél said.

"I do too," Lydia said. "Okay, I'll approve it." She bent over, took a pen from Noél, and scribbled her initials on it. "Think we'll have a jacket of the book by then?" she asked Kate.

"Yes," Kate said.

"Good," Lydia said, pouring some Pellegrino water into her glass and taking a sip, "then we'll have a big blowup of the book there and I'll announce that all royalties from the book are going to charitable causes for children."

Kate smiled. "Very nice."

"Yes, I thought so," Lydia said, sipping her water.

"Mort will have an absolute stroke," Noël said, making a note to send the invitation back to Bestar. "I can hardly wait."

"And if you come out for the party," Lydia said to Kate, "I'll fix you up with Wesley Hart."

"Wesley," Noël croaked, collapsing on the desk as if she had died.

"Noël, dear," Lydia said, looking down, patting at the perspiration on her forehead with the towel, "are you perhaps trying to tell us something?"

From her deathlike position, Noël nodded. "This is not Dream Date she's suggesting, Kate. He likes to tie women up."

Lydia's face was blank. "What?" she said.

"You're such an innocent sometimes, Lydia," Noël sighed, sitting up. "You've got to be the only one who doesn't know. Ask Gary if you don't believe me."

"Good morning," Gary said, appearing as if on cue in the doorway with a mug of coffee in hand.

Lydia put her glass down and unslung her towel from around her neck. "Did you know that Wesley ties up women?"

"Uh—yes," Gary said.

"She was going to fix him up with Kate," Noël said, laughing.

"No, Lydia," Gary said, vigorously shaking his head, "no."

Noël looked at Lydia's shocked expression and said, "He doesn't hurt them or anything. He just sort of—well, ties them up." She cracked up again.

"Don't you remember that time when April Lyttleton guested?" Gary said.

Lydia's expression was now one of abject horror. "Do you mean to tell me that those marks on her—?"

"I told her she was the only one who didn't know," Noël said.

"Oh, God!" Lydia cried, throwing her towel to the floor and thumping herself down on the windowsill. "How can I ever look at him again?"

"So are you guys ready to work or what?" Gary said, looking at his watch.

"Doesn't *any*one have a good old-fashioned marriage anymore?" Lydia wailed.

Kate reached for the tape recorder on the table and turned it on.

"Okay, Lydia," she said, pushing it in her direction, "tell us—what, in your mind, constitutes a good old-fashioned marriage?"

"Maybe you should ask me," Noél said, waving her hand. "My marriage lasted longer than most of Lydia's did."

Lydia looked at her.

"Maybe you and I should wait in the breakfast room," Gary said, pulling Noél out of her chair and into the hall.

And so there they were, Kate sitting at the table, Lydia sitting on the windowsill in her leotard, tape recorder running, with the question of what Lydia thought a good old-fashioned marriage was still in the air.

Her track record in marriage, Kate knew by now, had been this:

Lydia married in Florida, at age nineteen, and was divorced at twenty-one. She had been too young, she said.

She married again in New York, at age twenty-seven, and was divorced less than two years later. She had been too afraid of living alone, she said. That's why she had married.

She married a third time in 1978 to Texas land baron Bill Lakersdale. How old Lydia was at the time of this marriage was a little confusing since she couldn't have *still* been twenty-seven years old five years after she said she had gotten married for the second time at age twenty-seven, and so, for the moment, they merely said in the manuscript that this third marriage had taken place in 1978, that it had been a widely publicized ceremony in Central Park, and that Lakersdale hadn't wanted to leave Texas and Lydia hadn't wanted to move to Texas and so, in 1984, they had amicably ended the marriage.

"I haven't the slightest idea what a good old-fashioned marriage is," Lydia said, "but I think if the husband and wife both believe in God, then that is a start."

Pause.

"And you believe in God," Kate said. Religion was not something they had really discussed—basically because Lydia said she hadn't been brought up on anything.

"Of course I do," Lydia said. "I would have killed myself long ago if I didn't—and in a *merciful* God. I don't know any beautiful women who live long after forty who don't." She frowned slightly, looking at Kate. "What's the matter?"

"Nothing," Kate said, averting her eyes.

Lydia pushed herself off the windowsill and reached to turn off the tape recorder. "Yes—there was something," she said to Kate. "I saw it in your eyes—when I said not many beautiful women live past forty who don't believe in a merciful God."

Kate looked at her.

"What is it, Kate?"

Kate lowered her eyes to the table. "I was thinking about my mother. She believed in God when I was little—I remember." She looked up. "She killed herself, I told you that, so what you just said—well, I just wonder. I never thought about it before—about her belief in God. That maybe she stopped believing in God and that was why she . . ." She shook her head, letting her breath out slowly, looking back down at the table.

Lydia had the strangest effect on her sometimes.

"Your mother was beautiful, wasn't she?" Lydia said.

Kate nodded. "Yes." And then she added, "I know everybody thinks their mother's beautiful—but everybody agreed about Mom. Before—that is, before she really fell into the drinking—yes, she was beautiful." Pause. "That's why my father married her, I think."

"How old was she when she died?" This was barely a whisper.

"Thirty-nine," Kate said.

Lydia nodded and then stood up, turning to look out the window. Resting her hand on the window sash, she said, "So you know what it can do to a beautiful woman to see that she's losing her looks." Pause. "Some idea of the loss of power she feels—power she always denied having, but had become accustomed to having anyway." She shook her head, slowly. "As long as the world is ruled by men, beautiful women will have fleeting power." Pause. "And then they have the unhappy decline—the loss of power."

Kate didn't say anything. She was looking down at her hands, thinking how this was true, that she remembered very well the anguish her mother had over losing her looks—the tears, and then her absolute refusal, the last two years of her life, to have her picture taken. Fleeting, ghostlike images of her mother running away from cameras, cringing, hands trying to cover her face, passed through Kate's mind.

Kate had not looked at pictures of her mother in years.

Because they brought it all back. How desperately unhappy her mother had been; how slow, how cruel her decline had been.

If only someone had said something.

If only someone had done something. Kate. Her father. Sissy. Matt. The maid. Someone.

But no one had.

And her mother had retreated to the guest room to live. With the television. With the curtains drawn.

And she had died there. Alone.

If only there hadn't been so many pills in the house. *You'd think a doctor would be more careful,* she remembered one of the neighbors saying.

Lydia turned around. "I will not despair over losing my looks, Kate. I won't. Like your mother, beauty was my ticket out, too. But I've made plans—important plans about how I want to spend the rest of my life." Pause. "You shouldn't think women like your mother died for no reason, Kate. Some of us learned from them—some of us refuse to pass family tragedy on." Pause. "Like you, Kate."

Kate felt her throat tighten. She felt close to Lydia. Didn't she, in fact, remind her of her mother?

Lydia dropped down into the chair next to Kate. "Haven't you ever wondered why everyone calls me Mrs. Southland?"

"I don't know," Kate said, "I guess I thought you were following an old theatrical tradition—sort of like Mrs. Siddons in the eighteenth century."

"But Mrs. Siddons was married to a Mr. Siddons," Lydia pointed out, "and Southland's my maiden name."

"Like Mrs. Jordan, then," Kate said, thinking of the comedienne of the same period, also at the Drury Lane in London, who had assumed the name of Mrs. Jordan without ever having been married to a Mr. Jordan. "Although," Kate added, "I'm not quite sure you'd pattern yourself after an actress who had thirteen illegitimate children."

"There is no such thing as an illegitimate child," Lydia said. "An illegitimate liaison, maybe—"

"Yes, of course," Kate said quickly, "you're right. Excuse me, I didn't mean it that way." Pause. "Anyway"—she cleared the air with her hand—"why do people call you Mrs. Southland?"

"Because," Lydia said, "Lydia Southland will never be allowed to grow old—but *Mrs.* Southland will be able to."

Kate looked at her. "And so you'll be Mrs. Southland when you leave the show."

Lydia nodded.

"Lydia," Kate said, "do you think you'll ever get married again?"

No response. Lydia was looking out the window. She did that often when asked a personal question: stare off into space.

"Or—*do* you want to get married again?" Kate rephrased it.

"I don't know," Lydia said slowly. "I did once—want to get married again." She broke off her stare and shrugged, bringing her eyes back to Kate. "But I'm very happy the way I am now."

"But how about when you retire?" Kate said. "Is someone going to go with you to the horse farm?"

Actress or no actress, Kate recognized a flash of pain when she saw one—and she had just seen one in Lydia's eyes.

"I don't know," Lydia said quietly, getting up. She looked at her watch. "We better get to work, don't you think?"

— 25 —

All this new high-tech razzmatazz in the office had to have its downside somewhere, and for Noél it had come in the form of Mark Fiducia talking her into signing up for something called "Bay Cafe" in New York City. For a nominal fee every month, or so he said (forgetting the long distance phone charges since they were in L.A.), Noél could have the computer dial ATDT 718-769-6787 and be presented with all kinds of activities to do, from chatting online to people in New York—with code names like Zeron and Buxom and Flash—to playing trivia games, fantasy adventures, and storytelling games, and, most fun of all, scanning bulletin boards for things like personal ads.

Given her nature, Noél was already hopelessly addicted. It was near two in the morning and here she was in her robe and slippers, chatting on City Lights to some nice guy whose real name, he said, was Barry. His code name was BarryNYC. (Noél's code name was RedHot.) Barry was explaining different commands to her and their conversation was going like this:

REDHOT: So I just push return after?
BARRYNYC: Yes. By the way, u haven't filled out bio yet. U should do that. But don't put last name or #. We have a few strange ones on here.
REDHOT: K. Hey—do u know if u have anybody in AA?
BARRYNYC: Don't know. Why don't u put note on bulletin board? If there is, he will leave a message in your mailbox.
REDHOT: Neat!

"Oh, Noél," Lydia sighed, coming into the office later in her nightie, robe, and slippers too, "you're not down here talking to that pervert in Queens again, are you?"

"No," Noél said, "I got rid of him days ago. I was talking to a really nice guy before, Barry. He has something to do with City Lights. I think he helped create it or something."

"Now you know why he was so nice to you," Lydia said. She pulled a chair up alongside Noél and sat down. "What's that?" she asked, pointing to the screen.

"A user questionnaire," Noél explained. "So we can look each other up and get some idea of what kind of person we're talking to."

Lydia squinted. "Your favorite TV show is 'Murphy Brown'?" She looked at Noél. "You're fired."

Noél grinned, typing in that her favorite movie was *Swiss Family Robinson*.

Lydia squinted at the screen again. "*Swiss Family Robinson?*"

"Uh-huh," Noél said.

"Noél, dear," Lydia said then, getting up, "get off that thing and come into the kitchen. I want to talk to you."

"A lot of people like *Swiss Family Robinson*," Noél protested.

"No, no, that's not what I want to talk about," she said, leaving the room.

Hmmm. Chances were it was not good. Lydia did not get up in the middle of the night to talk to her about nothing. Something was up.

Noél sighed, left a thank-you note in BarryNYC's mailbox, and logged off the computer. She turned off the machine and turned off the lights in the office, then walked down the hall, down the stairs into the living room, through the breakfast room, and through the swinging door into the kitchen.

Lydia was at the stove, stirring a little honey into a saucepan of skim milk. "I'm making you a cup to take to your room, okay?"

"Thanks," Noél said, relieved because this meant Lydia planned on going back to her room and so whatever she wished to talk about would not take long.

"Things are going really well on the book, don't you think?" Lydia said.

"Yeah," Noél said. She hiked herself up to sit on the counter, watching Lydia.

"But you're not happy," Lydia said, stirring the milk with a wooden spoon. She looked over at Noél. "Are you?"

Noél shrugged. "I am."

"But not really happy," Lydia said.

Noél shrugged again, not knowing what to say. As far as she knew, she was as happy as she had ever been.

Lydia went back to stirring her milk. Without looking at Noél she said, "Do you ever think about talking to Holly? Seeing how she is?"

"I saw Holly—at the studio."

"When?"

"The day you re-shot that scene."

"Oh, right," Lydia said.

Silence.

Eighteen months after admitting she drank insanely, took drugs like an insane person, and slept around like someone who could only be insane, how could Noél rationalize, after all this time, feeling even more in love with Holly when she could scarcely remember having fallen in love with Holly in the first place, because she had been so crazy at the time? What sense did that make? An ongoing love for someone Noél could not remember clearly, had not talked to in a year and a half, had seen but once in passing?

But yes, that was the situation. And every time Noél heard Holly's name it grew worse: the ache of loss, the anger that everyone—Lydia, Gary, everybody—could see and talk to Holly and know how Holly was doing, while Noél, scourge of the earth, it felt like, had to spend the rest of her life avoiding the places where she might see her.

Because it hurt. At the sound of her name, Noél's stomach would drop, a pain would stab at her heart, and she would feel like crying. It was so bad sometimes she wondered if it was really about Holly or whether it was about her past life in general. That Holly stood for all the gifts, both precious and wonderful, that had been burnt, wasted, run through by Noél in her self-centered drive to destruction.

Holly . . . Holly . . . Could it really have ever been that Noél had slept in her arms? That Holly told her, over and over, how much she loved her, how she would do anything if only Noél would get help? How Noél would disappear after such a discussion, to teach Holly a lesson, to reappear a few days later and find Holly a mess, eyes a wreck, shaking like a leaf? And that Holly would not get angry, but would only hug her, holding on to her, kissing her like a lost child, crying that she needed Noél, she'd do anything to make her happy.

Holly had gone into heavy-duty therapy after Noél went into Betty

Ford. That's why, Gary said, she refused to see Noél when she first got out. Of course this had infuriated Noél, making her wonder who the hell this therapist was, interfering in their relationship like that. But was that what it was? Using and abusing Holly, being Mort's mistress, screwing around with anybody who could produce a couple good lines of coke—that was what constituted a *relationship* with Noél? In fairly short order guilt had rushed in to replace Noél's anger. And then after that the anger at Holly returned. Shortly after that, Noél found herself on a seesaw of guilt and then anger, guilt and then anger, at Holly, at herself, at everybody, only to go back the next moment to guilt again. And then, finally, after that, after about a year, all Noél felt about Holly was loss, grievous loss. And now, most recently, chilling fear at the thought of Holly: fear of running into her, fear of being in love with her still, fear of being rejected, fear of—well, everything.

And the ache in her heart would start again and she would start to cry, knowing, yes, that she would give anything if only to be able to talk to Holly a little, to hold her hand a little, and maybe just to know that Holly did not hate her.

Lydia looked up from the saucepan. "She'd like to see you, Noél."

Noél dropped her eyes and didn't say anything.

"A lot of time has passed," Lydia started.

"I'm not sure there will ever be enough time to undo what happened," Noél said. "The things I did."

Lydia's eyes were on the saucepan, stirring, stirring, stirring. "It's never all just one person's problems in a relationship, you know."

Noél sighed. "Some relationship."

"It wasn't just you, Noél," Lydia said, "and I hope you understand that." She looked up. "There was something very wrong with Holly—it wasn't just you."

A small flash of anger swept through Noél. "Holly's wonderful," she protested.

Lydia smiled. "I know she is. What I meant was that it was not good for her to stay in that relationship with you—and she did. And it was a signal she couldn't ignore. She needed to learn how to take care of herself better. At least, get the neurosis out of her relationships to see what was really there."

Noél frowned. "I don't like how you say that."

"I know you don't. Because you love her—"

"I didn't say—"

"You didn't have to," Lydia said quietly. She took the saucepan off the heat, turned off the burner, and looked at Noél. "I've been there, Noél. I've been where Holly's been. I had my turn falling in love with an alcoholic. I know the work I had to do on myself—I know it wasn't all him." Pause. "And I'd like to see you and Holly encourage each other in what you're doing. In your recoveries."

One tear spilled down Noél's cheek. She did not blink; she did not wipe it away.

— 26 —

"I'm sorry," Lydia said in the driveway, "but I can't stand this—I hate this," and abruptly she turned away from Kate and went back to the house, Cookie and Cupcake trotting after her.

Gary touched Kate's arm. "She doesn't do well with good-byes sometimes."

"But I'll be back," Kate said, standing next to her car. "It's not as if I'm never going to see you guys again."

"But things change," Noél sighed, slinging her arm through Gracia's and leaning against her.

"Yes," Gracia said, nodding, looking sad, "and the señora does not take well to change, no she doesn't."

"Unless *she's* inflicting the changes, that is," Noél added.

They all laughed. And then Kate shook Gary's hand and kissed him on the cheek, gave Noél a big hug and Gracia a smaller hug, thanking them for all their hard work. Then she got into her car and drove down the driveway, looking in the rearview mirror, giving a last little wave to the house on Benedict Canyon.

On the airplane the FASTEN YOUR SEAT BELT light went off. Kate loosened her seat belt slightly, and then reached down under the seat in front of her for her briefcase. She was pulling out some work to do when the stewardess stopped by her seat. "Ms. Weston?" she said.

Kate looked up. "Yes?"

"This is for you," the stewardess said, handing her a small gift-wrapped package and a card. "A friend of yours asked that we give it to you once we left Los Angeles."

Kate opened the box. It was a gold fountain pen. A real gold fountain pen. And there, on the side, in discreet script, blending into the engraved pattern on the pen, she saw the initials, KGW. She hefted the pen in her hand—never having held such an exquisite writing instrument in all her life—and opened the card.

Dear Kate,
        Please accept this as a small expression of my thanks.
        You've been a wonderful influence on us all—
        and you've been a wonderful friend to me.
                    I'll miss you.
                                        Love,
                                        Lydia

THREE

Chemistry

— 27 —

Instead of arriving at Kennedy airport at midnight, Kate's plane landed near six o'clock the following morning. There had been the little matter of New York being socked-in with a major storm, the little matter of lightning streaking everywhere in the sky as they circled and circled, waiting for clearance to land, the little matter of the passengers pretending they weren't scared as the plane bucked and heaved and shook in the winds and then, finally, there was the little matter of having to fly to Newburgh before they ran out of fuel.

"This is what the Avianca flight should have done," the man sitting next to Kate remarked. "If they had they wouldn't have crashed and all those people wouldn't have died."

"Oh," Kate said, smiling politely, thinking, *Oh, God, please, I do not want to die yet,* and very discreetly, as the plane shuddered and heaved in the winds, she wrote a will on the legal pad in her lap.

My books and papers to Mark Fiducia. My typewriter also. Letters too. (Don't be too shocked by some of what you find. I couldn't tell you about *everything*.) Also, I'd like you to have my desk and chair. And the bookcase with the glass doors—the ones that have those glass dust cover things that pull out and then down over the shelf.

The pearls Grandmother Weston gave me should go to Sherry Berman Meyer. (Berman, it's the only thing of mine I ever remember you liking. So please, keep them and know how much I love you.)

To my assistant, Sarah Steadwell, $10,000 from my estate—on her promise she'll give book publishing one more year. (If she won't, give it to her anyway—who can blame her for wanting out!)

At this point she was stuck. What to leave Harris? Hmmm. Finally,

I leave my IRA fund to Harris so that he will take that fishing trip to Scotland he always dreamed about.

There, that was good. He'd love that.

Also, Harris, please, take the beautiful bracelets and necklace you gave me and give them to your daughter on her eighteenth birthday. (But for heaven's sake, don't tell her they used to belong to me! Just tell her they've been "in the family.")

Okay, now, what about everybody else?

Dad, Matt, Sissy, there's nothing special that I could leave you— except, perhaps, the knowledge that I love you. Mom's jewelry will go to you guys—Sissy, Matt—right? Anyway, it should. And I would also like you two to take that footlocker of mine that's up in the attic. It is full of children's books—but for collectors, not kids! There's a first edition of *The Wizard of Oz* and a signed first edition of *The Cat in the Hat* in there that you should especially keep an eye on. The books are all sealed in plastic and my recommendation is they not be opened until one of you or your children is ready to become a collector, or all of you agree to sell them.

The remainder of my money—my B, F & C life insurance policy, my travel insurance from AmEx and my savings—I leave to my stepmother, Kimberly Sorrel Weston, for having been so wonderful to me when she married my father. Kimberly, you've spent your life doing for others; I think it's time you had money of your own to spend as you wish.

There. Kate read this over, satisfied, and then she had a rather startling thought. She considered it for another moment and then smiled, knowing that this person had never been left anything by anybody. So she added:

And my Empire sofa is to go to Lydia Southland.

*

She dragged into Harris's apartment at 7:45 A.M. dog tired. He had already left for LaGuardia to catch the shuttle to Washington.

Dear Kate,
    Welcome home. Wish I could have seen you this morning— how I've missed you! You've been away FOREVER! I love you. And I love you. And I love you!

I'll call you later.
H

She longed to crawl into the big bed and go to sleep, but knew she would be better off if she simply pushed on through the day. So she stripped off her clothes, did ten minutes on the NordicTrack machine in the bedroom, showered, washed her hair, and got dressed in a cheery spring suit. Stuffing her purse and excess work stuff from her suitcase into a big canvas bag, she slung that over one shoulder and hefted her briefcase in her hand and set out on the fourteen blocks down Central Park West to work.

One of the benefits of Bennett, Fitzallen & Coe being owned by Heartland Communications America was that the Japanese partner owned a significant number of "trophy properties" in New York, one of which was the Anderson Building at Central Park West and Sixtieth Street. It was into this building B, F & C had been moved three years ago and it was here now that they enjoyed views unbeaten in all of book publishing from some twenty-four floors above Central Park.

It was too cold for the spring suit Kate had chosen to wear. In fact, she realized, she should have worn an overcoat. It was freezing out.

No doubt about it, she thought as she walked faster, *New York mornings are not like mornings in Southern California.* It was not warm, it was not sunshiny, and people were not pleasant. Of course there were many parts of Los Angeles in which one would be terrified to walk. But then, this part of New York, Central Park West, was one of the most exclusive residential areas in Manhattan. If people weren't pleasant here, where on earth would they be?

And it seemed to Kate there was more than Central Park West's share of ugly people out this morning. One such person Kate saw on the corner of Seventy-second Street, outside the Dakota, giving her little son a smack on the side of the head because he asked why couldn't they walk a different way to school. Kate saw another on Seventy-first, telling a doorman to go to hell, he'd park where he damn well felt like it, who the hell did the doorman think he was? She saw another on Seventieth, pushing his way past people on the sidewalk, muttering about assholes, so goddamn slow, why the fuck didn't they get out of his way? And then on the corner of Sixty-seventh Street, there was a charming soul bundled up in several layers of clothing, screaming at passerbys that Jesus Christ was going to kill them.

Kate saw a young boy, perhaps eight, standing off to the side, watch the screaming woman with anxiety. Kate bent close to the boy and whispered, "Don't worry, you know Jesus Christ can only love—he could never hurt anyone."

The boy looked at Kate, shifting his little knapsack on his shoulder. "But I'm Jewish," he said. "She said he's going to kill all the Jews."

Kate smiled. "But Jesus Christ was Jewish—did you know that?"

The boy's eyes got wide. "He was?"

"Uh-huh," Kate said, nodding. "And he would never hurt his brothers and sisters, never. So don't listen to her. She's very ill and doesn't know what she's saying."

The boy turned to look at the woman again.

"Jesus Christ is going to get you, filthy whore!" she was screaming at a woman passerby, following her with a pointed finger.

The boy turned back to Kate. "She's sick," he said, as if to make absolutely sure of this fact.

"Yes," Kate said, nodding.

"Then why doesn't someone take her to the doctor?" the boy asked.

"Oh," Kate said, sighing, feeling oddly close to tears for some reason. Straightening up, she patted the boy on the shoulder. "I don't know."

"Maybe Jesus Christ could take her to the doctor," the boy suggested.

Kate dashed up the stairs of the Anderson Building, went in through the revolving door and was waved through by security. ("Hi, Miss Weston, how was California? You look tan." "Great thanks, but it's nice to be back," she said, walking on to the elevators. "Aren't you a little cold, though? In those California clothes?" "I'm a warm-blooded Easterner," she laughed, getting onto the elevator.)

"Kate, hi," the art director said to her. "How was California?"

"Great," she said, nestling into the back, people flooding in behind her. The doors closed.

The art director leaned close and whispered. "Lydia Southland's finishing the book, is that true?"

"I think so," Kate whispered back.

Almost every head in the elevator turned to look at her.

Kate smiled, focusing on the man in front of her. "Would you buy Lydia Southland's autobiography?"

"For my wife, I would," he said. "I don't usually read that kind of book myself."

Kate nodded. She looked at the woman to her left. "Would you?"

"I'd read it," she said. "I don't know if I'd buy it—not in hardback. In paperback I would though."

"And you?" Kate said to the man standing on the other side of the art director.

"I'm afraid I don't know who Lydia Southland is," the man said.

" 'Cassandra's World,' " someone in the front of the elevator said.

The elevator stopped at the twenty-first floor.

"Oh," the man said. He leaned forward to see past the art director to Kate. "Is she the blonde?"

"Yes," Kate said.

"I think my kids watch that show," he said.

"Great," Kate said, smiling. She turned to the art director, lowering her voice. "I brought some pictures back. I thought we could maybe design a jazzy sales brochure for the reps."

"Great," he said, "I'd love to see them." He got out on twenty-three.

Kate got out on twenty-four. "Good luck with the book," the woman who would not buy it in hardcover said. "I'll look for it."

"Let us know if she comes in!" called a man as the doors closed.

"Well, look who's here!" the receptionist, Emma Lou, said. "How was California? Are you going to be on the show?"

Kate laughed. "It was great, Emma Lou, but no, I'm not going on the show."

"We missed you," Emma Lou said. "Mr. Mark would get so lonely he'd come out here and sit with me."

"And eat candy, no doubt," Kate said.

"Do you want some?" Emma Lou said, picking up the candy dish in front of her and offering it to her.

"Not quite this early, but thank you," Kate said, backing her way down the hall. "I'll stop by later and get all the gossip."

Kate made her way down the hall toward her office. She popped her head into Mr. Rushman's office—he was on the phone, so she waved and indicated she'd stop in later; she popped her head into Rebecca's office—she wasn't in yet; she popped her head into the associate publisher's office, Dick Skolchak—he wasn't in yet; she popped her head into the managing editor's office, Eugene Doherty—he was on the phone so she just waved; and then, while she was coming down the hall, leaping into the hallway, wearing sunglasses, was Mark.

"Hey, baby," he said, flinging his arms out to the sides, "it's like, Kate Weston—famous Hollywood type, here to take a meeting!"

"Hey baby," she said, giving him a kiss on the cheek and pushing her briefcase into his stomach for him to take it.

"Geez, what's in here?" Mark said, weighing the briefcase in his hand, following her into her office.

"Oh, what's this?" she said, seeing carnations on her desk. On closer inspection she found they were not terribly fresh looking.

"They're from Adesca," Mark said, throwing himself down in a chair.

"Adesca?" Kate said. For the second time that morning Kate felt close to crying. Adesca was the lady who cleaned the offices at night; she barely spoke English. Since Kate worked late almost every night, she saw Adesca almost every night. Adesca didn't understand half of what Kate said to her, but they chatted a lot nonetheless.

("So are things going okay with your children?" Kate would say.

"Yes"—smiles—"maybe warmer tomorrow."

"Your son—what is his name?"

"Ah!" Eyes shining in delight. "My son. Engineer—is goot job."

"That's so wonderful, Adesca," Kate would say.

"Yes, goot—goot boy. My son.")

"I'm afraid I didn't even get you a bagel," Mark said, taking off the sunglasses.

"What kind of Italian are you, anyway?" Kate said, thumping down her canvas bag on the floor and pulling out her chair.

"I'll buy you an Italian lunch," he offered.

"Can't," Kate said, sitting down and then holding up her calendar to read, "Lunch with Mr. Rushman and agent Sasha Freed."

"Oh, yeah, she's mad at us," Mark said. "Somebody told Rushman she liked you."

"What did we do this time?" she asked him, eyes scanning the call sheets Sarah had left on her desk.

"I think Dick canceled some author of hers," Mark said.

"You can't cancel an author," Kate said, looking up. "That would be murder."

"Well, you never know around here," Mark said, shrugging. "Hey, listen, what about an Italian drink after work?"

"Done," Kate said, opening her mail folder.

"Hi, Kate—welcome home," Sylvie Botnik called on her way down the hall. Sylvie was an editor specializing in lifestyle and etiquette books. She was a great fan of Kate's and kept threatening to send her out on tour instead of her authors.

"Kate's back?" another voice said. (Kate and Mark looked at each other. Ugh. It was Tad Haskins, a tacky sort of an editor with a tacky sort of a list, suffering from a disease more commonly known as Chronic Boardinghouse Reach.) "Kate, I have a proposal I need you to read," he said, poking his head in her office. "Can you read it tonight?"

"Good morning, Tad," Kate said to him.

He blinked. "Can you?" he said.

Kate smiled. "Yes, Tad, I can."

"Thanks," Tad said, disappearing. In a moment, they could hear him calling down the hall, "Rebecca! Rebecca! I need to talk to you!"

Kate and Mark looked at each other again and started to laugh.

"Kate, hi!" Sarah said, rushing in. She and Kate exchanged a brief hug. "I wanted to get in before you, but the subway—"

"Oh, Sarah, don't worry about it, it's only—" Kate looked at her watch. "Oh, great," she said, "according to my watch it's five minutes to six." She looked at Sarah. "So you're very early, my friend. Hey, listen, you guys, I brought you some presents," she said, reaching down into her canvas bag and extracting two packages. "Sarah, this is for you, and Mark, this is for you."

They opened them. Sarah got some silver earrings and a baseball hat that said CASSANDRA'S WORLD on it, and Mark got a framed picture of Lydia Southland in a bathing suit, with the inscription:

> *Dearest Mark,*
> *Thanks for the great weekend.*
> *Love, Lydia*

"I don't believe this," Mark said.

Kate smiled. "She said you may use it as a reference."

He stood up. "This goes up in my office right now." He started for the door, stopped, turned around. "Maybe I should accidentally send it to Carla with the last of her things?"

Kate smiled, shaking her head. "Use it for better things to come." She winked.

"Ah, yes," he said, "good choice of words."

"Oh, Mark," Kate said, reaching into her bag again, "give this to Dale, will you? It's just a little something I got for him."

"Yeah, sure," Mark said, taking the package from her.

"Oh, Kate, thank you," Sarah said, bending to kiss Kate on the cheek as she took one of her earrings off. "I'm going to go try these on now, okay?"

"If you don't like them—"

"But I do!" Sarah said, skipping out.

The phone rang and Kate picked it up. "Kate Weston," she said.

"Why don't you come down and discuss this Seth Roberts novel you're so keen about," Mr. Rushman said.

"I'll be down in two seconds," she said, reaching into her bag again. She had brought Mr. Rushman a present from California, too—a G-string from the Mata Hari episode of "Cassandra's World." (It was not the one Lydia had actually worn. It was one of five hundred copies that had been made up by an ingenious publicist. "They always work," Lydia had assured Kate. "Give this to him and the man is ours.")

Kate went in to see Mr. Rushman and gave him his present. He roared. And he blushed. And he loved it.

It was not a particularly bad day at the office, yet Kate couldn't pretend she felt very happy about being back. Her three-and-a-half-week absence had put her office under siege, with authors and agents and in-house people all demanding to talk to or see her *now!* In the meantime, she was desperately trying to make an offer on the Roberts novel after B, F & C (read Rebecca) had been screwing around with it in her absence.

"Start with this offer and see their reaction," Mr. Rushman had said to Kate.

"Their reaction will be to tell us to go fly a kite while they go to auction," Kate had replied.

"If they wanted you as the editor enough to submit it on exclusive," Rebecca had said, "then surely, Kate, you can use this offer as a starting point for discussion."

Kate had looked at Rebecca. "This offer is not only late, it's insulting."

"The offer is reasonable," Rebecca said.

"The offer I want to make is based on what we will make on the book," Kate said.

"Says you," Rebecca said.

"Says the people who are supposed to know," Kate said. "Sales and sub rights—and I have that memo from Kip about the chains' commitment to Seth Roberts."

"Ladies," Mr. Rushman said, holding up one hand. He looked at Kate. "Start with this offer, Kate."

"I don't want to lose the project, Mr. Rushman," she said. "You're telling me to lose the project. He's a very important author. He'd be a wonderful addition to the list."

Rushman looked to Rebecca.

"If they think you're so special, Kate, they'll negotiate with you," Rebecca said. "Use the offer to open negotiations."

Kate was about to scream, "Oh, fuck you, you stupid conniving bitch! First you stall the offer and now you're killing it!" but she didn't. Instead she sighed and looked to Mr. Rushman. "I'm sorry you won't support me in this. God knows, we need this book."

Rebecca looked to Mr. Rushman. "See? *This* is what I have to deal with—this attitude of hers."

Mr. Rushman turned back to Kate. "You have your instructions. I expect you to carry them out. Tell Dick to come in on your way out."

She was dismissed.

"Thank you," Kate said, wishing she had handled this meeting better. It wasn't wise to cross swords openly with Rebecca—and lose. Mr. Rushman paid more attention to things like that than he did about whatever was being discussed. Of course, Mr. Rushman, to a large extent, was still rather ignorant of how book publishing worked—and of how to get people in book publishing to want to work with Bennett, Fitzallen & Coe while he was running it.

The industry was still buzzing over his appearance last year at the American Booksellers' Association convention. There had been a special breakfast organized to introduce him to booksellers and to let him wow them with his revolutionary new discount distribution plan. What Mr. Rushman had done for Klicky Kart™ Toys he evidently wished to do for the books of Bennett, Fitzallen & Coe. Unfortunately, when the plan was presented a near riot broke out, with booksellers jumping to their feet in disbelief at the concept that if they returned books to B, F & C, they would henceforth have to buy B, F & C books from wholesalers because their account with the publisher would thereby be closed.

What kind of tactics were these? booksellers cried, and in no time there were flyers circulating the convention floor with cartoon characters clad in World War II uniforms, evidently depicting the Italian, Japanese, and German partners of Heartland Communications America running a publishing house called Bennitzio, FitzTojo & Kraut.

"Harris is holding on two from Washington," Sarah said when Kate returned to her office.

Kate frowned, wondering what was up. She had already talked to him once today. She went into her office and picked up. Harris had to stay for a State Department dinner, late, so he thought he better stay over. "I'm sorry," he said, "I didn't know I would be invited—and it's important, Kate."

"Of course it is," Kate said, surprised at the relief she felt. She assured him she understood, said she needed a good night's sleep anyway, promised they would have a fun time tomorrow night—

"Kate," Sarah whispered from the doorway. "Sorry to interrupt, but Lydia Southland's holding on the other line."

"I'll take it," Kate said to Sarah. Back into the phone, "Harris, I have to run—"

"Love you," he said.

"Love you," Kate said, pushing the button to switch lines. "Lydia, hi! I love my pen! I've never seen such a gorgeous thing in all my life!"

With that funny faraway sound that speaker phones tended to have, Kate could hear Noél say, "What pen is this?"

"Sounds like a present," Gary said.

"You never gave me a pen," Noél said.

"Well, Kate," Lydia said, "nothing like talking to you to create a little discord in the ranks."

Kate laughed.

"Hello, Señorita Weston! We miss you!" Gracia called.

Kate heard Cookie and Cupcake barking in the background.

"Okay, now that you've said hi, everybody," Lydia said, "let me talk to Kate alone for a few minutes."

The speaker phone switched to the regular phone and after some noises and a chorus of good-byes, Lydia said, "Okay, here I am."

"What's up?"

"I'm thinking maybe I want to rewrite the section about my childhood," Lydia said.

It would be nice if we had your date of birth while you're at it, Kate thought. "What did you have in mind?"

"Talk a little about my father's drinking."

"It would help other people, Lydia," Kate said. "And it would also make a lot more sense about what happened to your father's career."

"But I don't want to talk about other stuff," Lydia said.

What other stuff? Kate wondered.

"My mother's dead and everything," Lydia said, "but I don't see any point in bringing up my father's womanizing. And I don't think it really affected me one way or the other."

Oh. "I don't see any reason to talk about that," Kate said gently, "but Lydia, I don't think it's wise to pretend to yourself that it didn't affect you."

"Kate!" Sarah whispered from the door. "Jeff from CAI's on the phone and he's got to talk to you—*now!*"

Kate hesitated. Decision time.

She covered the phone and said, "Tell him I'll call back, Sarah—this is important."

— 28 —

It didn't take much for Kate to get a little high. Two vodka tonics on an empty stomach, to be exact.

"Why are we playing pinball?" Kate thought to ask about eight forty-five, as Mark helped her jiggle the machine so the ball would go where she wanted, into a lit bonus hole to score ten thousand points and a free game.

"Because it's good for your soul," he explained.

Indeed. He was probably right. A little change was always good for the soul and Lonely Mama's was certainly a change.

Lonely Mama's was an old New York hangout where mostly off-duty policemen, firemen, construction workers, and civil servants came to drink, watch TV, shoot pool, and play pinball and American shuffleboard. (No electronic game would *ever* cross the threshold of Lonely Mama's). Kate was the only woman in the place tonight besides Lonely Mama herself, a large woman of fifty-six with a chest beyond belief, who was always behind the bar, good-naturedly gossiping and guffawing with "the boys." Her real name was Elena Maria Bolenetti but everyone called her Mama. Mama had opened the bar some twenty years before, using as the down payment the death benefit she had received as the widow of a slain policeman.

Mama was an adept businesswoman. Fifteen years ago, before the neighborhood had fallen (or risen, depending on who was speaking) to a wealthier New York nouveau elite, Mama bought the building the bar was in, not only protecting her primary place of business but also expanding her career as a landlady to—as she called them—"the Swishy." On one side of the bar was one of the most expensive boutiques on the Upper West Side, which came not to mind the proximity of the bar since twice already off-duty cops had stopped robberies in progress. On the other side was a unisex hair salon; beyond that a gourmet delicatessen where a ham sandwich cost $8.50; and, on the end, there was a video rental store that specialized in classic movies. Upstairs there were six apartments renting for prices Kate couldn't believe anyone would pay to live over a bar on Columbus Avenue.

But they did.

Mama knew more about what went on in the city than anyone, the mayor included. Mama knew what the new territory divisions were between the various branches of Italian, Irish, Jewish, and Hispanic organized crime organizations; she knew what buildings had paid to skip inspections and would soon be falling apart (she also knew which developers were most likely to skip town—if they hadn't already); and she certainly tended to know the most interesting things about the private lives of city officials, as told to her firsthand by the policemen who were assigned to protect them: who was into drugs, who was a closet gay, who was playing around, and who was just asking for trouble.

Mama, as a matter of fact, was rumored to have tipped reporters off about the story potential of the Bess Mess.

Mark had been encouraging Mama to commit her story to paper for years. "No, no Marco, no," Mama would say, wiping the bar with a damp cloth, sighing a sigh that would make her chest heave in the low-cut white blouse she always wore, "the secrets I know I will take to the grave. The fellas here trust me." Then she would smile at Mark and lean over the bar to touch the softness of his beard, gold hoop earrings swinging forward from under her hair, her chest more exposed than ever. "I want you to bring your friends here, Marco. I want more nice customers like you—publishing big shots, a new clientele."

At first meeting, however, Mama had looked as though she were more apt to break a bottle over Kate's head than to shake her hand, but after Kate talked to her for a while and Mama found out that Kate knew Dennis Smith, *the* firefighter/writer of the century, and after Kate played pinball with Mark—making a point to show how she could manhandle the machine and not tilt it—Mama had been won over. Kate had been here maybe six times since then, always bringing, with Mark, others from the office to play pinball. Tonight, when they had walked in, Mama said loudly from behind the bar, "Who says we're not a class establishment? Look here, gentlemen, and behold

American royalty. She has a whole town named after her in Connecticut."

"What time do you have to be home?" Mark said, taking his turn at the machine, yanking the plunger back and releasing it.

Kate shrugged. "Harris had to stay over in Washington, so it doesn't really matter. I'm tired, though—and hungry."

"Then let's have dinner," Mark said. He turned to the guy in the red flannel shirt who was watching him play and said, "Take our games, okay?" and stepped back.

"Thanks," the guy said, putting his icy beer mug down on the glass and just making it behind the machine in time to save the ball with a flipper.

"Dinner," Mark said, holding out his arm for Kate to take.

Off they went, leaving a generous tip on the bar on the way.

The air was nice outside (Lonely Mama's tended to be a bit smoky), but within a block Kate started to shiver.

"Cab?" Mark said.

"No, walk faster—it'll wake me up," Kate said. And so they did, up Columbus Avenue nine blocks to eat in a nice, quiet, dark Italian restaurant where they had eaten before.

The food was delicious. They shared a bottle of wine. Kate was exhausted but pleasantly so, laughing and more than a little giddy with so little sleep.

"California was good for you," Mark said after they finished eating, looking at her over the candle. "I've never seen you so happy as out there—or here, tonight."

"It was good for me," Kate agreed. She yawned, happy, comfortable, settling back in her chair. "And this, us, here—this feels like California too." She smiled. "Different, special, relaxed."

He smiled too. "I'm glad."

They looked at each other for a moment longer and then Mark's smile faded and he looked down at the table. "Carla and I nearly moved to Los Angeles once," he said.

The waiter came with the check.

"We'll split it," Kate said, reaching down to the floor for her bag.

"We were going to do it to get a new start," Mark continued. He took Kate's credit card from her, placed it on the back of the check with his own, and handed it to the waiter. He looked at Kate. "I had an offer in the story department at Metropolis Pictures. But she wouldn't go in the end—and you know why?"

Kate shook her head.

"Because I wouldn't make enough money. Out there, she said, it wasn't like New York. Out there it mattered how much money you had and we'd be nobodies."

Kate sighed, shaking her head. "It's so strange . . ." Her voice trailed off and then she looked at Mark. "Sometimes I have to wonder how on earth you ever married her. She's so unlike you."

"And so unlike you," Mark said.

"Thank you," Kate said. "And you know, Mark, don't you, that no matter how much money Carla has, that she'll always be a nobody? You know that, right? And that you'll always be somebody by virtue of exactly who and what you are?"

"I knew there was a reason why I love you so much," he said.

She smiled and looked around for the waiter. She was tired.

"Why are you with Harris?" Mark suddenly said.

Kate looked at him. "Because I love him."

"But don't you love other people too?" he said. "I mean, why Harris?"

Kate sat forward, resting her arms on the table. "What's wrong, Mark? What's going on?"

He dropped his head, sighing. "Oh, I don't know. I guess it's having to pack the rest of Carla's stuff."

"You still haven't done it?" she said. "I thought you did that last year!"

He shook his head. "Just haven't been able to do it." Pause. "But I've got to. Her lawyer's screaming."

"You're not kidding you've got to," Kate said. She shook her head. "No wonder you've been so slow to start dating—you're still haunted over there."

The waiter came back and they both signed a charge slip for half the dinner.

"I'm giving her the silver," Mark said, handing the check and receipts back to the waiter.

"No Mark, you give her half the silver," Kate said.

"What am I going to do with half the silver?"

"Eat with it," Kate suggested. "Or give it away—I don't care, just don't give it to her. It was given to you too." When he didn't say anything, but only stared down at the table, Kate said, "Mark, you've *got* to move on."

He raised his eyes. "I went out on a date while you were away."

"You did?" she said, eyebrows rising.

"Yeah," he said. Pause. "I almost slept with her."

"Almost," Kate repeated, eyebrows slowly coming back down.

"But I didn't," Mark said, eyes falling to the table again.

"Well, you shouldn't sleep with anyone on a first date anyway," Kate said.

He looked at her.

"Except maybe if she comes with my recommendation and a clean bill of health like Miss Loola did," she added, winking. "So, are you going to see her again?"

He shook his head. "I don't think so. I talked about Carla the whole night." Pause. "And so she told me when I was ready, I should call her again." Pause. "But not until then."

"She sounds nice," Kate said.

"She is," he said, raising his eyes. "And very pretty—so what's the matter with me?"

"Not a thing," Kate said, reaching across the table to take his hand, "not a thing. You just need a little more time." She let go of his hand and stood up. "Come on—let's go clear Carla out of your life once and for all," she said, looking at her watch.

They got a cab and shot across Central Park on Eighty-sixth Street to the East Side. Mark's apartment was on Eighty-fourth Street between First Avenue and York. Kate had never liked it. It had low ceilings and no character, which was, she thought, an awful lot like the person who had picked it out—namely Carla, she who refused to live anywhere but on the Upper East Side. (*Oh pardon me*, Kate used to think, listening to Carla go on and on about it, as if the former Miss Carla Palermo of Bayonne, New Jersey, would be banished from the Social Register or something. Honestly.)

When Mark opened the door to the apartment, Kate shuddered a little, realizing at once that he probably had not used the living room since Carla left. With the exception of some folded boxes and a roll of duct tape sitting in the middle of the floor, the room was in perfect order. There wasn't a magazine out, or a coaster—not even an indentation in the sofa cushions.

"Oh, Mark," Kate sighed, putting a hand on his shoulder. "Oh, Markie-Mark-Marco," she whispered, "we have to get you out of here."

He didn't say anything. He just dropped his briefcase on the floor, tossed his keys on the table, and walked into the kitchen. "I've got some wine in here, I think."

"No more for me, thanks," Kate said, putting her bags down and heading down the hall to the bedroom, "but I'll take some ice water." She pushed open the bedroom door and flicked on the light—and breathed a sigh of relief. It was the kind of mess editors tended to have where they lived—books, magazines, manuscripts, bound galleys, records, tapes, legal pads, and videos, all precariously balanced here and there and everywhere with some sort of method to the madness. (Kate kept an antique toy chest in Harris's bedroom in which she housed her current "interests." Disarray made Harris nervous.)

Mark's bed was made—good sign; a few shirts were thrown over the back of the chair; there weren't any plates or food in the room. Good, good, good. Kate went into the bathroom and opened the medicine cabinet.

A box of condoms.

Good.

But prescriptions were what she was looking for, Valium specifically, or anything in the Valium family—Librium, Ativan, Xanax—because they were the good suicide drugs to take with alcohol. She knew this because of her mother, and so whenever Kate was worried about anyone being depressed, she immediately and shamelessly checked out their medicine cabinets to see what was what.

Okay. No Valium. No tranquilizers. No sleeping pills. Just some aspirin.

Good. Good.

"What are you doing?" Mark said from the bedroom.

"Checking your medicine cabinet for suicide drugs," she said, coming out.

He laughed. Little did he know.

"I take it all of Carla's things are out of here," Kate said, walking over to him and taking the glass of water from him. "Thanks." She sipped.

"Yeah," he said, sipping from the wineglass in his hand.

"Smart," Kate said, walking past him to the hall. "Okay, so where is it?"

"Under the sofa, front hall closet, in the cabinets, and on the shelves in the living room," he said, following her. "And the buffet in the dining room—there's junk in there too."

Kate started assembling boxes and packing them, ordering Mark around as she did so—get this, get that, does that go? Then bring it here. What else? Get it, let's move it. Okay, what else?—and when they ran out of boxes, she instructed him to get out the sheets she knew he couldn't bear to have on the bed. (She knew this because the day Carla left him was the day Kate had gone over to Macy's and bought him new sheets and a comforter and had gone home with him to change this aspect of his bedroom so he could at least sleep in there.) And so they tied up the rest of Carla's belongings in linen bundles—photo albums, records, books, miscellaneous silver and pewter stuff—and, in four trips, took everything down to the basement where they piled it neatly by the laundry room.

"Now you call her," Kate said, picking up the phone and handing it to him. "And you tell her that her stuff is packed and ready to go and that the doorman will show her where."

Mark looked at Kate for a long moment. And then he swallowed, nodded, took the phone from her, and did exactly as she instructed. And then, after hanging up the phone—it was the Wall Street Whiz Kid he had talked to—Mark sat down on the couch and cried. He took off his glasses and buried his face in his hands and wept openly. Kate sat down next to him, arm around his shoulders, and she cried, too. "Oh, Mark, darling Mark," she whispered, rocking him slightly when he did not stop, "I promise you, you will get through this—and you will have a happier life, happier than it's ever been. This is all happening for a reason. It's pushing you in the direction you should be going."

"But why does it still hurt?" he said. "I should hate her."

"It hurts because you're trying to hate her," Kate said gently, rubbing his back. "You can't just close your heart to someone you love. But that's what we try to do—and that's why it hurts. It's not in your nature to hate anyone, Mark. So don't try."

He was groping around in his back pocket; found it, a handkerchief. He wiped his eyes and blew his nose. He cleared his throat, took a breath, and then put his glasses back on. He stuffed his handkerchief back in his pocket, turning to Kate. "I won't forget how you helped me tonight."

She smiled, giving his hand a squeeze.

"Tomorrow," he said, "this apartment will be different for me—it'll be mine."

"Tomorrow," Kate said, "we call a real estate agent friend of mine and start looking for a new place. This apartment's no more for you than the man on the moon."

"Think so?" he said.

She nodded. "Know so. You should live somewhere that's—well, like the Upper West Side. Hey," she said, sitting up straight, "maybe you should take over my apartment." And then she frowned, shook her head, and fell back against the couch. "Well, maybe not quite yet."

"Kate," Mark said.

She looked up and it was an instant before she realized that he was kissing her. And once she realized that, she didn't know what to do.

She gently pushed him back. "Mark, this isn't what you really want. You're tired. We're both tired."

He was kissing her again and this time her mind was registering mild panic because she was responding. Because she liked how it felt to have Mark kissing her. And it shocked her. For some reason she had never thought of him as kissable. He was too—short? Too nice? Too vulnerable? And yet, here he was kissing her and here she was responding, somewhat marveling, in fact, at this mouth that was pressing against hers.

She pushed him back slightly and tried again. "This isn't a wise thing to do, Mark."

He took off his glasses, twisted to put them on the coffee table, turned back around, took her chin in his hand, and kissed her again. But for real.

And she was lost. She knew it. Whatever sense of morality and ethics she had, it was no longer there because all she could feel was the thudding excitement in her chest that she was going to make love with Mark, the very worst thing she had ever done in her life. Her friend. Her best friend. Her colleague. Her pal Mark whose wife had dumped him. While Harris planned on her marrying him, while Harris was in Washington missing her, Kate was being sexually aroused in a way she hadn't been in years.

She'd had no idea. None. It had not hit her like this before, not after all the hours and hours they spent together.

But maybe that was part of it. Having worked together for so long, having played together so long, and then suddenly, as if it were some new invention, Mark was suddenly a sexual creature and she was insatiably curious about him. She didn't care. She just didn't care about anything except feeling what she was feeling right now.

Mark was all over her now, sensing, she knew, that he would have to keep her from talking if he were to keep her there. And so he did a good job. He kept his mouth glued to hers, and when he tried to move his lips down onto her neck, she started to say something and he came right back up to her mouth and stayed there, letting his hands roam instead. Through her hair. Down her neck. Over her breasts, her stomach, her thighs. Then he had her blouse open. He had her bra undone. He had his hand first on one breast and then the other, and she became aware of just how hard his hips were pressing into her side and it seemed as though a thousand editorial meetings floated past her eyes, egging her on: Mark, this is Mark, you're having sex with *Mark*.

Mark? This was Mark? Hiking her skirt up, pressing rhythmically against her, pulling her panty hose down so that he could touch her? He groaned with her, when she felt his hand on her, and it seemed so unreal, so unbelievably thrilling and unreal that she was actually reaching for his belt, fumbling to undo it, dying to get inside, feeling him starting to tremble. She got the belt undone—his mouth was back on hers—and she undid the clasp on his pants, and she undid the zipper, and eased her hand down past the elastic of his shorts, sliding down in the heat to find—

Him.

God, this was Mark?

How could he be so much bigger than Harris? Could this be? Yes, yes, it could and it was and she could feel Mark smiling in his kiss. He knew, he knew, he knew she was taken back by what she had found—

"Don't give me time to think," she said, breaking off their kiss, "please don't let me think." And he was up on his knees in a second, pulling off her panty hose and tugging her panties off and then, still kneeling, Mark pulled his pants down to his knees.

She couldn't take her eyes off him.

But then she did. And looked up. And saw him smiling. And she thought her lower body would die.

He crawled up on her and she started to reach down to guide him, but he whispered, "Don't worry, he knows exactly where he wants to go," and he was right, that part of him did know, because Kate felt it nudging at her gently, and then pushing slightly, and pushing a little more, starting to spread her—"Okay?" Mark whispered, "are you okay?" and she said, "Oh, God, yes"—and in one gliding motion, he pushed himself all the way in, spreading her in the most marvelous way, making her feel as though this were it, heaven, surely, surely, this was heaven, God how it felt—and in a moment they were both moving, hard, after it, and Kate groaned and didn't care because this was not polite, this was not political, this was not social, she thought, grinding herself into Mark, this was serious. This was it, this was what it was all about, this incredible feeling from head to toe, this not caring about anything but only letting go, feeling the release, to let him go all the way inside of her and fill the ache and make her—

And make her—

Come.

Yes. She arched, helpless, feeling it come, in waves, over her, through her, totally, wholly, and done.

"Mark," she said, letting her body fall, gasping for breath, and Mark twisted and thrust harder and then stiffened, immobilized—and then he jerked back and pushed back up inside her again, straining, and Kate felt a new warmth spreading through her. "Oh, God, Kate," Mark gasped, collapsing on her and then clutching her, squeezing her hard in his arms. "Oh, God, Kate," he said.

— *29* —

"No, it's not much," Lydia said, pointing with her pencil. "Just this part—take this part out."

"Okay," Gary said. They were sitting at the big table in the office and Lydia was pointing to the paragraphs that said how happy her childhood had been.

"And put this in," she said, handing him a yellow legal pad. "Kate and I've been working on it over the phone and I think I've finally got it right."

On the top page, in Lydia's dynamic, graceful script, he read:

Imagine the confusion if a play had a second director that was invisible to all, but which had the power to change the script, torture the players, and blow up the stage at will. That is what alcoholism is like in many families, unrecognized, denied, the invisible force tearing apart what to the naked eye appears to be a normal situation. Until I came to understand the nature of my father's illness, the plot of my life was periodically insane, but once I was taught how to recognize the invisible director at work, everything came to make perfect sense: my father's personality changes, my mother's personality changes, the financial ups and downs, the fights, the tears, our insecurities in relationships with others, and—the toughest one—my own sense of self-worth, which is to say almost none for years and years.

"Lyddie, this is beautiful," Gary murmured, looking up.
"Noël will type it up—my handwriting's not the greatest," she said matter-of-factly, standing up.
"Wait," he said, catching her arm. "Come, sit a second, tell me what this is all about."
She sighed and dropped down in the chair. "What's what about?"
He met her eyes. "This is very courageous of you."
She shrugged, looking down. "I don't think I'd better think about it much or I'll change my mind." She looked up, and smiled. "I don't know, it's what Kate kept saying about leaving a written record behind, explaining how I got to where I am today."
"I love you," Gary said.
"And you know how much I love you," she said, leaning forward to kiss him on the cheek. Then, abruptly, she got up and walked toward the door. She stopped and turned around. "Gary?"
"Yes?"
"Should I be scared?"
He turned around slowly. "Of what?"
"Of what we're doing?" she said.
He didn't know what she meant. Rather, he knew she could mean any number of things: writing the book, spending so much time together, thinking about the past . . .
He swallowed. "No," he said firmly.
She looked at him a moment longer. "Okay," she said. And she left the room.

— 30 —

"Would you please go get a Xerox machine?" Lydia said.
"Okay," Noël said, as if she could just dash out to the backyard and pick one from a tree. "What kind do you want?"
"One that works," Lydia said, hitting the machine that was presently in their office with the palm of her hand.

Yes, well, some days working on the book went better than others. This morning, perhaps, Noël shouldn't have asked Lydia if she was going to discuss plastic surgery in the book. (It *was* one of the most frequent subjects her female fans wrote to ask about.)

"I think you better rent such a machine first," Gracia later advised Noël in the kitchen. "You know how the señora can be."

"Tell me about it," Noël said, slinging her purse strap over her shoulder.

"That was so very awful," Gracia said, "the time the señora left us with that man and all those tennis cannons to test."

"Don't worry," Noël said, "I've got it all worked out—Bestar's going to loan us one."

"Loan us one?" Gracia said, one eyebrow rising.

"As long as she works there, we get to Xerox here," Noël explained. "Then when she leaves the show . . ." She shrugged. "I guess they come wheel it away."

"Little señora," Gracia warned, waving her finger, "you make sure this is above the board."

"Of course it is," Noël said. "Max said we could have one, as a branch office of the studio. I just have to run over and pick one out and sign some stuff."

"You watch out for that bad you-know-who while you're over there," Gracia said.

"I will," Noël promised. "After I see Max, I have one quick appointment and then I'll be home."

"Appointment to do what?" Gracia said, sounding suspicious.

"To make an amend, if you must know."

Gracia frowned. "Make what?"

"To apologize to someone."

"Who?" Gracia said, bringing a hand to her hip.

"You don't trust me at all, do you?" Noël said.

"I trust you," Gracia said, "but the señora will go into outer space if you're going to see that bad man, you know she will."

"I am *not* going to see the bad man," Noël said, heading for the door, "I'm going to Max's office and then"—she turned around to look at Gracia, hand on the door—"Mrs. *Nosy* Rodriguez—I'll be in Holly Montvale's trailer."

"Achee," Gracia said to the ceiling.

"What?" Noël said.

Gracia looked at Noël, shaking her head. "The señora will—"

"Approve," Noél said, cutting her off. "She's the one who suggested it. Holly's in for costume fittings for her movie and we're going to have tea, that's all."

"That's all," Gracia repeated, turning to the sink, adding under her breath, "I am not going to be the one to tell the señora that you are with Señora Montvale while she is undressing in her trailer, no I am not."

"I'm having *tea* with her," Noél said.

Gracia turned around. "She is very important to the señora's program—you will remember that."

"All right! All right!" Noél said, walking outside, slamming the door and starting up the path around the side of the house.

Geez. It was like a prison around here. Interrogation. Work schedule. What to eat. When to go to bed. When to get up. Who she could see, who she couldn't. The trust level in her was just enormous, wasn't it?

"Little señora!" Gracia called as Noél reached her car.

"What?" Noél yelled, wheeling around.

Gracia was standing on the path in the side yard, wiping her hands on a dishcloth. "Good luck with your apology."

Noél sighed. How could anyone be mad at Gracia? "Thanks," she said.

"And make sure to do only what will contribute to your future happiness," Gracia added. And then, with a little wave of the dish towel, she disappeared down the path.

Noél sighed again, shaking her head, and climbed into the car, the BMW Mort had given her two years ago. She should have gotten rid of it by now, but she hadn't, basically because it was such a gorgeous thing to drive and there was no way she could ever afford a car like this herself, not if she continued avoiding the question of what she was going to do with her life.

Just when *was* she going to start living on her own? she wondered as she drove to the studio. Lydia had always said there wasn't any hurry, but it had been almost a year and a half now and Noél was still here, still being told what to do—when to do it, how to do it—and living an utterly luxurious life on, as usual, someone else's money. First her parents. Then her drug-dealing husband. Then her drug-dealing girlfriend. Then Mort—the cars, the trips, the shopping sprees ("Mr. Pallsner's account," the boutique owners would say quietly, nodding once just to check), the tickets to anything, access to everywhere. The money Mort wrote off through the studio was endless. And now, at Lydia's, stone-cold sober, here was Noël, still living like a millionairess and working as a glorified secretary.

The afternoon guard at the gate of Metropolis Pictures knew Noël pretty well. He was a part-time coke dealer. He smiled when he saw her car, tipped his hat, and told her how beautiful she looked. Noël smiled, thanked him, and handed him her studio pass, not for the first time handing him along with the pass a meeting list of Cocaine Anonymous meetings in L.A.

"No thanks," he said, trying to hand the meeting list back to her.

"Tuck it away somewhere," Noël said. "You never know—you might have a friend who needs to know where he can get some help."

"I don't have any friends like that," he said, absently wiping his nose with the back of his hand.

"You look like hell, Joey," Noël told him.

"Thanks," he said, giving his cap a hard yank so that it came down practically over his eyes.

"My number's on the back," Noël said, nodding toward the meeting list in his hand. "Call me. I'll take you to a meeting and then we can have dinner. You don't have to do anything, stop anything, if you don't want."

He scribbled a lot number on a visitor's parking pass and handed it to her without comment.

"Hey," Noël said softly. He looked at her. She gave him her warmest smile. "If it worked for me . . ."

He smiled a little. "You were pretty bad," he remembered.

"Yeah," she said, nodding, "I was pretty bad." Pause. "But not anymore—so know how good it has to be on this side for me to stay off it."

The car behind her honked.

"Call me," Noël said, pulling out.

She drove back through the studio streets to the Bestar visitor's lot, waving here and there to people she knew. Some she had worked with; many she had partied with. She parked and skipped up the stairs of the main "Cassandra" production office building.

"Hey, gorgeous girl," the receptionist said to her.

"Hi, Darlene, how are you?" Noël said, wishing she knew for sure why Darlene always looked at her the way she did, whether there had been some secret thing between them that Noël failed to remember.

"Sign in, please," Darlene said, pushing the register to her. "We're under martial law these days."

"Okay," Noël said, bending to do so.

"Max said you'd be coming in."

"Ya ya," Noël said, straightening up. "May I go back?"

"Just let me call," Darlene said, holding up a hand to keep her there.

"I thought I heard your voice," Max said in a minute, coming out to reception himself. "You're looking better and better, lovey," he said, leading her back.

Noël nodded and said hello to everyone they passed on the way, making her feel a little lonesome for the place. She may have been a terror on wheels when she worked here, but everyone had liked her.

"So what does Lydia need the machine for?" Max asked her when they were settled in his office.

"Her book, mostly," Noël said.

Max winced and covered his head. "Did you have to tell me that? If Mort finds out you're using one of our machines—"

"He won't find out," Noël said.

Max dropped his arms and rolled his eyes. And then he smiled, eyes twinkling. "So how is it? Have you read it?"

"Not only have I read it, I'm *writing* some of it," Noël said.

Max laughed and leaned forward. "So what does she say about Mort?"

Noël shook her head. "Sorry. But it's not finished yet."

He looked disappointed.

"But you'll be the first to know when it is, Max, I promise."

"Oh, lovey," Max sighed, sitting back in his chair, "I miss having you around. Not that little stunt at the end, I don't miss that, but I do miss that irresistible face of yours."

The "little stunt at the end" Max was referring to was the time Noël had demanded to make love with Holly in her trailer and when Holly had pleaded that she had to go to the set, Noël grabbed some scissors and started screaming she would kill herself. Holly had gone to the set anyway and Noël continued her tantrum, following her through the soundstage with the scissors, yelling at the top of her lungs, until Gary and Skip took the scissors from her and literally dragged her away.

It was hard to explain to people outside AA or CA how scenes like that could happen. That Noël that day had not wanted to have sex at all with Holly. That what really had been going on was that Noël had been feeling dead inside and so she thought to try to have sex in order to feel *something,* but when that was refused rage came instead, and she had gone with the rage, hoping it might wake up something inside of her so she wouldn't feel so much like she was dying.

No, there was no explaining to normal people what it felt like to be dead, listening to yourself scream but not really hearing it, knowing your body is shaking and trembling but not really feeling it, seeing the perspiration break out all over your body but not being able to feel a goddamn thing.

And so you ranted. And raved. And lashed out, yelling, running, screaming, not caring, only hoping to God that something might wake up inside so you could be alive again.

But it never did.

Not until the alcohol and drugs stopped. And what a long road it was to get to that point. It had nearly killed her. It had killed a lot of the acquaintances she had made in those years.

"I have to say," Max told her, "I was upset it didn't work out about you coming back. I know it was part of Mort's push to get Lydia to re-sign, but I'd like to see you back in production. You're good, lovey, you're good with people—we could have used you."

Noél frowned. "Come back? You mean here?"

Now Max frowned. "Why do I get the feeling, lovey, that you don't know what I'm talking about?"

"Because I don't," Noél told him.

"She didn't tell you." It wasn't a question.

"Tell me what?"

Max blinked. He hesitated and then said, "And Gary didn't say anything to you?"

Noél shook her head.

"Lydia should have told you," Max said. "But I understand why she didn't. She's trying to protect you." He sighed. "Maybe she's right— maybe it wouldn't be such a hot idea to have you around Mort again. He's got *two* kittens here now, you know. Eyes so glassed-over Peggy Fleming could skate on 'em."

"Let me get this straight, Max," Noél said. "Mort offered me a job here and I never even heard about it."

"Lydia was trying to protect you," Max said.

Noél thought about this for a moment. "You're right, Max," she said, "Lydia should have told me."

"Knock-knock," Noël said, cautiously opening the door a crack.

The door opened the rest of the way very quickly.

And Holly was there. Smiling. "Look at you," she murmured. "My God, Noël, you look so wonderful."

Noël shrugged and said, "But they say it's an inside job"—she met Holly's eyes—"so I'd be careful. I may not be how I look." Then she made a sound of frustration, looking down at the ground. "Now why did I say that?" She looked back at Holly. "I *am* better, Holly. *Different.*" And then her voice softened. "But I'm nervous."

Holly leaned forward and gently kissed her on the cheek. "I'm different too. Come in," she said, stepping back and holding the door open.

Holly was that perfect supporting actor on a TV series, wonderful to look at but only as a complement to the star. She was about three inches shorter than Lydia, Noël's height, five feet five; where Lydia's hair was long and fair, Holly's was very dark, very thick, and cut just above her shoulders; and where Lydia's blazing blue eyes dazzled, Holly's large soft brown ones only warmed. Oh, Holly was pretty all right, but on "Cassandra's World" her job was to endear rather than compel.

Still, she was gorgeous.

Very early on Holly had become aware of the effect her looks could have on people and very early on, even back in Ohio, Holly had broken hearts both male and female. Then, at age nineteen, a forty-six-year-old man slipped an engagement ring on her finger and whisked her off to Los Angeles to become an actress, where, shortly thereafter, he died of a heart attack in a hot tub. The whole tragic story as depicted by the tabloids for months did more to launch Holly than any of her acting skills had. Better yet, since she had always known that she liked women better than men, she got to play the grieving widow part for almost ten years—until, that is, rumors began circulating in ominous proximity to the mainstream press and she knew she had to marry.

Her "fairy tale marriage" to her publicist, Kent Patterly, prompted more than a few chuckles around town, but the public at large had avidly been following it in the supermarket stands for seven years now:

Holly heartbroken over not being able to conceive; Holly going to France for a secret operation which did not work; Holly going for artificial insemination, getting pregnant, but then miscarrying; Holly separating from Kent and then joyfully reconciling; Holly and Kent trying again to have a baby. Considering that Holly didn't want any children and had never even had sex with Kent—though, quite often, on the road they did sleep together in the same bed, and for three nights once in L.A. too after Kent's mother died—Holly considered herself extremely lucky to have the press creating such an active marital life for her.

The only thing that had ever rocked their "marriage" had been the advent of Noél Shaunnessy in Holly's life. "Get rid of her!" Kent had told Holly after her first dalliance with Noél, an intended one-night stand that ended up with Holly staying at Noél's for three straight days. "She's trouble, Hol. She's using, she's Pallsner's mistress, the setup couldn't be worse—she'll ruin us before she's through."

But Holly had not gotten rid of Noél. She had simply tried to put more time in between her liaisons with her. But then, as time went on, the liaisons got more frequent and a hell of a lot more dangerous as Noél's behavior became more unpredictable, Noél became more obsessive, and Noél started acting out, first in private and then in semipublic. And then, finally, Holly had panicked completely, running to Gary to do something before everything was lost—Noél's life to drugs and Holly's career to Pallsner or the whole wide world.

And I was mad at her for not wanting to see me when I got out of Betty Ford, Noél thought.

"Did you really want tea?" Holly was saying from the little kitchen area of her trailer. "I'll make it if you like, but it's a little warm today—I thought I'd have some seltzer."

"Seltzer would be great," Noél said, sitting down, looking around, wishing she didn't feel so uncomfortable. It was just Holly, she kept telling herself—but then her mind would scream, "That's right— Holly! Holly! As beautiful and wonderful as ever!" And then she got that sick feeling in her stomach—it was fear, she knew, and then she knew for sure, yes, on this side of sobriety she was going to be in love with Holly. But maybe for real now.

Oh, God. What to do with this heart in this body in this world.

Holly turned. "There's no need to be nervous," she said quietly. "It's only me, Noél. It's okay."

Noél nodded, swallowing.

Holly fixed them both a tall glass of peach-flavored seltzer and, after giving Noél hers, she settled down in the chair across from Noél to hear why Noél had agreed to see her.

"There's a thing in AA called a ninth step," Noél said. "It's where you go back to someone you felt you've harmed in the past—and you go back to them to at least try and explain the circumstances of what happened. And you try to accept the responsibility for what you did." Pause. "And you try and make an amend to that person—not just by saying you're sorry, but by doing your best to make reparations—or making sure that whatever you did never happens again."

Holly nodded slightly. "Yes."

"So I came here wanting to make an amend to you," Noél said, swallowing.

"Yes," Holly said.

"Which I guess should be to leave you alone," Noél said, looking away.

Silence.

"But why?" Holly said. "What would you do to me now?"

"I don't know," Noél said, "but my motives about why I want to make an amend to you seem to be changing by the second."

Pause. "What new motive do you think you have?" Holly said.

"I knew I would screw this up if I saw you in person!" Noél said, jumping up and going over to the bookcase, standing there with her back to Holly. She touched the base of an award on a shelf and sighed, dropping her head, murmuring, "Am I never going to get things straight with you?"

"Noél—"

"I want to make things right, Holly," Noél said, starting to cry. "And now that I see you all I want to do is try and mess your life up again. And what kind of amend is that?"

Holly came over to her, handing her some tissues. Noél took them and wiped her eyes, blew her nose. "I'm not making an amend at all," she said, sniffing. "I'm just trying to get back into your life, I know I am, and that's not what I'm supposed to be doing."

"It's okay," Holly whispered, touching her shoulder.

"No! It's not!" Noél said, pulling away from her. "I'm sorry," she said, softening her voice, backing away a step. "Holly, it's not you—it's me. I have to try and make things right in my life. Coming over here and trying to seduce you is no way to make an amend."

Holly looked sympathetic—but then she laughed a little. "But you tried, Noél, that must count for something." She held out her arms. "Maybe you should just come here and let me hold you."

Noél knew that look in Holly's eyes. Very well. In a second they'd be all over each other.

"You've been clean for a long time now," Holly said, moving toward her.

"I can't," Noél said, backing away toward the door.

Holly stopped and lowered her arms. "You are clean, aren't you? Noél, you haven't—"

"No, I haven't," Noél said quickly. "I've been sober for eighteen months."

Holly looked into her eyes. "And I've so missed you."

"Oh, God, Holly," Noél sighed, turning away and banging her forehead on the door once and then letting it rest there. "I can't do this. Not like this. I have to do things differently now."

She felt Holly's hand on her shoulder. "And you are."

Silence.

Holly squeezed her shoulder and then released it. "Take your time, baby," she said.

Noél turned around, wiping a tear away with the back of her hand.

"Take your time," Holly repeated, pulling Noél's hand away and then wiping her tears away herself. "What is it they say?" she murmured, looking at her. "A day at a time?"

Noél nodded, swallowing.

"A day at a time, then," Holly said, kissing her on the forehead. "In the meantime, we can be friends again."

Friends again. Friends again. Had they ever been that?

— *32* —

She wished to God she had handled it better.

She could have stayed a few more minutes than she had. She could have said something. She certainly could have done something more than cry, flee to the bathroom, come back out, kiss a stunned Mark, and run out of his apartment.

But she hadn't known what else to do. What she had done was wrong. So very, very wrong.

And with Mark.

With *Mark*.

She had gone to Harris's, drunk a snifter of brandy, thrown up, taken a bath, and gone to bed, falling into a dead sleep. In the morning she had been awakened by Sarah calling to find out where she was. She was supposed to be in a planning meeting.

For the first time in her life Kate lied and did not go into work. She was very ill, she told Sarah. And then Kate hung up the phone, burst into tears, curled up into a little ball around a pillow, and shivered and shook and cried.

Yes, she was ill, she decided about noon, after she got out of bed and found that her legs were wobbly and her hands were shaking. She was ill with guilt. She sat down with coffee in the kitchen, holding her face in her hands, wondering why she had done what she had, wondering how she could make things go back to the way they were.

She had cheated on Harris and it would kill him if he knew.

And with Mark. Poor, vulnerable Mark, distraught over Carla still, supposedly her best friend.

What kind of monster was she?

Sarah called in the afternoon to tell Kate what was going on in the office, what she had missed, what Sarah was trying to reschedule—did Kate think she would be in the office tomorrow? Things were a little crazy, she admitted, since Kate had been out of the office for so long.

"Yes, I'll be in tomorrow, no matter what," Kate said. "I just need today to kick this thing."

"Mark's sick, too. He didn't come in either," Sarah said.

The week did not improve. On top of Mark's being out ("He's really got the flu bad," Dale told Kate, making her want to kill herself), Kate was forced to make Rebecca and Mr. Rushman's offer to CAI on the Seth Roberts novel.

The silence on the other end of the phone when Kate made said offer was deafening.

"Kate," the agent finally said, "be fair. We shouldn't be dealing with Bennett, Fitzallen & Coe at all, should we?"

Pause.

"I'm sorry," Kate said.

"I'm sorry we wasted so much time on you," the agent said, hanging up.

"I made your offer," Kate said, striding into Rebecca's office and throwing Rebecca's memo of instruction on how to make the offer back down on her desk. In red felt pen Kate had written across it:

CAI: I'm sorry we wasted so much time on Bennett, Fitzallen & Coe. We won't make the same mistake again.

"What's this?" Rebecca said, jumping to her feet.

"They won't be doing business with us again," Kate said.

"Of course they will," Rebecca said, angry, "there're only seven houses left in town—they have to."

"If that's your feeling on the subject, then nobody should be doing business with us," Kate said, turning on her heel and walking out.

It was a very stupid thing to do. Very stupid. But Kate was beyond caring today. Everything she cared about was going to hell anyway.

She had betrayed Harris.

She had betrayed her friendship with Mark.

And she had greeted Harris the following night as though nothing had happened.

And she had slept with Harris.

And Harris had told her he loved her.

And she had told Harris she loved him, too.

And she had yet to speak to Mark at all.

"Lydia Southland's holding on two," Sarah said now as Kate came back to her office.

The interoffice mailman stopped his cart and raised his hand. "I'll talk to her," he volunteered.

"Lydia, hi," Kate said on the phone in her office.

Pause. "Good grief," Lydia said, "what's the matter?"

"Do I sound that bad?" Kate said.

"You sound that mad," Lydia said.

"Oh, it's just the usual office bullshit here," Kate said, sighing, dropping down into her chair and swiveling around to look out the window. "On to brighter subjects . . . And so how are you? Writing your head off, I hope."

"Oh, we're doing okay," Lydia said.

Pause.

Kate sat up straighter in her chair. "What's wrong?"

"Oh, nothing, really," Lydia sighed. "Nothing I can really put my finger on."

Pause. "All this thinking about the past—is that starting to get you down?" Kate said gently.

"Yeah," Lydia said, sounding vague, "that may be it."

"It's very normal, you know, to feel some sadness while writing a book like this."

"I didn't before," Lydia said.

"You didn't tell the truth before," Kate said.

Pause. "I thought I'd feel happier," Lydia said then. "The revenge parts about the industry and all that."

"Then maybe we should cut back on the revenge parts," Kate suggested.

"Kate?" Lydia said.

"Yes?"

"What would happen if I decided I didn't want to publish the book—not right away?"

Kate hesitated, thinking, *Then we are in BIG trouble here,* but said, "We would work it out, that's all. What's best for you is best for us."

"Thanks, Kate," Lydia said. "Hearing that makes it easier somehow. Takes the pressure off."

Kate heard someone clearing her throat and she swiveled her chair around. Rebecca was standing in the doorway. Their eyes met: Rebecca moved to close the door behind her, and then turned back around, arms crossed over her chest, holding the memo that Kate had thrown down on her desk.

"I've got to go, Lydia, I'm sorry," Kate said. "Should I call you later?"

"If you want."

"I will then. In about an hour."

"Great."

Kate hung up the phone and looked at Rebecca, wishing she did not feel as unnerved as she did by her expression.

"Your behavior is completely unacceptable," Rebecca said.

Kate didn't say anything.

"Don't you *dare* come into my office again without knocking," she whispered, creeping up to Kate's desk, "don't you *dare* talk to me in that tone of voice and don't you *dare* hand me a memo like this again." She slapped the paper on Kate's desk and leaned forward, resting her hands on the desk. "Your ass is on the line and right now I don't mind telling you, Kate—the only thing that's keeping you afloat around here is the Southland book."

Kate's face flushed scarlet. "The only thing that's keeping me afloat," she repeated. She stared at Rebecca for a full moment. "And just how many editors do you have around here with a list like mine?"

Rebecca leaned closer. "The list belongs to the house, not to you—it would not be hard to replace you, Kate. Not when we already have the books." She looked at Kate a moment longer and then slowly straightened up. And then she turned around and walked out.

She came home ranting and raving, promising to murder Rebecca before the month was out. It was a scenario that brought out the best in Harris. Of course Kate was right. Of course Rebecca didn't know jack shit about anything. Of course Rebecca was a sleaze. Of course Rebecca was an insecure little know-nothing, a cheat and a liar and a crook—she was going to steal Kate's list, right, yes, that's what she was doing and the stupid jerk knew contractually how those authors were tied up with the house and—

"Damn her, damn her, damn her!" Kate said, smashing the ice holder on the counter, sending ice cubes flying everywhere.

Harris took it from her, murmuring something about her sitting down, he'd fix her a drink, but Kate went on ranting and raving, walking around and around the apartment, going on and on about the state of affairs at Bennett, Fitzallen & Coe and that she knew she couldn't put up with it much longer—while thinking, at the same time, privately to herself, that if future life at B, F & C meant being estranged from Mark then there was no reason—none—for her to go on working there. There was no Bennett, Fitzallen & Coe without Mark. Today had just been a sample of what life was going to be like.

Harris's loving eyes on her at this moment were not helping either. The Kate he loved was steadfast and true, temperamental yes, but the woman he had been looking for all his life, the woman who loved him and would stay with him, the woman who would not go crazy on him like his first wife.

So Kate had responded to his love and commitment by betraying him. She had sex with Mark. She had an orgasm with Mark like she had never had with poor Harris.

And Harris loved her.

And Harris was a good man.

And Harris was the only relationship that had ever worked for her.

"Oh, Harris," Kate sighed, sliding her arms around his waist, resting the side of her face against his smooth pale blue shirt, "I feel so out of control—so angry." His arms tightened around her and she closed her eyes. She felt him kiss the top of her head and she started to cry, softly. "I love you," she said.

Harris said they were going out on Saturday night. It was a surprise. He wouldn't tell her anything more but that she should put on her little black number and pearls and be ready at seven.

Saturday arrived and promptly at seven Harris took Kate downstairs to the lobby. A horse-drawn carriage was outside, waiting for them. It was a lovely red gig, pulled by a large white horse, and the driver, a woman, wore a big black top hat. Tucked in under a blanket, Kate and Harris were slowly driven—clip-clop, clip-clop, clip-clop—down through Central Park.

Kate didn't know why—was it the trees? the temperature? the light? what?—but while riding in the carriage, she suddenly thought of the time that, instead of taking the bus home, she had waited for her mother to pick her up at school to take her to the dentist.

Only her mother had not come.

Not after a half hour. Not after an hour.

When Kate's teacher saw her standing out there, she brought her in to call her mother. The line was busy. "Oh, she'll come as soon as she's off," Kate told her teacher. "She's probably talking to my father."

Her father. Ha. Her mother and father never talked anymore. She didn't even know where her father was. All she knew was that her mother cried all the time and asked Kate, over and over, who did she love better, her or her father?

"You, Mommy, I love you best," Kate would say, trying to calm her.

In any event, her mother did not come in two hours. The secretary from the principal's office made her come in at five and call her mother again. Now there was no answer. "She's on her way," Kate assured her. And the secretary had gone home, too.

It started to get dark.

Kate had done her homework, had finished her library book, and had built a little fort out of sticks on the stone wall.

What time was it when Mom had come? Kate didn't know. It was dark, she remembered, and she had by that time hidden herself in the bushes because she did not know what to say if anyone else came by and saw her still there.

And then the station wagon had come tearing up to the school. And there was Mom, crying, hugging her, saying, "My baby, my poor baby, I'm going to take you home now."

They never discussed it again.

"I couldn't believe how much I missed you when you were away," Harris said, holding Kate in his arms, kissing her once about every three minutes through the park.

"But I'm home now," Kate said, nestling her head into the side of his neck. It was so lovely out, so lovely clip-clopping along, the trees starting to bud, the warm blanket over her knees, Harris's arms around her.

Everything was in the past, Kate told herself. Even her mistake with Mark. She wouldn't make it again. It had only happened for her to make sure it was Harris she wanted. And it was Harris she wanted.

Harris, who never failed her. Harris, who was always, always there for her. Maybe he was short on emotion, but he was very long on reliability. And he loved her. And she loved him.

"I missed you so much I thought about how I could change," he said. "About the ways I could make you happier."

Kate sat up a little to look at him. "You make me happy now." She kissed him. "You don't have to change," she murmured, settling back against him, thinking again about what she had done with Mark and how it would kill Harris if he knew. And how lucky, lucky, lucky she was to have someone like Harris to love her.

The carriage clip-clopped down through the park, down Seventh Avenue, and then over to Rockefeller Center.

"Miss Weston, hello," the maître d' of the Rainbow Room said as they walked in. He knew her from all the publishing events that were held there. Harris thought it was funny. His big treat and Kate knew the maître d'.

They had a wonderful dinner. And they danced. Harris loved ballroom dancing and he was a wonderful dancer. Around and around and around they went, like a forties movie, with older couples smiling in approval and younger ones watching in a self-conscious comparison that was flattering.

"I love you, darling," Harris whispered in Kate's ear, turning her again on the dance floor.

At about eleven they went back downstairs. And there, waiting for them, was their carriage again. But this time, under the blanket in the seat, was a present. Kate opened it. It was a copy of *Pride and Prejudice*, protected in a new leather slipcase. Kate took it out, looking at it in awe under the streetlight.

It was a first edition. A *first* edition.

"Harris," she said, overwhelmed.

He tilted her chin up so that he could kiss her. "For the best damn editor in New York," he said.

They clip-clopped over to Fifty-ninth Street and then down and around the Plaza Hotel driveway. "Last stop," Harris announced as he hopped down and reached up to help her.

"Aren't we going to the Oak Room?" she asked him, puzzled when he led her into the lobby instead of straight back down the hallway.

"No," he said, smiling, "we're going to our room."

The room was a suite overlooking the park, enormous and exquisitely beautiful and, Kate knew, outrageously expensive. There was a bottle of champagne on ice and they drank a little of it, snuggling on the couch in the living room.

"We must get you a new job," Harris said to Kate, kissing her neck.

"Yes," Kate agreed, finishing the champagne in her glass.

"We're tired of you being married to that place," Harris said, trying to pull down the zipper on the back of her dress.

"Yes," Kate agreed.

"We must make love right now," Harris said.

"Yes," Kate agreed, trying to get her glass on the table.

"Kate, darling," Harris said, lying to the side of her, warm wetness lying against her thigh, "I want you to stop using the pill."

Silence.

"They say it takes a while for your system to start up again," he whispered, kissing one of her eyelids and then the other. Pause. "Kate, darling, look at me."

She opened her eyes.

"I want to have a family with you," he said. "I want us to have children together."

She looked at him.

"Kate," he said, "I'm asking you to marry me." He swallowed. "And I think it's the last time I'll ask." Pause. "Because I know you're ready. Ready for us"—he kissed her—"ready for children."

Her eyes were filling.

"And what about *Reader's Digest?*" he asked her. "People say that's a good place to work for people with families."

"Oh, Harris," Kate said, closing her eyes and hugging him while laughing. "Me at *Reader's Digest?*"

"It was just a thought," he said. He reached back to open the drawer of the bedside table and got something out of it. "Here," he said, rolling back toward her and handing her a small box. "We go all the way this time."

Kate examined the box in her hands. She felt oddly safe. Safe, loved, vaguely excited by both. She had been mistaken, she thought. She had not dug deep enough with Harris.

The box was from Tiffany.

"Open it," he whispered.

She did. And the ring was beautiful. A rock, really, but such a gorgeous pear-shaped diamond, the size seemed only exactly right.

She looked at Harris, pushing some strands of his hair back over his forehead. "I want to do the right thing, Harris."

"Then say yes."

She looked at the ring again.

He took it out of the box and slipped it on her finger. It looked even better on. Harris kissed her hand and then simply held it there, at his mouth, eyes rising to meet hers. "Say yes, Kate," he whispered.

She looked into his eyes. "Yes," she said.

— *33* —

"Katherine, I couldn't be more pleased," Dr. Weston said over the telephone. "I think Harris will make a fine husband."

"Thanks, Dad," Kate said, "I think he will too."

"He's Episcopalian, is that right?" Dr. Weston said.

"Yes," Kate said.

"Good," Kimberly, her stepmother, said cheerfully on the extension, "then there's no problem with Reverend Walker performing the ceremony at St. Matthew's."

"That would be wonderful," Kate said. "Harris likes him."

"We'd like to give you an engagement party," Dr. Weston said. "We'd like everyone to get a chance to meet Harris."

"Yes, okay," Kate said. "That would be great."

"Oh, it sounded so romantic, Kate," Kimberly said. "He told us all about his plans—about the carriage and the Rainbow Room and the Plaza. Oh, and Kate, it was so cute, your father told him he better buy you a book *and* a ring if he wanted to win you over."

"Kimberly knew you would like the ring," Dr. Weston said.

"He asked me to come in and see it before he bought it," Kimberly added. "Oh, Kate, it was so exciting. I just knew you two had sorted things out."

Kate smiled. "So you were all in on it."

"Hoping," Dr. Weston said, "only hoping. It's your life, Katherine, I've always told you that. But we're very, very happy for you. You've made an excellent choice and I'm proud of you."

"We were somewhat hoping for the third Saturday of September," Kimberly said. "It's perfectly gorgeous at that time of year and we could have the reception outside—or at the club, if you prefer. But you're going to have to let me know—soon, dear—if we want to reserve it."

"I vote for the club," Dr. Weston said, "at least to delegate part of the insanity to those accustomed to dealing with it."

"It wouldn't be insane, dear, if we had it here at the house," Kimberly told her husband. "Harriet would take care of everything. They would come the night before with the tents and the dance floor and then bring in the food and flowers the next morning. And there's the orchestra, Kate. I was thinking of young Paul Earlin—he played at the ball this year and it was lovely."

"Sounds fine to me," Kate said. And then she did a double take. "Wait a minute," she said, "are we talking about *this* September?"

"Oh, God, I don't believe it!" Sherry Berman Meyer screamed, making one of her kids start screaming too. "Jonathan! Jonathan!" she called. "Kate's getting married!" She laughed. "Jonathan wants to know, 'To whom?' "

"Harris," Kate said, laughing.

"Harris. She's marrying, Harris. Wait, hold on, Kate."

"Katie girl, congratulations!" Jonathan said.

"Thank you," she said.

"He's a very lucky guy," Jonathan said, "and if he doesn't know it, I'll be sure to set him straight."

"Yes, you do that, Jonathan," Kate laughed.

"Okay, here's Sherry."

"Do you have a ring?" Sherry asked.

"I sure do," Kate said.

"What's it like?"

Kate described it to her.

"Where did he get it?"

"Tiffany's."

"Kate, look, we've got to get this guy straightened out—he just threw away your first child's first year of college. We could have gotten him a deal through my cousin."

"Oh, Sherry, you know Harris, he's just not like that," Kate said.

"What's not to like about saving money? I thought he's supposed to be a banker. What kind of banker doesn't want to save money?"

Kate laughed. "I'm afraid Harris does things the way his father did them. You know, he went to Tiffany's for his engagement ring so Harris goes to Tiffany's—"

"Right," Sherry said, "WASP insanity in action—let the children fend for themselves."

"Listen, Berman, I would like you to be my matron of honor."

"And I'd like very much to be it," she said. "Thank you, I accept." Then she dropped her voice to add, "It'll be worth the price of admission just to see your father's face—a Jew on the altar in Windy Hills!"

"Oh, Sherry—stop it!"

There was the murmur of a young voice on the other end. "No, sweetie pie," Sherry said, "I said 'shoe.' Aunt Kate and I are talking about what to wear to her wedding." In her normal voice, she said, "So what's the date, Kate?"

"I'm not sure," Kate said.

"I don't mean to be a party pooper or anything," Sherry said, "but generally speaking, Kate, when one wants to get married one sets a date to do it." Pause. "You do want to marry him—Harris—right?"

"Of course I do," Kate said.

Pause. "Are you sure?"

"I'm sure," Kate said.

"Hold on, then, the children want to say something."

"Congratulations, Aunt Kate!" the children cried.

"Sarah said you had some news," Lydia said over the phone. "I thought it would be about the book but she said, no, it was personal. I said, 'Kate has a personal life? How dare she! She should be working on my book around the clock—we are!' "

Kate laughed, looking at her watch. It was just after eight. She was dressed for work, having a bite of breakfast in the kitchen, waiting for Harris. They were late starting this morning. They had lingered to make love. Again.

"What are you doing up at five in the morning?" Kate said.

"I'm working on the section about dating in Hollywood," Lydia explained. "I'm afraid it makes me sound like a public flirt and nothing else, but I'm afraid that's just about the extent of it these days. When Noél gets up I'll have her fax the pages to you—I think you'll like them."

"Great," Kate said.

"But enough about the book," Lydia said. "What's your big news?"

"I'm getting married," Kate said, smiling at Harris, who had just come into the kitchen.

"To who?" Lydia said.

Kate was about to say, "Why does everyone keep asking me to who? As if you don't know I live with Harris!" but she didn't because Harris was standing right there. She covered the phone and said to Harris, "There's a bran muffin in the bread box," and then came back to the phone. "Thank you, thank you," she said into the phone enthusiastically. "Yes, we're very happy."

Harris beamed.

"Sitting right there, huh?" Lydia said. "This is that Harris guy, right? Well, listen, Kate, I'll go along with you on it if it's what you think's best. But we'll talk about it more later."

"What?" Kate said. "Why?"

"Well, I don't know," Lydia said, "you always say that to me when you're not sure about something I'm doing in the book, so I thought I'd say it back to you now to see how you liked it."

Kate laughed.

Harris was whistling, pouring himself coffee.

And then Kate realized she shouldn't have laughed. Because Lydia, she realized, had not offered any congratulations; Lydia, she realized, did not approve.

"Mark, I have to talk to you," Kate said over the phone. "I have to see you before you come into the office."

"Maybe it would be best if you simply said whatever it is you have to say," he said, sounding horribly distant.

Oh, God, how could she do this? How could she explain how she went to bed with him one night and got engaged to Harris a few weeks later?

By just telling him. *Do it.*

"Mark," she said, "I'm going to marry Harris."

"So I surmised," he said coolly.

"How?" she asked, surprised.

"Call it mental telepathy," he said. "Or consider your running out of my apartment and avoiding me for weeks a small hint that you made your choice."

Pause. "And I'm wearing a ring," Kate said. "I wanted you to know that before you saw it."

"You're very thoughtful, Kate."

Silence.

"Why, Kate?" Mark said then.

"Because I love him," she said.

"You know it won't work," he said. "You know it—deep down you do. The guy's very nice and all, but we both know he can't keep up with you. Or maybe there's something about him I don't know—some secret life, perhaps? Some deeply expressive, soul-searching creativity he expresses in his work but fails to show in his private life?"

"There's a lot you don't know about Harris," Kate said, angry.

"Oh, so you've been radiantly happy with him," Mark said. "I'm sorry, I must have missed that part over the past year."

"I've been happy," Kate said defiantly, "I've been happier with Harris than anyone else—ever!"

"Oh, right," Mark said, "and we all know what a happy life you've led."

Kate was so angry she couldn't see straight. "How dare you!" she finally said.

"And this has been the honeymoon," Mark said. "This is as romantic as it will get, Kate." Pause. "So how dare you pretend that this is what you really want—to be bound to this poor guy for the rest of your life. I mean, who do you think you're talking to? Kate, I *know* you. I'm not Harris—I'm no fool. I'm a full-fledged emotionally functioning human being."

"I can't believe you're saying these things to me!" Kate said, starting to cry. "I understand that you're upset—but you're supposed to be my friend."

"Upset?" Mark said. "Why should I be upset? It only means that I don't have the slightest idea who you are. If all it takes is the right last name, money, and being emotionally shut down to marry you, Kate, then this is a marriage made in heaven. I'm *happy* for you, Kate."

"Mark, stop it!" Kate sobbed. "Stop saying these things!"

"Good luck, Kate," Mark said. "You're certainly doing your father proud." And he hung up.

And Kate hated him.

— *34* —

They were seeing too much of each other, he knew that. Even the best of friends could grow grouchy with one another, wishing the other had something new to say besides what they had already heard at least ten times before. But the book just kept going on and on, the work just kept going on and on, and so did they, day after day, night after night, draft after draft, revision after revision. "These dates still don't add up," Gary would sigh, pushing the pages to Lydia's side of the table in the office. "Kate says she has to have them right for the sales presentation."

Lydia would look at the pages, her reading glasses down on her nose (she had long since given up trying to pretend she didn't need them), and she would say, "What dates?"

"These—when you were born, when you graduated from school and stuff," Gary would say.

"Oh, God, not that again," Lydia would sigh.

And then Gary would look at her and Lydia would look at him and they would burst out laughing.

"Oh, hell, Steiner," Lydia would groan, dropping her head on the desk, "how did I ever get us into this? Why didn't we just stay on in 'Parson's Crossing' in New York?"

And then he would smile, rubbing her back with his hand, and he would murmur something like, "Yeah, well, if we did, I'd be dead and you'd be sick to death of daytime," and then something would lurch in his chest and he would look at Lydia, at the back of her head, and he would feel almost ill with emotion. And then he would try to dismiss it and, fairly soon after, make a point of going home and trying to forget about it—about what he felt—and get his head back on track before seeing her again the next day.

Lydia was his friend. Lydia was his family.

And his track record with women was horrible. His most recent girlfriend, in fact, had informed Gary that he didn't date women, but took hostages. And that if any woman agreed to such an obsessive arrangement he was bound to lose interest in her. This had to stop, this girlfriend had said. She knew all about it. Her friends had warned her about him. "And now," she had said one night, while driving with him in his car, "you're trying to do it to me."

"Do what to you?" Gary had said, irritated, speeding up on Santa Monica Boulevard.

"Trying to take over my life," she'd said. "Gary, whatever happened to getting to know each other? Dating you is like dating a storm trooper."

He had looked at her. Hayley had been her name. Named after Hayley Mills no doubt. The era was about right for a daughter of Pollyanna. "I thought you liked me," he had said.

"I do," she had said. "But I still don't know you very well." Pause. "Not enough to go move in with you certainly."

When Gary didn't say anything, but continued to race up Santa Monica, Hayley had added, "I know what you're thinking and yes, you're right, plenty of great-looking women would love to move in with you."

"Oh, fuck this!" Gary had yelled, swerving to the side of the road and stopping. "What are you, Dr. Joyce Brothers?"

"I'm not trying to hurt you, Gary," Hayley had said, "I'm just trying to explain to you why I don't feel comfortable having my life taken over by you." Pause. "I'm not used to someone trying to use me, either."

"And what's that supposed to mean?" he'd asked her.

"It means I don't know who you're hung up on," she said evenly, "but I do know that I don't want to be a stand-in." Pause. "So either be willing to get to know me or let's forget the whole thing."

In the end they decided to forget the whole thing.

Before Hayley, Gary had lived with a woman named Ellen. She had been in Alcoholics Anonymous, too. Well, sort of. She went to meetings and got her car keys on a good seat early enough, but she didn't seem ever really to get AA—which is to say that after about six months Gary noticed that Ellen seemed to be getting more unhappy instead of happier, which was usually a sign that certain steps in AA had been missed along the way.

Gary had really cared for Ellen. Well, sort of. The sex had been out of this world, but after she moved in the sex got progressively worse until, after a year, there was no sex at all. At least not between the two of them.

When Gary had thrown up his hands to his friend and sponsor, Skip, and said it was all beyond him—that he hated relationships, period, he couldn't maintain one if his life depended on it—Skip had come up with an interesting point. "How hopeless can you be if at least one of your relationships is of a duration, depth, and strength that few people ever have with anyone?"

Huh?

"Lydia," Skip had said. "You've put a lot of work into your relationship with her. You two have taught each other a lot—built a great deal."

"But I mean a *real* relationship," Gary said.

"It *is* a real relationship," Skip said. "Sex has nothing to do with a relationship—forming one, I mean."

Huh?

True, he had known Lydia for an awfully long time. And true, he had his most intimate talks with Lydia. About how he felt, his frustrations, how he was emotionally. Lydia knew about his work life, of course, because she was there in it, but she also knew who were his AA buddies; she knew the areas where he tended to get depressed if he didn't do better than anyone else; she knew without his having to say what kind of mood he was in. And Lydia talked to him more freely than she did to others—certainly about her work, but, admittedly, little about her love life. But then, Gary didn't talk about his love life to her either.

"How's Hayley?" Lydia would say.

"Fine," Gary would say. "How's Steve?"

"Good."

End of discussion.

He first became aware of Lydia watching him the afternoon he played singles with her new business manager on her court. Gary had just served (an ace, thank you) when he saw Lydia watching from the window of the exercise room. She quickly moved away from the window and Gary pretended not to see her, acutely aware, for the rest of the match, that she was still watching, and that she did not want to be seen watching. (Choke, choke, choke—he lost the next two sets.)

Last week, while waiting for Lydia to return from a benefit luncheon in the Valley, he had decided to take a swim. Flipping over on his back to do the backstroke for a few laps, he had caught Lydia out of the corner of his eye, standing in the window of one of the guest rooms upstairs. Again, she had been watching him. She did though, that time, come down later to say hello, but he noticed that she made it appear as though she had only just arrived home at that moment.

"What are you looking at?" he said to her, toweling dry.

"Your foot," she said.

"Prehensile toes, as my dear ex-wife used to say," he said, wriggling them. "Said she always knew I must have come straight down from the trees."

"They are very long, aren't they?" Lydia murmured, studying his toes to a degree that made him feel uncomfortable.

"They're not ugly," he protested.

"No, they're not," she said, raising her eyes. "Not at all."

"My grandmother used to say it was the rape of the Russians," he said.

"Oh, that's awful," Lydia had said, turning away.

A couple of days later, he and Noél were working together outside on the table by the pool, going over the notes Kate had faxed back about their most recent pages. "Don't look now," Noél said under her breath, "but the boss lady is watching us."

"What?" Gary had said, raising his head.

"Don't look," Noél had said. "She's in her room." Pause. "She's been at the window for about a half hour—just sitting there, watching us."

"So?" Gary said, resuming reading.

After a moment, Noél said, "The more we work on this book, the stranger she gets—you notice?"

"Look," Gary said, stopping reading and facing Noél, "I'd be a little overwhelmed too if I had to commit my whole life story to paper."

"Sad," Noél said softly. "I think that's what she's been. Sad. Getting sadder. The farther we get with the book, the sadder she gets."

"Oh, I don't know about that," Gary said, collecting the papers and tapping them on the table in tight order.

"Kate thinks so too," Noél added.

Gary looked at her.

"She thinks Lydia's maybe having second thoughts about the book."

Gary thought a moment and then shook his head. "I don't think so." He paused, putting the pages back down flat on the table. "No, if she's having second thoughts, it's about leaving the series. I think it's dawning on her how much of her identity is wrapped up in her work."

"Maybe," Noél said. "Boy," she said, "that would make Mort happy, wouldn't it? If she re-signed after all this?"

"It'd make me happy, I know," Gary said.

"And me too," Noél said. "Then I could go back to work at Bestar."

Gary looked at her. "You know," he said.

"Yeah," she said. "Max let it slip a few weeks ago—about *my* job offer you guys never thought to tell me about."

"Don't be angry, Noél. She thinks she's protecting you."

"I'm not angry," Noél said. "I'm just wondering what I'm going to do. I can't stay here forever."

"It'll work itself out," Gary assured her.

Noél shrugged.

They resumed reading pages. They made a couple of corrections and then Noél said, "She's still watching us."

"Stop it, Noél."

A sigh. And then, "Gary."

"What?" he whispered under his breath, exasperated.

"She is acting strange—admit it."

"Okay, Noél," he said, rubbing his eyes, "she's acting strange."

"Something's up," Noél said to herself. She looked at Gary. "Are you sure you don't know what it is?"

He dropped his hand to the table. "No, Noél, I don't. Okay? Can we go back to work now?"

"Sure," Noél said, picking up the papers again. After a moment she looked sideways at him, adding, "She's still watching."

"Oh, what difference does it make!" Lydia said to Gary impatiently, throwing more things out of the trunk and onto the guest bedroom floor. "Who could possibly be interested in this?"

"Kate is—and the sales force too, evidently," Gary said, trying not to smile. Lydia was down on her knees in front of an old wooden footlocker, wearing a white leotard and sweatpants, and he was sitting on the double bed, watching her, holding a desperate, handwritten fax from Kate that said, "FLORIDA SALES REP SAYS YOU GRADUATED IN '66, NOT '71. HOW DO I REFUTE?"

Having to interrupt Lydia in the middle of her sacred workout was bad enough, but forcing her to look for her high school and college diplomas was turning her mood absolutely foul. "If I never answered any of Kate's questions to begin with, we'd never be in this mess," Lydia said, tossing an old pair of pink ballet slippers on the floor and diving back into the trunk. "What is this sales rep anyway, a private detective? How the hell does he know when I graduated?"

"He went to your high school, I think," Gary said.

"He works for Bennett, Fitzallen & Coe—you'd think they could control him," she said. She flipped through an old photo album and sneezed.

"Bless you," Gary said.

"Well, here's my old stuffed monkey," Lydia said, waving a dilapidated rag doll through the air. "I suppose Kate will want a picture of this in the book, too, to show more deep psychological insights into my character."

Gary laughed, getting up off the bed. "I think maybe I better get you some fortification for this ordeal. What would you like?"

"Something hot and good and nonfattening, please—as if there is such a thing," she muttered.

Gary went downstairs to the kitchen where Gracia and Noél were making chocolate chip cookies for one of Noél's CA meetings. Billy and Cathy were over, in the breakfast room doing their homework. Gary relayed Lydia's request to Gracia and then sidled over to the counter where Noél was standing over a bowl of raw cookie dough, which maybe, just maybe, was his favorite thing to eat in all the world. He sneaked a taste.

Noél looked at him, lofting an eyebrow. "Anything going on I should know about?" she asked him.

"Hmmm?" he said, finger still in his mouth.

Noél looked up at the ceiling, to where Lydia was upstairs, and then looked back at Gary. "*Something's* in the air—and I figure it's got something to do with you."

"What do you mean?" Gary said, feeling as though he were falling out of a plane. There was something about the way Noél said it that thrilled him. Thrilled and terrified him.

"Now *both* of you are acting sad and strange," Noél told him.

"Little señora is not doing her job," Gracia scolded, coming over and picking up the spatula off the counter and shoving it back into Noél's hand. Then she handed Gary a plate of quartered oranges and some napkins. "Take these up to the señora, please," she said, "and tell her that I will bring her up a hot surprise she will like."

"Ten to one the hot surprise is already with her and she likes it fine but doesn't know what to do with it," Noél said.

Gary felt his face burn. Without looking at Noél or Gracia, he took the plate of oranges and went upstairs. "She sent some oranges," he reported, sitting down on the floor by the footlocker and handing Lydia a napkin, "and some sort of hot surprise is coming up soon."

"Thanks," Lydia said, taking a piece of orange and settling back on her haunches to bite into it. "Gare," she said after a minute.

"Hmmm?" He was eating orange too.

She patted her mouth with her napkin. "What am I going to do about my graduation dates?"

He looked at her.

"If I lie, they'll catch me. If I don't . . ." She made a face indicating imminent disaster.

"Then we'll finesse it," he said. "We won't give dates—we'll just gloss over the whole first part of the book. I know what to do, don't worry—but you will have to practice fielding questions about it when you promote the book."

Lydia smiled, pushing back her damp hair over her shoulder and reaching for another piece of orange. She looked at it for a moment and then raised her eyes to look at Gary. "How old are you again?" she said.

"Forty-two," he said. "Forty-three in—"

"November," she said. "Yes, I know." She dropped her hand to her lap, balancing the orange on her knee. "Gary."

"Yes?"

They were looking into each other's eyes. "I'm not really thirty-nine," she said. Pause. "I'm forty-two."

After a moment, still looking into her eyes, he said, "Are you sure you want to tell me you're forty-two?"

She winced slightly. "Why? Do you think I'm lying?"

"Well," he said, smiling, "I think you're careful."

"Oh, you," she sighed, dropping her eyes. "Okay," she said then. She looked up. "I'm forty-three—now you know. And I'll be forty-four—"

"In July, I know." He touched her arm. "Thanks for trusting me," he said softly.

"And I do," she said, covering his hand with hers. "I do trust you, Gary."

They sat there, hand over hand, looking at each other.

"Señora," Gracia said, standing in the doorway with a tray, "I have brought you some hot chocolate."

"For Gary, you mean," Lydia said, quickly withdrawing her hand and returning her attention to the trunk. "You know I can't eat chocolate."

"No, señora," Gracia said, smiling, coming in with a tray, "I have some hot chocolate for you—there is no real chocolate in it, but what is in it is very much like it and is very good, yes, it is, I promise."

Lydia turned around, looking interested.

"And I have some other wonderful things," Gracia continued, bending to show Lydia her creation. It indeed looked wonderful. A hot steaming mug of something that looked like hot chocolate with something that looked like whipped cream on it, all sitting prettily on a doily in a saucer, a teaspoon and linen napkin lying beside it.

Lydia leaned over and sniffed it. "And what's that lethal-looking stuff?" she asked, looking at the other mug, which had some sort of gunky brown stuff in it.

"That is real chocolate," Gracia said. "That is for Señor Steiner."

Lydia examined both mugs again and, apparently convinced that she was indeed getting the better bargain of the two—Gary's had no special little doily and special teaspoon or linen napkin or anything—she accepted her "hot chocolate" with a murmured, "You are so very good to me, Gracia. Thank you. I appreciate it."

"You're very welcome, señora," Gracia said, turning to serve Gary his mug.

"Thanks, Gracia," he said.

"Mmm, this is delicious," Lydia said, tasting hers. "What did you say it was again?"

"I did not say, señora," Gracia said. "Under the advisement of Señorita Weston. She says if I am ever to write the Benedict Canyon cookbook, I must stop giving away my secrets."

They laughed.

Gracia bent over to pick something out of the trunk and before Gary could see what it was, she had put it on her tray, shielding it from view. "This does not belong in here," she said, walking to the door.

"What doesn't?" Lydia said absently, focused on her drink.

"What was that, a photograph, Gracia?" Gary said.

Gracia stopped in the doorway, but did not turn around.

Puzzled, Gary looked to Lydia.

"Gracia," Lydia said, "what is it?"

"An old photo, señora," Gracia said, moving on into the hall, "which I will put in your room."

"Maybe we should look at it for the book," Gary said. He turned back around to look at Lydia.

Her eyes were down on her mug and she was shaking her head. "It's probably an old boyfriend or something. I don't think she wants you to see it."

Gary looked at her, not understanding. "Why?"

"Oh, I don't know," Lydia sighed, putting her mug and spoon down.

She did know. He knew she did. What could that picture have been? Who could have been in Lydia's past that he didn't know about already?

Gary put his mug down and moved closer to her. "Lyddie," he said gently, brushing a lock of hair back off her forehead, "what's wrong?"

"I don't know," she said, closing her eyes and shaking her head. "All the talk about the past, I guess." She opened her eyes and he saw the tears that were there. "I do love you, Gary," she said.

He blinked. There was a very different sound to this. It was different in a way that called back a long, long time ago. A way that he had been trying to banish from his mind, but which kept coming back, again and again. "And God knows," he said, taking her hand, "I love you." After a moment, he brought her hand up to his mouth and kissed it.

"I'm scared," she whispered.

"Don't be," he whispered.

"But there are things I have to tell you," she said, swallowing. "And I can't—not yet. I need time."

His heart was pounding.

"Can you wait?" she whispered. "Can you be patient?"

He nodded. "As long as it takes—I mean it."

She closed her eyes and a tear spilled down over one cheek.

He wiped it away with his hand. "Lyddie?"

She opened her eyes.

"Do you want me to leave now?"

"Would you mind?" she whispered. "I'd like some time alone."

"No," he said. "I understand." He hesitated and then leaned forward slightly, and then she leaned forward the rest of the way. They kissed, softly, their lips barely touching. And then they parted, looking at each other a moment longer.

Gary smiled, reached for his mug, and stood up. "Back to work tomorrow, I guess, or Kate will have our heads."

Lydia sniffed and smiled. "Tomorrow."

"Tomorrow," he repeated, and walked to the door.

"Gary," she said.

He turned around.

"You should know," Lydia said, "that I'm really forty-four."

He smiled. Broadly. "I know," he said.

— *35* —

After all these years he didn't even bother saying it. He simply took the broom out of Kate's hands and demonstrated the way he preferred to see people sweep the garden walk, the systematic cleaning, line by line, of each row of brick, rather than the swish-swash-every-which-way method of Kate's. If Dr. Weston had said it, it would have sounded like this: "Katherine, if you sweep in one direction, you move the dirt in one direction, and everything will be neat and tidy and the refuse will end up in the garbage, not in the garden." And then Kate would have said, "I know, Dad, but dirt belongs with dirt—this is silly throwing away dirt that's only blown out of the garden," knowing full well that what her father meant as refuse were the pieces of dead leaves and stalks, and that he hated to have bits of dead leaves and stalks swept back into the garden, even if he couldn't see them, because he was, after all, a surgeon.

Right.

It was always like this at home in Windy Hills. Her father pretty much ignored Kate until the second she decided to do something. Then he couldn't get close enough. Thus far today Kate had made coffee incorrectly, Kate had emptied the dishwasher incorrectly, Kate had held the newspaper incorrectly, and Kate, her father was sure, must make Harris crazy by replacing the toilet paper in the bathroom so that the end came out the bottom. (Harris and Kate wisely did not say anything about how, after she had moved in with Harris, she had been told to do it this way because it was the way Harris preferred it.)

Kate had thought a reprieve was coming in the afternoon, when her father was to take Harris to play a short nine holes, but then her brother-in-law, Sissy's husband, Steve, called for a game and Dr. Weston generously allowed those two to go ahead and play a full eighteen. "You boys should know each other better," Dr. Weston had said, patting Harris on the back. "Steve's on the membership committee and we're thinking a golf membership would perhaps be a good wedding present for you. Then you could come out and play anytime—bring some of your clients."

"A lot of my clients already belong to your club," Harris said.

"Good boy," Dr. Weston said, patting him again on the back.

And so Harris had gone off to the club with Steve, wearing his pale-blue-and-lime plaid golfing shorts and pale blue shirt. He looked good. He certainly looked right for the Windy Hills Country Club. Kimberly, in the meantime, had offered to take Kate with her to the hairdresser and then to some shops around town on errands, but Dr. Weston announced that he was sure Kate wanted to stay home and read. And so Kate said thank you, but she thought she'd stay home and read a manuscript.

As soon as Kimberly left, Dr. Weston had gone into his study. Kate had waited around in the kitchen for a half hour or so, wondering if her father wanted her to come in, or wait for him or what, but when he didn't reappear she knew he was busy doing something and that he had not wanted to spend time with her, he had simply wanted to know that Kate was around, that she hadn't left.

He was like that, her father. When he was around, he liked people to be around. But he didn't want to have to talk to them or anything.

And so Kate had put on her bathing suit and gone out on the back terrace, catching some rays, reading a manuscript, and finally, not being able to stand it anymore, went to the garage to get a broom and sweep the brick path that wound through Kimberly's cutting garden. (Kate was not without neat and tidy inclinations of her own. Perhaps it was genetic?) The minute she had started sweeping, however, her father appeared to supervise, and here they were now.

Dr. Weston handed the broom back to Kate. For seventy-nine, he was in incredibly good shape. He had worn glasses all the time after about age sixty-five, but his eyesight was still pretty good. He was still operating, at any rate. "Maybe time you got a bathing suit that was more appropriate for your age," he said.

Immediately Kate felt the urge to sock him. She had grown up with this urge, to one day just haul off and smack her father when he used that tone of voice with her. The criticism, the judgment, the constant tone of disapproval. "I don't wear this in public, Dad," Kate said, knowing she had been a fool to bring out this two-piece, even though her father had seen her wear one for years and years.

"I would hope not," he said. He gestured to the broom. "Sweep, sweep. You started the job, now finish it."

Kate started to sweep, trying to be "systematic and neat and orderly" about it, feeling horribly uncomfortable because she knew her father was watching her, judging her, not only her sweeping, but for herself, her thirty-three-year-old unmarried self in a two-piece bathing suit, judging her weight, judging her fitness, judging her attractiveness.

"Dad, could you please go watch something else while I finish this up?" she finally said, stopping again and turning around to look at him.

"Finish up? Why, you haven't even started." He turned around and pointed. "I thought you were going to do the terrace—that needs sweeping too. Harris is here and I thought you wanted the place to look nice."

Kate looked at him. And then she smiled. "Yes, I do, Dad. So I'll do just that." Pause. "So why don't you bring out a chair and talk to me while I do it?"

"Oh, no," Dr. Weston said quickly, "I have work to do inside."

Works every time, Kate thought to herself.

Theirs was a wonderful old house and Kimberly had done much to brighten it up. She was thirteen years younger than Dr. Weston and although she had been a widow with three grown children of her own when they married, she was then—and still was now—younger than springtime in spirit.

There was one room in the house that still remained largely unused, however. A bedroom. Upstairs. Kimberly had it completely redone, with yellow-and-white wallpaper, white lacy curtains, a king-sized bed with a handmade cotton quilt spread, and other lovely pieces of furniture. The shades were never closed and sunlight streamed in for most of the afternoon, more often than not glinting off the brass fender set surrounding the white marble fireplace. It was a very beautiful, appealing room. Still, though, the only time it was used was when Kimberly could pack it with happy, laughing little grandchildren. Otherwise, it was never used.

It was the room where Kate's mother had died.

Kate sat down on the bed and looked around. This room sure had changed. In her mother's day it had largely been red and was almost always dark because her mother would draw the red velvet drapes against the light.

It was strange how the light had become an enemy to her mother toward the end, the sun that her mother had always loved before, craved to have streaming into the house. ("How many times do I have to tell you?" Kate remembered her father yelling when she was little, when he found all the drapes open in the living room during the day. "It fades the carpets and ruins the furniture! If you want sunlight, go outside!")

She had worn sunglasses all the time near the end. Kate remembered that. One morning she remembered laughing at her mother for wearing sunglasses in the kitchen. Her mother had said her eyes hurt. Kate believed her and stopped laughing, because her mother had taken off her glasses and her eyes had looked like two hot burning coals, killing her. She talked of pressure behind her eyes, of steel rods burning through her brain; some afternoons she talked of dying of some horrible disease, which was why she couldn't go to the doctor about it, didn't Kate understand? The doctor would send her away, send her away to a hospital, and Kate wouldn't like that, would she? Or would she rather go live with her father in New York and be with that woman?

What woman her mother had always talked about, Kate had never really been sure. Matt said their father had had mistresses, none of them serious, simply local outlets near the hospital in the city to relieve pressure. Their father did not drink, after all. Not at all. So it was all very strange why he was under pressure and didn't drink and Mom was supposedly a lady of leisure and drank all the time. But her father stayed away and Kate came eventually not to care much about what he did or did not do.

Then there was the day Kate had come home from school to find her mother lying unconscious on the living room floor. At first she had thought someone murdered her and had run over to her. Her mother had groaned and rolled over, then, and sat up, rubbing her eyes, and then she had proceeded to vomit all over Kate and herself. That was the first time, Kate thought, the gray veil had come—that wonderful gray veil of numbness that descended over her when things were just too horrible to be fully comprehended, that wonderful gray veil that allowed Kate to go on, mechanically, as if nothing had happened.

She remembered walking out of the living room that afternoon, letting her mother fend for herself, stripping her own clothes off in the laundry room and getting into the shower. Then she took her time getting dressed in her room, and she stayed in her room, reading, for one, maybe two hours, and then her mother appeared at the door. Kate's strategy had worked. Mom was unwell still but okay and on her feet; there was no trace of sickness on her or in the living room and even Kate's clothes by that time had been sudsing merrily along in the washer.

It never happened. Her father would not be needed after all.

Another afternoon Kate ran in the house to ask if she could play next door and found her mother repotting plants in the kitchen. At least, that was what she was trying to do. Still in her nightgown at three in the afternoon, she was sobbing over a broken pot, and potting soil was all over the kitchen table and floor. A glass was there beside her, a glass with water in it? The gray veil dropped; Kate went back outside and told her friend she couldn't come and play, she had to go shopping with her mother. And so Kate went back inside and went to her room and read all afternoon, waiting for her mother to appear at her door to signal she had pulled herself together.

It didn't get better. Dr. Weston came home one weekend, toward the end, and Kate had awakened because her father was screaming at her mother. He had found a vodka bottle stashed under a cushion in *his* study! "What do you want me to do, bring Kate in here and show her what her mother is?"

"No!" her mother had wailed. "Please, Arthur, please!"

"Please, what? You're the one who's doing all the drinking."

"I can't help it!"

"Of course you can help it—you just want to destroy everything!"

"If you were here, maybe—"

"Lies, lies, lies, I'm sick of your lies, Elizabeth. What am I going to do with you? Lock you away? Handcuff you to the bed? Put you in an insane asylum?"

"Please, Arthur, please," her mother sobbed.

"Get this thing out of here," her father ordered, and there was a crash and the sound of glass breaking and a wail from her mother. Her father said something, her mother cried again, and then there was murmuring, soft voices. And then Dr. Weston came out of his study and tripped over Kate. "Go back to bed, everything's fine," he said to her.

But Kate hadn't moved. And Dr. Weston had gone into the hall linen closet and rumbled around in the boxes he kept on the top three shelves and then brought something back to the study. "Your mother isn't well, I'm going to give her some medicine," he said. "Now go back to bed, Katherine."

And Kate had. In a manner of speaking. She had curled up on the floor of her room, holding herself and pressing her forehead against the carpet. She didn't know why she did this except it felt better than anything else. And she had stayed like that, thinking, *This is what's happening, Mom is drinking, that's what's the matter, Dad said so.* And Kate wondered what she was supposed to do. You were supposed to do something when someone drank. Somewhere she had heard that. But who was she supposed to tell? Mrs. Potter at school? But Dad knew and if he didn't do anything, who would? The minister? Could she call up Reverend Walker and tell him? But how? Her mother would kill her for telling on her—and so would her father.

"The victorious Arnold Palmer Pondfield is home!" Harris called in the front hallway of the house.

Startled, Kate jumped to her feet and looked around. She realized she was crying and hurried into the bathroom to wash her face.

They had drinks in the sun room before going to the club for dinner. Harris made them at the bar. White wine and Perrier for Kimberly, mineral water and lemon for Dr. Weston, a scotch and water for Harris, a vodka tonic for Kate. It was pleasant. Kimberly always made things pleasant; she had this marvelous way of simply rising above Dr. Weston's comments and judgments.

But her father was always pretty good around Harris. Finally Kate had his complete approval on something. Oh, he didn't approve of Harris's having an ex-wife and children, but of everything else he did.

"You should have seen him, Arthur," Harris said. "There we were, standing at the eighth hole, and I say to Steve, 'Nice thought, but I'm afraid that's not your ball. Yours is over there somewhere.' 'Well, whose is this?' he says, and a voice from nowhere comes, 'It's mine and I'll thank you not to touch it.' "

Hahahahahaha.

"What is that you're wearing?" Dr. Weston suddenly said to Kate.

"What, this?" Kate said, standing to show him the dress. It was short.

"Harris gave it to her," Kimberly said quickly, knowing that Dr. Weston was about to say something awful.

"I like the dress," her father said, "but I'm not sure it looks right on you, Katherine. Are you gaining weight?"

"Would you like me to change, Dad?"

"No, no, you don't have to," he said.

Harris glanced at Kate and said, "I think she looks fabulous."

"Well then, by all means wear what you're wearing," Dr. Weston said. "I only thought it looked—well, never mind."

"I think Kate looks lovely," Kimberly said.

"But maybe your father thinks it's a little much for the club," Harris said to Kate.

Kate looked at him. Blink. "I thought you were pleased I was wearing it," she finally said.

"I am," Harris said.

"It is a little much for the club, I think," Dr. Weston said. "I haven't seen any dresses like that on any of our friends."

"I disagree," Kimberly started to say, "I think it's—"

"I'll go change," Kate said.

"You don't have to," Kimberly said.

"Kimberly, if she wants to change, let her change," Dr. Weston said. "She'll feel more comfortable if she's dressed properly."

The Westons, it was clear, had told everyone they knew at the club that Kate's fiancé was coming to dinner with them. At least twenty people stopped by their table to congratulate Kate and meet Harris. It was, after all, quite an event. Of all her parents' friends' children over age twenty-five, Kate was the only one who hadn't married yet. This was a social triumph for the Westons then, of sorts, at last closing the chapter on Kate—the only remaining worry whether or not the *New York Times* would say that Harris's first marriage had ended in divorce. A friend of Dr. Weston's had told him Harris's first marriage was on the data bank at the *Times*. But this, Dr. Weston assured Kimberly, who assured Kate, was something he felt confident he could remedy.

She played tennis with Harris early Sunday morning and went out to breakfast. At the restaurant they ran into people they knew, clients of Harris's; it was pleasant.

When they got home they found Kimberly and Dr. Weston and some lady named Harriet who organized weddings sitting in the sun room, calendars in hand. Dates, dates—they needed to settle on firm dates today. No excuses, let's go: engagement party; wedding; reception; honeymoon, the whole bit. What days could Kate meet Kimberly in the city to look for a wedding dress? Bridesmaids—

"Sherry *Berman Meyer* is going to be the matron of honor?" Dr. Weston said. "What about your sister?"

"She'll be a bridesmaid. Like I was in her wedding," Kate said.

Dr. Weston looked at Kimberly.

"And I'd like Lucy and Anne to be bridesmaids too," Kate said, looking at Kimberly. Lucy and Anne were Kate's stepsisters.

Dr. Weston looked at Harris. "Who is your best man?"

"John Halifent, a longtime friend," Harris said. "And, of course," he quickly added, "I'd like Matt and Steve to be ushers. And my brother, Jim."

"We're hoping Peter would sing," Kate said to Kimberly, speaking of her stepbrother. "And I thought Chrissy could be a flower girl, and little Stevie the ring bearer."

"That would be lovely," Kimberly said.

"And Sherry Berman Meyer will be your matron of honor," Dr. Weston repeated.

Kimberly said to Harris, "What about your children, Harris? Would they like to come?"

Harris smiled. "It's a nice thought, but I'd rather not risk it. They might get upset."

"Where does Sherry Berman Meyer live?" Dr. Weston asked Kate.

"Greenwich, Dad, with her husband and children."

"Greenwich," Dr. Weston repeated, frowning.

"Excuse me," Kate said, quickly rising from her seat. "I'll be right back." And then she ran upstairs, Harris coming quickly after her.

"Don't explode, Kate, don't explode," he urged her, whispering, reaching her in the hall.

"I could kill him," she said. "I don't care how much he knocks me, but God damn it—if he says one more word about Sherry—"

"He won't, he won't," Harris whispered, taking her into his arms. "It's okay, Kate. It will all go fine."

"He's such a stuck-up, bigoted, goddamn asshole jerk!" she hissed. "No wonder he drove my mother crazy. Who could live with him?"

Pause. "Kimberly can," Harris pointed out.

Kate frowned. This was not the response she had expected. Or wanted.

They caught the four-forty train back to New York. They sat in a two-seater and Harris sat on the aisle and did the *Times* crossword puzzle while Kate sat with a P. D. James novel in her lap, head against the glass of the window, looking at the green of Fairfield County flashing by. The train stopped in Darien and more people got on, people, Kate thought, who looked an awful lot like them—except younger. At thirty-three and forty-three, Kate knew, she and Harris were a little old still to be living in New York. That is, if one were to have a family. These riders on the trains were young at the game of New York. And those who weren't were merely invited out by married friends.

Kate closed her eyes, head rattling against the glass, and she thought, *Why do I feel so unhappy? Why do I feel like there is nothing to look forward to? Why do I feel like it's all over, everything's at an end?* She opened her eyes and watched the passing trees. And then she closed her eyes again and remembered a version of a prayer she had once read. *Dear God,* she said inside her head, *please help me to do your work and your will. And please help me, God, to know what that is—to know why I am here on this earth and what it is I'm supposed to do.*

There. If He couldn't help her, no one could.

— *36* —

"Lydia's decided we're going out tonight," Noél reported to Gary, "you, me, Lydia, and Skip. Chasen's at eight and the Cinegrill for the ten-thirty show. We're supposed to be surprised and delighted."

Gary smiled. "And aren't you?"

"I told her I had nothing to wear to go out with such a big star," Noél explained, "but we seem now to have that under control. Chico's coming over from wardrobe to whip me up in TV star–like fashion."

Gary laughed. He was happy. It sounded like a wonderful idea.

Gary and Skip arrived together at Lydia's at seven, officially rang the doorbell, and were greeted by Gracia, dressed this evening in a long-sleeved blue gown. She showed them into the front living room—the really formal one, with the Victorian sofas—and Imelda appeared, first to offer iced cocktails—an exotic planter's punch, sans alcohol of course—and then three rounds of equally exotic hors d'oeuvres. Gracia then reappeared, trotting in her grandchildren and their friends to say hello.

It was a tradition around the Southland home that when the señora was looking forward to going out and having a really good special time, that Gracia was to bring her grandchildren over here, with one friend each, to have a really good special time, too. The children were allowed to slam old tennis balls in an effort to play tennis, use the swimming pool if it was warm enough, cook hot dogs and hamburgers outside, romp downstairs in the playroom and play with anything they found down there, and, closing the evening, watch a video on the big TV, complete with freshly popped popcorn.

Gracia's grandson, Billy, was almost ten now and a really nice boy, a little quiet maybe, but smart and athletic (Gary had taken him to Little League practice a couple of times). Cathy—or Catalina as her grandmother called her—was seven and a veritable little chatterbox. The children had come to Los Angeles from Mexico City to live with Gracia a little over five years ago, shortly after Gracia had begun working for Lydia. Their parents, evidently, were dead.

Actually, the past and present of Gracia and her grandchildren were still somewhat of a mystery to Gary. He *assumed* Billy and Cathy's parents were dead, because the rare time Gracia ever spoke of them it was in the past tense. And how Gracia could afford the nice, neat little house and yard she maintained in nearby West Hollywood for the three of them and the private schools the kids attended was utterly beyond him. But then, of course, when one remembered the wild card in the game called Lydia, it all made perfect sense.

Billy and Cathy had very nearly no accent now, although they did crisscross back and forth from English to Spanish effortlessly, something their grandmother encouraged. They had the classic good looks of Mexico, too, but in all other aspects were thoroughly Americanized, bordering on preppie elite. And their friends! Another mystery. The boy Billy was introducing to Gary was named Jackie Smaltzen, and Gary *knew* he had to be Jack Smaltzen the movie director's son.

Lydia made her entrance at seven-twenty, her usual breathtaking self, sweeping into the living room in a white silk number, but she waved off the men's compliments, urging them to wait and see who was coming in behind her. And then Noél made her entrance and Gary and Skip broke out into whistles and applause. Lydia and Chico had made her into a kind of tidier, younger, and slimmer Ann-Margret in a wonderful green dress that somehow enhanced Noél's red hair.

"Hubba-hubba," Gary said, showing Ms. Shaunnessy to a seat.

"But am I devastating?" Noél wanted to know, sitting down and turning to Skip. "I always wanted to be devastating."

"You're devastating," Skip assured her, straightening his tie. (Skip had just been telling Gary that his wife had been a little wary about this outing. "Some AA function," she had said, "Chasen's and the Cinegrill with Lydia Southland, who's not even in the program.")

Lydia was just standing there, sipping the punch Imelda had brought her, beaming over the top of her glass at Noél.

"I don't look like a whore, do I?" Noél asked her.

Lydia nearly choked on her punch, laughing. "Darling," she managed to get out, "you've never looked so elegant in all your life. This is what it means to be a lady—in a very glamorous way."

"Then why do you keep smiling at me like that?" Noél said.

Lydia looked surprised. And then a little hurt. She turned to Gary. "I'm only smiling because I'm proud of her."

"For what?" Noél said. "All I did was sit there and get 'done' by you guys."

Lydia looked at her. "I'm proud of you, Noél," she said, "because you're you again—your own person." She paused and then raised her glass. "To Noél."

"To Noél," everybody said, raising their glass.

"Oh, little señora," came a sigh from the doorway.

Everyone turned to look. Gracia was standing there, weeping, dabbing her eyes with a tissue. "I am so proud of you," she said.

Noél looked around the room. "What's going on around here?"

A limousine drove them to Chasen's on Beverly Boulevard. At the front door, under the awning, a lone photographer dawdled, waiting to see who would emerge from the car. Gary got out first, turning around then, holding his hand out to Lydia.

She took it and her eyes met his and something went through him.

A flash went off. "Miss Southland," the photographer said, "hi! It's Greg Blynn from *Shooting Star.*"

"You are not," Lydia told the photographer, getting out of the car. "You're that guy Scowlski or something—the one who sold that picture of me looking so awful to the *Enquirer.* You made me look like I was a hundred and nine."

The guy was caught. "Uh," he said, back-pedaling, blocking the way into the restaurant, "Skalchi's the name. Jim Skalchi. Let bygones be bygones, okay, Miss Southland? Come on, pose for one with your boyfriend? I've got to make a living too."

"Okay," Lydia said, putting her arm through Gary's and pulling him close. They smiled. The flash went off.

He dropped the camera on the strap around his neck and whipped out a pad and pen from his jacket pocket. "Name?" Skalchi said, letting them pass.

"Bernard Kleindorf," Lydia said, pulling Gary along into the restaurant. "B-e-r-n-a-r-d-k-l-e-i-n-d-o-r-f. Make sure you get it right—a portrait painter from Heidelberg."

"Thanks, Miss Southland," Skalchi said, jotting this information down. "You won't regret it."

"Well aren't you going to take my picture?" Noël wanted to know.

"Who are you?" Skalchi said, looking at her over his pad.

"I'm Helen Hatter," Noël said. "I'm starting on the new season of 'Cassandra's World.' "

"That's right," Lydia called back. "Helen Hatter."

"And this is my husband Matazza," Noël said, gesturing to Skip.

Dutifully Mr. Skalchi wrote this information down and then took Helen's picture with her husband, Matazza Hatter.

"Mrs. Southland, hello, hello, your table is of course ready for you—right this way," the maître d' said to Lydia, showing her the way. As soon as Lydia entered the green-and-red main dining room, the diners looked up, put their eating utensils down, and began to applaud. Three men stood up. Such was the respect for the star of a hit TV show. Lydia paused a moment, smiled and nodded in humble acknowledgment, and then continued on her way.

The maître d' led them to the back terrace, to a large round table tucked in the corner. Gary at first thought the maître d' was making a mistake because there were already two people sitting at the table— but no, apparently it was no mistake, because Lydia was soon kissing both the man and woman hello. She turned and made introductions all around.

Evidently they were having dinner with Lise and Manny Kellerman, the executive producers and creators of last year's surprise hit sitcom, "Kelly Girls."

Gary recognized their names, naturally, but he also recognized Lise as simply "Lise" from an AA meeting near his house in Pacific Palisades. She had been sober a long time—eleven, twelve years. He had had no idea that "Lise" was the Lise who had created "Kelly Girls" any more than she had known that "Gary" was Gary Steiner, head writer and story editor of "Cassandra's World." Such was the world of AA.

Gary said hello, waiting to see if Lise wanted to acknowledge their having met before. Gary was always very careful to respect anonymity when meeting someone again in the outside world.

"I think we've met before, Gary," Lise said, shaking his hand.

"Yes, we have," Gary said, letting her know that it was okay with him.

Lise went on to shake hands with Noél and Skip, neither of whom she seemed to recognize. Apparently they had not crossed paths at meetings; Gary would not say anything to either one of them then.

Introductions complete, they sat down for a wonderful meal. Lydia had chicken; Noél and Lise had spinach salads; all three men had steaks. As dinner went on, Gary noticed how Lise and Manny's attention seemed to be focused on talking to Noél. And then he noticed how Lydia kept steering the conversation back to Noél, who handled it all very well. (Noél liked attention.) She related stories about early production problems on "Cassandra's World," about some of the problems she saw with the show now, about loving having worked with Lydia all this time; but—when asked by Manny—she admitted that she missed production.

There was nothing unusual in the exchange, except it did seem a little odd to Gary that with the star, producer, and story editor of "Cassandra's World" all sitting there that Lise and Manny might have asked one of *them* how they thought the show was going.

When coffee was served, Manny turned to Lydia and said, "You're right, Lydia. She's smart, funny, and charming."

"And capable," Lydia said. "A little rusty, but the best."

Noél blinked. "I beg your pardon?" she said to Lydia.

"Noél," Lise said, "Lydia told us that you turned Pallsner down about coming back to 'Cassandra's World.' " She smiled. "I can't say that I blame you."

Noél blinked again, expression unreadable.

"Max tells us you'd be quite an addition to our lot," Lise continued.

"Max did," Noél said.

Gary finally understood what was going on. "We wanted her back for good reason," he told Manny. "Her strength, you know, is getting the cast and crew psyched. They'd do anything for her. And with some of the morale problems we've had of late . . ."

Manny nodded and turned to Noël. "Holly Montvale also gave us a big recommendation," he said.

Pause. "Recommendation as what?" Noël said.

Gary laughed and Lydia kicked him.

"She's very good with the talent," Skip said.

"I'll say," Gary said. This time Noël kicked him.

"She's been indispensable to me, as you know," Lydia said, sipping her coffee. She put her cup down. "She's also been incredible on my book—she's gifted when it comes to working with writers."

"Yes, she is," Gary said.

Manny cleared his throat. "We have a pretty full slate, Noël, but Lydia said you might consider joining us—in a lesser capacity than you're used to, I'm afraid—but she said you might consider it since you'd be making the switch to half-hour comedy. It's a different beast, you know. And with a live audience—"

"I don't know," Skip said, leaning forward to look past Noël at Lydia, "I think Noël could do more with us at 'Cassandra's World.'" He looked over at Manny. "Sorry, but I do have a show of my own to look after."

"But Lydia said Noël turned Pallsner down," Lise pointed out.

"Pallsner is not necessarily the last word at Bestar," Gary said.

Everyone looked at him. This was a lie and they all knew it.

"Where Noël is concerned," he added, "Lydia has the final say."

"But you're leaving at the end of next season, aren't you?" Lise said.

"Yes," Lydia said. "That's why I'd rather see Noël with your outfit."

Gary got the picture now. The Kellermans were angling to sign Lydia for when she left "Cassandra's World." Lydia was angling to get them to offer Noël a job now. And Gary had a feeling that Lydia also probably knew that Lise had been sober a long, long time, because the job, as the Kellermans had described, would be for Noël to work as Lise's right arm.

Yes, it was all making sense now.

Yes, it would be a wonderful opportunity for Noël.

No, Gary had never loved Lydia more.

"I'm so happy I won't be mad at you for being so devious and mean and horrible to me in the process!" Noël said in the limo, throwing herself at Lydia to hug her.

Noél had herself a job. In a month she'd be starting as an associate producer on "Kelly Girls."

"I'm so proud of you," Lydia said, patting her back. "You handled the evening beautifully."

Noél threw herself back against the seat and looked at Gary. "I did, didn't I? Don't tell me I have my brains back?"

"They're back," Gary assured her, opening the limo bar. He pulled out a bottle of Loka sparkling water. "Time to celebrate."

"Time to call Gracia and tell her the news," Noél said, reaching for the phone. She punched in the number and turned to look at Lydia. "She knew, didn't she?"

Lydia smiled. "She knew," she said.

The Hollywood Roosevelt Hotel was finished shortly before the crash of 1929, was closed in 1984, and reopened in 1986, completely renovated to its original plush art deco grandeur. The Cinegrill, the hotel's nightclub, was a throwback to when nightlife was truly glamorous, and this evening it was glamour on high again since Ann Hampton Callaway was in from New York to perform. The place was packed; with Lydia heading the procession, they were snaked through to the very front, to the lone empty table that had been held for them. There were excited whispers and murmurs as they made their way through; Lydia smiled slightly and nodded to people who caught her eye.

"Uh-oh," Lydia said after she was seated, "that guy James Spada's here, the biographer."

Gary turned around. "Where?"

"Over there. The cute one with the beard. Who's smiling. At me. Oh, well," she sighed, eyes returning to the table, "I guess I'll just have to be on my best behavior so he won't have anything to write about."

"He writes books about legends," Noél said, "so I hardly think you have anything to worry about."

Lydia looked at her. "Are you perhaps implying that I'm not a legend?"

"I don't think you're Marilyn Monroe or Princess Grace yet, if that's what you're asking. I mean," Noél added a second later, "you're not dead yet or anything."

"Oh, I'm not dead yet," Lydia repeated. "Noél, dear, shall we continue this discussion, or should we merely be grateful that you've found another means of employment?"

They ordered drinks—a glass of champagne for Lydia, grapefruit juice and mineral water for Skip, a café au lait for Noél, and a glass of tonic water for Gary—and after they were delivered, the lights lowered and the cabaret star was introduced.

Ann Hampton Callaway was a tall, very beautiful young woman who dressed the torch singer part to the hilt. At times in her act she was hilariously funny, but first and foremost she was a singer extraordinaire, capable of warming the coldest heart with songs of love, capable of breaking the strongest heart with songs of love now lost.

After opening with a jazzy, swinging number that had the whole club clapping, Callaway smiled slightly and then started to sway, slowly, as her accompanist started the piano intro into what Gary just knew was going to be a wrist slasher. He had heard Callaway before, at the Algonquin in New York, and there was good reason, he knew, that they called her the Dangerous Diva. First she had you laughing, then she had you crying.

With a voice of incredible purity, Callaway held the club mesmerized as she sang,

> *How do I trust my heart*
> *when it tells me that you're the one?*
> *Whatever brought us together*
> *is also keeping us apart*
> *how do I trust this ache inside my heart?*

Gary felt Lydia's hand under the table. He turned to look at her. Her eyes were on Callaway, but her hand was finding its way into his.

Gary swallowed, turning back to the stage.

> *How do I find the way*
> *to show you that I love you?*

He felt Lydia squeeze his hand.

> *How do I find the strength*
> *to keep all my love inside?*

Gary squeezed Lydia's hand back and held it very, very tight.

"Kate's getting married, did I tell you?" Lydia said, sitting in the dark in one of the chairs by the pool.

It was nearly two in the morning. Skip was long gone; Noél had just gone to bed. They were drinking seltzer in the dark, Lydia sitting across from Gary, the cat in her lap and the dogs asleep at her feet. All was quiet except the hum of the pool filter.

"Noél told me," he said. He couldn't see Lydia's face. There was no moon tonight; there was only one light on in the living room and it was not enough to see her by. "She said you weren't thrilled about it."

"I'm not," she said. "I think she needs someone more . . . Well, an investment banker and Kate—I just don't see it." She sighed. "But what do I know?"

"A lot," Gary said. "At least now, I hope."

She laughed softly. There was the tinkle of ice as she sipped her seltzer. And then, "We have to go back to work soon—can you believe it?"

"I know," he said.

"You haven't even had a vacation," she said. "You've been working nonstop."

"So have you," he said.

"But it's my book," she said, "I'm supposed to work on it."

"I've enjoyed every moment of it," he said.

"Me too," she said. "Not the book so much, but being with you. Every day."

He swallowed. "That's what I meant, too." Pause. "Something has healed, hasn't it, Lyddie? In us, between us."

"Yes," she said. "But Gary—" She didn't finish.

"But what?" he said.

Pause. "Can you still be patient?" she said. "A little while longer? Until I get things sorted out on my end?"

"If you'll kiss me good night," he said.

"Of course I'll kiss you good night," she said, surprising him by jumping out of her chair—making the cat and the dogs jump, too. "It's okay," she told the animals, plunking her glass down on the table and moving toward Gary in a swish of silk. And then she was sitting in his lap, arms around his neck. "Okay, dear Gary," she said, and kissed him.

Really kissed him. In a way he didn't even remember from the old days.

And then she was up and out of his lap, walking into the house, whistling for the dogs to follow and psst-psst-psst-ing for the cat. "You'll lock up on your way out?"

"Yes," he said. "Good night, Lyddie. Thanks for the wonderful evening."

She was at the french doors. He saw her silhouette. "Thank you—for being so wonderful, period." She went into the house with the animals and closed the doors behind her.

He smiled, resettling in his chair, still not quite believing any of this yet. He sat there, recrossing his leg to the other knee, finishing off his seltzer, smiling in the dark.

"Psst," said a voice.

He turned.

"Does this mean," Noél's voice whispered from an upstairs window, "that I may be asked to move out sooner than expected?"

"You fuck!" Gary whispered up at the window, jumping up out of his chair.

"How else am I supposed to know what's going on around here?"

"By spying?" Gary hissed up at the window.

"You gotta admit," Noél whispered, "this would make a hell of a last chapter for her book—she falls for the writer at the end."

"I'm going to kill you," he promised.

"Well," she whispered, "I'm going to go to sleep now, so you'll have to kill me tomorrow." Pause. "Big Gare?"

"What?"

"I'd do anything for you—you know that, don't you?"

"Yes," he said.

"And I'd do anything for her," Noél said. "So I guess what I'm trying to say is that I'd do anything to see you guys together."

Gary smiled. "Me too."

— 37 —

She didn't know why she couldn't come. Harris had touched her everywhere; Harris had kissed her everywhere; Harris had been making love to her tonight for a long, long time.

And it wasn't working. He knew it, too, and had been holding back, hot, sweaty, determined, diligently carrying on, demonstrating incredible control, Kate thought, to say nothing of physical fitness.

She couldn't fake it, she just couldn't. But she knew Harris would not give up on her. He was like that. He wanted her to have everything he did, to get every ounce of it that he did.

But it wasn't working. And she was tired and sore and hot and detached.

And then her thoughts drifted to Mark.

And she thought of Mark. About Mark.

That night.

On the couch.

When he had pulled his pants down.

And in seconds she came—quickly, violently—and Harris said, "Oh, yes, yes, my love, your best ever," and then he came himself.

FOUR

Upheaval

It was a hell of a morning all round, so bad that by eleven o'clock even Sarah was slamming the phone down outside Kate's office, swearing under her breath.

If Sarah was losing her patience, things were not just bad, Kate knew, they had to be teetering on the disastrous.

"Kate," Sarah announced, appearing in her doorway, "the art department says no jacket revision on the Beauchamp book and that's final. If you want to fight about it, they say go fight with Rebecca."

"Okay, fine," Kate said, jumping out of her chair and sending it banging into the radiator, "I'll go fight with Rebecca."

"You have to fight with me first," came from the doorway behind Sarah. It was Dick Skolchak, the associate publisher, holding some papers in his hand. "I have a bone to pick with you, Kate."

"Oh, Dick," Kate sighed, "what would our relationship be without your bones?"

"It's about that car you rented in L.A.," Dick said.

"Oh, no!" Kate said, whirling around and throwing her arms over her head as if to protect herself. "Sarah, please—deal with him before I punch somebody."

"But Kate," Dick said with great determination, "you know you're only supposed to rent an economy car. You can't rent convertibles—"

"Kate paid for the difference between an economy car and the convertible," Sarah said, explaining it for the twentieth time. "They lost her check in accounting."

"Well, there's no record of payment here," Dick said, frowning, looking through the papers.

Kate remained standing, arms over her head, trying not to explode.

"I will give you a copy of the memo and the check she sent to accounting two months ago," Sarah said.

"Two months ago?" Dick said, looking confused. "It says here your expense account on American Express is way overdue. It says you haven't done your expenses in three months."

Kate remained standing, arms over her head.

"That's because Rebecca refused to approve the rest of Kate's expense account until the car rental matter was cleared up," Sarah said.

"But your card will get canceled," Dick said.

"Yes, we know," Sarah said.

Kate remained standing, arms over her head.

"Maybe you better write another check, Kate," he said to her.

"She did," Sarah said to him, "but accounting returned it, saying that Rebecca had frozen all matters regarding Kate's expense account until the matter of the car rental is cleared up."

"What are you doing for an expense account then?" Dick asked Kate.

"She's using her own money, waiting for someone to reimburse her," Sarah said. "Perhaps we could persuade you to sign—"

Dick sighed in frustration and walked out, muttering, "I don't know why your office always has so many problems, Kate."

Kate dropped into her chair and banged her forehead on her desk, making a muffled screaming sound in her throat. Sarah, at least, laughed a little. But Kate didn't.

It was unbelievable how many fights she was having in the company suddenly. Never, not once in twelve years in publishing, had she ever had bad in-house relations with other departments, and yet now she did. Even her editorial colleagues were starting to act funny around her because they knew Rebecca was gunning for her. They had seen Rebecca start "papering" a file on an editor before. And the worst part was that since Kate and Mark weren't talking, it looked as though Mark was distancing himself from Kate too, something all of editorial couldn't help but notice since the two had always been so close.

Well, Rebecca would not get her out of here easily, if at all. Kate had already talked to one of Harris's lawyers ("If he can break Texaco, he can advise you on dealing with Bennett, Fitzallen Coe," he assured her) and she had begun to "paper" a file of her own. There were ways, Kate was told, to protect herself. Perhaps more importantly, there were ways to get them to pay her for the trouble of leaving, if that's what she decided she had to do.

Yes, it was that bad.

But what would she do then? Work at another publishing house? She wasn't sure that she wanted to. The way things were going in the industry, it could be a little like changing seats on the *Titanic*. But was it really the industry that got her down? Or was it rather that she didn't like the kind of editor she had become in response to a changing industry?

Or the person she had become.

Or maybe had always been.

She just didn't know anymore. Not about any of it.

The day got worse. "N-O, no!" on a book she wanted to buy. Yelling from the managing editor about late title information sheets. Yelling from marketing for the catalog copy on a biography of Edith Wharton, copy Kate had said she would rewrite since theirs was so horrible. Yelling from the mail room because they didn't like the way Sarah stapled Jiffy bags (!?). Kate fled to lunch with an agent who lit into her about the new contracts at B, F & C and never stopped with complaints, not through lunch or coffee or the walk back uptown. "I have done books with Bennett, Fitzallen & Coe for twenty-one years," the agent said, "and I have tried to be patient, but Kate, I'd have to be mad to voluntarily do business with you people again."

Kate stopped, right there on the sidewalk at Columbus Circle. "Then mean what you say and stop selling to us. All of you. That's the only way anything will change. They just sit there and listen to your threats and say, 'Oh, they'll sell to us—they *have* to,' and sure enough, if you don't get the money you're looking for at the other houses, then there you are, back on our doorstep saying you'll make an exception this time. You're *all* making exceptions *all* the time. So stop it. Don't make exceptions. Mean what you say and effect a change."

The agent looked flabbergasted.

Kate sighed, turning to walk on, slinging her arm through the agent's like a comrade after a great war. "My bet is Rushman will be out within the year," she said, pulling the agent along. "But I'm afraid it's going to have to get worse to get better—it will take at least a year to undo what's being set into motion now." Her voice caught on the last word and she was embarrassed but not surprised that she felt like crying. It was treason, what she had just said. One could always criticize the house on the inside, but never *ever* did an editor badmouth her house to the outside world.

"I didn't know things were that bad," the agent finally said.

Kate didn't say anything and they continued walking. Outside the Anderson Building he gave Kate a hug. "I'm putting the word out that you're looking," he whispered.

On her way back to her office, Kate stopped in the marketing department to negotiate a truce over the Edith Wharton copy she hadn't rewritten yet, their version of which made the biography sound like a Jackie Collins novel of manners.

"Oh, that's all right, Kate," the marketing director told her. "The copy's been approved and sent out."

Kate felt her face flush hot. "Sent out where?"

"To the printer. Rebecca approved it."

"She approved that copy?" Kate said.

"Well," he said, sounding rather nasal, "she approved this." He handed her a piece of paper. "I can't guarantee it's whatever copy you're talking about."

Kate was about to explode, but she counted to three in her head, let her shoulders relax, and smiled. "Thank you," she said, and then she went on to her office, thinking of all the ways she would take out her revenge on that smug son of a bitch.

This is not helpful, Kate, she told herself. *Hating everyone in the company is not a way to fix this.*

"Get somebody to cover the phone and come into my office," Kate said to Sarah. "Now, posthaste, let's go." Kate went into her office, threw her purse down in the corner, and sat down at her desk with the catalog copy she had been given. In a moment Sarah came in, closing the door behind her. "Okay, come on," Kate said, "we've got to rewrite this thing and call it into the printer's. Who do we talk to in marketing?"

"Sid's office."

"I already talked to *him*. I mean, who actually gets things done?" Kate said, already penciling in changes in the copy. Then she made a little noise of horror and slashed a line through most of the rest of it. "You know, the hands-on person."

"Maki," Sarah said.

"And does Maki like us?" Kate asked, eyes still on the copy.

"Loves us after the ballet tickets we gave her."

Kate paused, looking up. "We gave her ballet tickets?"

"The ones you and Harris couldn't use while you were away."

Kate smiled. "God bless you, Sarah Steadwell." She resumed writing while Sarah called Maki and talked her into giving them the top-secret number of the person who could make changes at the printer. They finished rewriting the copy, read it aloud twice, and then Sarah called the new copy into the printer to replace what they had received.

"Okay, it's done," Sarah said, hanging up.

"Thank God," Kate said, sighing with relief.

"Kate," Sarah said then.

"Yes?"

"What are we going to do?"

Kate closed her eyes for a moment. "It's pretty bad, isn't it?"

"More than a little Kafkaesque if you ask me," Sarah said.

Kate smiled and opened her eyes. "I didn't know it was going to be like this when I hired you, Sarah. I swear I didn't."

"I know. No one did," Sarah said. "When I came here for the interview the guy in personnel told me you were going to be the next publisher."

"Who was that?"

"Harry."

"Oh, the one that got fired," Kate said. "Figures." They both laughed.

"I better get back outside," Sarah said, standing up. She started to move to the door, stopped, turned around, and came back. "Kate?" she said quietly.

Kate's eyebrows went up.

"What's happened with you and Mark?" In the next second Sarah apologized, saying it was none of her business, and Kate let it go at that—but Kate did notice that as Sarah asked about it, she had been looking at her engagement ring.

So Sarah knew. At the very least, she knew Mark used to live in her office, and that he hadn't come near it or her since she got engaged.

And God, Kate missed him.

And God, was Bennett, Fitzallen & Coe unbearable without him.

Before, they had always had their own little subdivision over here, their two offices, shielding each other against the rest of this depressing company. But now Kate was alone at B, F & C, and now Kate hated it at B, F & C. Without Mark, there was nothing here for her.

There was a knock at the door and before she had time to reply, speak of the devil, there he was, Mark. "Kate," he said, "I'm sorry, but it's important—I just saw this." He was walking over to her desk, carrying an afternoon edition of the *New York Post*.

"What is it?" Kate said.

"Lydia Southland's sister."

"Lydia doesn't have a sister," Kate said.

"Well, she does now and apparently she's dead," Mark said, placing the paper on the desk in front of her. The headline said:

TV STAR'S SISTER ONE OF L.I. DEAD

The half sister of beautiful TV star Lydia Southland was one of six people killed in Tuesday night's fiery crash on the Long Island Expressway, the Post has learned. Angela Clarke, 37, and her husband, Christopher, 41, were pronounced dead on the scene after the explosion of a Halycon Gas Truck near Exit 24 sent the couple's station wagon careening over the median into oncoming traffic. The Clarkes had been on their way home to Westhampton Beach after celebrating their fifteenth wedding anniversary in Manhattan.

"Oh, no" Kate said, turning the page. "Oh, no," she repeated.

"This is awful," Sarah said, reading over Kate's shoulder. "Poor Lydia."

"Kate," Mr. Rushman said, suddenly appearing in her doorway, "did you see this?" He was holding a copy of the *Post*.

"Mark just brought it in," Kate said.

"Does this mean the manuscript's going to be late?"

Kate looked at him.

"Kate," the head of publicity said, charging in through the door and nearly smashing into Mr. Rushman. "Whoops, sorry." She too was holding a copy of the *Post*, and Rebecca was right on her heels.

"Oh, hi, Mr. Rushman," Rebecca said. "You've seen it too." She looked at Kate. "So what's the story?"

"You know as much as I do at the moment," Kate said.

"You haven't talked to her yet?" Rebecca said.

"No," Kate said.

"Call her," Rebecca said.

Now Kate looked at her.

"Get fifty copies of the front page for the sales kits," Rebecca said to the publicist while waiting for Kate to respond. She turned back to Kate. "Well? What are we waiting for? Get on the phone—find out if this will affect the delivery of the manuscript. There isn't an hour of air in that production schedule."

"I can't call her two seconds after her sister died," Kate said.

"She died Tuesday," Rebecca said. "Look, Kate, we've got three hundred and fifty thousand advance orders for this book already—you've *got* to keep on top of this manuscript."

"I *am* on top of it," Kate said.

"How on top of it can you be," Rebecca said, "if the manuscript pages you showed us say she's an only child and here her sister's dead on the front page of the *Post?*"

She had Kate there.

Rebecca looked at Mr. Rushman. "This book has gotten way too complicated for Kate to handle."

"What?" Kate said, standing up.

"Your fact sheets are late, your expense account is all messed up, you've got to edit the Beauchamp manuscript," Rebecca said, not even bothering to look at Kate, but keeping her eyes on Mr. Rushman. "You're behind on everything, Kate, and we can't run the risk of the ball being dropped on this book—you need help."

"Help from who?" Kate said. "*You?*"

The tone of her voice made both Rebecca and Mr. Rushman look at her.

"Lydia fired Rebecca off the book in the first place," Kate reminded Mr. Rushman.

"Oh, that's right," he said, turning to look at Rebecca. "She won't work with you, will she?" His eyes moved on to Mark. "Can you help with the follow-up?"

"Yes, of course," Mark said without hesitation.

"Okay, Rebecca?" Rushman said.

Rebecca nodded, making a face indicating that Mark might be better than nothing, but clearly he was not the choice she had in mind.

"Thank you, Mr. Rushman," Kate said, "Mark would be an enormous help."

"All right," Rebecca said to Mark, "come to publicity with me."

"For what?" Kate said.

"For a meeting Mark is coming to," Rebecca said, "while you call Southland and find out what the status is on the manuscript."

"I'm not calling Lydia today!" Kate said.

"Tomorrow then, and no later," Rebecca said, walking out of the office. "Mark!"

"Coming," he said.

"So everything's under control," Mr. Rushman said to Kate.

"Yes, everything's under control," Kate said.

After he left, Kate whipped through her Rolodex, picked up the phone, and dialed a number. "Amoy Allen, please," she said. Pause. "Amoy? It's Kate Weston calling. Listen, I need a big favor. Could you find out how fast Crown could turn a four-hundred-fifty-page manuscript into a finished hardcover book and publish?" Pause. "Why?" A sigh. "Well, to be honest, I've got a big book in big trouble and I need something to compare the production schedule with that's being forced on me here." Pause. A smile. "Thanks, Amoy. Thanks a million."

— *39* —

The night the phone call had come from back east, Lydia had been on her way home from Denver, where she had hosted a fund-raiser for a pilot tutoring program for children.

"Oh, Gracia," Noél had said over the phone in a panic, "I didn't know Lydia had a sister—I thought it was some kind of a joke. I kept saying, 'Yeah, right, and your mother wears army boots.' But the police captain was for real—Lydia's the next of kin for this woman in Long Island. Oh, God, and it's so awful—the husband's dead too and there's a little girl. What do I do? Try and reach Lydia on the plane or at the airport? Her flight's supposed to get in around now."

"First you will calm down," Gracia instructed her, "and then you will call Señor Steiner and tell him what has happened. Then you will go downstairs and make a pot of tea and by that I time I will be there."

"But what if Lydia gets here?"

"Then you will do the right thing, little señora, and you will say the right thing, and you will be the right person to be there."

"Okay," Noél said, not sounding at all sure about this. "Gracia?" she said then. "Did you know Lydia had a sister?"

Gracia hesitated. "I knew there was a relative in Long Island."

Noél called Gary. He said he remembered something about someone out in Long Island, years ago, but he thought it had been a cousin of Lydia's or something. He asked when Lydia's flight was to arrive; Noél said right about now. He said he was on his way over.

Gracia arrived before Lydia, thank heavens, but not much before. She had only just joined Noél in the kitchen when the dogs started barking outside, signaling that Lydia's limousine was rounding the drive. It's always heartbreaking to see someone bounding in, flushed and happy with the events of her day, when one has to deliver some very bad news. There is the hesitation, then, on her part, the little flash of fear that crosses her eyes while her smile is still in place, somehow sensing that something is wrong.

"What is it?" Lydia said, dropping her bag.

"There was an accident in Long Island tonight, señora," Gracia said.

Lydia's face went white. "Not Allyson."

"No, señora," Gracia said gently, "but her mother and father."

Lydia swallowed. "Are they dead?"

"Yes, I'm sorry, señora."

"There was a trucking accident on the Long Island Expressway," Noël said. "They were killed instantly. They didn't know any pain. It happened just before midnight—their time. The police called less than an hour ago."

Lydia nodded absently, reaching—rather unsteadily—for a chair. Gracia helped her down into it. "Angie and Chris," Lydia said, folding her hands together in her lap.

The news was beginning to sink in.

"The police called," Noël said, "because you're listed as next of kin." She hesitated and then added, "The police captain didn't know how long he could keep that out of the papers—but he said for at least twenty-four hours he could. After that, he didn't know."

"Oh, God," Lydia said then, looking up at the ceiling, tears flooding her eyes, "that poor little girl, left all alone." In the next instant she was up and out of the chair, running through the swinging door. "Get me on the next flight to New York."

When Gary came through the gate he had to swerve to the side to avoid crashing into Lydia, who was barreling down the drive in her Mercedes. She stopped and rolled down her window, saying in a weird, strained voice, "I have to go, Gary, I've got a flight to New York to catch."

"You're going now?"

"I've got to go," she said, tears rising. She was rolling the window back up. Gary jumped out of his car and tried to open her door. It was locked.

"Lydia, open the door," he said.

She was moving the car ahead, saying something—words muffled inside the car—about having to go, having to go, she had to go to the airport.

"Open this door!" Gary yelled, pounding on the roof of the car.

She stopped the car, unlocked the door, and then fell forward on the steering wheel in a heap, causing the horn to sound.

"Oh, Lyddie, come here," Gary said, reaching in to undo her seat belt. "You can't drive like this." He grabbed her under her arms and pulled her out of the car.

"Oh, Gary," she wailed, sobbing on his shoulder, "her parents are dead. That little girl is all alone out there—she doesn't know they're never coming home again."

"Shhh, yes, I know," Gary murmured, holding her tight and rocking her, feeling tears burn in his own eyes. "I know, I know, I know."

"I have to go to her," Lydia whimpered.

"Yes, of course, you do," he said, "and I'm coming with you."

Lydia started. "No!" she said, pushing away from him.

"Okay, okay," he said, trying to calm her. "Then let me drive you to the airport at least. Let me get you on the plane."

She nodded then, head down, crying. While Gary turned off his car, Lydia went around to the other side of the Mercedes and tried to get in. The door was locked. Gary reached across the driver's side and unlocked it and then went around to help her in. Once he closed her door he heard something up the drive.

It was Noél, coming down out of the shadows, holding herself, looking as though she had been crying, too. "Good, you're taking her," she said.

"Only to the airport. She won't let me go with her."

"We've got a car meeting her on the other end," Noél said. "Gracia's leaving first thing in the morning. The kids are going to come here and stay with me."

"I'll come back after seeing her off," he promised.

— 40 —

The talk of death did funny things to people. Harris came home from work early. He brought flowers. He brought oriental chicken and a salad from Zabar's. They ate by candlelight. He made love to her on the living room floor. They took a shower. And now here they were at ten o'clock, in their robes, she trying to read a manuscript on the couch, he doing Sunday's crossword puzzle in his chair.

It was so quiet.

Kate looked over at Harris. She had never seen him so happy. So content. So *smiley*.

Kate didn't know what was wrong with her. She felt scared inside, panicked, and it wasn't just the talk of death in the air.

Did she feel trapped?

But this was what she had always wanted.

Wasn't it?

And this ring means I've done it, she thought, looking down at her hand. *I've made a promise, a commitment.*

The phone rang.

"Hello?" Harris said into it. His eyebrows went up and his eyes sparked delight and with a very big smile he said, "Yes, hello."

At this point, Kate was on her feet, thinking for some crazy reason it might be Mark.

"Yes, it is," Harris said. Pause. "Thank you—we're very excited about it." He looked up at Kate. He smiled again. "Good—it's nice to know she behaves herself when she's away from home." Pause. "She's told me a lot about you, too." Pause. "Yes, she is. Hold on. But wait—Ms. Southland? I—well, please accept my condolences about the terrible accident. I—well, as Kate will tell you, we've both been thinking of you, and our prayers are with you." Pause. "You're welcome. Yes, she is—hold on." He handed the phone to Kate.

"Lydia," Kate said, taking the phone, "I'm so glad you called. I've been so worried about you."

"I'm fine," Lydia said quietly.

"Are you here? In the East?"

"Yes. In Long Island." She sounded terrible—beaten, exhausted, spent.

"I'm just so sorry, Lydia," Kate said after a pause, resisting the impulse to ask just who, exactly, this had been who had died. "Is there anything I can do, anything at all?"

"Well," Lydia said, "you could come to the funeral on Monday. I could use a friend there." Pause. "Things are a little crazy right now. I had to move my niece out of my sister's house because the press was hanging from the trees. We're at a friend's house now, in Quogue."

"I'll be there Monday, you can count on it," Kate said, plucking Harris's pencil out of his hand. "What time and where?"

"Eleven in the morning, the Presbyterian church on Meeting House Road." She went on to give directions.

"Would you like me to come earlier?" Kate asked. "To help with anything?"

"Gracia's here," Lydia said, "we're fairly squared away. But thank you." Pause. "After, I was hoping you might come back to the house—my sister's house. We're going to have a thing there, you know, food and all. So I was thinking maybe you might want to bring someone with you. I was thinking maybe you could bring Mark."

"Mark?" Kate said.

"I wish you would," Lydia said. "I feel comfortable with him."

"I'm sure he'll be there if he can," Kate said.

"Besides," Lydia said, "Rebecca tells me he's working on my book now, too. Is that right?"

"*Rebecca called you?*" Kate said.

"She called the house and Noël talked to her. For something to take my mind off things, I called her back this evening."

"Oh, my God," Kate said, "Lydia, I apologize. On behalf of the house—on behalf of every rational person in America, I apologize."

There was a quiet laugh on the other end. "Relax, Kate, it's just revolting Rebecca—I've had to deal with her before, you know."

"Lydia," Kate said, eyes starting to fill, "I just think you're the greatest. And if there's anything, anything at all I can do . . ."

"Thanks," Lydia said. "You know, it's funny—but you're the only one who hasn't asked."

"Asked what?"

"Who Angela was."

"I figured you'd tell me when you were ready."

"She was the daughter of one of my father's girlfriends. We didn't know about her until after he died—when her mother contested my father's estate."

"Oh, Lydia, I'm sorry," Kate sighed.

"No need," Lydia said. "Angie was a wonderful person and we actually became rather close in later years, after my mother died." Pause. "We've kept quiet about our relationship because of her family. With my fame and everything it only promised to generate a lot of unpleasant publicity, and Angie wanted to spare her daughter that until she was old enough to explain it all to her. About our father and all."

"I see," Kate said.

Lydia sighed. "But it'll all come out now, I guess." Pause. "How anyone can call a child illegitimate, I don't know—but that's what they'll be calling my sister, won't they?"

— *41* —

"Red alert, Kate," Mark said over the phone Sunday night, "Rebecca just called for directions to the funeral in Westhampton."

Furious, Kate tracked down Mr. Rushman at his home in Greenwich to say—as politely as she could muster—that no, Rebecca and Dick Skolchak's presence at Lydia Southland's sister's funeral would not be necessary tomorrow, and would Mr. Rushman please call Rebecca and tell her so before she irrevocably damaged the house's relationship with Ms. Southland beyond repair?

"Rebecca feels that Bennett, Fitzallen & Coe should be represented at the service," Mr. Rushman said.

So what were she and Mark, Kate wondered, editors at Simon & Schuster? "Yes, I see her point," Kate said, "but Mr. Rushman, this isn't *Lydia's* funeral—it's her sister's."

"But a great deal of press, I understand, will be there."

Kate brought the phone down to look at it and then brought it back to her ear, tempted to say, "What planet are you from, anyway?" but she didn't. Instead she said, "Would you please talk to her, Mr. Rushman? I'm asking you for the sake of the house—you must believe me."

No response. Some woman in the background on his end was laughing and moving pots and pans around, making quite a racket.

It was in this moment that Kate realized that Mr. Rushman had made up his mind that she was expendable. It was in this moment, in fact, that the chill running down Kate's spine told her the impossible might indeed be happening, that she might indeed be on her way to getting fired.

She.

Kate Weston.

Kate Weston getting *fired?*

Could Mr. Rushman fire someone he had just promoted not so long ago?

"I don't think Rebecca needs to attend," Mr. Rushman said finally. "I'll give her a call now."

Kate breathed a sigh of relief. "Thank you," she said.

— 42 —

Kate dressed in a black Chanel suit she had lucked into on Orchard Street. She took pains with her hair and makeup; careful not to put on too much of anything, including perfume and jewelry, she wore a single strand of pearls and matching earrings, plain black heels, and carried a simple black bag. From the parking garage around the corner, she picked up Harris's car, which was, interestingly, black as well.

Mark was waiting for her on the corner of Ninety-sixth and Third, near the entrance to the FDR Drive. He was dressed in a navy blue jacket and gray pants and was holding a bag that turned out to have two cups of coffee and two cartons of yogurt in it. "How did you know I forgot to eat?" Kate said, pulling away from the curb and heading down toward the entrance ramp.

"Because I know you," Mark said simply, opening the bag.

Uh-oh. It wasn't going to be that kind of ride, was it? Because if it was, then Kate was going to let him out at the tollbooth.

Pulling out the cup holder from the dash, Mark added, "And given the current environment at B, F & C, I'm seriously considering the option of becoming a caterer." He took her cup of coffee out, removed the lid, sipped the top off of it, and then put it in the holder for her.

She glanced over at him, making the turn onto the ramp. "So it's not just me."

"Nope," he said, taking the top off her yogurt. He stirred it with a plastic spoon and stuck the carton and the spoon in the second hole in the cup holder. Then he unfolded a napkin and dropped it in Kate's lap. "There's a rumor we're for sale."

"I heard that," Kate said, looking back at oncoming traffic and accelerating to get on the FDR, "but we're always hearing that."

"Honnersby-London says the Germans and the Italians want to build printing plants in East Germany."

"Now that I hadn't heard," Kate said.

"So they're looking for cash," Mark said. He sipped his own coffee and swallowed. "The Japanese partners are not in the least impressed with us, as we know—although they do seem to like my baseball books. I got another note from Kasada the other day."

"So everybody wants to sell us," Kate said, moving over into the left lane for the turnoff for the Triborough Bridge.

"But not necessarily with any problems attached," Mark said. He looked at her. "Problems like editors with large salaries."

Kate made the turn for the bridge before responding. She was trying to make sense of what Mark was saying.

"They want the list and the backlist and the name of the house to sell," Mark said, "but not expensive employees."

Kate frowned, slowing down for the toll. She reached across Mark to get a token out of the glove compartment and then, waiting in line, picked up her yogurt and took a few hasty bites. Then she put it back in the holder and turned to Mark. "I found out that if I was doing Lydia's book at Crown, I could have another two weeks in my production schedule."

"Are you kidding?" he said.

"Even more," she said coldly, eyes ahead on the road, "if absolutely necessary."

"And they deal with the same printers we do," Mark said.

"Yes," Kate said, her mouth pressing into a line.

They made good time, turning off Route 27 at the Westhampton Beach exit at 10:25. Kate hadn't been to Westhampton in years. When she was very little one of her aunts had taken a house in Quogue one summer and since there was no real town in the town of Quogue, the twins would ride their bikes over to Westhampton Beach to hang out. The problem was they always had Kate—some eight years younger— to drag along on these journeys.

"Oh, come on, Kate!" her brother would yell from what seemed like fifty miles up the road. And then, finally, exasperated, Matt would ride back to her, hide Kate's bike in the bushes, stick her on the top of his handlebars, and ride her to Westhampton himself. She would make the rest of the trip clutching the handlebars, hair blowing back flat in the wind, red Keds sneakers balanced precariously on the front fender. To this day Kate could remember the cramps in her hands and the pain in her rear from those terror rides.

They stopped at a gas station and filled the tank, and Kate and Mark used the rest rooms. They drove on then, following Lydia's directions, and found the church easily, a beautiful old white Presbyterian relic. It would have been pretty hard to miss, actually, since the entire church grounds had been set off by police barricades, with reporters, photographers, thrill seekers, fans, vans, and minivans with microwave antennas pressing in on them.

"This is scary," Kate said, driving slowly through the crowd. She gave their names to a guard, who checked them off on a roster and directed them into the church parking lot.

Kate was fine until, as they approached the church, she heard the organ starting to play. Funerals were not her strong point. She hesitated at the stairs. Mark touched her back and they went in.

Lydia was right inside the vestibule. Her hair was up and she was wearing a pale coral dress and short jacket, pearls, pearl earrings, and white gloves. The colors, for some reason, seemed more appropriate than the black Kate was wearing. Funerals were supposed to be part of the grieving process, Kate knew, a healthy way of saying good-bye to a loved one. But to Kate they were scary and dark and grief-stricken occasions, eminently suitable for the black, black, black she always wore no matter how tradition had changed. For Lydia's sake, though, she was glad to see that Lydia didn't share her outlook.

Lydia hugged her hard, murmuring, "Thanks for coming."

"I'm glad I could be here," Kate said.

"Mark," Lydia said, releasing Kate and holding out her hand to him, "thank you."

He took her hand and leaned forward to kiss her on the cheek.

"You'll come back to the house—after," Lydia whispered, looking back and forth between the two.

"Of course," Kate said.

"Señorita Weston," someone called softly.

Kate turned around and saw Gracia, somber though smiling, dressed in a long-sleeved black dress and with a black lace veil over her head. "Oh, Gracia," Kate murmured, giving her a hug.

"Señor Faith and Trust," Gracia said over Kate's shoulder.

Mark smiled.

Kate released Gracia and she and Mark moved along toward the interior of the church.

"Why does she call you that?" Kate whispered to him.

"What?" he whispered back.

"Mr. Faith and Trust."

"Speaks Italian, I guess," he said, handing her off to an usher.

The church was very crowded. But then it was a double funeral. Kate tried not to look at the coffins as the usher showed them into a pew on the left, about halfway down the aisle. Kate walked in first and sat down. Mark came in behind her, stood there a second—he was looking for the kneeling bench, Kate knew—and then sat down next to her. As if it were the most natural thing in the world, he took her hand.

He knew how she was about funerals. In recent years they had attended several together. Many of their friends and colleagues in the industry had died of AIDS-related illnesses and so by now there had come to be three kinds of funerals to Kate: the ones for people who had died at peace; the ones for people who were at peace only now that they were dead; and the ones for people she could never believe were dead because they had only been her age.

The coffins lay side by side in front of the church, an American flag draped over the husband's casket, Lydia's sister's coffin made of a beautiful mahogany. Kate swallowed, letting her eyes deliberately go out of focus, wanting to be respectful and attentive, but not really wanting the scene to register. The organ played on; Kate heard a woman crying behind her; Mark was clearing his throat.

And the service hadn't even started yet.

This music.

Mark released her hand and then came back to it, pressing his handkerchief into it. He noticed more than she did. Like the fact that she had tears in her eyes.

There had been two funerals for her mother. One in Windy Hills shortly after she died and then one in her hometown of Cosgrove Springs, Texas, followed by a graveside ceremony. Kate remembered nothing of the service in Windy Hills except how the shoulder of her uncle Sam's suit had smelled and tasted. Of the funeral in Texas, she remembered everyone beforehand pumping her sister and her brother and then her for, "What were your mother's favorite hymns?" and all Kate could think of was how much her mother had loved singing, "Around the World in Eighty Days," "Itsy Bitsy Teenie Weenie Yellow Polkadot Bikini," and "Hey, Look Me Over," none of which, she had been pretty sure, were what her relatives had in mind.

No.

And so they had played all these Southern hymns—not even "Men and Children Everywhere" which, too late, Kate remembered her mother had loved to sing—and the service had gone on and on and Kate had been hot and confused, not even knowing that it was her own mother they were talking about until her mother's name was said; and even then, the way it was said made it sound like someone else's name, someone old and quiet and sad, not her mother because her mother had often been loud and funny and slightly eccentric. And so instead of talking about what a loving wife she had been, Kate wished they would say something about the way Mom *really* was—talk about the time, maybe, that she talked to a wrong number on the telephone for two and a half hours.

And then Kate remembered sitting in the backseat of a limousine with Sissy and Matt after the funeral, waiting to go to the cemetery, seeing her mother's coffin being loaded into the hearse, Kate sobbing and sobbing, uncontrollably, with various relatives jumping into the front seat of the limo trying to calm down "K-k-k-Katie," as they called her down there.

I want to die, I want to die too, Mom, take me with you! she remembered crying in her head, looking at the wet on her white gloves in the back of that limousine, realizing that people were talking to her and expected her to care that they were, but she just didn't care anymore about anything because Mom was dead, Mom was dead and she wasn't coming back and Kate couldn't believe Mom would leave her like this, what would she do? Never ever—she would never ever see her mother again?

Stop it, Kate told herself, clearing her throat and looking up to the cross on the altar in the church in Westhampton.

She had never been back to the cemetery. Not once in all these years.

Oh, Mom, she thought, pressing Mark's handkerchief to one eye and then the other, *I miss you so much.*

The music stopped and Kate looked up. And then back. An older couple was slowly making their way down the aisle. Behind them were seven or eight younger people. The older couple sat down in the front row on the right side; the others behind them in the second row.

They all stood there, the congregation, looking back, waiting for Lydia. But she did not come.

But then the door to the left of the altar opened and everyone turned around toward the front. There was Lydia, gently leading the Clarkes' little girl in by the hand. Kate craned her neck but couldn't get a good look—there were too many people—but she could see that the little girl was blond and that she wore a pale yellow dress with a sash that tied in the back.

And then Kate smiled—as her heart broke a little too—when she saw that under Lydia's arm she was carrying a coloring book.

Now why couldn't she have had an aunt like that at her mother's funeral?

But she had been a lot older than this little girl. She had been eleven, old enough to be expected to sit there and listen and participate in the funeral that had gone on so interminably.

How would Allyson feel twenty years from now? Kate wondered, watching as Lydia and the little girl sat in the front pew and the minister came out to greet the congregation. How well would she remember her mother and father? And would she remember this day? Would she remember Aunt Lydia sitting beside her, her arm protectively around her?

The most terrible thing about losing your mother, Kate had found, was the life sentence of never feeling as though you belonged to anyone or anything ever again. From the day her mother had died, Kate had felt like an outsider everywhere, a guest who had to earn her place by what she did.

She remembered that day. That day when she had come home from school and found a neighbor at their front door. "Hi, Mrs. Taylor," Kate had said, and Mrs. Taylor had burst into tears and grabbed her.

And Kate had known. Right then.

Her body wasn't there in the house anymore, of course. It had been taken to the hospital for an autopsy. Kate's father was home, behind the closed doors of his study. Sissy and Matt were on their way home from college. Grandmother Weston was being driven down from Springfield. Uncle Sam and Aunt Caroline were driving down from Providence. People were in the kitchen, whispering, and, passing through, Kate overheard enough words like "pills," "hall closet," "vodka," "practically a pharmacy," to know what had happened.

And so Kate had gone upstairs to her bedroom and closed the door, walked over to the window, and rested her arms on the sill, letting her forehead rest against the glass. Looking out over the fields and woods, she still didn't believe it.

And she had stood there a long, long time, until the evening light began to fade, and it began to sink in that maybe what they said was true, that Mom was never coming back.

Kate fell forward in the pew, covering her face with her hands. She felt Mark's arm around her, pulling her toward him, and she turned to him and buried her face in his shoulder.

He brought his other arm around and held her as she cried. And they stayed like that through the rest of the service and later, when Kate could calm down a little, she would think how odd it was, but the shoulder of Mark's blazer seemed to smell and taste just like Uncle Sam's had so many years before.

— *43* —

When the service was over and they left the church, Kate's exhausted grief turned to anger. Outside cameras were clicking and whirling, the crowds of reporters and photographers and onlookers straining over the blockades as the coffins were loaded into the hearses. Kate looked around for Lydia but didn't see her. Mark nudged her and she followed his eyes.

Lydia was standing to the side of the church, talking to the minister.

Kate turned back around to look at the road. Could all of these people and cameras really be there to witness one person's grief? "Where's the little girl?" she asked Mark.

"Gracia took her out of the church just before the end of the service," he said.

"Oh," Kate said.

"I thought they carried him out well, didn't you?" a woman said to Kate as they walked across the parking lot to the car.

"Excuse me?" Kate said.

"Chris was a big man," the woman said, "I thought they needed six to carry him, but Ace insisted. They wanted the old gang you see, the old gang to carry Chris."

Kate realized she was talking about the husband's coffin.

"My John was the one with the mustache," the woman said. She smiled. "They still call him Ace."

"So they were in the military together," Mark said. "I wondered about the flag."

"Air force," the woman said.

Chris had been a navigator, it turned out, stationed with Ace, this woman's husband, here at Westhampton Air Force Base. When their tour of duty was up, they had both gone civilian, choosing to stay in Westhampton to start new careers, Chris in landscaping and Ace in construction.

"You can follow me to the cemetery if you don't know the way," the woman said.

"Thanks," Kate said. She handed the car keys to Mark.

The hearses were first to leave the church parking lot, followed by four limousines. They could tell which limo was Lydia's—the third one—because the police had to bodily remove reporters from it so it could drive through. They were way back in line, about the twenty-fifth passenger car or so. Kate said, "Mark, the lights," and he turned them on.

Kate looked out the side window then, embarrassed that she might still have tears left to spill. This was incredible, this little scene today, and she didn't feel well. Certainly not up for a cemetery.

The funeral procession got moving and as they crept along Old Montauk Highway, Kate knew Mark was watching her. Suddenly she felt the car swerve and she saw that he had turned off the road.

"We'll meet them at the house," he said. "We don't have to go to the cemetery too."

He drove down to the beach and stopped at the guardhouse. "We're not residents," Mark said to the guard, "but we just went to a funeral and I was wondering if maybe we could walk up to the beach for a breath of fresh air before going to the reception."

"You must have been at the Clarke funeral," the guard said, nodding. "Really sad, what happened."

Following the guard's instructions, they parked the car on the other side of the drawbridge, left Mark's jacket in it, and walked back. The guard scribbled a pass, which they showed at the bathhouse to be allowed through. There was a marvelous wooden porch off the bathhouse, and Mark left Kate sitting there, in the shade, looking at the dunes. When he reappeared it was to hand her an ice cream cone.

They sat together in silence, eating the ice cream.

Kate started to feel better. Mark was so smart sometimes. She looked at him. "Thank you," she said.

"Want to walk down to the water?" he said.

"I'd have to take my stockings off."

"Ladies locker room is right over there," he said.

"Do you believe in God?" he asked her.

They were standing in the wet sand, the waves first crashing and then stretching up the beach, just reaching their feet. Kate was holding her dress high; Mark's pants were rolled up around his knees.

"Yes," Kate said.

"Me too," he said. He paused, looking out at the water, and then he turned to her, his hair blowing in the wind around his glasses. "Do you think your mother is here? With you, I mean."

She looked at him, wondering how on earth he knew thoughts of her mother had gotten her so upset. But then, what else would it be? *How about the state of your life?* she asked herself, and in the next instant she wondered why she had thought that because everything in her life was fine now.

Wasn't it?

"Mom's around," Kate said, nodding. "I don't think any mother ever really leaves her child—do you?" A sigh. She looked out at the water. "I just wish I could see her sometimes."

"But you can't," Mark said. "So you feel her presence and know she's there—don't you? Feel her presence like you have to with God."

Kate looked at him and smiled. They certainly had some strange conversations sometimes.

— *44* —

The Clarke residence was a charming white-shingle-and-stone split-level house on Aspautuck Road. Surrounded by a split-rail fence, it had a big front yard with wonderful shade trees, and around the base of the house were beautiful flower beds. They parked the car down the road and walked to the house. Kate stopped once on the way, complaining she had sand in her stockings, and Mark asked her what did she mean, look at his pants, all crinkled and wet around the knees. They made their way through the reporters milling around the property, gave their name to a guard at the end of the driveway, and went in.

There was a swarm of people in the house and Kate took the lead, looking for Lydia. They found her in the kitchen, besieged with friends of her sister's who had brought food. Gracia, with an apron on, came bustling in from the dining room, asking them to please take the señora out to circulate.

Lydia led Kate and Mark through the dining room—past the turkey and ham and potato salad and cole slaw and squash and bread and lettuce and tomato and sliced onion and molded salad and tossed salads and cheese and tuna casserole and pasta salad and olives and antipasto and pickles and chicken salad and pâté and fried chicken—through the living room, and then downstairs into a playroom where a bar had been set up.

"Oh, good," Lydia said, looking outside by the pool, "there are some people I know you'll love talking to." And after Kate and Mark got themselves a soda, she took them outside. There was a tall privacy fence all around the backyard—with wonderful azalea bushes and lilacs and Kate didn't know what else along it—but around the pool area itself was a short chain link fence, about four feet high.

Oh, the little girl, Kate thought, figuring it out, *it's to keep her from going into the pool unsupervised.* "Where's Allyson?" she asked Lydia.

"She's beautiful, isn't she?" Lydia said. "She behaved like an angel through the service." Her eyes teared suddenly and she looked away.

"Yes," Kate said gently, "she did—and I think she'll always be grateful you let her come."

Lydia looked at her, blinking rapidly. "You think so? I debated."

Kate nodded. "Oh, yes, it was the right decision."

"She's over at the other house now," Lydia said, regaining her composure. "I want to keep her away from the crowds and all those crazy people out front. Shirley, Shirley!" she called to a woman standing with a large group of people. "I have some people I want you to meet." She pulled Kate and Mark over to the group. "This is my editor I told you about, Kate Weston, from Bennett, Fitzallen & Coe. And this is Mark Fiducia, who's also an editor there."

Shirley VanDeroef was the director of the Westhampton Free Library, where Lydia's sister, evidently, had been something called a Friend of the Library—and evidently a very popular one. Every librarian had shown up for the funeral, and Kate and Mark met them all, with Lydia showing off her skills as a quick study (even the librarians couldn't believe it when she rattled all the names off). "Kate, Mark— I'd like you to meet Robert Allard, Jan Camarda, Elva Stanley, Phyllis Acard, Kathy Roggeveen, Nancy Foley, Karen Hewlett, Jane Vail, Susan LaVista, Mary Ann Bilyk, Josephine Silverman, Anne Realmuto, and Maurice Alberts, their computer systems expert." Kate and Mark shook hands with them all, and while Lydia went off to talk to other guests, they had a wonderful time talking about books, publishing, library buying habits, and interlibrary loan systems.

"Good grief," Lydia said, coming back later, "you can't all still be talking back here!" and the group laughed. Yes, indeed, they could be,

Kate said. Book people were very much the same, she'd always found. Good-byes were said and Lydia took Kate and Mark back into the house to introduce them to two special friends of her sister's—"Irene Barrett, my sister's wonderful friend and doubles partner at the tennis club, and Hortense Sarot, who is also a special Friend of the Library"—and then they moved on to the dining room to get something to eat.

Kate and Mark and Lydia loaded up plates of food and sat at the top of the stairs, eating and talking, watching the crowd in the living room below.

"If you can wait a little longer," Lydia said, "I'd like to take you over to meet Allyson."

"Wonderful," Kate said, "we'd love it."

Lydia smiled, but then something caught her eye in the living room. She squinted, expression growing serious. She put her plate down, excused herself, went down the stairs, and out the front door. When she reappeared it was with a policeman; she pointed to a man standing by himself at the fireplace, eating a sandwich off a paper plate.

Kate and Mark watched as the policeman went over and said something to the man. The man looked very surprised; he swallowed his food and said something, nodded and then smiled. But the policeman said something that took the smile off his face and in the next moment both the man and his sandwich were being escorted out the front door.

Mark turned to Kate. "Want to go see?"

She nodded and they went down to look through the living room window. The policeman and man were out in the driveway. The man was a bit red in the face. He sighed then, handed his sandwich over to the policeman, and got out his wallet.

"The damn *Inquiring Eye*, I bet," Lydia said from behind Kate and Mark. "It would be just like them to crash my sister's funeral."

"Oh, that's awful," Kate said.

"We'll know soon enough," Lydia said.

Lydia went outside and the policeman called over another policeman to stand with the man while he—still holding the man's sandwich plate in his hand—walked over to talk to Lydia. He said something and Lydia's face darkened. She looked at the man, back to the policeman, shook her head, and then made a motion with her hand indicating that whoever he was, she wanted him away from here.

They watched as the policeman escorted the man down the driveway to the road and did not, Kate noticed, give him his sandwich back.

Lydia came back in the living room shaking her head. "A private investigator, can you believe it? Working for guess who."

"The *Inquiring Eye?*" Mark said.

Lydia shook her head. "No—working for Bestar."

Kate and Mark looked at each other.

"I know," Lydia said. "Oh, the hell with this," she said then, taking Kate's arm, "I've had enough for one day."

— *45* —

They slipped through a gate in the privacy fence out back, walked through the woods to a neighbor's property, sneaked around their house, crossed over to the next backyard, and, once past that neighbor's house, crept through a grove of trees in the side yard to reach Harris's car unobserved. ("I feel like we're filming an episode of 'Cassandra,'" Lydia said at one point, as Mark flattened himself against the side of the house, peering around the corner to see if the coast was clear.)

Mark drove out Aspautuck Road and, following Lydia's instructions, turned left on Main Street. They went over a bridge with a startlingly beautiful view of a bay, followed the road past some nice houses, and then the road made an extremely sharp turn to the left; they made the turn and drove straight on, passing through a heavily wooded residential area. Lydia told Mark to slow down and then had him turn into a drive they otherwise probably wouldn't have seen.

They drove back through the woods on a narrow lane, turned left into a driveway, drove around the corner, and then a big gray-shingled house swung into view. It was gorgeous back here, sprawling grounds with fantastic trees and bushes—all in bloom—and a charming brick wall running along the far side of the yard with an old-fashioned wood door. The house itself was three stories—a converted turn-of-the-century barn, Lydia explained—and it was warm, friendly, extremely inviting. Across the driveway was a separate gray-shingled garage; behind it a pool house, and beyond that a swimming pool area, beautifully landscaped with rocks and flowers and a red-brick walk.

"Your friends must do very well," Kate said as they walked to the house.

"They do," Lydia said. "And one of them is in book publishing."

"No way," Kate said.

"She is," Lydia said, leading them up a walk to the kitchen door. She said a name that Kate recognized. The woman had been a fabulous editor for twenty-five years at one of the biggest houses and now was a literary agent.

Kate looked at Mark. "Clearly this is handwriting on the wall."

Lydia unlocked the door and they went inside. She picked up a note off the counter, read it, smiled, and checked her watch. "Okay, out," she said, shooing them outside again, "we take a walk."

"But I want a tour," Kate said.

"Later," Lydia said. "I want to take you somewhere." She took them back down the driveway and through the woods again on the lane. When they reached the main road, they walked a bit and then crossed over to two horse corrals. No one was riding. Some of the horses started walking in their direction in hopes of a treat.

"Oh, darn," Lydia said, looking around, "I thought we'd be in time to see her. Come on, we'll go back around this way." She walked them around the smaller corral to a barn set back in the woods. As they came around the side of it, they saw Allyson in a riding habit—complete with a black velvet hat and little riding boots—helping a woman unsaddle a small black-and-white horse. When she saw them she ran over, her unfastened chin strap swinging.

"Hi, sweetheart," Lydia said, giving the child a hug and a kiss on the cheek.

"Aunt Lyddie," Allyson said, "I forgot the carrots for Apache."

"Oh, I'm sorry," Lydia said, "had I known I would have brought them."

"Hi, Mrs. Southland," the instructor said, walking over, leading behind her presumably the carrotless Apache.

"Hi, Barbara," Lydia said, straightening up, holding one of Allyson's hands. "I'd like you to meet my editor—and my friend—Kate Weston, and her friend—and mine—Mark Fiducia."

They exchanged hellos.

"And I'd like you to meet my niece—Kate, Mark," Lydia said, pulling her forward slightly, "this is Allyson Clarke. Allyson, these are my friends Kate and Mark."

"Hi," Allyson said to them. Her hair was very blond and she had the most wonderful brown eyes. She was not a pretty child, but was very pleasing to look at. Sweet. Infinitely huggable.

Kate bent slightly to offer Allyson her hand. "Nice to meet you."

Allyson shook Kate's hand, but while doing so looked up at her aunt.

"What am I going to do about Apache? I wanted to give him a good-bye present."

Kate straightened up, noticing that Barbara was smiling. Broadly.

"Allyson, darling," Lydia said, squatting down to look at the little girl eye to eye, taking both of her hands into hers, "we have the best good-bye present for Apache of all."

"We do?"

"Yes, sweetheart, we do," Lydia said, pushing a piece of hair back off the child's forehead, back under the rim of her riding hat. "We're not going to say good-bye at all. Apache's coming with us."

Little Allyson's face remained blank for a moment. And then she blinked. And then she turned to look back at Barbara, who nodded, and then Allyson looked at Apache, and then her head swung back to Lydia. "Apache . . ." her voice trailed off.

"Is coming with us," Lydia repeated.

"Oh, Aunt Lyddie!" Allyson suddenly cried, throwing her arms around her. The poor little girl was crying for real now, sobbing, and everyone knew it wasn't about the horse.

Over Allyson's shoulder, Lydia was crying her own tears. After several moments, she looked up and met Kate's eyes. She nodded, turned to kiss the side of Allyson's face—awkwardly bumping her nose against the riding hat—and returned her chin to Allyson's shoulder. "Yes," Lydia said, "Allyson's coming home to California—and Apache's coming too."

— 46 —

It was very strange being the head of Lydia's household, to say nothing of acting as guardian to Gracia's grandchildren. This was Noél Shaunnessy? she would ask herself, waking Billy and Cathy in the morning, fixing breakfast and driving them to school in the station wagon. This was Noél, making lists, shopping at the supermarket, making sure the breakfast room table was clear so the children could get right to work on their homework when they got home, setting out graham crackers and milk for a snack? Cooking dinner, seeing that clothes were cleaned and pressed and ready for the next day? Organizing the gang, when homework was done, to play a little Canadian doubles outside—running them around the tennis court (correction, *being* run around the court. "Oh, Cat," Billy would say, "did you see that? Aunt Noël did a two-handed back-over-the-cliffer!")—and organizing a shower for Billy and a bath for Cathy, jammies, one hour of TV, hot chocolate, teeth brushing, prayer saying, fifteen minutes of reading and then lights out, good night!

"And please bless Allyson," Catalina said one night in her prayers. "And please, God, don't let her be scared. Tell her you will protect her and Aunt Lyddie will protect her and so will Grandma and so will we."

Sitting on the edge of her bed, Noël smiled.

It was a miraculous thing for someone's heart—namely Noël's—to have reawakened to the subtleties of life. Only now, in moments like these, listening to this child's prayers, did Noël have a glimmer of all she had missed. She had never known anything of trust before getting sober; she had never known anything of peace, of quiet happiness, of joy at just being alive. Certainly she had known nothing of faith.

She did not have to drink or drug anymore. She did not have to find money to support her habit and she did not have to endure the humiliation that had gone along with getting it. She did not have to do emergency work on her body all the time—ice packs and tissues for nose hemorrhages, inhalers for absence of breath, eating stomach antacids like candy, aspirin too, Kaopectate when things went one way and Ex-Lax the other. She did not have to plan the early part of her day around the certainty that she would have to throw up. She did not have to awaken and find that her morning was going to start at two in the afternoon. She did not have to swallow something to knock herself to sleep and she did not have to snort something to knock herself out of bed. She did not have to swallow and snort, swallow and snort, snort and swallow, snort, snort, snort, to talk, to walk, to function. To be normal.

For some people it was booze, for some it was coke, for Noël it had been both, a constant balancing act, with first one drug, then the other ravaging her life. The problem of being addicted only came out at two times: when she took too much and when she had too little. When she had just the right amount, then she had been "herself," normal, no one suspecting that too much, more than usual, was wrong with her.

Cocaine used up all the natural chemicals in the brain that the body needed to create a feeling of well-being; it literally consumed the body's capacity to produce a positive emotion. So the only way to avoid suicidal depression once addicted—and, indeed, it took many people that way, the unexplained suicide one heard about that made no sense until the missing piece was fit into the puzzle; yes, ah-ha, cocaine—was to take more cocaine or be safely holed up somewhere where people wouldn't let one kill oneself while waiting for one's body to replace the resources the drug had robbed his or her body of.

But nobody ever said being an addict was an easy way to live.

No.

And now, dear God, it blew Noél's mind sometimes that she could just eat and work and exercise and sleep and laugh and cry and do something worthwhile once in a while like help other people get over the fence that she'd had to. Show them that it could be done. And help them have the faith that there was a life beyond their dreams on this side, one well worth the terrors of giving up their drug(s) of choice.

"Aunt Noél?" Cathy said, breaking into her thoughts.

"Yes, Miss Pie?" Noél said, tucking her in.

"Thank you for taking care of us," she said.

"You're welcome," Noél said, kissing her lightly on the forehead. "Thank you for making me so happy."

"You didn't look very happy when Billy got you with the hose tonight," Catalina whispered, smiling, sleepy, turning on her side.

"Sleep tight, little one," Noél said, turning out the light.

"Not a bad life here, is it?" Billy said, playing Mr. Big Shot in Lydia's enormous bed, hands back behind his head on the pillows. "I like that Monet on the wall."

Billy had been moved into Lydia's room because the second guest room was being cleaned out, painted, and recarpeted in preparation for Lydia's niece. Lydia was bringing all of Allyson's bedroom furniture from Westhampton so the little girl wouldn't feel so strange here.

"Put the furniture in storage for now," Lydia had said over the phone, "and then when you get settled in your new place, you can take it."

Right, her new place. Ever since the announcement that Allyson was coming back to live with Lydia and that there was going to be a nanny moving in, too, Noél had gotten the distinct impression that day zero was about to arrive and she was expected to move out.

"I'm also shipping back some of my sister's things—furniture and the like," Lydia said, "so there will be some more things from the house you can have."

BENEDICT CANYON

Considering how Lydia's taste ran in furniture, this was no minor offer—but it only confirmed to Noël that it was a bribe to hurry up and move out.

So Noël had gone out looking for a place to live, returning home the first day to call Lise Kellerman and ask her, how much would she be making again? Oh. Hmmm. It was a very good salary; she could afford more than she thought. Gary came over and helped her write out a budget, figuring out how much she could pay for rent and still be saving.

"Saving?" Noël said to him.

"Yes, I know," Gary said, "it was a word foreign to me too in the beginning."

Noël chaired an AA meeting on Saturday nights in Westwood and Gary offered to give her the night off completely. "Have dinner with your sponsor after, go to a movie or something, stay out late and whoop it up," he said. Noël took him up on his offer to baby-sit, but lined up Imelda to come over, too, to fix dinner for the gang and help with the baths.

"Oh, great, this is great," Gary said when he arrived Saturday evening. "I need practice with Allyson coming and all."

Noël looked at him. "Planning to spend a lot of time here, are you?"

He blushed. "Go to your meeting," he said, pushing her toward the door.

It was a good thing Noël got to the meeting early and unlocked the church meeting room because the coffee guy wasn't there yet and it took at least an hour to prepare the amount of coffee they needed for a meeting as large as this—plus brewed decaf and water for tea—and AAs got sort of crazy when they expected coffee at a meeting and it wasn't there. While Noël started the coffee, members ran in to leave car keys on seats to save them while they dashed across the street for an early dinner. Others came in: the *real* chairpeople, which is to say the man and woman who were in charge of setting up the chairs; the refreshments committee arrived, carrying in cookies, crackers, sliced fruit, and cheese; the secretary, with his notebook and announcements; and last, but not least, the treasurer with the bank deposit bag.

There were no dues or fees in AA, but at every meeting they passed the hat, so to speak, to pay rent to the church, temple, community center, or wherever it was they met; to buy literature and meeting schedules, which they sold to members and gave away to newcomers;

and, if any money was left over, to send a contribution to their regional AA administrative offices, the national headquarters, too, and to special branches like the institutions groups or world services branch.

Almost all officers of an AA meeting changed every six months. Noél had been slightly shocked when she had been elected to chair this meeting this term, but then later she figured out people had only elected her because they thought she needed to get more involved. It had been true; since she also went to Cocaine Anonymous meetings, for a long time she had felt funny about being in AA too.

"Let's face it, Gare," she had said in the beginning, "I can qualify for every twelve-step program there is, plus some that haven't even been invented yet! What am I supposed to do? Belong to everything?" "Don't drink," Gary had told her, "don't drug—and go to meetings, that's what you do. AA will help you with the drinking, CA with the coke, and the twelve steps in both will save your ass, period."

Noél was supposed to go to dinner after the meeting with her sponsor, but her sponsor, when she arrived, didn't look too enthused about it. (The reason why Noél had chosen this particular sponsor, frankly, was because she almost never talked to her and that seemed fine with the sponsor—which certainly was *not* the recommended relationship, but Noél always figured that Gary was her real sponsor anyway and if she chose a woman she really liked a lot—instead of this one, whom she did not like—then she'd probably end up in bed with her.) Noél took one look at her sponsor's face and suggested they have dinner another time. Her sponsor brightened immediately and agreed.

The meeting was terrific; they had a wonderful speaker who had driven down from Carmel, and Noél, after helping others to clean up, felt very good. They locked up the room and talked a while in the parking lot, and then Noél hopped in her car and was on her way.

Driving to Beverly Hills, though, Noél felt the urge come over her to do something.

But what?

Oh, she knew. She knew what she wanted to do.

She drove past Benedict Canyon and continued on Sunset Boulevard for another mile, turning left on Laurel Canyon and driving up, up, up, and then right onto a short road. Holly lived on this road. Noél drove back and forth in front of her house four times. The house was set close to the road and the lights were on. One car was in the driveway, Kent's. Finally Noél stopped at the gate and pressed the intercom.

"Hello," Kent's voice said.

"Kent, hi, it's Noél Shaunnessy."

Pause. "Well, well, well," Kent said, sounding surprised. "Let me check with the madame and see what she says. Hang on."

Noél sat in her car, waiting. She was glad Kent was here. This way she was just an old friend stopping in to say hi.

Yeah, right.

"Noél Shaunnessy, come on in!" Kent reported, the gate buzzing open.

They had been sitting out back, just the two of them, Holly and Kent, having some wine on the terrace. Rather, Kent had been drinking wine and Holly had evidently been giving him a hard time about his expenditures of late because there were bills all over the table, weighted down with plates and silverware.

Holly was very good with money. Kent was not. They lived separately together largely on what she made.

"Saved by the bell, Kent, literally," Holly said, standing when she saw Noél coming down to the terrace. "I told him to tell whoever it was to go away, but then he said it was you—at first I didn't believe him." She gave Noél a hug and a kiss on the cheek. "Hi," she said, holding her arm, "you're looking wonderful."

"Thanks," Noél said, "you do too."

And how. Holly was in a short silk dress that fit her to perfection. And although she did have on gold hoop earrings, as usual when she was home, Holly's hair was an untidy and exotic mess, her makeup was scarcely detectable, and she was most elegantly barefoot. The cumulative effect was that of a *Cosmo* girl who had been abducted into a haystack for a couple of hours. But then, Holly had grown up on a farm.

"I guess we better continue our discussion tomorrow, Hol," Kent said, moving toward the table.

Holly lunged to catch Kent. "Oh, no you don't," she said, pulling him back and turning him around, "those receipts stay with me."

Kent laughed.

Holly gave him a mock punch in the arm. "It's not funny. What if Lydia left the show right now? We'd be in big trouble."

"No, we wouldn't," he said. He looked at Noél and smiled. "She's still the same—if she has less than enough to buy Fort Knox she goes into a panic."

"Fort Knox, ha," Holly said, looking at Noél.

It always overwhelmed Noél when she saw Holly, as if she always forgot what she looked like. Was like. And standing here, meeting those liquid brown eyes that were so incredibly gentle and lovely, Noél felt her stomach do something, felt her breath get a little short.

"Kent, love," Holly murmured, turning to him and holding his arm, "maybe you'd like to go out for a while."

Kent looked to her, back to Noél, and then back to Holly. "All right, love," and he kissed her on the forehead. Kent turned to Noél and held out his hand. Then he smiled and came forward to give her a hug. "I'm so glad you're doing so well with"—he released her—"well," he said, "you know, the other."

"The other" meant drugs and alcohol.

"Thanks, Kent," Noél said. And then she heard herself add, "I wouldn't be here tonight if I thought there was any chance it could be otherwise." Pause. "With, you know, the other."

"I'm sorry about this," Holly apologized, paperclipping yet more bills and putting them in her leather folder, "but Kent hides bills and thinks they'll go away. Every couple of months I have to go through his closet and find them and go over them with him."

Noél smiled. She was resting her chin in her hand, elbow propped up on the table.

It was all coming back. Sitting here, in the gloom of nightfall, one single porch light on, Holly in the shadows. She looked much the way Noél remembered her from the first time she had seen her up close, when they had literally crashed into each other in the bushes in the darkness, trying to sneak out the back of one of Mort and Beatrice Pallsner's dreadful parties. Then, as now, Holly had turned those doelike eyes on Noél, hesitated a moment, and then, seemingly, had melted. Later, when Noél saw Holly in daylight, she would come to know that *that* look, the one of melting, was always accompanied by a flush that started in her cheeks and burned its way down to her chest.

Holly closed the notebook, folded her hands on it. "Penny for your thoughts," she said.

"I'm trying to guess what you're thinking," Noél said truthfully.

"Why?" Holly said softly.

Had she just leaned closer? A little?

"Because," Noél said, looking into her eyes, feeling herself getting lost in them, as always, scared to let herself, though, because, "I don't want you to send me away." Pause. "I want to stay here with you. Close to you. Right here. Like this."

Holly sighed, lowering her eyes. "But this may not be a good idea."

"Not for you, no, I understand that," Noél said.

"No," Holly said, looking up, "for you. I know what you want, Noél, and I'm not in a position to give it to you."

"Maybe I've changed," Noél said. "Maybe you don't know what I want."

"I know what you need," Holly said.

"I don't need you," Noél said, "I know that."

Holly looked at her.

Noél put her hand over hers. "I used to need you, Holly. But I don't need you now—so now I know I only want to be with you because I love you, not because I need you."

Holly swallowed. Then she touched the side of Noél's face with her hand and held it there. "I love you—you know that," she said.

Noél nodded.

"And you know I can't leave Kent," she said.

Noél nodded.

"And that I can't ever live with you—at least not for some time."

Noél nodded. And then she leaned forward, hesitating. She had been staring at it for a while now, Holly's mouth. She looked up and met Holly's eyes again. And then she kissed her. Gently. And retreated. And kissed her again. And retreated. And then she waited. After a moment Holly reached over and pulled Noél back to her mouth and held her there.

How could Noél explain it? After so much sex with so many people over the years, how could it be that it was only with Holly that it had ever felt overwhelmingly right? So wonderfully deep and sexy and yet somehow not like sex at all as Noél had always known it, but like some new warm, moving, living thing, some incredible new feeling of otherworldliness? Where Noél forgot everything and couldn't think, knowing just that she only wished to operate somehow as one with Holly, as one mind, one heart, for at least just a little while?

Holly was undoing Noél's blouse, her mouth on Noél's neck, pausing to whisper, "It's been so long," and then pulling her blouse apart. Her hands went to the middle of her bra—no catch; Holly's mouth was in her ear; her hand slid around to Noél's back to undo the clasp there. Hand sliding back; hand pushing Noél's bra up; hand on Noél's breast, feeling it; a sigh from Holly; mouth traveling down Noél's neck.

Before they had ever gone to bed with each other, Holly had asked Noël what fantasy about the possibility turned her on more than anything. Noël had said without hesitation, "The idea of your mouth on my breast." It was true then. It was true now. And Holly remembered.

Sitting there, stroking the back of Holly's head, Noël felt herself let go. She was no longer frightened. Not in the least. And as if she heard her thoughts, Holly suddenly stood up, pulled Noël out of her chair, led her two steps, and then pushed her down on a narrow strip of sod between the terrace and the bushes. Noël laughed at this. Holly did too. Kneeling next to her, Holly reached back around to unzip her own dress, take it off, and throw it behind her; next her white lacy bra was off and in the air; and then there she was, kneeling, smiling at Noël, breasts hanging full.

"What are all these clothes you have on, Noël?" Holly said then, sounding exasperated, working to get Noël's shorts and panties off, but not bothering with her blouse and bra. She simply pushed them higher over Noël's chest and lay down on her, breast to breast, slipping her leg in between her thighs and kissing her full on the mouth.

After a while Noël eased a bit to the side to try to touch Holly, but Holly said, "No, let me touch you—I want to touch you," but that didn't work out very well since within minutes of touching Noël, Holly was rhythmically flexing around Noël's thigh, and then Holly was faltering with Noël, trying not to come but leaving Noël stranded in the process, both of them about to climb the walls; and then, mercifully, their bodies figured it out for them and they found themselves holding each other, moving with each other, and in a minute Holly was groaning into Noël's ear, and Noël, silently clinging, was in moments coming too.

Noël didn't know who laughed first, then, she or Holly, but one started and then the other one started and they lay there, soaked with perspiration, all tangled up with each other on this narrow strip of grass, laughing. And then their laughter wound to a stop and they kissed for a while and then that too wound to a stop and they simply lay there, looking at each other.

"I could wake up to this every morning," Holly whispered, touching the side of Noël's face. "I could wake up to this face every morning and be very happy."

That was when Noël began to cry. But only because she was happy.

He could hear Kate's sigh three thousand miles away. "So even if Lydia does resume work on the book when she gets back, you can't."

"Kate, I'm sorry, but there's nothing I can do," Gary said. "I have to go back to work on 'Cassandra' and Noél has to start over at 'Kelly Girls.'"

Another sigh on Kate's end. The manuscript was supposed to be in production and the book wasn't finished. "Well," Kate said, "I guess I'll just have to finish it."

"What?" Gary said. "But you've been telling us all along that you're no writer."

"Oh, I know," Kate said, "I always say that. If I didn't I'd be finishing everybody's book. You can't imagine how many writers balk at revisions."

"I thought you could write," Gary said. "A lot of that so-called line editing of yours seemed like completely rewritten material to me."

Kate laughed.

"Okay, you're hired," Gary said. "Pack your bathing suit and come out."

"Well, let's see how things go," Kate said. "Lydia's got her hands full at the moment."

"More than you know," Gary said. "The studio's hoping she'll start work soon."

Kate groaned.

"Look, we'll work it out somehow," Gary told her. "Just come out."

Just come out and get Lydia to start talking again, he thought.

Lydia always acted funny when she was hurt, but her reaction to her sister's death had completely thrown him. Rather, Lydia's behavior toward *him:* her refusal to let him come to the funeral, her refusal to discuss her plans with him, her refusal to call or write. He understood how painful it was for her, the newspapers dredging up a painful past: about her father's girlfriend, about this other daughter of his, Angela, about Mr. Southland's death and, later, the death of Angela's mother, the death of Lydia's mother; and then the two half sisters getting in touch again when Lydia lived in New York—secretly—Angela not wanting to be known as the illegitimate daughter of Lydia Southland's father.

But now Angela and her husband were dead and in their will they had asked, in the event that something ever happened to them, that her half sister, Lydia Southland, raise their daughter. And now it had come to pass and Lydia was bringing the little girl back to California and suddenly everything had changed between them and Gary didn't understand why.

Wasn't he good enough? Was that it? That Lydia didn't want certain kinds of people to be around the child? Like him?

But no, he couldn't believe that. But her attitude—the night she called when he was baby-sitting for Gracia's grandchildren—had been so awful.

"What are you doing there?" Lydia had said when he answered the phone.

"I'm baby-sitting," he said. "I sent Noël to a meeting and dinner. Besides," he added, "I need a little refresher course in baby-sitting. Seems like I might be doing some in the near future."

Silence.

And then, "Gary, I appreciate what you're trying to say, what you're trying to do," Lydia said, "but I have to tell you, I'm in no shape to deal with anything or anyone except Allyson right now. So I'd appreciate it if you could give me a wide berth."

"Well, yeah, okay," Gary said.

"What was that?" Lydia said, in response to shrieks coming from the front hall.

"The kids are tying Imelda to the banister, I think," Gary said.

"Gary, they should be in bed by now!"

He looked at his watch. "Whoops, I guess they should be. Don't tell Gracia, I'll put them to bed now."

"You better." Pause. And then, her voice softening, "I'm sorry I can't talk with you now—or maybe for the next couple of weeks. You understand, don't you? That I just can't handle any more right now?"

"Yes," he said, although he didn't. He felt shut out, unneeded, discarded. And it hurt.

His sponsor, Skip, though, had an interesting angle on it. He asked Gary if anyone had ever tried to seduce him while he was writing on deadline. Gary laughed and said that was just about the only thing he knew of for sure that could kill his sex drive and make him angry.

"Then think how Lydia must feel," Skip said. "Leave her alone, Gary. She'll be back to you when she's finished dealing with the crisis she's in."

Yeah. Skip was probably right.

But still, it hurt.

Gary was summoned to Pallsner's office for a meeting soon after. Mort wanted to know how Lydia was, if there was anything the studio could do for her. No, Gary said, he was pretty sure there wasn't.

"We'll be making a significant donation in her sister's name to whatever charity Lydia wants, of course," Pallsner said, sounding horrendously friendly about it, throwing a piece of gum away under his desk and popping fresh pieces in his mouth.

"I'm sure she'll appreciate that," Gary said, bringing his ankle up to rest on his knee, wondering why Pallsner was in such high spirits. Something was up.

"Yes," Pallsner said. He looked around on the desk. And then he frowned suddenly and—chewing—looked at Gary again. "Other business," he said sternly. "There's something else I need to talk to you about."

Gary nodded, indicating that he was to talk away.

"Noél's working over at 'Kelly Girls,' " Pallsner said.

"She starts in a week," Gary said.

"And she's clean—right? Absolutely one hundred percent drug free?"

Gary nodded. "Yes."

Pallsner leaned forward, clasping his hands together and knitting his fingers. "And can I be assured that she's going to stay out of trouble?"

Gary nodded. "Yes—I'd stake my life on it, in fact."

"Good," Pallsner said, sitting back, "good. But in any case"—he raised his finger and pointed it at Gary—"I want you to tell her that she better be damn careful with Holly."

Gary blinked.

Pallsner stood up. It was a cue, and so Gary stood up, too.

"I've got plans for Holly," Pallsner said, still pointing at Gary, "and her reputation can't take another hit—understand? I also don't want her showing up here all weepy in the morning like the old days."

Gary nodded, very much taken aback, wondering how the hell Pallsner knew that Noél was even talking to Holly again.

"Good," Pallsner said, walking to the door. Hand on the doorknob, he turned around. "I mean it, Gary. And tell Noël I mean it." And then he resumed chewing his gum and opened the door.

Gary went to his office and called Noël immediately. "I just saw Pallsner."

"Oh, Mr. Charming," Noël said, "do tell how he is."

"He told me to tell you that he didn't want any trouble from you where Holly was concerned—and he wants both of you to be very careful."

Silence.

"Noël?"

"That son of a bitch," Noël said. "He's still at it."

"But how does he know?" Gary said.

Noël sighed. "He knows, I bet, because he still has enough private investigators on retainer to watch a small country." She made a sound of contempt. "He always did say he liked to keep an eye on his investments."

Gary looked out his office window, a creepy feeling coming over him, the kind he always got when he realized he was involved with a sicko.

Was Pallsner watching him? Was he watching Lydia too?

— *48* —

She knew something was wrong when Emma Lou, the receptionist at the front desk, avoided her eyes and said under her breath, "It's a shame certain people aren't nicer. There was nothing I could do."

"What was that, Emma Lou?" Kate said, stopping.

Emma Lou looked at her and sighed. "It all happened right out here. I wanted to say something but—" She shrugged. "Poor Sarah."

Kate was off like a shot, striding down the hall toward her office. Two assistants were standing out in the hall, whispering; otherwise it was dead quiet on the floor. "Have you seen Sarah?" Kate asked them.

"She's in your office, I think," one said.

The door to Kate's office was closed. She opened it and found Sarah standing behind her desk, on the telephone, tears streaming down her face. Upon seeing Kate, she gave a small wail, dropped the phone, and ran around the desk to throw her arms around her. "I'm so sorry, Kate," she said, crying, "but I couldn't take it anymore!"

Kate sat Sarah down in a chair, closed her office door, and then sat down next to her to find out what was going on.

What was going on was that Sarah was leaving. What was going on was that Rebecca had jumped on Sarah as soon as she had come in this morning, snarling at her in the reception area that a certain sales presentation of Kate's was, "Stupid, cliché-ridden, and totally unacceptable," and stormed off, and Sarah—after all these months—finally lost her cool, calling Rebecca a bitch loud enough so that Rebecca could hear it.

Rebecca's response had been to wheel around and tell Sarah she was fired.

Sarah's response had been to wheel back around and tell Rebecca that that was fine with her, it had never been her aspiration to work for white trash like her anyway.

White trash? Kate repeated in the privacy of her own head, forcing herself not to smile because Sarah was so upset and the situation itself was so upsetting. *But white trash?* Oh, but to have missed the moment when Rebecca was called white trash!

Rebecca's response evidently had been cold fury and a diatribe that Sarah did not care to repeat—except the part about how she had to be off the premises by ten o'clock this morning.

"Oh, Sarah," Kate sighed, rubbing her face (and knowing she shouldn't, that all of her makeup was coming off), "I don't know what to do." She dropped her hand. "I can probably get it undone—but, quite frankly, I'm not sure that would be best for you. If there's a chance for you to take some money with you from here—"

"Kate, I love you," Sarah said, cutting her off, "I love the books, I love the people—most of them, anyway—but I hate that bitch and I'm not staying here another minute."

"But do you mind being—let go?" Kate said, knowing that it had to bother Sarah a lot because that's the way Sarah was—like Kate. Used to praise, not being fired.

"Not if it means some severance pay and a ticket out of this hell hole, I don't," Sarah said.

Kate couldn't help it. She had to smile because in the fifteen months Sarah had been here, Kate had never heard her call her office anything like that before.

As if reading her thoughts, Sarah's expression softened and she said, "I'm sorry, Kate, it hasn't been a hell—"

"Oh yes it has," Kate said. "Listen, what do you think you want to do? If you want to give publishing another try—which I wish you would—I've got some good friends at Random House and I think that might be a good place—"

Sarah was shaking her head.

"What about agenting?" Kate said. "I wish you'd call Morgan Barnes and—"

Sarah was shaking her head. "I want to go back to school," she said. "I was hoping to go out west, to where my cousin is, but I think I'll focus on Columbia now, work on my master's in English."

Kate smiled. "Sounds as though you've been making plans."

Sarah winced slightly. "Sorry."

"Sorry nothing," Kate said, "I'm just glad you have enough self-respect to move ahead. Some of us—" She waved her hand in the air and dropped it. "I don't know, sometimes I think some of us are going to get buried here in our offices before we look elsewhere."

Sarah blew her nose in some Kleenex and then lowered her hands, smiling a little. "You really should get out of here, Kate. Not to hurt your feelings, but the wear is beginning to tell."

"I know," Kate said. And then the realization hit. Sarah was leaving. Today. Like right now. And tears came and Kate gave Sarah an enormous hug—rocking her—and said, "Oh, but am I going to miss you! And I'll never, ever forget how wonderful you were to me. And if I can ever do anything for you—" She released her to look at her. "Listen, you have to promise me you'll let me set up a meeting with Ann Douglas at Columbia."

"Who wrote *Feminization of American Culture?*" Sarah's eyes were very wide. She was impressed.

Kate was heartbroken.

"Knock, knock," Mark said, poking his head in Kate's office.

"Hi," she said.

"I heard about Sarah," he said, slipping in and closing the door behind him. "I thought you might need some cheering up."

"True, I do feel like killing myself," Kate acknowledged, turning away from the typewriter, where she had been rewriting the offending sales presentation that had caused so much grief this morning. Kate had recently inherited the book it was for, and Rebecca was right. The sales presentation was stupid, cliché-ridden, and totally unacceptable because the novel was stupid, cliché-ridden, and totally unacceptable; but no one would let Kate cancel it because it was written by a friend of somebody in corporate and Kate had not wanted to mislead the sales force into thinking it was anything but stupid, cliché-ridden, and totally unacceptable.

"What are you going to do?" Mark said, sitting down in a chair.

"I get a temp tomorrow," Kate said, "and then I guess I start interviewing."

"There's a hiring freeze," Mark reminded her.

Kate looked at him for a full moment. "Oh, damn," she finally said, "you're right. I bet—" And then she closed her eyes and shuddered. "No," she said, opening her eyes, "I'm just going to have to go on blind faith. If I think about any of this a second longer I'm going to start screaming."

Her door suddenly opened and Dick Skolchak's head appeared. "Sorry—Kate, is or is not the Southland book going to make it into production this week?"

"The week after next," she said. "Rebecca knows—so does production. And Eugene. Pub date's late November now."

"I didn't know this," Dick said.

"Sorry," Kate said, "but I thought you would have read the memo I sent to everyone."

"You didn't send it to me," Dick said.

"Yes, I did," Kate said. "Sarah will show it to you." Pause, eyes close. Reopen. "Scratch that—*I* will get you another copy of it."

The door closed and then reopened. "When?" Dick said.

"Within the hour, Dick," Kate said.

The door closed and then reopened. "By the way," Dick added, "we've decided not to hire Jaqueline Deval to promote the Southland book. We're going to use our people."

"No way," Kate said. "Lydia's met Jackie and loves her and thinks she's working with her."

"Well, she's not now," Dick said.

"But she has to!" Kate said. "Jackie's already started work on it."

"Then have her undo the work on it," Dick said, "because we no longer have allocation of funds for outside publicists—all publicity and promotion will be handled in-house now."

"*What?*" Kate said.

"Oh, come on, Dick," Mark said, "publicity couldn't book Johnny Carson on the 'Tonight Show'!"

Dick frowned at Mark. "I expect that kind of sass from Kate, but not from you, Mark."

"Dick," Mark said.

"What?"

"Go fuck yourself," Mark said.

Dick slammed the door closed.

Kate turned to Mark. "Thank you."

"You're welcome."

"Well," Kate sighed, "now what do I do?"

"You could marry me," Mark suggested.

Kate looked at him, her face reddening.

"Don't marry Harris, Kate," Mark said. "At least promise me you'll consider it."

Kate's face grew darker, but she said nothing.

Mark looked at her for a moment longer and then he shrugged. "I can't help it if I love you," he said. And then he went back to his office.

— 49 —

"Passion is hot, neediness is not," Lydia Southland said over the phone.

"I don't know," Mark said, sounding doubtful. He was behind the closed doors of his office. "She'll probably never talk to me again after what I just said."

"What's wrong with telling someone that you love them?" Lydia asked him.

"Nothing," Mark said, shrugging, "except Kate's sort of—"

"Mark, you've *got* to wake her up before she gets in any deeper."

"But maybe she *should* marry Harris," Mark said.

"Mark, listen to me," Lydia said, "if Kate really wanted to marry her father then she should just move home with her father. She doesn't have to marry Harris to reenact the family nightmare."

"So you think she's re-creating family history," Mark said.

"Who *knows* what she's doing?" Lydia said impatiently. "The important thing to remember, Mark, is that Kate has a tendency to make her personal decisions based on her fears—not on what she wants or what she needs."

"Yeah, but Kate—"

"Yeah, but nothing," Lydia said. "Did you call Traci?"

"Yes," he said.

"And she'll go to the dinner?"

"Yes," Mark said.

"Good," Lydia said. "Now don't make a big deal out of it, but do it, Mark. Let Kate see what life's going to be like if she marries this guy."

He sighed. "Okay, if you say so."

— 50 —

Oh, God.

Kate nearly turned around and left. Mark was here with a *date*. And a very, very pretty one.

"Mr. Rushman," Kate said, standing in the foyer of his apartment, "you remember my fiancé, Harris Pondfield."

"Of course, of course," Mr. Rushman said, shaking his hand. "And congratulations."

"Thank you," Harris said.

"Set a date yet?" Rushman asked, leading them to the living room.

"October," Harris said. "And we're hoping you'll come."

Kate looked at Harris in horror.

"We'd love to," Mr. Rushman said.

"You must be Kate Weston," an Englishman said, coming over to her and extending his hand.

"This is Kate," Rushman confirmed. "And Kate, this is Louis Kern, publisher of Hatfield & Stephens."

They shook hands. Kern was a kind of English equivalent of Rushman, a new publisher for an old house, one who had never worked in book publishing before either; but Kern, at least, had worked in the newspaper business. He was, however, about as welcome in British publishing circles as Rushman was in American, and Kern was here in New York to prove himself on a buying trip.

Kate and Harris were the last to arrive and so they were taken around the living room to say hello to everybody: Kern's dreary wife,

Evelyn; Rebecca, of course, with her husband, Cliff; Dick Skolchak and his wife Mary; and then—thank heavens!—at Kern's request, because she was editing a book he was desperate to buy, Rushman had invited Shaye Areheart, a senior editor at Doubleday, and her husband Jaime Bernanke. And then there was Mark, of course, and his date, an *actress* named Traci Daugs. Rushman's young second wife, Gigi, finally came stumbling out of the kitchen to say hello, where, Kate surmised, she had been having a cocktail party of her own.

Kate would be damned if she would ask Mark about his friend. And if they were so comfortable with each other—which clearly they were—then why hadn't she ever even *heard* of this Traci before? She was gorgeous. Blonde, terrific brown eyes, body beyond belief, great voice, too. And Kate soon found that she was smart, funny, and utterly winning as well, which only increased Kate's resentment tenfold. Who *was* this woman? One day Mark sits in her office and says he's in love with Kate and the next he shows up with—

"Looks like Mark's doing very well for himself," Harris murmured to Kate as they went in to dinner.

It was an interesting dinner if for no other reason than the guest of honor and the host left in the middle of it to "discuss some things" in Rushman's library, and then their hostess excused herself to get something in the kitchen and never came back. The butler, left on his own, just went on serving them. Rebecca and her husband were talking to Harris at one end of the table. (Harris, Kate knew, was trying to charm Rebecca on her behalf.) Dick and his wife were talking to each other down at the other end. Kate, in the meantime, was trying to ignore Mark and Traci, who were sitting across from her in the middle, but since they were having a wonderful time talking and laughing with Jaime, who was sitting next to Kate, this was no easy feat. Poor Shaye Areheart, in the meantime, was stuck trying to make polite conversation with Evelyn Kern, who might as well have been dead, for all her personality.

"Evelyn," Shaye said, "will you have a chance to do some things in New York while you're here?"

"I don't know," Evelyn said.

Shaye tried again. "There's a wonderful new exhibit opening at the Met—an Impressionist collection you might enjoy."

Harris leaned down the table. "We're going to the opening," he said. "Some of my clients are underwriting it."

"Black tie?" Mark asked Harris.

"Black tie," Harris said, turning back to Rebecca and her husband.

Mark looked at Kate. "You'll have to tell us all about it, Kate. I've never been to an opening like that. Not black tie."

Fuck you, she looked at him.

"I have a pass to the exhibit if you'd like to see it," Shaye said to Evelyn.

"Oh, I don't know," Evelyn said.

"Traci and I will probably go to the exhibit," Mark said to Kate. "But like normal people do."

"Ha," Kate said. She looked at Traci. "Do you like art?"

She nodded, smiling. "Very much."

"Do you like normal people?" Kate said.

Traci's smile broadened. "I like people," she said, neatly avoiding the trap.

Stop it! Kate told herself. *You're acting like a child. Leave her alone. Ignore him.*

"Kate," Shaye said, "isn't Bennett, Fitzallen & Coe publishing a biography of Monet soon?"

"I don't know," Evelyn Kern said, no doubt out of habit.

Conversation ceased at Rebecca's end of the table. She was looking at Kate. So was Dick Skolchak. They were doing so because they had canceled the Monet book because they didn't think it was commercial. The agent had then sold it for three times the money to another house, for which it was a lead book for the fall. It was the kind of failure on the administration's part that one did well not to dwell on for long if one wished to remain employed.

"It didn't work out," Kate said.

"Oh, that's too bad," Shaye said.

Dinner staggered on. Rushman reappeared, but only to ask that Rebecca join him and Kern in the study.

When Kate shook hands good night with Kern in the foyer, the British publisher leaned forward and whispered, "I'm thrilled we'll be doing the Southland book."

Kate looked at him. This was news to her. The Southland book had been sold to another English publisher three years ago—and it sure as hell hadn't been Hatfield & Stephens.

Mr. Rushman and Rebecca simultaneously appeared on either side of Kate then. She looked at Mr. Rushman. "Louis was just talking about Lydia's book."

"Yes," Mr. Rushman said under his breath, smiling at Kern, "we've made a deal."

"And a damn good one, I think," Kern said.

Rebecca whispered, "Eight hundred," in Kate's ear and stepped back, beaming.

Oh. So that was it. Hatfield & Stephens had offered eight hundred thousand dollars for Lydia's book. The contract they had with the other English publisher was only for two hundred fifty plus escalators. Presuming the manuscript due date hadn't been changed on the first contract, and that manuscript delivery date had long since come and gone, Bennett, Fitzallen & Coe, Kate bet, was going to declare the contract void.

Nice. Nice move.

Kate Weston, Executive Editor, Sleazebag Publishing, Inc.

"Harris, let's go," Kate said abruptly, taking his arm. "Good night, everyone."

"We'll go down with you," Mark said, guiding his gorgeous young Traci to the door.

Oh, God. Kate rubbed her eyes as she went out into the hall, wishing this night would end. She was near tears. When she reached the elevator and pushed the button, she dropped her hand and turned around to find that Traci was standing there.

"Lydia staged this," Traci whispered. "It's not what you think."

Kate stared at her for a moment. *Lydia* had staged this? Mark and Traci? Here? Tonight?

"Oh, brother," Harris said to Kate as he and Mark joined the women at the elevator, "you've taken me to some weird publishing dinners, honey, but that was the weirdest."

"The wife never did come back from the kitchen, did she?" Mark said.

"No," Harris said.

Kate looked at Mark and smiled. "I like your friend, Traci," she said, reveling in a look of astonishment.

FIVE

Forgiveness

With everything else going so badly, the black tie opening at the Metropolitan came as a welcome diversion. Kate changed into a dress at the office, changed her jewelry, brushed her teeth, put on new makeup, tried to jazz up her hair a little, and then met Harris downstairs at seven. They took a cab crosstown on Sixty-third Street, through the park, and headed uptown where they were dropped at Parioli Romanissimo at Eighty-first Street.

They were dining with Harris's great friend, John Halifent, and his wife, Ramona. John was in investment banking, too, and Ramona was some sort of an artist—Ramona was so vague about it, about whether she was a painter or a sculptor or what, and no one had ever been invited to her studio to see anything—and, as they usually did, Kate chatted with Ramona about art books and cookbooks while the men discussed deals and golf.

Dinner was delicious and Kate was not aware of feeling any kind of distress. In fact, she enjoyed herself.

They walked over to the museum shortly after ten and Kate's spirits rose, marveling at how beautiful the Metropolitan was under the night lights, the fountains spraying, the stairs rising as though an altar to the gods. They walked in through the front door, handing over their invitations, and what was normally the hustle-and-bustle lobby mobbed with tourists was now a kind of fairy land where everyone smiled and looked pretty and handsome. The light—how much more flattering could it get?—was soft and the music from the orchestra there in the central lobby rose up through the great domed hall and then outward, down through the wings of the museum, rolling over marble, through eons of time past.

There were many small tables set up in the lobby and people were already sitting at them, drinking. The exhibit was upstairs, on the second floor, and it was while climbing that front main staircase that Kate's heart began to sink. It was something about Harris's friend, John. John was a shuffler, and an uncomfortable one at that. And Kate didn't know why, but it always seemed to fall to her to move John around the museum—or wherever they were with the Halifents—and try to interest John in the goings-on. He never was, though he was always unfailingly polite about it—always standing at attention, trying to keep out of everyone else's way, smiling a little, waiting for someone to direct him where to go next.

Harris, on the other hand, was always taken away by Ramona, and she would—and did tonight—use sweeping dramatic gestures and a tiny whispering voice to cast all the light on the paintings for Harris that her mysterious artistic sensibilities were capable of. Harris, smiling always, would listen.

"That's you, waiting for Harris to come home from work," John whispered to Kate, laughing, as they stood in front of a picture of a woman washing clothes on a riverbank while her baby played in the grass.

"I hope not," Kate said, moving on, knowing she would have to come back to see the exhibit again. She was getting into a horrendous temper now, feeling like punching John's dopey face, pulling Ramona's hair, and giving Harris a swift kick in the rear. The Halifents were awful, she decided during the exhibit; she also decided she probably hated them.

They walked back to the main staircase and began their descent. Kate loved coming down these stairs, always, inexplicably, as long as she could remember, slipping away into the fantasy that she was the queen of England coming down the palace stairs to greet her subjects. (Kate had no idea why, but this fantasy also always occurred while descending one of the main staircases in the New York Public Library.)

People were dancing in the lobby, a fox trot—which was sweet, Kate thought; she really did love this side of New York, this part that liked to fox trot. The tables around the orchestra and dance area were draped in white tablecloths, and with one low burning candle on each, their cumulative effect was magical.

"Thank heavens you love to dance," Ramona said, slinging her arm through Harris's and leaning her head on his shoulder, "because John, as you know, hates it. Not that he knows how."

"I danced at our wedding," John said.

"Danced once in eleven years, hooray," Ramona said.

Kate had heard this same exchange perhaps eight times now since she had met the Halifents.

They found a table and, as Kate sat down, Ramona pulled Harris away to dance.

"What would you like?" John asked Kate, sitting down next to her.

"White wine," Kate said. "Harris will want a brandy."

"Two white wines and two brandies," John said to the waiter.

They watched Harris and Ramona on the floor. They were very good, both of them, fluid, clearly enjoying how good a dancer the other one was.

"Do you dance well, Kate?" John said.

"Not as well as your wife."

"Nobody dances as well as Ramona," John said. "At least, that's what they tell me."

Kate looked at John. He was straightening his dinner tie, looking around at the other tables. "What *do* you like to do?" she asked him.

"Besides making love?" he said, turning to her, grinning.

She smiled politely.

"Golf, squash, tennis, you know, the usual," he said.

The number ended and Harris and Ramona clapped, but didn't return to the table. They waited for the next number to begin and resumed dancing.

The drinks arrived at the table.

"We're going to throw Harris's bachelor party at the seaport," John said. "We want everyone from the office to come."

Kate looked at him over the rim of her glass.

"Harris said he thought October twenty-third—that sound about right to you?"

Sipping wine, she nodded. She swallowed, lowering her glass. "But please remember, we'll be having a very long week."

"You mean don't tire the old man out," John said, chuckling, bringing his calendar and pen out of his breast pocket to make a notation. "Yep," he said, snapping it shut and putting it back in his pocket, "we're not as young as we used to be."

John had been Harris's best man at his first wedding.

"If you'll excuse me," Kate said, standing up, "I have to visit the ladies' room," and she took her clutch bag and circled the lobby, making the long walk through the ancient sculpture hall to find it.

She did not really have to visit the ladies' room. She really just had to get away from John for a few minutes.

"Kate Weston, isn't it?" a young woman said to her in the hall.

Kate smiled. "Yes." The woman was stunning and Kate knew she recognized her from somewhere.

"Dani Shapiro," she said, holding out her hand, "we met at Margo's book party."

"Oh, yes, hi," Kate said, shaking her hand, "nice to see you again. I don't suppose you're ready to consider changing publishing houses yet, are you?" And then she caught herself. She released the woman's hand and shook her head. "No, you stay right where you are. You're at a great house."

"Yes, I know," the woman said. Pause. "I'm sorry if I seem a little confused; it's just the last time we talked, you made Bennett, Fitzallen & Coe sound like the new heaven on earth."

"And I was wrong," Kate said flat out.

The woman blinked, clearly thrown by Kate's attitude.

They exchanged a few more words and then each went on her way, Kate feeling worse than before. She was not accustomed to being a traitor to the publishing house she loved. Had loved.

In the ladies' room lounge she tried to make herself look a little more festive. But it wasn't working. There was a peculiar connection in Kate's biology so that whenever she was very tired or depressed her hair went flat. It was flat now. And she looked pale, too, and . . . and blech.

"Blech," Kate said, looking at herself in the mirror.

"What I wouldn't give to be your age," the woman next to her said. She was one of those raving New York beauties now in her late sixties or so, clearly older, but somehow even more beautiful now after years of practice in carrying herself. She was thin and terribly elegant, with white hair swept up on the back of her head in a way that made Kate suspect she had been blond and had worn her hair the same way in yesteryear too. Like Grace Kelly.

Kate smiled at the woman in the mirror. "And what would you do if you were my age? Believe me, I'm open for suggestions."

The woman laughed a sparkling, lovely laugh and met Kate's eyes in the mirror. "I think," she said, "I would not have spent nearly so much time on things I later found out were not really worth my time at all."

"Such as?" Kate said.

The woman glanced back over her shoulder and then looked at Kate again in the mirror, hesitating.

"Tell me the truth now," Kate said, smiling, "it's important."

The woman smiled and looked as though she were going to say something—but she didn't. She shook her head instead, inhaling sharply through her nose, and turned away from the mirror. "I'm sorry," she said to Kate, "but I'm afraid that's between me and my

Maker." She paused. "Good luck," she said, gently laying a hand on Kate's arm.

"Thank you," Kate said, watching her go out.

Well.

Walking back to the lobby through the great hall, the museum seemed haunted now to Kate, the echoes of music and talk and laughter reverberating around her like a testament to lost souls—one of which, she felt, she might be rapidly becoming.

She returned to their table and saw Harris laughing with John and Ramona. He looked very distinguished in black tie. He looked very handsome. And when he saw her he smiled, standing up immediately, and Kate felt as though her heart might break.

They went straight into the bedroom as usual, Kate to toss her purse down and take off her shoes, Harris to throw his jacket on the bed and use the bathroom. When he came out, zipping up his pants, Kate glanced over from the closet and heard herself say, "Harris, I'm sorry, but I don't think I'm going to be able to do it after all."

Would that always be how Kate would remember him? Standing there in the bedroom, hand on his zipper, a stricken look on his face as though she had just shot him?

"I don't think I can get married," she said.

He recovered quickly, coming quietly over to sit with her on the bed, to say all the right things. Of course she was scared, of course it was happening too fast, of course they could postpone the wedding—maybe push it to the spring? But she was not to worry, they would take their time. He loved her and she loved him and it would all work out, she should just wait and see.

When she had blurted her news out, at first it had felt good. But now, as Harris talked on, Kate realized that if she were not careful she would let him bend this conversation back to the familiar path: back to where they would decide they should not decide anything tonight, they'd sleep on it and talk in the morning. Only if they did that, Kate knew, they would not talk in the morning. They would simply go on as if Kate had never said anything.

Kate was shaking her head. "No, no," she was saying, "I do love you—and that's why I know I shouldn't marry you. Harris, I don't love you the right way. Not the way you want."

Harris laughed at this, giving her a hug, saying, "Oh, Kate, your self-esteem is so low, darling. And you're tired. You're not supposed to worry about me—you should worry about yourself, what you want."

Kate pushed him back, held his face in her hands, and said, "I am, Harris, I am doing what I want. And I'm sorry, but I can't get married." A tear spilled down her cheek. He didn't move. She kissed one side of his face and then the other, reached for her bag, and got up.

"Kate, listen to me," he said, grabbing her hand, "I know you want to get married—I know you want to have children."

And then, clear as a bell, as if she were standing right next to her, Kate heard her mother say, "Your father said the same thing to me." Kate whirled around and looked at Harris. *Dear God,* she thought, *that's it, isn't it?*

"Kate," Harris said, jumping up and taking hold of her arms, shaking her, "Kate, what's the matter with you?"

"I don't know," she said, pushing his hands away and walking into the hall. "But I know I have to go home and think."

"But this is your home!" he said. It was close to a wail.

"Harris, please," she said, walking to the front hall closet, "let me go tonight. Let me go home and think things through." She opened the hall closet, reached to the key rack for her apartment keys. When she came out, she found him blocking the way to the door.

"Kate," he said, "don't go."

"I have to go," she said. Pause. "Please."

Slowly he stepped out of her way. When she moved past him and opened the door, he blurted, "You can't just walk out!"

"I'm not walking out," she said, frozen, standing there in the doorway, eyes on the carpet in the hallway. *Go, go, you've got to go.*

"You are!" Harris said. "You're walking out instead of talking it out. It isn't fair, Kate. You have to stay and talk this out with me."

She didn't say anything.

"Then go ahead!" he shouted. "Go on! Get out of here, if that's what you want!"

And so she did, closing the door behind her. Numb, tears streaking her face, she pushed the button for the elevator and fumbled in her purse for a tissue.

"Kate, I'm sorry," Harris said a second later, running out of the apartment and taking her by the arm. "Darling, please, come back inside—let's talk."

"I can't, Harris," Kate whispered, "not tonight."

The elevator arrived and when the door opened, the attendant stood there, not knowing quite what to do.

Harris let go of her arm.

Kate got in the elevator. The doors closed behind her. She didn't turn around until the elevator reached the ground floor and the attendant said, "We're here, Miss Weston."

— *52* —

"Home again, home again, jiggedy jig!" Lydia called, coming into the house through the kitchen door.

"Hi!" Noél called, running in from the breakfast room. She stopped short on the other side of the swinging door, realizing she might scare the little girl.

Oh, she was a sweetie. Cute, but not pretty like Noél thought she would be. She was more—huggable. And her eyes, she had the brownest eyes. And she had the blond hair of the sisters.

"Allyson, darling," Lydia said, "this is my friend Noél. Can you say hello?"

Noél didn't think Allyson looked very enthused about the idea. In fact, she looked decidedly uneasy, sidling closer to Lydia.

But when Noél leaned over and smiled and said, "How was your plane ride? I'm afraid to fly, how 'bout you?" the little girl came alive.

"It was very good except when the plane hit a bump in the air and then everyone got scared," she said. "But not really because there was nothing to be scared of, Aunt Lyddie said so, and I told her I knew that and I wasn't scared at all and so then we played cards—go fish—and I won. Look, they gave me the cards to keep. And these—these wings they gave to me to keep too."

Just what we need, Noél thought, smiling, as Allyson stepped forward to show her her treasures, *another chatty female around the house.*

Gracia, who had flown back the week before, now came into the kitchen, saying, "Ahhh, my little señorita! Welcome home!" and Allyson ran to her and jumped up in her arms. Meanwhile, the driver appeared at the kitchen door, carrying their bags, and Gracia and Allyson went off to show him where to put them.

"So what's new?" Lydia said, pouring herself a glass of water from the cooler.

"Pallsner called again," Noél said.

"Let him call," Lydia said, raising the glass to her mouth. "I told him I'd start working as soon as I can."

"He's adamant about seeing you tomorrow," Noél said, "not to work—for a meeting."

Lydia drank the whole glass down. She took a breath, lowered the glass, and said, "He called you at your job?"

"I'm not starting until August," Noél said. "Lise said with everything that's happened, she figured you could use me a little longer."

"That was very nice of her," Lydia said, scanning the bulletin board on the wall for new things.

"Lydia," Noél said, "Mort's not kidding—he's determined to see you tomorrow."

"Then I'll see him the day *after* tomorrow," Lydia said, turning around, "you can tell him that." Pause. "I'm sorry about this, Noél," she said then, walking over and putting her glass down on the counter, "I'll get a new assistant in here as soon as I can."

"Listen, I'm just glad I'm here," Noél said. Pause. "You know, I'm going to kind of miss working with you—a lot."

Lydia smiled then. "Me, too, Ms. Shaunnessy, me too."

Noél awakened at five the next morning and couldn't go back to sleep. She gave up trying, finally, put on her robe, and went downstairs for something to eat. As she walked through the living room she was surprised to hear Lydia's voice in the kitchen.

Of course she's up, Noél thought, *the time difference with the East Coast.*

"How long was it before Billy and Cathy really understood?" she heard Lydia say.

Noél froze in her tracks. She didn't know why, but Lydia's tone of voice told her she shouldn't be listening to this. There was nothing to listen to though, at the moment; evidently Lydia was on the phone with Gracia—who else had a Billy and Cathy?

"So will she go all through it again?" Lydia said. "Crying and everything?"

Silence.

"Yes." A sigh. "I hope so. But I'll make an appointment with Dr. Glasson right away. I remember how much she helped Billy." Pause.

"No, she went right to sleep. Later I went in to check on her and I sat on the bed and watched her for a while—" Lydia's voice caught and she paused again. And then she said, "And I wondered—what will I do if she never stops crying for her mother?"

Lydia spent the morning helping Allyson arrange her room the way she wanted it. Noél, in the meantime, stayed downstairs in the office to take all the calls Lydia refused to take: Gary, Max Zacharius, Lydia's agent, Helena from Pallsner's office, Lydia's lawyer, Aaron Platz, Chico the costume designer, Lydia's makeup lady, Holly—

"Holly, hi," Noél said.

"Hi gorgeous girl, how are you? Now that the children are away, can you come out and play? Like tonight?"

"Aren't you shooting tomorrow?"

"Not until three."

"Tonight," Noél said.

"Tonight!" Holly said. "Eight, okay?"

The other line was ringing and Noél took it. It was Kate.

"I know she must be busy," Kate said, "but I thought I'd call anyway and see how things were going."

"You know?" Noél said, "there's a chance you just might be the exception to the rule this morning, hold on." For what seemed like the ninety-ninth time Noél walked to the bottom of the stairs. "Lydia, Kate's on the phone," she called.

"I'll talk to Kate," Lydia said, appearing at the top of the stairs. "Allyson, sweetheart," she called down the hall, "I'm going downstairs. When you finish come down and we'll have lunch, okay?" Lydia came skipping down the stairs. "She's so smart, I can't believe it," she said to Noél. "Just the smartest little lambkin."

They went into the office and Lydia swept up the phone. "Kate, hello!" she said. Smile. "Oh, we're just terrific. How about you?" She listened for a moment and then her smile faded. "What's the matter?" she said. "You sound terrible." She turned to Noél and winced, sending the signal that this would better be taken in private.

Noél closed the door to the office and went upstairs to see how Allyson, a.k.a. smartest little lambkin, was doing. Gracia was in there, giving her opinion as to where Bernardo the Bear should go, on the foot of the bed or on top of the bookcase.

"I think on the bed, little señorita," Gracia said. "I think it is softer to sit there."

"Okay," Allyson said happily, skipping over to put Bernardo on the foot of her bed with what looked to be twenty or so other stuffed animals.

"I leave the little señorita in your hands," Gracia said to Noél, going out.

By the time Lydia came back upstairs, Noél and Allyson were sitting in a sea of books on the floor.

"And we just got those organized," Lydia sighed, smiling, resting her shoulder against the doorway.

Allyson looked up at her aunt, brown eyes sincere. "I'm sorry, Aunt Lyddie, but Noél wanted to know what books I had. I was showing them to her."

"Yes, that Noél can talk a girl into anything, I hear," Lydia said, pushing off the doorway and coming over to squat down next to Allyson. "Can't she?" she said, tickling Allyson a little and then giving her a big kiss on the top of the head.

"I'll put them away," Noél offered.

"No," Allyson said, "I took them out, I'll put them away."

Lydia beamed. "And after you finish, we'll have lunch." She stood up and Allyson began her task. "Guess what?" Lydia said to Noél, who was still sitting cross-legged on the floor, "Kate's not getting married anymore."

"No?" Noél said.

"No, and she's pretty upset," Lydia sighed. And then, making sure Allyson wasn't looking at her, she made a pantomime of utter jubilation.

"And I'm sure this all comes as a complete surprise to you," Noél said.

"Why yes, it does," Lydia said, starting to laugh.

Noél stood up and gave Lydia a disapproving look. But then she smiled. "Well, I have to admit, he didn't sound right for her."

"And Mark is pretty wonderful," Lydia said.

"You can't make Kate's choices for her, Lydia," Noél said.

"Of course not." She turned to Allyson. "Allyson, do you remember Mark who came to the riding ring with Kate?"

"Yes," she said, filing a book away.

"Did you like him?"

Allyson nodded, turning around. "He made jumps in the front yard."

Lydia turned to Allyson. "He had a horse show with Allyson in the front yard."

"But did he jump the jumps?" Noél said. "That is the question."

"Not only did he jump the jumps," Lydia said, "but he made Kate take off her shoes and stockings and jump the jumps too."

"Well then, that's it," Noél said, throwing up her hands, "you can't make Kate's choices for her, Lydia, but Allyson can. Mark wins by a landslide."

They had lunch outside on the patio, salads and mineral water for Lydia and Noél; peanut butter and honey and wheat germ on raisin bread for Allyson, plus a glass of milk and a dish of fresh fruit salad.

"Excuse me, señora," Gracia said, coming outside, "but Mr. Pallsner is on the telephone and says it is an emergency."

Pallsner was the only man in the world Gracia called mister and everyone knew she meant it as an insult.

"It's Pallsner on the line himself?" Lydia said.

"Yes, señora."

Lydia glanced at Noél. "Okay, I'll take it," she said, getting up and going into the house.

Whatever Mort said to her, it had to have been a lulu because when Lydia reappeared fifteen minutes later, she was dressed in a pale gray suit, with her hair up—her elegant businesswoman attire—announcing that she had to run down to the studio for a meeting.

"I have to go to work, honey," she said to Allyson. "I'll be home in time to eat dinner with you." She kissed her, glanced at Noél— shaking her head, indicating she didn't want any questions—and left without further comment.

The hair on Noél's neck was up. Something was wrong.

"Gary," Noél said, speaking on the cordless phone while sitting on the little hill in the woods out front where Allyson's dolls were having a Robin Hood tea party with Maid Marion, or so Allyson said, "something's wrong. Lydia's on her way in to see Mort."

"You said she wouldn't come in until tomorrow."

"Exactly. I don't know what he said to her, but I don't think it's good. Something's up."

"I'll see if I can find out anything," he promised.

At three-thirty Gary called back to say he had missed Lydia, that she had her meeting with Pallsner and left, presumably on her way home. But Lydia was not on her way home because four o'clock rolled by, and then five o'clock, and then, finally, just before six the Mercedes came up the driveway.

Lydia looked terrible. Noél thought she might be ill, she was so pale.

"Sweetheart," Lydia said quietly to Allyson, "why don't you take your dolls inside to Gracia and wash up for dinner. I need to talk to Noél for a moment."

"Okay," Allyson said, picking up her things.

When she disappeared through the front door, Noél said, "What's the matter? What's happened?"

Lydia turned to address her, but avoided—Noél thought—meeting her eyes. "I had to make some decisions today," she said.

Noél waited.

"First," Lydia said, "I've re-signed with 'Cassandra's World' for another two years. Allyson needs continuity and I think we should settle into a routine here for a few years longer."

Pause. "You signed a new contract?" Noél said. "Today? Just like that? One phone call from Mort and you went down and signed a new contract?"

"And two," Lydia said, continuing, "I'm going to repay the advance to Bennett, Fitzallen & Coe—the book is off."

"What!" Noél said.

"There's more than one life to be concerned about now," Lydia said, looking down at the ground. "And I need you to call Kate first thing tomorrow and tell her—and tell her I'll call her later this week."

"But Lydia—"

"Noél, please." It was scarcely a whisper; it was definitely a plea. Lydia raised her head. "I need your help."

Noél nodded. "Okay."

"Thank you," Lydia said, and she walked into the house, leaving Noél standing in the yard, utterly dumbfounded.

"And just how do you propose we unsell the three hundred fifty thousand books the sales force has taken orders for?" Mr. Rushman wanted to know.

Needless to say, the news of Lydia's decision to repay the advance on her book and not publish her autobiography after all was not going over very well at Bennett, Fitzallen & Coe. They were in an emergency meeting, Mr. Rushman, Kate, Rebecca, Dick Skolchak, and Mark, trying to figure out what to do.

"Three hundred *ninety* thousand," Rebecca said, correcting him. "The new advance figures came in this morning."

"We're wiped out, that's it," Dick said to no one in particular. "We have no lead book—we have no books on the fall list."

"What I want to know, Kate," Rebecca said, "is what did you do out in Long Island that has her backing out now?"

Kate looked at her. "And what is that supposed to mean?"

"It means if this book turns up at another house, Kate Weston, and you happen to turn up working at that other house," Rebecca said, "we're going to be suing you from here to Timbuktu."

Kate blinked. "You think I'm getting her to cancel the book so I can take it to another house."

"How dare you!" Mr. Rushman exploded.

"Mr. Rushman," Kate said, turning to him calmly, "Rebecca was just making a point. No one is stealing this book, I assure you."

"Then why is she canceling the book?" Rebecca said. "Explain it to us, Kate."

If Kate had felt like herself at that moment, she would have said, "Because I think she's trying to protect the little girl. I don't think she wants to go on record about Allyson's mother's past, the circumstances of her birth; I don't think Lydia wants to pick fights with industry people who might somehow take their revenge out on Allyson." But since Kate was not feeling like herself, but was instead so thoroughly sick of Rebecca, Kate decided to put Rebecca in the hot seat to see how she liked it. Two could play at this game.

"Why are you asking me?" Kate said to her. "You were the one who called Lydia the day we found out that her sister died. Maybe you'd like to tell us what it was that you said to her."

"You called Lydia Southland?" Rushman said. "Rebecca? I thought we agreed that you wouldn't call her."

"She called her," Kate said, thoroughly enjoying how red Rebecca's face was getting.

"I called," Rebecca said, "only because I couldn't trust Kate to do what we agreed upon."

"And what was that?" Kate asked her.

She turned to Kate, eyes narrowing slightly. "To find out if the completed manuscript would be delayed."

"So you called Lydia after her sister died to find out if she would be late with the manuscript," Kate summarized, "and now Lydia wants to cancel publication with Bennett, Fitzallen & Coe. Gee, I wonder if there's a connection."

Silence.

"Well, I guess that's that," Kate said, getting up out of her chair.

"That's not it," Rushman said. "You get on a plane to Los Angeles and get that manuscript, Kate."

"She can't go," Rebecca said, "her office is a mess."

"Who am I going to send," Rushman said, "*you?*"

Rebecca shut her mouth.

Rushman turned back to Kate. "I don't care what it takes, Kate, but get that manuscript and signed releases. Cut the shit out of it—anything she's nervous about, yank it out!—but we *have* to publish something or we're sunk." Pause. "And I mean sunk. Dick's right, the fall list is for shit."

"I'll do my best," Kate said, going to the door.

"An economy car, remember!" Dick said.

As Kate walked down the hall, Mark came flying out of Rushman's office after her.

"Kate, wait—wait up a sec," he said.

She waited for him to catch up. "What?"

"I have to go back," he said, pointing with his thumb back at Rushman's office, "but I have to ask you something."

"What?" Kate said.

"The ring," he said.

It didn't register for a moment.

Mark took hold of her left hand. "It's gone," he said. His eyes came up to hers—looking hopeful, but also a little scared.

"Oh, that," Kate said, instinctively pulling her hand away and hiding it behind her.

"Yes, that," Mark said.

"This isn't the time or place," she said.

"Just tell me," he said.

"And it doesn't have anything to do with you," she said.

"Just tell me," he said.

"It's off," she said. "I gave him the ring back." And then she walked back to her office. As she turned the corner, she heard Mark give the muffled cry, "Yes! Yes!" and Kate, once she closed her office door, couldn't help but smile.

— *54* —

Lydia had been so clear in her wish to avoid him, Gary didn't want to offend her anymore than he already knew he would by showing up at the house and so, for the first time in three years, instead of punching in the security code at the gate and letting himself in, he pressed the intercom. If Lydia was too angry, he'd simply drive away, he decided. If she was only half-angry, he'd talk his way in to see her.

He had to know what was going on. He was happy to hear she had re-signed with "Cassandra's World," but was utterly confused about why or how she had come to make that decision. Rather, why or how she could have made it without discussing it with him first. A month ago it would have been unthinkable. A month ago it would have been unthinkable that a day would go by when they wouldn't have spoken.

Had he pressured her too much? Was this her way of telling him to back off or he was out of her life for good?

"I'm sorry, Señor Steiner," Gracia said through the intercom, "but the señora is not here."

"Oh," Gary said. He sat there not knowing what to do. "Well, do you think she'll be home soon?"

"I do not think so," Gracia said. "She had a meeting in the Valley with her lawyers. She said it would be a long meeting."

"Oh," Gary said.

"Señor Steiner?" Gracia said.

"Yes?"

"Why are you talking through the intercom? Why don't you come in? Is there something wrong?"

"Oh," he said. So Lydia hadn't banished him from the kingdom after all. She wouldn't talk to Gary, but everybody else was allowed to apparently. "I don't know," Gary said, "I guess with the little girl and everything I thought I should be a little more formal."

"Then now you have been formal," Gracia said, "and now you come in," and the gate buzzed open.

He found Gracia in the kitchen. Noél was out apartment hunting, she reported, and Allyson was upstairs helping the new nanny unpack.

"I haven't even met her," Gary said, helping himself to an oatmeal cookie from the jar on the counter.

"Oh, she is very nice," Gracia said. "Very proper. She is a genuine English nanny. The señora said she went to nanny school."

"I meant Allyson," Gary said, biting into the cookie. "I haven't even seen her yet."

"Yes, well, the señora has been careful not to overwhelm her," Gracia said. "The little señorita has had a lot of changes—and so quickly."

"Gracia?" an English woman's voice called.

"In here, Señorita Twickingham," Gracia called.

There was a chuckle from a woman and the sound of a little girl giggling. "Such a big house," the English woman's voice said, "such a lovely big house, I am lost!"

"I know the way!" the little girl said, and an instant later, the two appeared through the swinging door.

"Oh!" the nanny said, seeing Gary. "I didn't know we had company."

Allyson only looked up at Gary with a puzzled expression, as much as to say, *You're not Noél—who are you?*

"Little señorita," Gracia said, "I want you to meet one of your aunt's dearest friends. This is Señor Steiner."

"Gary," he said, squatting down on his haunches to say hello. He held the half-eaten cookie up and smiled. "Alias, Gary the cookie snatcher. Gracia makes the best cookies in all of Los Angeles and I come over to snatch them."

Allyson smiled tentatively, backing slightly toward the nanny. She was an irresistible little girl. Tall for her age, on the thin side, with the blondest hair and the biggest, brownest eyes. She was dressed in pale lavender shorts and a T-shirt that had dancing bears on it.

"And I'm Judith Twickingham," the nanny said, holding out her hand. "I'm Allyson's nanny. Please call me Judith."

"Hi," Gary said, standing to take her hand. "Welcome. Gary Steiner. As well as being an old friend, I work with Lydia at the studio."

"Señor Steiner is the story editor," Gracia said.

"Oh, indeed," Judith said. "It is all so very exciting. But we are one year behind in the show, you know, in England."

"Want to see my room?" Allyson asked him.

Gary looked down, delighted at this unexpected invitation. "Well, sure," he said, "I'd love to."

"This way," she said, skipping back out the swinging door.

Gary followed Allyson upstairs. Boy, had things changed up here. The guest room where he and Lydia had gone through her trunk that evening was now Allyson's room. It was pale pink with white trim, and the four-poster bed was gone, in its place a white trundle bed. There was a white dresser, some white bookcases, tons of books, and a lot of stuffed animals and dolls.

"This is my dog, Doggert," Allyson said, holding out a brown stuffed dog to him to hold. "And this is Rudolf the cat. And over there are their friends Misty and Woody—and this is Bernardo. He sits here because it's softer."

Gary said hello to each.

"And this is my mommy," Allyson said, going over to the night table and picking up a picture frame. She brought it over to Gary to look at.

"She's very pretty," Gary said, thinking that maybe, vaguely, Angela Clarke resembled Lydia.

"She's in heaven now," Allyson explained, walking around to her desk. "And this is my daddy. He's with Mommy in heaven." She brought this picture over to Gary too.

Daddy was about forty, seen in the picture putting together a jungle gym. He was laughing. He looked like a good guy. A big guy. "He's a very handsome, very strong man," Gary said. He looked at Allyson. "Should I put these back now?"

"No, I'll put them back," she said, taking them from him and walking over to the dresser and replacing her father, and then trotting over to the night table to put her mother back.

Gary glanced at Judith, who was now standing in the doorway. She looked very moved, very locked in to this little girl already. But who wouldn't be? Gary could understand now why Lydia was so protective.

"Are you a good swimmer?" Allyson asked him next, standing on one foot and holding the other in her hand behind her.

"Very good, as a matter of fact," he said. "How about you?"

"Oh, Judith," Allyson said quickly, turning to her, "please can Gary take me swimming in the swimming pool? He's a good swimmer."

"Oh, but Allyson—"

"I do have a suit here," Gary said to Judith. "And I wouldn't mind—not at all."

"Oh please oh please oh please?" Allyson said, dropping her foot and clasping her hands in a plea.

Judith smiled. "Well, if Mr. Steiner says it's all right with him, I suppose we all could go outside."

"Goodeee!" Allyson squealed, jumping up and down.

"I do not have a bathing costume yet, you see," Judith explained.

"I'll go down to the pool house and change," Gary said. "You guys come down when you're ready."

As he walked down the hall to the front stairs, he poked his head into what used to be the second guest room and found that that room too had completely changed; it was now Judith's room, wallpapered in a cheerful flower pattern. In it was the four-poster bed from the other former guest room.

He went downstairs whistling, stopping in at the kitchen to tell Gracia he was taking Allyson for a swim, an idea that met with her approval. She told him that the señora had only swum with the little señorita once, briefly, and that she wished to have her wear one of the life jackets until she was absolutely sure of her swimming ability.

Gary went out to the pool house and changed out of his clothes. For a lousy day, it was fast improving. But then, kids were like that. Kids tended always to be in the place where AA was constantly urging its members to be—not dwelling in the past, not projecting into the future, but here and now in the present, experiencing life. Kids did it naturally and were pretty happy until, of course, some adult taught them otherwise, taught them how to dwell in the past or be terrified about the future so they could be unhappy like adults too.

Gary rummaged around in the storage area of the pool house and not only found a life preserver for Allyson, but an eight-foot-long inflatable alligator, which was currently as flat as a pancake. He was dragging this out when Noél arrived home.

"Hey, Tarzan, it doesn't look like much of a match," she said from the patio.

"You got a bicycle pump or something for this thing?"

"Only if you invite me to swim with you," she said.

"You'll have to ask Allyson," he said.

"Allyson!" Noél called up to Allyson's window. "May I go swimming with you and Gary?"

A little face appeared at the window. "Sure!"

"Great," Noél said, "I'll get the pump from the garage." She stopped and turned around. "Hey, Gare, guess who thinks she's found a house to rent?"

Gary straightened up and turned around to look at her. "A house?"

"A little house," Noél said. "It's only two bedrooms, but it has a neat little yard—"

"What do you need two bedrooms for?" Gary said. "And who's going to mow the lawn?"

She put her arm on her hip. "I haven't even moved yet and you're already criticizing my house and yelling at me for not cutting the lawn. Man, talk about stinking thinking, Steiner, you're the pits."

Gary laughed. "Sorry. Where is it?"

"North Orange Grove," she said. "Near Gracia."

"Sort of near someone else too, if I recall," he said, knowing that North Orange Grove was maybe all of ten minutes from a certain little lane off Laurel Canyon. "I don't suppose Holly helped you pick it out."

"And what if she did?" Noél asked him.

"Then I approve," he said, returning his attention to the deflated alligator, kicking it with his bare foot. "She's good with money."

Now Noél's other hand came up to rest on her other hip. "And how, pray tell, do you happen to know that?"

"Lydia told me once," he said.

"And how would Lydia know?" Noél said. "Holly never talks about money."

"Maybe that's how she knows," Gary said. "Come on, Noél, I've got a hot customer for this thing. Get the pump, will you?"

Allyson came down to the pool wearing a white terry cloth robe, flipflops, and Mickey Mouse sunglasses. Gary burst out laughing. "Oh, Allyson, what a glamourpuss you are. You look just like your Aunt Lydia."

Allyson smiled and Gary could have sworn she started swaying her hips a little as she walked. Good grief. She could do a pretty fair imitation of her aunt's walk already.

"Are the dogs terribly ferocious?" Judith asked him as she came down to sit at the table under the shade of the umbrella.

"To strangers, they are," Gary said. "But that's the point. Once they get to know you, you'll be glad they're around. They're good company."

"Mrs. Southland said they're going to be retrained," Judith said. "That a man is coming to teach us too—how to talk to them—and then train the dogs to respond to us."

"Doggie school," Allyson giggled, slipping off her robe. Her bathing suit was red-and-white striped with a big blue sailboat on it.

"I think you're going to need some suntan lotion," Gary said, noting how white her skin was.

"She has sunblock on," Judith said. "Number fifteen."

"Good," Gary said. "Now Allyson, you're going to have to wear a life preserver, okay? Your Aunt Lydia—"

"I know," Allyson said, kicking off her flipflops, "I have a pool at home and I always wear one in Daddy's boat. Aunt Lyddie said I had to wear one here until we swim some more."

Gary's heart did a little lurch, wondering how a little girl like this could lose her parents. It seemed so unfair.

Allyson padded over to pick up the life jacket. She put it on and then stood there, waiting, arms out. "Will you do me up?"

"Sure," he said. He looped the belt through the hinge and tightened it back. "Not too tight?"

She shook her head.

He smiled, touching the tip of her nose. "You're getting freckles already, you know that?"

"I get them every summer," she said.

"Here comes the bicycle pump to save the day!" Noél announced, skipping down the stairs in a white bikini. Judith looked at her and then looked again.

"I'm not embarrassing you, am I, Judith?" Noél said, handing the pump to Gary and then turning around.

"Oh, no," Judith was quick to say. "Everything that needs to be covered is covered." Pause. Smile. "In a manner of speaking."

"My baby-sitter in Long Island has a suit like that," Allyson said. "It's a bikini, Judith." She reached out and touched Noél's stomach. "Look. She has millions and skillions of freckles."

"What do you mean?" Noél said. "Those are beauty marks. And what did you say—*skillions* of them?"

Allyson laughed, taking Noél's hand and pulling her to the pool.

It turned out that Allyson was a pretty good swimmer. After they messed around a while with the alligator—it seemed to take forever to blow up—Gary took Allyson's life jacket off and she swam two whole lengths of the pool with Gary swimming sidestroke beside her.

"You better not let the señora catch her without that life jacket on!" Gracia warned from the patio, coming out with a tray of lemonade.

"I'll take responsibility, Gracia," Judith said. "I think she's quite safe with Mr. Steiner and Noél."

"Gary!" he called from the pool. "How many times do I have to tell you? Gary—call me Gary." He pulled himself out of the pool and then turned around for Allyson. "Come on, Allyson, we better get that life jacket back on, just in case. We don't want your aunt Lydia to blow a gasket on Judith's first day." He took her hands and in one fell swoop pulled her up and out of the water, setting her down on her feet. He walked over and picked up the life jacket and held it for her while she slipped her arms through it. Then he turned her around and knelt on one knee to fasten the belt.

"Ouch," Allyson said, swatting her ankle.

"What, a fly?" Gary said.

"I don't know," she said.

"Here, let me see," he said, pulling her hand away from her ankle to look.

And that's when he saw Allyson's feet.

He blinked and looked again.

No, he wasn't imagining it, Allyson had the same kind of toes that he did, the ones his ex-wife had always teased him about.

"Oh, hello, señora," he heard Gracia say, "the little señorita is just getting the belt on her life jacket tightened."

Gary looked up the stairs at Lydia.

She was standing there, immobilized, a look of panic on her face like he had never seen before.

"Hi, Aunt Lyddie," Allyson said. "Do you want to swim with us?"

Gary looked back at Allyson—at her eyes, her nose, mouth, chin, neck, and ears—

And in one wild moment he knew it all.

Allyson was his. And Lydia was her mother.

— 55 —

Noél was sitting on the alligator, trying to paddle along, while Gary was helping Allyson put on the life jacket. Gary said something to Allyson; Lydia appeared on the patio; Gracia said something to her; Allyson asked Lydia if she wanted to come swimming; and then next thing Noél knew, Lydia was running into the house and Gary, dripping wet, was running up the stairs into the house after her.

"Allyson," Noél said instinctively, "are you going to ride this wild alligator with me or not?"

Allyson was looking up at the house.

"Yes, dear," Judith said, standing up, "Gary had to see your aunt Lydia. Until they come back, why don't you play on the alligator?"

"Your full name *is* Allyson Alligator Clarke, is it not?" Noél said.

Allyson giggled and walked over to the stairs of the pool.

Lydia ran up the front stairs and Gary threw himself around the end of the banister, scrambling up after her. He heard her bedroom door slam as he reached the top of the stairs; he flew down the hall, trying to get to the door before she—too late—locked it.

"Lydia, let me in," he whispered, jiggling the doorknob.

Silence.

"Lydia," he whispered, "I know. You know I know." Pause. "I saw her feet—her toes. I know. And you knew I'd know. That's why you've kept me away."

After a moment the door opened and Lydia just stood there, shoulders slumped, eyes to the ground.

It was in that moment Gary realized he had tears in his eyes. When Lydia looked up and saw it too, she let out a low wail and sank to her knees. Gary stepped forward and Lydia grabbed his leg, pressing her face into his thigh, sobbing, "I wanted to tell you. Oh, God, for so long I've wanted to tell you."

He squatted down next to her and took her in his arms, holding her as she sobbed.

After several minutes she said, "I thought, at first, if he gets sober, if he stops drinking—" She closed her eyes, tears spilling down her face.

"But I did, Lydia, I did stop drinking," he said.

"But not for a long time, Gary, and then when you did," she said, opening her eyes, "you were such a mess—chasing all those women, always so depressed, saying you were going to kill yourself, I just didn't know if—"

The anger hit from nowhere. He stood up and jerked Lydia to her feet with him. "And who said you were God, Lydia? Who said it was your decision to make that I shouldn't know I had a daughter?"

A spark of anger flashed through her eyes. "Lower your voice," she said.

They glared at each other.

"It's lowered," he said, still holding her by the arms. "Tell me."

"I told you," she said.

"Tell me!" he said.

"What do you want me to say?" she whispered. "I need to spell it out? The kind of parents we would have been? You, drunk most of the day, and me, a neurotic mess with three husbands already?"

"It wasn't your decision to make by yourself," he said.

"It was!" she said. Then she lowered her voice. "Angela and Chris were that child's parents from the day she was born—and they were wonderful parents." She jerked away from him, stumbling and then regaining her balance. "I did what was best for Allyson."

"That still didn't give you the right," Gary said.

"To spare her what I had to go through having a drunk as a father? I would have done anything to protect her from that—you *bet* I had the right!"

She had hit him in his most vulnerable place. His guilt. All the guilt and remorse he still carried about the things he had done in his drinking years. It didn't matter that it had been well over five years ago. What Lydia said was true. He would have been a nightmare as a father—if he would have owned up to paternity at all. Chances are he would have demanded Lydia have an abortion or sign a paper clearing him of all responsibility. That's what he had been like in the old days.

That's what he had been like even in the early days of sobriety, too. Hadn't he?

"You were wrong," Gary finally said. "You should have told me."

"I couldn't," she said.

He sighed. "We're going to have to talk."

"No, no—I can't deal with this now," Lydia wailed, covering her face with her hands. "Please go away." And then she rushed into the bathroom, closing and locking the door behind her.

———

"No, I'm sorry, Allyson, but I have to go," Gary said, coming back out of the pool house in his clothes. "I promise though," he said, squatting down and taking her hand, "that we will be swimming lots more times together. Because I like swimming with you—and I like you." And then he kissed her on the cheek.

"Okay, bye," Allyson said, turning back to the pool. "Will you catch me, Noél, when I jump in?"

"Sure," Noél said, making her way toward the shallow end. "Hey, Gare—will I see you tonight at the meeting?"

"Yeah, sure," he said. "See you later, Judith, it was nice to meet you."

"It was lovely meeting you," Judith said.

As Gary climbed the stone stairs around the house to the driveway, he could see Lydia upstairs out of the corner of his eye. She was just standing there, at the window. Watching.

Noél knocked on Lydia's opened bedroom door.

"Yes?" Lydia said.

Noél went in. Lydia was sitting on the sofa by the window, reading one of those big blue books of hers, the ones that had something to do with miracles. "Judith would like to know how you would like Allyson to dress for dinner."

"Why," Lydia said, putting the book facedown on the couch beside her, "I'd like Allyson dressed the way Allyson would like to dress for dinner."

"I didn't know if there was a special way you wished to have her dress, Mrs. Southland," Judith called from down the hall. "Some parents do, you see."

Lydia got up and came over to the door. "Let Allyson choose what she would like to wear," she told her.

"Very good," Judith said, disappearing into Allyson's room.

"Lydia," Noél said, when Lydia went back into her room, "I need to talk to you."

"What about?" She was walking back to the couch.

"Despite everything I said to Kate," Noél said, "you should know that she's on her way out here."

"I told you to tell her—" Lydia started.

"*Believe* me, Lydia, I told her—and told her and told her," Noél said. "But I think she has to come out for at least the sake of appearances."

"Appearances?" Lydia said, sitting down.

"Well"—Noél shrugged—"I can't imagine Bennett, Fitzallen & Coe is very happy with her after all the time and money and energy she put into your book. I think she at least has to make a show of trying to talk you into publishing it—or some version of it."

Lydia's eyes drifted over to the windows. She didn't say anything.

Noél knew that look. Lydia was not about to explain anything. "You will at least see her," Noél said.

"Yes, of course," Lydia murmured. She brought her eyes back. "What is it, Noél? Why are you looking at me like that?"

Noél hesitated and then, dropping her voice, she whispered, "Exactly what has happened, Lydia? Why are we junking the book?" She looked toward the doorway and then back at Lydia. "Because of Allyson?"

Lydia nodded.

"But we can fix it," Noel said. "Kate said we could. We could just start the book in New York or something, not say anything about your family. And we can take all the negative stuff out—" She smiled. "We'll have to take all that stuff out about Mort, that's for sure. You can't go on working with him if—" Noél stopped herself; Lydia looked as though she was about to be sick. "What is it, Lydia?"

Lydia only shook her head, indicating that whatever it was, she wasn't talking about it.

"Please don't shut me out," Noél said. "I can't stand this."

There was a twinge in Lydia's face. "Noél," she said quietly, "you're moving on in your life—and enormous changes have just moved into mine. There's got to be a period of readjustment."

Pause. "By shutting me out?"

"By giving me time and room to think."

"Okay, fine," Noél said, hurt and angry about whatever the hell it was that was going on.

— *56* —

Gary was fifteen minutes late to the meeting. It was a round robin, where they went around the table, taking turns sharing on the topic— which tonight was gratitude—and when it got to Gary, he only shook his head, looking terrible, murmuring that he would pass tonight. As the meeting went on, Noél's concern grew. Gary wasn't listening to what was going on, she knew. He wouldn't meet her eyes; he was like someone she saw in the back of meetings all the time but who had never been Gary before. Tonight Gary looked like one of those beaten, depressed alcoholics, barely sober, who were trying to decide whether or not they should just kill themselves.

After the meeting Noél tried to talk to him. He said he was very tired, he just wanted to go home. And then, watching him walk across the parking lot toward his car, shoulders sagging, Noél remembered how Gary had been with her on her really bad days and she thought, *Help him, he's in a bad way,* and she ran to catch up with him, taking his arm when she did. "I can't let you go home like this," she said.

He stopped.

"Gary, you know you can tell me anything. Anything."

He turned to her and in the streetlight, Noél could see that he was crying.

"Come on," she said, pulling him on, "let's sit in your car."

It was after midnight and Lydia was still up; she was outside in the garage with the lights on, unpacking cartons from her sister's house. "Hi," she called as Noél parked the BMW. "Come give me your opinion, will you?"

Reluctantly Noél walked over. Lydia held up a picture. It was a paint-by-number of a horse in armor of some kind. And it wasn't very good. Not at all. Somebody had gotten the color scheme all screwed up so the armor was brown and the horse was silver. "Is this just too awful to put up in the playroom?" Lydia asked her.

"Who did it?"

"Allyson doesn't know, but Angie had it up in their playroom so it must have been somebody special." Pause. "Allyson calls it Charger." Lydia grimaced then, and then smiled, turning to the painting to say, "Well, I guess that decides it, Charger, up you go in the playroom." She put it on top of the station wagon. "How was your meeting?"

"Good," Noél said.

Lydia was pulling another box over. "Did Gary go?"

"Yeah."

Lydia opened the box. "Did you guys have dinner after?"

"No," Noél said.

"So where have you been?"

"A bunch of us were talking after the meeting," Noél said, quickly moving over to a pile of stuff in the corner. "What's this?" she said.

Lydia straightened up, wiping stray hairs off the back of her forehead with the back of her hand. "Noél," she said.

"What is this, a neon sign?" Noél asked, pulling the thing out of a box.

"Noél, look at me," Lydia commanded.

Noél looked at her.

"He told you," Lydia said, "didn't he?"

Noél didn't say anything. After a moment, she put the neon sign back in the box.

Lydia turned and kicked the fertilizer spreader, smashing the metal side against the wall of the garage with a bang. "Damn him," she said.

"Well, what was he supposed to do?" Noél wanted to know.

"He could have talked to anyone but you," Lydia said, turning away. "This does no good for anybody."

"No good for you, you mean," Noél blurted out. "What do you want Gary to do, go off and kill himself just to make your life a little more convenient?"

Lydia whirled around, pointing a finger. "If you do or say *anything*, Noél," she said through clenched teeth, "that could possibly hurt that child, I swear I'll—" She stopped herself and dropped her face in her hands. "I'm sorry," she said, turning away. "Oh, Noél, I'm sorry. Of course you won't do anything—I know that. I'm just so tired." She turned around to look at Noél with weary eyes. "I'm sorry," she said again.

"I'm sorry too," Noél said.

There was a long silence.

"Under the circumstances," Lydia said, looking down, nudging the corner of the box with her foot, "I guess it would be best if you took the lease on that house."

"First thing in the morning," Noél said.

Lydia looked at her and swallowed. "Please try to understand."

There was another long silence as the two women looked at each other.

"I'll try," Noél said. And then she walked back to the house. Crying. She couldn't believe what Lydia had done.

Kate wasn't sure what she should do. When she arrived at the airport Friday she called the office at the Benedict Canyon house and instead of getting Noél, she got an answering machine. Then when she called Gary at his office, he said, "Look, I wish I could help you out, but I haven't the slightest idea what Lydia's up to. Noél's moving out and I'd appreciate it if you left me out of it, and if you need any more explanation than that, Kate, I'm sorry, but you're going to have to get it from Lydia." And then, when she called Lydia's personal line at the house, Gracia answered, who said, sounding not like herself at all, "Can you give the señora a day? There are many balls in the air around her head right now."

What was going on? Clearly something was wrong, but what to do except wait for Lydia to call her?

And so Kate got into her car (another convertible LeBaron—*Screw you, Dick Skolchak*) and drove to the Hotel Shangri-La in Santa Monica where at least Dino and David were glad to see her again. She stayed in that night, line editing a manuscript she had lugged along, waiting for Lydia to call.

She was sitting in the same place on the couch at ten Saturday morning when Mark called to see what was what. "Nothing is anything," she said, cutting his call short because she did not know what to say to him if he said anything about anything that had to do with her.

One crisis at a time, please.

Besides, she was beat. She had had a horrendous scene with Harris at his apartment before leaving New York. It was supposed to have been a talking session to put things in some sort of holding pattern between them until they had time to sort things out, but it had turned into a shouting match instead, with Harris telling her to go to hell, what a bitch she was, god*damn* but was he lucky to find that out in time!

The phone rang again around two and Kate answered it. It was Mark again. No news, she told him. And again, she hurried off the phone.

Mark.

Mark.

She couldn't think about Mark. It was too complicated. Too confusing.

She called her answering machine in New York and got halfway through a stern message from her father about Harris when she said to hell with it and hung up.

The phone rang again and Kate snapped it up. "Hello?"

"Kate, it's Mark again—don't hang up. Listen a minute, will you?"

"Sure," she said, trying to sound cheerful but feeling more like jumping out a window, crying, "I'm too confused to handle this life! I don't know what I'm doing!"

"I don't want you to be afraid of me," Mark said.

"I'm not afraid of you," Kate said, knowing as soon as she said it that he was absolutely right, she was scared of him.

"So whatever it is you need to hear from me that will stop you from being scared of me," he said, "well, I'm prepared to say it. Even if it means pretending that I'm not in love with you."

Kate sighed. "Mark, be fair."

"I'm trying to be, Kate."

She knew he was. And she knew she had no reason to be angry with him. Or afraid of him. But she wasn't sure of what to say, either. She wanted to stop Mark from talking any more because she was aware that he was prying open that old part of her that had always been open to him—that part of her that was friend, pal, confidante, playmate—and forcing it wider, spreading it to that other part of her that she had always safely, until *that* night, kept away from him. It was odd, though. She felt both safe and threatened by him right now, happy and scared that he had called again, vaguely aroused and partly frozen— and angry with herself for not being able to control any of this.

"I can't just turn off over a year of my life like a TV set," Kate said. "I can't just snap my fingers and say, okay, Harris, you're out, and then say, okay, Mark, you're the one—and that's what I feel like you're asking me to do."

"I never asked to be the one," Mark said quietly. "In fact, if you ever felt I was *the* one, then I'd know for sure I wasn't. I'd know then I was just like all the rest."

"You can't dismiss Harris that easily," Kate said.

"Oh yes I can," Mark said. "Because I wasn't the one who loved him."

Pause. "So you do believe I loved him."

"I think you thought you loved him," Mark said.

"And what about you?" Kate said. "How do you think I feel about you?"

"I think you love me for all the right reasons," he said. "I told you—you should marry your best friend. I learned the hard way—a lot of us have."

"Sherry is my best friend," Kate said.

"Then you should have married Sherry years ago," Mark said, starting to laugh.

"Hey, listen, with my track record," Kate said, "it's not as if I haven't thought about it—it certainly hasn't worked very well with men."

"It doesn't have to work with men," Mark said, "it only has to work with me."

"True," Kate heard herself say, feeling a wave of warmth washing over her.

Stop it, stop it! she told herself. *You don't want to get into this!*

"And you always said you'd have to get married to become publisher," Mark reminded her.

"True," Kate said.

"And what better person to marry than the one you love working with best?"

Kate smiled. "You mean I should marry Sarah?"

He laughed. He was relieved. Kate was too. Something was okay now. The dangerous stuff had been brought up. They could live with it like this for a while.

"But she's not in publishing anymore," he said.

"The way things are going, I soon may not be either," Kate sighed. Silence.

"Oh, Mark," Kate said, "I miss you." She looked out the window. "It's so different out here—so light. So far away from everything. Of course," she said in the next moment, bowing her head slightly, "it's not real, is it? This isn't the real world out here."

"If you're there, if you're present, it's real," Mark said.

"So this conversation is real," she said, looking back out to the water. "And it's real that I'm telling you that I miss you and wish you were here." She paused and then smiled. "Funny, it doesn't feel very real saying that. It feels like I'm dreaming."

"What do you mean?" he said. "I feel like *I'm* dreaming! Kate, did you just say you wished I was there?"

"Yes. Yes, I did," she said softly, nodding.

There was a knock on Kate's door.

"Someone's at the door, hang on," she said. She put the phone down and went over to answer it.

No. It couldn't be. This was like a bad movie.

It was Harris.

— 58 —

She told Harris to come in and went back into the living room. "I'll have to call you back," she said into the phone.

"Is it Lydia?" Mark said.

"Okay, I'll call you." Kate hung up. "Well," she said, turning around to look at Harris.

"I needed to see you," he said.

She gestured to the couch. "Would you like some water or something?"

He shook his head.

She watched him sit, wondering why this seemed so normal. They could have been in Connecticut. She sitting around in shorts and a T-shirt, Harris in a pale yellow polo shirt, khaki pants, and Top-Siders. She sat down in the chair next to the couch and waited.

Harris was leaning forward, resting his arms on his knees, looking down at his hands. Finally he looked up. "I think we're making a mistake," he said quietly.

She didn't say anything.

"I saw your parents," he continued. He lowered his eyes again. "Kimberly thinks maybe we rushed you." Pause. "Your father doesn't know what to make of it." Pause. "He seems to think once the excitement's over and you've had time to think, you'll change your mind." Harris brought his eyes up to look at her. "I think so too."

"No, Harris," Kate said.

Harris looked surprised. "But he said . . ." And then his voice trailed off, as if he sensed that Kate would not like what he was about to say.

Kate sighed. "The fact that you would think my father knows anything about the way I feel pretty well sums up why it would never work between us."

He sat up. "I never said I thought your father knew how you felt."

"Then why did you talk to him instead of someone who knows me?" she said.

"What do you mean your father doesn't know you?" Harris said.

"And the reason why I can't marry you," Kate continued, "is because you don't know me either, Harris. If you did, you wouldn't be interested in marrying me."

"What do you mean, Kate?" Harris said, standing up. "Kate, I love you."

"You love the way I look and the way I talk and the way I do certain things," she said, eyes tearing, "but you can't stand my loneliness, you can't stand my insecurities, and you can't stand that my interests are so different from yours. So you don't let me have them, Harris—you make me hide everything from you. Only it's my problem, not yours. And if I'm to be me, and that's what I want to be—we both know you wouldn't be able to stand it."

"What are you talking about?" he said, angry now.

She didn't say anything; she let her eyes rest on the coffee table.

"Kate!"

She looked up.

"Kate, please," he said, dropping to one knee next to her chair, "don't throw the baby out with the bathwater. We can work this out." Pause. "I'll go to therapy with you—I promise, I will."

"It's too late," she said.

He screwed his eyes shut. "Kate, no," he whispered. "All our plans."

Kate hesitated a moment and then took him in her arms. She held him tight, and stroked his back. "It can't be, Harris," she whispered, "I'm sorry. But one day you'll be glad. You'll see. But it can't be."

"But I came all the way out here," he said.

Looking over his shoulder, Kate smiled a little. It was so like Harris to point this out.

That night, Kate sat and sat, trying to write a letter to her father. One draft after another went into the trash. And then, around midnight, she got a funny feeling and went to stand at the window. Looking out over the palms to the night ocean, she felt the strangest sensation. It was as if someone had taken a hundred pounds off her back and was saying, "See? See how light life can be?" She stood there a long time, not trusting this feeling at all. But the feeling stayed.

In the morning a note effortlessly wrote itself. It said:

Dear Dad,
    I didn't want to let you down about Harris, but I'm afraid I would have caused him and myself and everyone around us enormous pain in the years ahead. You'll have to believe me on this one, Dad—I'm not marrying him because of what's wrong with me, but because of all that's right with me.

I love you for caring.
Katherine

— *59* —

"Holly, I can't," Noél said, standing on a ladder, examining the hairline cracks around the living room air vent that were probably from the last earthquake. "It's between Gary and Lydia."

"If it's between Gary and Lydia," Holly said, holding the ladder, "then why are you so upset?"

Holly was in her irresistible "working at home" clothes, which meant designer blue jeans, a T-shirt that left absolutely nothing to the imagination, a work shirt casually open over that, and hair deliberately a mess—in other words, the vision of an at-home frump according to *Playboy.*

"I'm not upset," Noél said.

"You've only moved out," Holly observed.

"I was moving out anyway," Noél said.

"And accepting some furniture from Lydia as a gift," Holly said. "Now, suddenly, you won't take a bologna sandwich from her."

Noél put her hands on her hips, looking up at the vent. "I guess I'll have to replaster up here. Do you think I can do it myself?"

"Listen you," Holly said, gently placing a hand on Noél's derriere, "I thought this was a new beginning for us. I thought we were going to tell each other the truth."

Noél sighed and came down from the ladder. Holly was right. She owed her some explanation of what was going on—but how to do so without making things worse? The more people who knew, the bigger the danger, and there was the little girl caught in all this.

The more Noél thought about it, the angrier she got. Why did Lydia

bring Allyson to Beverly Hills? If she had wanted to spare everyone the big secret, she should have finished out her contract on the series and then moved back East to be with Allyson. But no, she brought Allyson here and re-signed with the series—it made no sense!

"Noél, come here a minute," Holly said, taking her hand. She led her over to the front picture window and sat down under it on the floor, pulling Noél down on the floor beside her. She put her arm around Noél, and with her free hand, steered Noél's chin so that she had to look at her. "If you can't trust me," Holly said softly, "what chance do we have?"

"I do trust you," Noél said, thinking that she had never in her life known anyone as lovely as Holly. And the idea that Holly had given her another chance, that she had still cared about her enough to give it another try, still seemed unbelievable. But then Noél didn't recognize herself these days, so who was she to judge who Holly should or should not care about and give another chance to?

"Then let's talk about it," Holly said.

"I swore to Lydia I wouldn't tell anyone."

"I think she'd understand if you told me," Holly said. "She's one of my closest friends."

"So you keep saying," Noél said. She shook her head, saying almost to herself, "I live in the woman's house for a year and a half and I don't even know she talks to you—and now you tell me she's one of your best friends."

Holly kissed her on the forehead. "It wasn't appropriate for you to know."

"That sounds like Lydia," Noél muttered.

"Baby, tell me," Holly said.

After a moment, Noél said, "Gary and Lydia went out for a while back in New York."

"I knew that," Holly said. "When Gary first came to the show, he always used to get drunk and talk about it."

"Charming disease, isn't it?" Noél said to herself. She shook her head slightly then, as if to shake the idea of Gary ever being drunk, and turned back to Holly. "Lydia got pregnant and had the child—and then her sister adopted it."

Holly's eyes first narrowed—and then widened. "Allyson's . . . ?"

Noél nodded. "And Gary found out—but only accidentally. Lydia never said a word to him about any of it. Ever. Left to her, he probably

never would have even met the little girl. Lydia would have just cut him out of her life." She snapped her fingers.

"But you don't know that," Holly said quickly. "You have no way of knowing what Lydia intended to do."

"Yeah, well, I know she could have told Gary something about his having a daughter some time in the past seven years."

"But you don't know that either," Holly said.

They sat there in silence for a while, each with her own thoughts.

"Poor Lydia," Holly sighed. "I can't even imagine what it's been like for her all these years."

"Poor Lydia nothing," Noél said, getting up to her feet and walking toward the kitchen. "Poor Lydia's been manipulating everyone and everything for far too long—including me."

After a moment: "Noél?"

"What?" She was in the kitchen.

"If it wasn't for Lydia," Holly said, picking at the knee of her blue jeans, "I wouldn't be here." Pause. "As far as I was concerned, I was never going to see or talk to you again."

Noél came walking slowly back out of the kitchen.

"If Lydia hadn't worked on me," Holly said, "there's no way I would have seen you again."

Noél leaned against the archway.

Holly winced slightly. "Sorry, but it's true. Lydia kept telling me that you were sober, that Betty Ford had worked for you, that you were involved in AA and CA and everything, and then—whether I liked it or not—over the weeks and months she kept telling me how you were doing, what you were up to, how much better you were getting, and then Gary started telling me the same thing, and so I knew—" She stopped.

Noél looked up. "Knew what?"

"I knew Lydia was probably right about two things."

"Which were . . . ?"

"That you were going to stay sober." Pause, swallow. "And that you really did love me. Even when you were so sick." Pause. "I never knew that, Noél. You did so many awful things."

Noél thought of the late night talks she had had with Lydia about Holly. About how guilty she felt, how much she missed Holly, how if she had ever loved anyone, it had probably, in her own insane way, been Holly.

After a long moment, Noél said, "So she always thought I should be with you."

"She doesn't think you should have to be with anyone," Holly said. "But she's always thought we should have a chance to—"

"And you find nothing presumptuous about this?" Noél said.

"Did it ever occur to you," Holly said, "that some people might love you and care about you and consider me to be a pretty dependable sort of lover for you to have, circumstances notwithstanding? It's complicated, yes, the situation is, with my career and Kent—but how I feel about you isn't. I care enormously about you, Noél. Enough at any rate to be sitting in this dusty house with you arguing about why you shouldn't be arbitrarily turning your back on Lydia."

"Arbitrary bullshit," Noél said, pushing off the archway. "Every day for seven years that woman made a conscious decision to betray Gary. How can anyone justify that?" she asked, walking away.

"So that's it?" Holly said, scrambling to her feet, following Noél. "No discussion, no nothing, just fuck you, Lydia?"

"How can I be close to someone who did that to Gary?" Noél nearly wailed, turning around. "How could I ever trust her again?"

"And how did you ever expect any sane person to trust you again, Noél?" Holly said. "My God! You lied, you stole, you cheated, you damn near destroyed my career with your filthy drugs, and now you're asking me how *you* could ever trust *Lydia* again? *Lydia?*" Holly shuddered with frustration, ending it by yelling, "God!" and walking to the archway and then back again. "You could at least find out what happened," she said to Noél. "You could at least wait until Lydia is prepared to tell her side of things before sentencing her. For God's sake, Noél, you could at least show her half the compassion you show to every bloody Tom, Dick, and Harry that stumbles down the stairs dead drunk into AA!"

Noél covered her face with her hands.

"Or don't AA principles apply to anyone outside of it?" Holly said. "Or isn't Lydia worthy of the same respect you show an alcoholic? I understand how you feel about Gary—but Noél, it's his life, not yours, and he sure as hell messed his up until very recently, and so did you, and as far as I can see, the two of you would be lost, if not dead, without Lydia, so I think this whole thing is not only ridiculous but cruel and uncaring and certainly not what I would call very sober behavior!"

Holly watched Noél cry for a while. Then she walked over to her and placed a hand on her back. "I'm sorry to yell at you," she said quietly, "but this isn't a time to pass judgment. It's a time for love and understanding. Give her time to explain her side." Pause. "And Noél?" Holly said, pulling Noél's hands away from her face and tilting her chin up so that she'd look at her, dabbing at Noél's tears with the sleeve of her workshirt. "I say this because I love you." Pause. "And baby, Lydia does too. You know that. Please don't turn your back on her—because if you did it would be like turning your back on me."

— 60 —

When someone knocked on her hotel door again Sunday morning, Kate almost didn't answer it for fear it might be Harris again. But she took a deep breath and answered it anyway.

It was Lydia, hair in a ponytail, wearing a Rams football jersey that came down to her thighs, short white shorts about the same length as her shirt, very large dark sunglasses and a baseball cap that said UCLA on it. "Hi," she said.

"I was just hanging up with one of my authors," Kate said, stepping back from the door. "Come in."

"Talking to authors on Sunday," Lydia said, sounding subdued, walking into the living room and looking around, sunglasses still on.

Kate quickly finished her conversation and hung up. She turned to speak to Lydia—who was gone. "Lydia?" Kate went into the bedroom and found her in there, sitting on the far side of the bed, looking out at the ocean. "Lydia," she said quietly. No response. "I feel like something awful's happened—and I want to help."

"Can we walk?" Lydia said without turning around. "On the beach?"

"Sure, let me just put some shoes on." Kate went to the closet to get her Top-Siders; Lydia got up and moved over to stand in the doorway—her sunglasses still on—to watch as Kate put on her shoes. When they were on Kate stood up.

Lydia just stood there, not moving.

"Lydia," Kate said gently, "what is it?"

Lydia took off her sunglasses. Her eyes were a wreck. Red, swollen, they looked as though she had been crying for days. "It's going to be a tough one for me to talk about," she said hoarsely. "But I want to tell you the truth. I need to tell you the truth. I need someone—" She stopped, shaking her head. "But the book—I can't—"

"Lydia," Kate said.

Lydia brought her eyes up.

"Forget the book," Kate told her, "it's over."

The two women went down to the beach to walk and talk, and they were glad that Kate had thought to bring Kleenex.

— *61* —

"Where's Allyson?" Gary said, following Gracia and Noél into the living room.

"She is with Señorita Twickingham at the stable," Gracia said. "Apache, her pony, has arrived from Long Island."

"Where's Lydia?" he said.

"She is not here. Now sit down," Gracia said to him, pointing to the couch, "and little señora"—she snapped her fingers—"you too. Sit."

Gary and Noél looked at each other and then did as they were told. Neither had ever heard Gracia speak to them in such a tone of voice.

"I called you here because someone has to talk sense to you," Gracia began. She was wearing a lemon-colored warm-up suit with bright green striping today, and a pair of white Puma sneakers. She began pacing in front of them, slowly. "I love you very much, you know that," she said, "but I must tell you, I love the señora more than anyone except my Billy and Catalina."

Gary and Noél exchanged looks again.

"I do not care if you think what the señora did was wrong," Gracia continued, "I only care that you know she did what she thought was right." She stopped and turned to them. Tears sprang to her eyes as the next words came out in a rush. "Because there is no one better in all this world than the señora, you know that. She made your lives better and she helped my Billy and my Catalina and she helped me and probably the little señorita Allyson too by what she did, I know she did." She punctuated the next sentences by beating her fist in the air. "I will not allow you to hurt the señora anymore! She needs you!"

"Gracia, we don't mean to hurt her," Noél began.

"I do not want to hear it!" Gracia shouted. And then she lowered her voice. "She made a mistake—or maybe she did not," she said. "Whatever happened, it is in the past now. It is over. Now is now."

Gary sighed. "Look, Gracia, you don't know all of it."

"I do, Señor Steiner, yes I do!" Gracia said, her voice rising again. She pointed at him with a trembling finger. "So if you want to hate the señora, then you hate me too. Because I knew about the little señorita"—she pointed to herself, thumping her finger on her chest— "Yes, I knew." She dropped her hand. "So if you think the señora is bad, you must think I am bad too."

Dead silence. Gary's mouth had parted. Noél looked pale.

"I lived in Mexico City with my husband, Nico," Gracia said. "My son, Guillermo, and his wife Latalla, they lived with us too, and Billy, who was three, and Catalina, who was a baby." She was sitting on the fireplace hearth now, hands clasped around her knees. "My husband worked in the Ford factory. My son was a scribe. Everyday he went to the square and set up his table and typewriter and people came to him to write letters and documents.

"September nineteenth," she continued, "nineteen eighty-five—" She took a tissue out of her pocket and blew her nose.

"The earthquake," Gary said.

"Yes, the earthquake," Gracia said, putting the tissue back in her pocket. She looked first at Noél and then at Gary. "A terrace fell on my son in the square, he was killed. Two days later another earthquake came—even stronger." Her voice had grown distant, her eyes too. "Our house fell, there was a bad fire. My husband got the children out and came back—" She paused for a moment and then looked at Gary. "My husband came back to find me and Latalla, but he could not breathe for the smoke. He died. Latalla died, too, next to me, under the rubble. Her body became a shield for me from the fire."

"Oh, Gracia," Noél murmured.

Gracia swallowed, lowering her eyes to the floor. "I was very bad when they found me. They took me to the hospital where the sisters took care of me." Pause. "I did not want to live. I was in so much pain they had to give me drugs. I did not know where I was for a long time." Pause. "And after I knew . . ." She shook her head.

"What about Billy and Cathy?" Gary said quietly.

There was a quiet sigh. Eyes still on the carpet, Gracia continued, "The authorities took them to a home to be cared for." She blinked.

"They did not think, you see, that there was going to be anyone to care for them." She raised her eyes to Gary's. "Not their dying grandmother."

Gracia cleared her throat. "That was when the señora came from America for the Red Cross. She was there with reporters to see the horrible things of the earthquake so that people in America would send food and clothes and medicine."

Gary smiled slightly.

"The señora tried to talk to me in the hospital. I could not talk well, I did not know much English, I was out of my head with the drugs, but the señora stayed at my side with an interpreter, determined to hear out my story." She smiled slightly and looked at Noél. "You know how the señora gets when she wants to know something."

"Yes," Noél said.

"Well," Gracia continued, stretching her legs out in front of her and then crossing them, proceeding to watch her feet as she flexed them, "she demanded to know what had happened to my grandchildren, where they were, why had not anyone brought them to see their grandmother. And the sisters explained to her—the señora later told me this—that they did not think that I would live, my burns were too bad, and even if I were to live I would not be able to function."

Gracia looked up, smiling, retracting her legs. "Well, the señora got in her head that this was not what she wanted to hear and"—Gracia shrugged, holding out her hands—"she decided that the grandmother had to live."

Gary and Noél both smiled.

"And so she came back after her tour was finished and told me she was bringing me to America with her and when I was well she would bring my grandchildren too." Gracia clapped a hand to the side of her face. "Oh, I was so very sick and confused—I thought the señora was crazy—I did—why did this beautiful lady want to take me to America?"

Gracia stopped here, pulling out her tissue again as if she knew how she would react to this part of the story. "And that is when she told me, Señor Steiner," she said. "That is when she told me about the baby. The señora said she needed a reason to live after giving her baby up." She wiped her eyes.

"Did she say she gave it away?" Gary said softly.

Gracia nodded. "She said the father was very sick and she did not know if he would ever get well. She said her sister had prayed for a child for many years. She said Señora Clarke and her husband would make the best parents in the world. She said—" Gracia paused, sniffing, lowering the tissue to her lap. "The señora said she was not good enough to be a mother." Pause. "And now you know why the señora wanted to be in Long Island." Swallow. "She would have done anything, Señor Steiner, to protect that baby from what she thought might hurt her."

Gary sighed, rubbing his eyes with his hand. "I know."

Gracia positioned herself then and, with a heave, hauled herself up to her feet. "The only way she could bring me to America was—and you will laugh, because it is quite funny in a very sad way—"

Gary looked up.

"The señora told the government that she had a job that only I could do. She said no one in all the world but me could run her life for her."

"She was right," Noél said.

"And when she got the papers, she brought me to Cedars Sinai Hospital for many operations, until finally I said enough, I am well enough, señora, no more operations, I want to see my Billy and Catalina, and I moved into this house—into your room, little señora—and soon my Billy and Catalina came too. And when I was healed, we moved into our house."

Gracia took a step toward them. "I want you to see," she said, unzipping the top of her exercise suit.

"No, Gracia, you don't have—" Gary said.

But Gracia unzipped the top of her warm-up suit down about three-quarters of the way, exposing the kind of massive brassiere that matronly grandmothers tended to wear, but also—

But also the sight that from her neck down, Gracia was almost a patchwork of scar tissue. She had had some skin grafts, that was evident, but then she had stopped—just as she had said she had—leaving patches of twisted, darkened flesh and moderately healed-over flesh, both of which were a little frightening to look at.

She zipped her top back up then and looked at Gary. "I know about miracles, Señor Steiner," she said. "And I know it is a miracle that God brought that child back to her—and back to you."

The dogs were barking outside.

"I have said all that I wanted to say," Gracia concluded, walking toward the kitchen. "I will leave what you want to say to the señora to you."

Gary and Noél looked at each other. Noél touched his hand and whispered, "Lydia loves you, too, Gare—you know that."

They heard the front door close and the sound of Kate Weston's voice.

"Well," Lydia said a moment later, standing at the top of the living room stairs with Kate at her side.

No one said anything.

"I guess you should know," Lydia finally said, slowly coming down the stairs, "that Kate knows it all now." Her voice was not confident. She stopped in the middle of the stairs. She was looking at Gary. Waiting.

Gary was looking at her. Waiting.

"Please say something," Lydia said to him.

"I love you, Lyddie," he said.

"I love you too," she whispered.

Kate came down a stair to touch Lydia's shoulder. "Tell them why you signed the new contract."

Lydia sighed, pausing a moment. Then she looked at Gary and said, "Promise me you won't do anything that would endanger yourself."

He looked confused.

"Promise me," she said.

"Okay, I promise," he said.

Lydia nodded then and said, "Right after Angela died, someone stole some files from the Suffolk County Courthouse in Long Island." Pause. "I had to have you on record as the biological father, Gary—in case Allyson ever had a medical emergency."

He nodded.

Lydia walked down the stairs and over to stand in front of him. She took his hands and squatted before him. "You've got to believe me, Gary," she said, "I was going to tell you about Allyson. Even before Angie was killed. And then when it happened I got scared and all I knew to do was to get to Allyson and be with her." She swallowed, eyes glistening. "The reason why I shut you out wasn't because I wanted to continue to keep her a secret from you—it was because I needed time to think—and then later, when I got back here, I needed time to think about how to deal with Pallsner. And so I signed his contract to gain time."

"Pallsner?" Gary said, frowning. "What does he have to do with it?"

"He has Allyson's birth records," Lydia said.

"That bastard!" Noél cried, jumping to her feet. "That bastard was going to blackmail you?"

"I think the present tense is more in order," Lydia said, eyes narrowing. She released Gary's hands and stood up. "He slapped a contract renewal notice in front of me and said if I signed it that afternoon, I'd have no reason to fear that Allyson's life story would be all over the papers—about her father—you—and what your past was, and about his mother—me—and my past."

"Bastard," Noél said again, suddenly tearing up the stairs and out of the living room.

"So I took the contract to my lawyers that afternoon," Lydia continued, "signed it, and returned it."

"Oh, Lyddie," Gary sighed, sounding very tired. He stood up and went to her, holding out his arms. She fell into them and he held her there, rocking her gently from side to side. "I swear, Lyddie, we'll get this straightened out—and I swear we won't let that son of a bitch get to Allyson."

Lydia didn't say anything; she just held on to him.

"Tell him what you did, Lydia," Kate said.

"What did you do?" Gary said, releasing her.

"Oh," Lydia said, moving to sit down on the couch, "I taped him."

"Taped him?" Gary said, dropping down next to her.

"With that dictation thing Kate gave me to use on the book. I gave the tape to my lawyer."

"Mort was dumb enough to say something after he knew you had seen your lawyer?" Gary said.

"No," Lydia said, "I taped him the first time I went in. He slapped the contract renewal in front of me and I was looking for my glasses in my purse and there it was"—she shrugged—"so I just turned it on. It's not really very good, but you can hear what he said and know it's him. Whichever way you look at it, my lawyer said, it's attempted blackmail, enough for a warrant."

"Okay!" Noél yelled from upstairs. They could hear her running down the hall. "Okay!" she yelled again, thumping her way down the front staircase. "I knew this would come in handy some day," she said, coming down the stairs into the living room and, slightly breathless, coming to a stop in front of Lydia. "Okay, Lydia," she said, "here's just about the best amend I can make to you," and she thrust a manila folder into her hands, some of the contents spilling to the floor.

"What's this?" Lydia said.

"Plane tickets, clothes receipts, jewelry, bank accounts, credit cards, you name it, it's all there," Noél said, bending to pick up the papers off the floor and dump them on the sofa next to Lydia. "All the people and places and things Mortie lied about that I knew about, all the places he took me as his wife, all the presents he bought me on his expense account—plus some dates we were with some of his shadier friends, what they talked about. Believe me, it's enough to give him heart failure."

Lydia was staring at all the date books, receipts, and notations around her. "How—?"

"He threatened to cut off my cocaine and so like any self-respecting drug addict, I was going to blackmail him. Only *some*body," Noel added, "or shall we say some*bodies*—had me carted off to Betty Ford before I could get to it."

"Noél," Gary said, looking at a piece of paper stapled to a large receipt, "Bestar paid for your BMW?"

"Yeah," she said, "but he always wrote stuff off as other things. What did he write that off as?"

"Miscellaneous overtime transportation costs on the Dolley Madison episode," Gary read.

Kate let out a whistle. "I like that miscellaneous convertible top myself."

"Noél," Gary said, clearing his throat, "I think it's time you got rid of that car."

"I guess so," Noél sighed, walking over and throwing herself down in a chair.

"And what's this?" Lydia said, looking at another receipt. "What did you get at Randelay's of Rodeo that cost six thousand dollars?"

"A fur," Noél said. "It was a present, actually—for Holly."

"What did he claim it as?" Gary said, looking over Lydia's shoulder.

"Miscellaneous wardrobe expenses for the Catherine the Great episode," she said.

Gary turned to Noél. "You better tell Holly to get rid of the fur."

"She doesn't have it," Noél said. "She wouldn't take it—she doesn't believe in fur coats."

"So where is it?" Lydia said.

"Don't look at me," Noél said, eyes wandering in the direction of the kitchen.

"Oh, no," Lydia said, "you didn't."

"I bet she did," Gary said. "Gracia! Oh, Gracia!"

"Yes, Señor Steiner?" Gracia said, appearing in the archway, wiping her hands on a dish towel.

"Gracia," Lydia said, "did Noél give you a fur coat?"

"I do not have it," Gracia said quickly.

Now it was Noél's turn to be puzzled. "You don't?"

"I gave it to Imelda," Gracia said, "and she gave it to her mother— her mother in Seattle." She looked at Gary. "It is very cold there in the winter, in Seattle." She looked at Lydia. "Her mother is, I believe, very old, señora. Very old." Pause. "And Imelda says she gets very cold." Faintly: "Way up there in Seattle."

Lydia looked at Gary. "Think Imelda's mother in Seattle can keep the fur?"

"I think Imelda's mother in Seattle can keep the fur," Gary said.

"Okay, that's settled," Lydia said, "and now I think I better call my lawyer."

— 62 —

Gary stopped in at an AA meeting in Santa Monica on his way home. There wasn't a seat left in the place and so he stood in the back and leaned against the wall, munching on a piece of pineapple, trying to listen.

The woman "qualifying" was telling her story to the group: a little about what her drinking days had been like, how she came to get sober in AA, and a bit about how her life was today. She was in her late forties, "sort of" blond, a faded looker, had been married once, left her husband to come to Los Angeles and become an actress and ended up with part-time work, full-time parties, and a lot of men, all of whom discarded her when she bottomed-out on booze, no longer a pretty young thing. She came into AA, stopped drinking, and had not a clue as to how to support herself. Three and a half years later she was working as a receptionist and going to college, hoping one day to become a high school counselor. "I'm even thinking of getting married," she said, smiling slightly. "I mean, to like a real guy—you know, who works for a living, doesn't play around, calls when he says he will, and means what he says—"

By this point the room had broken up into laughter, Gary included. It rarely failed, an AA meeting. If he was down, it brought him up a little. If he was way up, it brought him down a little. Just enough either way to calm Gary and to reassure him that life did indeed ebb and flow, and that all things, even this moment, would pass.

I'm a father. I have a daughter. Lydia had my baby. These thoughts kept intruding as he tried to listen to people share around the room. He had his hand up out of habit, mostly, because when the speaker called on him he felt totally unprepared. But then, that was how one was supposed to speak in AA. Unprepared. To simply share the truth of where you were.

"Hi, my name's Gary and I'm a grateful recovering alcoholic," he said.

"Hi, Gary," the people in the room said, many turning to see who it was speaking.

"I really don't have much to say—I just wanted to check in and hear the sound of my own voice say that I'm an alcoholic. This time of all times it's very important I remember that—remember what I was like, from where I've come and what a long, long road it's been." He was staring down at the back of the chair in front of him, not knowing what to say next. "I found out this week that I have a daughter from my drinking days," he said, as if someone else were speaking for him.

There was a murmur of sympathy around the room.

Eyes still down on the chair. "The mother—" He paused, his throat tightening. He swallowed and continued. "The mother was too scared to tell me because I was such a mess. She didn't want to have the baby by herself—she didn't want to have an abortion." Pause. "So she gave the baby up for adoption and never told me that the child existed." Pause. He looked up at the speaker. "And now the child is here—in my life. I can't pretend she doesn't exist." He closed his eyes, feeling tears squeezing out from under the lids. "And now I don't know what to do. How to be." He opened his eyes. "I don't know if I know how to be a father, even if anyone will let me try. And I think I want to. To be a father. But I'm scared. And I don't know what to do."

Someone put a hand on his shoulder and offered him a tissue. He shook his head, murmuring no thanks, pulling out his own handkerchief and wiping his eyes. And then blowing his nose.

"I'm really glad you shared," the speaker said. "Because so many of us, Gary, have so many 'surprises' from our past. You know how they say when you come in, to put things on the shelf for a while?"

Gary nodded.

"Well, I think we're all used to having things starting jumping down on us from that shelf after a while whether we think we're ready to handle them or not." People laughed; she smiled. "Chances are, Gary, you are ready. Your Higher Power has certainly brought you a long way to get you ready for this day, hasn't He? It's hard to believe your child wouldn't be better off knowing you as the man you are today."

After the meeting, many of the people murmured their identification to Gary. Lost families, old debts, sins one hoped were safely buried in the past . . .

Driving home, Gary felt enormously better. At least he didn't feel like such a wimp. It was normal to be scared, people told him. It was normal to be apprehensive, unsure of where things went from here. That's why it was important he do what the program suggested, to follow the steps. Turn what he couldn't control over to God. Pay attention to what he could do. Most of all, take things one at time, a day at a time, a minute at a time if he had to. That was manageable. Projection into the future always terrified; dwelling on the past always depressed; stay in the now, be present in your own life, be alive, be grateful, you will get through this.

He stopped at the deli and picked up a roast chicken and some salad and some ice cream and drove home. He had bought this house way up here in Pacific Palisades two years ago because the house was a steal. Well, yeah, in the mid-1980s maybe. Six months after buying it, the house devalued by about 20 percent as the housing market started to fall. But still, it was a nice house, three bedrooms, with a secluded yard in the back. And most important, Gary had bought it with his own money—well, the down payment, anyway; he still had a sizable mortgage on it—the first money he had had free and clear after so many years of debt.

Was it sick for someone to love to pay taxes? Gary often wondered. The feeling it had given him that first year, that first year his taxes were clear and honest and aboveboard and he had had the money in his account to write the check to cover them, he had felt indescribably wonderful. He was legit. And suddenly, after that, he found himself saying hello to police officers on the street (instead of crossing the street to avoid them), voting in every election, and reading the paper with a real interest in how the budget was—correction—*never* was shaping up in Washington and writing his senators and congressman his sentiments about it.

Gary Steiner was an upstanding American citizen.

The wiseass, jaded, cynical, beaten, angry, flash-and-dash TV writer with too much money and too much mouth and certainly too much booze in him was now the kind of person who did not flinch when the president of the United States said that the state of the union relied on the state of the individuals in it.

Gary was part of the solution, not part of the problem.

And man oh man, did that ever blow his mind.

What this meant, then, was that he was not someone who would be a minus in Allyson's life. He would be a plus. He could teach her things his parents couldn't teach him. About self-esteem, about coping with insecurity, about how to have fun, about what is real in this world and what is not, about making the most of her gifts and learning to change in response to realizing her drawbacks. And he would teach her about forgiveness—and about love and acceptance and about everything else that had so baffled him for so many years.

He stopped the car. Lydia's station wagon was in his driveway.

He sat there awhile, looking at it.

She had only been here three times before. With Gracia the day he found the house, with Noél the day he moved in, and at the party he threw to celebrate moving in.

Of course, he thought, pulling all the way in and parking, turning off the lights and then the engine, *she wants to talk about Allyson. About rules and boundaries.*

His was a one-story house, a white stucco with a red tile roof. Lydia wasn't on the front porch and so, knowing that the house was locked, Gary undid the latch on the gate and walked through the dusk around to the backyard. There she was, sitting in a lounge chair on the terrace—legs crossed, one arm on each arm of the chair. No, correction—there she was, *sleeping* in a lounge chair on the terrace.

As he approached, the crinkling of the paper bag in his arms awakened her. "Hi," he said, softly, sitting on the end of the other lounge chair.

"Hi," she said, eyes open, but otherwise remaining motionless.

He let the bag slip down through his hands to the ground. "It's been quite a day." Pause. "I stopped at a meeting and the store on my way home. Have you been here long?"

She smiled. Then she shook her head slightly, looking at him. "Who would have ever thought we'd be sitting in the backyard of your house after you had been to an AA meeting and the store?" she said. "I remember when you thought good nutrition was a pizza and beer—and the rent was something no one should bother you about for at least six months."

He scratched his ear. "Funny," he said, smiling too, "I was just thinking the same thing in the car."

Silence.

"I came because I wanted to try and help you understand exactly why I did the things I did, Gary," she said.

"Good," he said.

"Because I have nothing to lose now," she said, adding a moment later, "Nothing but everything. Because you've meant so much to me for so many years I don't know what I would do if I lost you."

He looked at her, not understanding. "Don't you think our—our relationship can survive this? Because if you don't, we need to talk about this, because Allyson's—she is my daughter and I want to be a part of her life."

"Yes, I know," Lydia said. "That's why I was hoping for more time to sort this out in my own head. Allyson comes first, of course, but I can't pretend that—that I haven't always—" She stopped. "None of it worked the way it was supposed to, Gary. I didn't mean for any of this to happen the way it did."

"What was supposed to happen?" he said.

"You were supposed to stop drinking when I left you."

"You didn't just leave me," Gary said, "you left New York."

"You forget," she said. "When I left, you swore you would stop drinking. And I said, fine, as soon as you get six months together, we'll talk."

It hit him like thunder. What she said was true. It was one of those vague distant memories that had thus far escaped being totally remembered. Until now.

"I was in Southampton for those six months," she said. "My sister found me a house near the ocean and there I sat, getting bigger by the day. Three weeks before Allyson was born, I called you and a woman answered. She was drunk. And so were you. And so I didn't call back."

"Oh, Lyddie," he sighed, dropping his head in his hands.

"No one except the doctor and a nurse and Angela and Chris knew I gave birth to Allyson in the master bedroom of that house. I wouldn't go to the hospital—I couldn't risk exposure. Because by then I knew I was in no shape to raise a child by myself. And I didn't have a job—I had quit the soap—I didn't know what was going to happen to me. And so I took my sister up on her offer, which was to take Allyson for a year while I tried to get settled." Lydia was crying now. "After she was born and I got back into shape, I went off to California and almost immediately got 'Cassandra.' My sister and I talked about them

[331]

moving to Los Angeles, but Chris didn't want to leave Westhampton. At that point, I got in touch with you again, but by that time you had been fired from 'Parson's Crossing' and—"

"And I was still drinking," Gary finished for her.

Lydia nodded. "Angela flew out to see me and she begged me to let them adopt Allyson. I could see her as much as I wanted, but this way Allyson could have real parents, a real home. And they had been trying to have children for years, and couldn't conceive and—" She paused, swallowing. "And I was in heavy-duty therapy then, trying to deal with all my problems—and so I thought, yes, that would be best." She added in a whisper, tears filling her eyes, "So I let them have her."

Gary raised his head. Lydia was struggling to compose herself.

"I met Gracia that year," she resumed, "and she and Billy and Catalina seemed—well, they seemed like what I was supposed to do. It seemed like they had been sent, that if I couldn't take care of Allyson, that I could at least try and help someone else's children." Pause. "Can you understand at all, Gary? How much I wanted to tell you? But what trouble you were in—and so was I?—and oh, God, Angela and Chris were so good, so loving and reliable. And she was my *baby*, Gary—and I loved her and I wanted her to have—"

She broke down completely. Gary moved over to sit on her lounge chair and hold her in his arms. He was crying too, pressing his face against the back of her neck, in her hair.

After several minutes had gone by, when both had quieted, Gary whispered, "But why did you get me the job at Bestar? Why did you bring me to Los Angeles?"

"Because I loved you," she said. "Because I've always loved you."

He squeezed his eyes shut. So it was true. All those fleeting moments over the years—he had not mistaken them.

Lydia's grip on him tightened. "But you were like my father, Gary, just like him—and I could see it all happening the same way." She raised her head, wiping her nose with the back of her hand. "But I couldn't just let you go down. I had to try to help you stop—" She sniffed. "And—after a time, you did it. It happened. You stopped drinking."

"But it was too late," Gary said, brushing the hair out of her face.

"To tell you about Allyson, yes," Lydia said, nodding. "Although in the last year, when things seemed to be, well, getting better between us—and both of us getting so much better—I knew I had to start rethinking things."

"The night we went through your trunk," Gary said, "was Allyson what you meant when you said there were things you had to tell me before we could go on?"

"Yes," she said, nodding. "When I was working on the book, I realized that it didn't matter what I thought was right or not right, that I had to tell you about Allyson. But I was so scared about interfering with Angela and Chris and their life with her, because—oh Gary, she's been such a happy little girl. But I knew, too, and they knew—Angela and Chris did—that Allyson would someday have the right to know who her real parents were."

The thought dumbfounded Gary. "You mean you're going to tell Allyson? That we're her real parents?"

"All I know for sure," Lydia said, "is that we—you and I—need a lot of professional counseling about it. Whatever we do, Gary, we have to make sure it's the right thing. What's best for her."

Gary nodded.

"And I always prayed that when I finally told you about Allyson," she said, "that you'd somehow find your way to forgive me. But even if you didn't, I always intended to ask for your participation in counseling. If you were sober, that is. I don't know what I thought I would do if you weren't."

"We'll go to counseling," he said softly, brushing the hair out of her eyes.

"Angela and I had just started talking about it on my last visit," she sighed.

"You used to visit," Gary said.

"Oh," she said, sniffing, wiping her eyes with the back of her hand, "but it never worked very well. I wasn't allowed to get too near, because—I'd get so upset and felt like I wanted to die if I couldn't be with Allyson—and I'd see that little face—" She started to cry again and Gary held her.

After a minute, he gave her his handkerchief and put his arm around her as she used it. "Lyddie? I have to ask you something."

She looked at him.

"All this time—all these years—all the help you've given me—you did it for Allyson?"

She shook her head, took a breath, and then let it out. "No," she said. "I did it for me." Then she nodded, "Yes, I think I told myself I was doing it for Allyson's sake for a long time—but I knew why I was doing it." She sighed, but smiled a little. "I'd do anything to keep you in my life, Gary."

"But you must know I've always loved you," Gary said.

She shook her head. "No, not always."

It was Gary's turn to sigh, lowering his head. "Yeah, well, when I look back at everything, I guess I didn't act very much like someone in love with you."

Lydia started to laugh.

Surprised, he looked up. And then he began to laugh too, because the concept of him demonstrating his love for Lydia was pretty ludicrous. He had been one mass of problems, and since he had moved to California not one of those problems had ever had anything to do with Lydia, except that it had always been poor Lydia on whom he had always dumped all his problems.

He hugged her. "God, I love you."

"And I love you," she said. And then she eased him back to look at him. "I need to take this slow. And I'm not sure exactly how to handle it with Allyson. But I think what I'd like to do—if you'd like to do it—is to spend some time with you, alone, just you and me."

His heart soared. "You mean go away?"

"No, no, I can't—we can't," she said, "not with work—and I don't want to leave Allyson any more than I have to right now. No," she said, touching his chest, "I was thinking maybe we could schedule some regular time together—at night maybe, after Allyson's gone to bed. Here, maybe. Or somewhere." She looked up. "Do you know what I mean?"

He smiled, heart pounding. "Oh, I know what you mean, Lyddie."

She smiled.

And he kissed her.

After, holding her, kissing her neck, he murmured, "I don't suppose you could stay an hour or two more tonight, could you?"

She brought his face up to look at him. "Yes, I could." And then she smiled one of her most dazzling smiles. "I've been waiting to make love with you for seven years, Gary—I'm not about to give up five minutes before the miracle."

Lydia stayed not two hours, but six, leaving his house shortly before dawn.

Singing.

Yes, he could hear her singing in the driveway.

It had not been like the old days. No, not at all.

SIX

Liberation

"Yes, Gary, what is it? I'm very busy," Mortimer Pallsner said, not bothering to get up from behind his desk.

"I wanted you to know that there're going to be some contract revisions on Lydia's renewal with Bestar," Gary said, tossing a large manila envelope on his desk.

"Nonsense, it's already signed," Pallsner said.

"Yes, well, a lot of things get signed," Gary said, "and a lot of things get revised and approved—just like Lydia's agreement will be."

"What, are you her lawyer now?" Pallsner said.

"You should read some of that," Gary said, pointing to the envelope, "and then you should call Lydia's people."

Pallsner picked up the envelope, hefting it in his hands. "What's in here?"

"Transcripts of certain conversations, receipts for certain things billed to Bestar, notes on meetings with people not considered by the authorities to be particularly upstanding."

Pallsner didn't seem fazed in the least. He looked at Gary as if he had said, "New script for the next show." (But then, what was this in a town built largely on blackmail?) "Okay," Pallsner said, "I'll give Lydia's people a call. But you can tell Noél from me," he added, "that she's a sneaky little fuck and I always knew she wasn't as out of it as everyone said she was."

Pallsner *smiled* as he said this last part.

"There's nothing unreasonable Lydia wants—you'll see that," Gary said. "She'll stay on for the extra two years, as she agreed." Pause. "See, she's not like you, Mort. She's interested in building, not tearing down—not tearing people apart."

"Don't be a fuckhead, Gary," Pallsner said. "There's only one person Lydia Southland's interested in building and that's herself." He opened his drawer, took out some gum, and popped it in his mouth. Over the chewing, he asked, "What about the book?"

"No book," Gary said. "At least—you won't be in it if there is one."

"Huh," Pallsner said, sitting back in his chair, chewing, considering this for a moment. "Huh," he said again. "So we go on."

"We go on," Gary confirmed. A second later he said, "That reminds me—I saw that woman from Fox yesterday and I think you're right, I think we should hire her. She said she could start in three weeks."

"Good," Pallsner said, and then he went on to reiterate his idea about how they could reorganize the writing team on "Cassandra's World" to safeguard it from burnout.

In five minutes their business was finished and Gary went back to his office and Pallsner went back to what he had been doing.

It was, after all, just another afternoon in La La Land.

— 64 —

Kate had spent the entire flight to JFK brooding, staring out the window, wondering what on earth she was going to do with her life. Her career was a mess; she had finished with Harris; her father wasn't speaking to her; and while part of her wanted to see Mark and explore that relationship, most of her wanted to run for the hills. Would that be her crowning achievement, on top of everything else—destroying her relationship with Mark, too?

She'd be thirty-four this year and she was beginning to feel like an aging prostitute or something.

Yes, that's exactly what she felt like.

If she ever got married, she'd have to wear black in honor of all the bodies she'd left by the side of the road.

Why was it other women could just get married? And some get married and divorced and married? And some, like Lydia, even have a child suddenly? True, Lydia's circumstances were extraordinary, but Kate couldn't help but be a little jealous. Lydia had a child. Lydia could or could not remarry one day; it wouldn't affect her having a child or not. Allyson was hers. Forever. And Lydia was wealthy. And Lydia was talented. And Lydia was loved.

And she earned every bit of it, Katherine Gates Weston, she heard her mother say in her head, *and had to endure a kind of pain you can't even imagine. Think of me having to give you away when you were a baby; think of how long I would have lasted then.*

After the plane taxied to the gate, Kate remained in her seat, looking out the window, waiting for everyone to get off the plane ahead of her. She felt as though she couldn't even look at anyone without it hurting. "We've landed," a stewardess said gently.

Kate looked over. The plane was almost empty. She undid her seat belt, lugged out her manuscript bag from under the seat, and made her way off the plane. "Thank you," she said mechanically to the crew at the door, "it was a lovely flight."

It felt cold in the gate. It was always cold in New York, Kate thought. Even on the hottest day of summer it was cold in New York.

She walked around the bend of the gate, down the ramp, and into the building wing, turning right and starting the walk to the main terminal.

She felt awful.

Following a group of people, she went downstairs to baggage, wishing like hell she only had carry-on luggage so she could go straight home. And then, looking at all the drivers waiting with signs for the passengers they were to pick up—AULT, GARNER, AUTHIER, HAYWARD— she wished one of those drivers were waiting for her.

And then she saw Mark. He smiled and gave a little wave. "I thought you missed the plane," he called. "Everybody and their brother's come through already from your flight."

"Hi," he said when she reached him, taking her manuscript bag and giving her a hug. She was in heels so they were almost exactly the same height.

He looked great. Young, intelligent, kind, funny, warm—he looked just like Mark. It *was* Mark. Just Mark. Kate looked down at his mouth and before she thought about it, leaned forward and kissed him there. And then she smiled, taking his arm and sagging against him slightly, starting over to the baggage claim area, saying, "You're an angel to come. How did you know what flight?"

"Lydia," he said.

Kate looked at him. "Lydia?"

He cleared his throat and said, "Listen, Kate, there's something I need to tell you—right away, I think."

From his tone, she knew it was going to be bad.

"I think you're getting fired tomorrow."

Kate stopped, swallowed, her brain falling into her stomach, or so it felt. "Well, I can't say it's totally unexpected, can I?" she said.

He tightened his grip on her arm. "I saw the paperwork."

Kate was in a daze. She sort of saw the airport lights. Was sort of aware of where she was going. But when they got into the baggage area, Mark had to steer her toward the right carousel because she was heading for the wrong one. She swallowed again. "How did you see that—the paperwork?"

"I don't know why," Mark said, "but Chaz brought it to me. Just came into my office, closed the door, handed me a file, and stood there while I read it. And then he took it away—never said a word."

Kate knew why Chaz had done it. He was paying her back. Chaz was a "permanent" temporary secretary in the personnel department (so B, F & C did not have to pay him benefits as a regular employee). When he had been there about a month, Kate had heard that he was secretly living in the offices—sleeping on the couch in the men's room lounge at night—having nowhere to go. He didn't have enough money yet for an apartment and he had broken up with the lover he had moved to New York with from Atlanta. After a character reference from Sarah, Kate had let him stay in her apartment for five weeks, rent free, since she had been living over at Harris's. No one else but Sarah had ever known about it.

Kate smiled. So Chaz had remembered a favor when Kate had forgotten all about it. That was the nice part of the story—the only part Kate could cling to right now. That is, if she were to get out of this airport without bursting into tears.

They took a cab to the office and arrived there about ten o'clock. They signed in downstairs—leaving her suitcase with the night guard—took the elevator up to their floor, and used her key to unlock the door. All was quiet. All was dark. They turned on the hall lights and made their way back toward their offices.

Kate turned on her office lights; Mark went into his office and came back with a Literary Guild canvas bag and then, for the next three hours, they went through Kate's files, searching for letters from authors she wished to keep.

"There's a handwritten note from Joyce Carol Oates in there somewhere," she said, handing Mark an OUTSIDE AUTHORS MISC file to look through. "And look for one from Herman Wouk." Pause. "I'm taking all of these letters from Lance in here, they have nothing to do with business. And there's a letter somewhere in Zalia's file that other people shouldn't see, about her husband. We need to find that."

They went through her Rolodex and Sarah's old Rolodex, pulling all of the cards with people's numbers and addresses Kate wanted, but making sure to leave duplicate cards of all the authors and agents she dealt with for inheriting editors. Mark went off in search of another canvas bag and in it they put Kate's office copy of the *Literary Market Place*, a copy of *The Perfect Résumé* ("And I thought I was getting this for Sarah," Kate sighed), and all of the personal papers Kate had in the middle drawer of her desk ("Look, Mark, here's the cartoon you drew for my thirtieth birthday").

As they were about to leave, Kate quickly flipped through her mail and stopped at a memo. "Well," she said, picking it up, "I guess this confirms it."

"What?"

"My requisition for a new assistant was denied," Kate said. She put the memo back down, closed the folder, and closed her eyes, not wanting to cry. But this was so humiliating. And infuriating. She felt as though she could kill Rebecca. Imagine; Kate was getting fired. There wasn't an editor at B, F & C who had made as much money as she had for the house and yet *Kate* was getting fired.

Politics. Office politics. She had risen too high, she made too much money, she had shot off her mouth to Rebecca too many times.

They turned off the lights, let themselves out, signed out downstairs, and walked over to Broadway. "So now what?" Kate said, more to herself than to Mark.

"I'll drop you off at home," Mark said, putting her suitcase down and waving for a cab. "You should try to get some sleep."

Kate looked at him. "Maybe you should try to get some sleep with me."

He looked at her, his arm still poised in the air.

"I don't think I'll be any good for romance, though," she said. "It's amazing how asexual you feel when you've failed."

"You haven't failed, Kate," he said. "But you shouldn't be alone."

Kate threw her head back and laughed. "Oh, God, are we a pair," she said, laughing still. She straightened up and parted her legs in a stance and threw her arm back if she was singing a song. "This is it, Mark Fiducia!" she said. "High romance at its best! A broken-down spinster who's getting fired tomorrow!"

He grabbed her arm. She looked at him. "Don't," he said. He let go. "And if inviting me over is part of beating yourself up—or giving up—then don't invite me."

"Oh, Mark," she sighed, resting her forehead on his shoulder. She raised a hand to his other shoulder. "No. That's not it." She raised her head. "I invited you over not because I'm giving up—but because the pretenses are rapidly falling apart in my life and I think what I need now more than anything else is a big dose of reality." There was a flicker of a smile. "Our friendship has been the only real thing in my life for a while now."

He smiled. "I know."

Kate's living room was about as lived-in as a hotel room. Boxes of stuff from Harris's were sitting there unopened; and although she did have a pretty oriental rug on the floor, a few pieces of nice dark-wood furniture—including her favorite, the long Empire sofa—and bookcases filled with books, it did not look as though anyone really lived here. There were no plants. There were no photographs, no pictures on the walls, no knickknacks; and there were shades on the windows but no drapes. The bookcases were freestanding. In other words, nothing was attached to the apartment itself.

Kate threw her stuff down and while Mark carried her suitcase into the bedroom, she walked into the kitchen to look in the refrigerator. "We have a big choice here—grapefruit juice or seltzer?"

"How about a little of both," he suggested, coming back to lean against the doorway.

"The worst part about moving home," Kate said, as she cracked the ice trays in the sink, "is that I always forget how I really live."

"Harris had an ice maker, huh?"

"Harris practically hired an ice maker," Kate muttered, putting ice in the glasses.

"Will you miss that?"

"What?"

"The way you lived with Harris. It's pretty much the way you grew up, wasn't it?"

She looked at him. "I make a good living." She winced. And sighed. "Well, I did. And I've saved."

"But you won't live the way you did with Harris."

"Good," she said. "Even if I did grow up in a comfortable family, look at all the good it's done me."

"And it's done you a lot," Mark said. "You're well educated, speak well, God knows you move well—the way you are, Kate, the people you know, the talents you have, you can pretty much go anywhere from here."

She finished making their drinks. "There's some vodka in the living room if you want some," she said, handing him his.

"No thanks," he said. "I want to keep my wits about me tonight."

"Mark," she said, taking her glass and walking past him to the living room, "I'm getting depressed. I'm getting fired tomorrow."

"Maybe not," he said, following her.

"Then why did you have me clean out my office?"

"Because I want you to be prepared for the worst."

She turned around. "I repeat, I'm getting depressed. Do something."

"Like what?" he said.

"Make love to me?" she said.

He shook his head. "I don't think that's the best idea."

"Oh, great," she sighed, dropping down on the Empire sofa, "now you don't want me either."

"That's not true, Kate."

She took a gulp of her drink, tempted to sling it with vodka.

"Come on," Mark said, holding out his hand.

"What?"

"Come on," he said, pulling her to her feet. "Take a bath and put on a nightie. I'll give you a massage and we'll go to sleep."

"Sounds good," Kate said.

"Go in and take your bath," he said, sending her off. "I'll turn off the lights out here."

Kate did as she was told. She took a very hot bath, covered herself with Oil of Olay, put on only a moderately sexy nightgown (white satin), and came out of the bathroom. Mark was in his undershirt and boxer shorts, sitting on the bed. "Come on," he said, patting the sheet beside him.

Obediently she stretched out on the bed and he started to rub her back.

"Hmmm, that's great," she said. "You know," she said a while later, "Lydia has a woman who comes and does this to her twice a week. Can you imagine?"

"You should get one once a week," Mark said.

"You're hired. I'll be on a rather strict budget as of tomorrow."

He chuckled, continuing to rub her back. "Kate," he said after a while.

"Hmmm?"

"I don't want to take advantage of you," he said. "I don't want you to think I'm moving in on you because you're vulnerable."

"I'm always vulnerable to you," Kate said. "Or don't you remember the night you found that out?"

He was starting down, massaging her legs through her nightie. It felt like heaven.

"Mark?" she said.

"What?"

"What am I going to do?"

"I don't know," he said, hands rising to her buttocks. They hesitated a moment and then he began massaging them too. "What do you think you want to do? I mean, *really* do."

"Oh, God," Kate groaned, "get a clean start. Be born again. Move to Siberia. I don't know, something. Even the thought of interviewing around town . . ." Her voice trailed off as Mark's hands came back up to her shoulders. "Oh, right there. Yes, that's wonderful."

"That's where I get really sore too," Mark said, swinging his leg over and sitting down on her lower back. "Is this okay?"

"Oh, it's great," she said as he massaged harder. "I guess most editors get the same pains in the neck, huh?" She smiled. She was also becoming keenly aware that it might be an erection that was lightly grazing her lower back every time Mark surged ahead in his massage. The thought went straight through her and she could feel her lower body turn on. Like ON.

"When you were in L.A., did you look around at all?" he said, rubbing and rubbing, rubbing and rubbing; and whatever it was that was so very lightly settling on her back and then lifting off again—that whatever it was that Kate imagined might be Mark's erection—was making her a little crazy.

For someone who thought she wouldn't be very good for sex tonight she sure was getting awfully aroused. There was something wildly exciting about the thought of Mark having an erection in boxer shorts. There was something wildly sexy about Mark having an erection, period. There was still that wildly sexy memory of how he had been with her that night at his apartment, a memory she had used to make herself come with Harris.

"Not really," she said, "I didn't have time. Besides, there's not really anything to do out there. I mean, what could I do?"

"You'd probably be a pretty good producer," he said. "You know commercial stories, where to find them, how to buy them—you work well with people—"

"So well I'm getting fired tomorrow," she said, but now actually feeling a little elation at the thought. After tomorrow, she might not have to deal with B, F & C anymore. It would all be out of her hands. It would be over, done with, and she would be forced to move on.

She wouldn't have to return her phone calls—hooray!

"Do you want to turn over?" she heard Mark say.

She smiled to herself, wondering what he would do. For someone who was once pretty shy, her friend had seemed to have gotten pretty confident in some areas.

"Sure," she said, and he slid off her back. She rolled over, smoothed her nightie, and opened her eyes, squinting against the light. It was funny to see Mark sitting on her bed in his undershirt. He looked so—well, undressed. "Sit," she said to him, patting her abdomen, "sit here," and then she closed her eyes, letting him make of that command what he would. And when she felt him complying, she let her left eye open a crack and—and she was right, there was the most marvelous erection in those boxer shorts, working to free itself through the opening. She closed her eyes, feeling a minor-major flooding event taking place inside her.

He massaged her temples, and her scalp, and while he was doing that, leaning way forward, Kate opened her eyes and smiled, marveling. She could see him through the opening—taut, straining, gorgeously elongated.

She couldn't help herself. She reached up and pulled his shorts down to free him. Mark froze there a moment—and then he resumed massaging her scalp. She touched the end of him with her fingers, stroked him for only a second, and then she held him fully in one hand and gently started to move. When he seized up slightly she stopped, let go of him, and, with both hands, pulled down on his boxer shorts to get them all the way off. He sat back then, looking at her with somewhat glazed-over eyes, and quickly moved to the side to kick his shorts off.

"Back," she said, patting her abdomen again, "sit here." And he complied, straddling her, all of him splayed out before her on the satin. She looked. Openly. And then she looked up at him and smiled. She didn't want to torture him, but the tension was exquisite. "You haven't massaged my breasts," she said, and he nodded, swallowing, and placed his hands on her breasts, over the nightie, and began to rub them. And rub them. Kate's eyes closed, the feeling extraordinary, and she felt his hands grow stronger, and then she felt him touching through the fabric to her nipples, and then squeezing them—that got a groan out of her—and he was sitting forward now, massaging her breasts and at the same time bending to kiss her. She could feel *that* part of him down there moving, skimming the surface of her stomach, questing. Aching. Wanting. And then while he was still kissing her, he suddenly shifted to the side and yanked her nightie up—up over her hips, over her stomach, up over her breasts to around her neck—and then he got back on her, hands on her bare breasts, himself lying across her bare stomach.

She was going to die, she wanted him so badly.

Still kissing him, his tongue in her mouth, she pushed at his hips with her hands, signaling to him. She hoped he got the message; he did, thank God he did!—and he lifted himself, reached down to spread her legs, and then stretched out on top of her. He felt around with his hand—touched her down there for a moment, finding where he was—shifted a little, and then brought himself up to her, poised for entry, brought his hand back up to her neck, and then—

And then he pushed his way in, each of them groaning into the other's mouth.

Like last time, their lovemaking was not in the least passive. Whatever this was between her and him, there was a sweetness above the sheets and franticness under them, which Kate supposed must be telling her something about something. There was nothing polite about how they were making love, nothing restrained. They groaned and perspired and went at it, banging away at each other, it getting deeper and deeper and wetter and wetter until Kate was sure she must have lost all feeling down there, but then Mark said in her ear, "It's you and me, Kate, doing it," and that shocked her but thrilled her, too, and way down there something was growing and then ballooning into view, a throbbing that grew larger and larger, rising along the base of her spine—

and he did it to her and did it to her and did it to her

—and it came barreling up then, leaving her wide open, the plunge absolutely complete this next time, making her cry out, "Yes, Mark, yes," and she came, coming in spasms around him, and then he stopped and then he started, faltering, and he said something, pushing up into her, pushing—and then he relaxed, gasped, "Kate," and surged into her again and held—shuddering—and he then pushed into her again gently—one, two, three times more. And stopped.

And stopped.

And stopped.

And she clamped her thighs tight around him and hugged him as hard as she could. "If this is what happens when you get fired," she whispered, "then I want to be fired twice a day for the rest of my life."

— 65 —

In the morning Kate and Mark made love again.

"Why does everything about you suddenly make me feel so—so ferocious?" Kate asked him afterward, a little chagrined about how she had been carrying on. This was not like being with Harris—or anyone that she could remember.

"I like ferocious," Mark said, grinning.

"But that's not me," Kate said.

"Well then, you must be someone else," Mark said. "Who do you suppose you are?"

She kissed him and then fell back against the pillow. "I'm a person who's getting fired today."

"You're a person who's ready for anything," Mark said, correcting her. "Besides, anyone who can make love to someone who has tennis-shoe mouth first thing in the morning is an amazing creature in my book."

Kate sat up. "But don't you understand?" she said, touching his face. "*Every* part of you seems absolutely amazing to me." She smiled. "I want to devour you, I think."

"Fine with me," he said.

They kissed.

"Kate," Mark said, looking at the clock, "I think we better be getting in."

Why she needed to hurry up to get in on time so she could be fired was beyond Kate, but she was so zonked in the head this morning that nothing seemed to make any sense anyway. She had probably slept all of an hour last night; she kept waking and finding Mark there and finding herself being incredibly happy about it. Then she'd settle down and be just falling off to sleep when she would feel Mark stir and then feel a gentle kiss—in the middle of her back, on her neck, on the top of her head—and hear him fall back off to sleep, leaving her wide awake again in wonderment.

But Kate was a woman who needed her sleep, and last night and the whirlwind trip to L.A. had left her dopier than she would like for what promised to be a difficult day. They showered together and Mark washed her hair (oh, golly, that could prompt a proposal of marriage out of her right then and there) and she took a lot of care in choosing her clothes. If she was going out of B, F & C for the last time, she was going to go out looking g-o-o-d.

"God, you look wonderful," Mark said when she finished dressing and came out into the living room. "You've got such wonderful color—did you go to the beach when you were in L.A.?"

"Mark," Kate said, laughing, going over to him and putting her arms around his waist, "the color is from you. I think it's called beard burn." She kissed him and then wiped a little lipstick off his mouth with her finger. "Shall we go?"

"Let's go," he said, taking her hand.

"Good morning, Emma Lou," Kate said in a singsong voice, stepping off the elevator. "How are you on this gorgeous morning?"

"It's raining," Emma Lou said, looking at Kate a little strangely. "Hi, Mr. Mark," she added, seeing him, "good morning."

"Good morning, Emma Lou-Lou-Lou!" Mark said, coming around her desk to give her a big kiss on the cheek. "It is the most wonderful morning I've ever had in my life." He straightened up, turned around, and followed Kate down the hall.

"Must be handing out happy pills downstairs," Emma Lou remarked to the next passerby, a secretary from administration.

"Well they didn't give me any," the secretary snapped.

"No, I don't think they did," Emma Lou said.

At the head of the hallway, Kate hesitated. She looked at the door to Dick's office and then the one to Rebecca's, toying with the idea of stopping in to see how they would react. Then she decided against it, continuing on to her office. The door was open, the lights on. Someone had been in here this morning.

Kate opened her umbrella and put it on the floor to dry, and then hung up her raincoat on the back of the door.

Dale, Mark's assistant, came in. "I brought you some coffee."

"What a saint," Kate told him. "Thank you." She took it and walked around her desk. And there, in her chair, was a handwritten note.

Kate, it said, *Mr. Rushman would like to see you at nine-thirty in his office.*

Kate's stomach flipflopped. She looked at her watch. It was eight-thirty. She had an hour left as executive editor at Bennett, Fitzallen & Coe. *You are not going to cry!* she screamed inside her head. *God damn it, Weston, you are not going to cry! You are going to go out like a lady!*

A lady? a different voice said in her head. *Sure you don't want to kick ass from here to Texas?*

The temp who had been manning the phones since Sarah was fired arrived at ten minutes to nine, carrying a large cloth bag and dressed in about twenty layers of multicolored clothing. She had dyed henna hair and was about twenty pounds overweight. She also had a tendency to be very loud. Her name was Catrell Hayes, although Kate sincerely doubted this was her real name. "Miss Weston, I have an audition at eleven o'clock, is that all right? I'll come back and work through lunch," she said, starting to unwind one of her many layers of festive clothing in the doorway.

She had on purple rubber rain boots, Kate noticed. "Sure," Kate said. "What's it for, a play?"

"No, and I'm so excited," Catrell said, coming right in and sitting down to tell Kate all about it. "It's a callback for a voice-over for a cat food commercial. Boy, if I get this"—she rolled her eyes—"I'll be on easy street."

"Oh Catrell," Kate said, "be careful. There is no such place. And if you ever find yourself on what you think is easy street"—her phone rang and Kate put her hand on it to answer it—"then pack your stuff and move on. You have to keep evolving. Complacency is the death of any artist, you know that." She picked up the phone. "Hello?"

"Mrs. Southland is here," Emma Lou said.

Kate blinked. "Here?" she said. "You mean *here* here?"

"Shall I tell her you will be coming out?" Emma Lou asked politely.

"I'm on my way," Kate said, hanging up the phone. "Catrell, get that umbrella out of here and this coffee stuff. Lydia Southland's here and I'm going to go out and get her."

"Lydia Southland!" Catrell said. "Ohmigod and I have an audition at eleven!"

Kate walked out of her office to find Mark standing in the hall. "Lydia's here," she whispered.

"I know," he whispered back. "She said she would try—she must have taken the red-eye. She said not to tell you in case she couldn't make it."

Kate looked at him.

"Come on," he said, pulling her down the hall.

"You've been talking to Lydia?" she whispered.

"Yeah," he whispered back. "She made me promise I'd call if things went badly for you over the book."

"Oh, hi, Mr. Rushman," Kate said, waving at him on her way by. "I'll see you at nine-thirty."

He didn't smile. He sort of nodded. Actually, he looked a little like Bambi caught in the headlights, which made Kate know it was true, that he intended to fire her this morning.

They sailed down the hall to reception and found Lydia standing with her back to the hall, looking out the window. She was in some kind of pale blue cloth rain cape.

"What are you doing here?" Kate said.

Lydia turned around with a dramatic flourish, her cape flaring out as she did. (It was definitely a Cassandra move.) "I have come to slay dragons," she said, bursting into a radiant smile. "Oh, Kate," she said, walking over, "what have I done to your career?"

"That's the lady on 'Cassandra's World,' " Emma Lou was whispering loudly to a passerby.

Kate was shushing Lydia, leading her back to her office.

"Hi, Mr. Faith and Trust," Lydia said, giving Mark a kiss on the cheek on the way.

"Hi," he said.

Behind Kate's back, Mark winked at Lydia, and her eyebrows went up. He nodded and her smile got even bigger. "Oh, Kate," Lydia said, putting her arm around her and marching up the hall, "I'm so proud of you."

"For what?"

"For I don't know, I just am," Lydia said.

"Oh, Mr. Rushman," Kate said, as they came around the corner and nearly crashed into him. He was with Dick Skolchak. "I'd like you to meet Lydia Southland."

He was clearly bowled over. "Uh, hello," he said, managing to get his hand out.

"So you're the famous Andrew Rushman Kate's told me so much about," she said, shaking his hand. "You have a big fan in Kate. Sometimes I think the only reason we've gotten as far on my book as we have has been because of the things she's told me about you." She smiled, still holding his hand. "About the kind of man you are."

It was embarrassing, how long she looked at him and held his hand.

"And this is Dick Skolchak," Kate said, "associate publisher of the company."

"Dick, hello," Lydia said, taking his hand.

Kate very nearly rolled her eyes. Lydia was really going overboard here with Mr. Dork and Twit here. One would think she was meeting Mel Gibson and Tom Cruise.

Dick's face had gone beet red. "Hello," he managed to say. "It's a plonor"—blink—"honor."

"And a pleasure," Mr. Rushman said. "And what brings you here today? Good news, I hope. We were all so saddened by the loss in your family."

"Thank you," Lydia said. She paused, licking her lips.

Well that lost the men's concentration for a moment or two.

"Actually, Andrew," she said, "I've come to see you. I wanted to talk to you about resuming the publication of my book."

"Oh, really," he said, surprised and delighted. But then a shadow fell across his face. "I'm afraid right now I have to go upstairs for a meeting with my CEO. The big guy," he added under his breath to her, as if she were in on some big secret. "Otherwise I'd be happy to meet with you this minute. Could you perhaps stay for—" He looked at his watch and then at Dick. "A half hour?"

Dick nodded.

He turned back to Lydia. "Could you meet with me in a half hour?" He looked at Kate. "In my office?"

Kate nodded.

He took Lydia's hand. "I look forward to it."

"And I do too," she said.

"If you'll excuse us," he said, moving on.

"Oh, Andrew," Lydia said, turning.

"Yes?"

"I would appreciate it if you did not have Rebecca at this meeting."

Rushman looked slightly stricken by this. "Okay," he said tentatively. And then more forcibly, "Of course. That will be fine. See you then."

Kate turned to Lydia. "What are you up to?" she whispered.

"I'm going to tell him I withdrew the book because of Rebecca," Lydia said behind the closed doors of Kate's office. "And I'm going to tell him that if I have Bennett, Fitzallen & Coe's promise—in writing—that you will continue to be my editor, I will go ahead and publish the book."

"But you don't want to publish the book," Kate pointed out.

"Well, no," Lydia said, "but I never intended on destroying your career either. But we can fix it, can't we? The book? And leave my family and Allyson out of it?"

"Sure we can," Mark said.

Kate was shaking her head. "No, it's too risky, Lydia. You can't publish your autobiography without setting off a whole chain of questions that can't help but further complicate your life with Allyson." Kate stood up and looked out her window, her back to Lydia and Mark. She sighed, then, and shook her head again. She turned around. "I really appreciate what you're trying to do—but no, Lydia, I won't let you do it. And that's final."

Lydia looked to Mark. "Is there anything else I can do?"

"You can still tell Rushman you withdrew the book because of Rebecca," he said. "And you can strongly *imply* that as long as you can work exclusively with Kate, then there's a good possibility you'll change your mind."

Lydia looked at Kate and nodded in Mark's direction. "I like how this man thinks."

Kate smiled. She liked how he thought too.

They rehearsed with Lydia what she would say to Rushman and how she would say it.

"No, don't say, 'She's a bad person,' " Mark said. "Say something like, 'It seems incredible to me that a person of your stature would employ a person like Rebecca as your personal representative.' "

"Rebecca is not a bad person, Andrew," Lydia said to the bookcase, "but if I were you, I would think seriously about the consequences of continuing to employ someone who has publicly humiliated your company and lost you hundreds of thousands of dollars in revenue from my book, to say nothing of severely damaging your personal reputation in Hollywood."

"Oh my God," Kate said, cringing, "I don't know, Mark—I think you've created a monster." And then she stood up. "Thank you!"

Mark wished them luck and Kate walked Lydia down to Mr. Rushman's office, encountering Rebecca on the way.

"Hello, Rebecca," Lydia said, not offering her hand.

"Hello, Lydia, what a pleasant surprise," Rebecca said. Pause. "I hear you're meeting with Mr. Rushman."

"Yes," Kate said. "Right now."

Rebecca looked at Kate and Kate thought, *Ha, ha, you're going to get yours now,* and then she thought she saw the tiniest flicker in Rebecca's eyes. A flicker of fear.

Of course you're scared, Kate thought. *Now you know how it feels.* "Well, we don't want to keep him waiting," Kate said, moving them along.

"Have a good meeting," Rebecca said uneasily.

Rushman closed the door and they sat around the coffee table in his office, Lydia on the couch, Kate in a chair, Mr. Rushman in another. The meeting began and, as they had rehearsed, Lydia explained that she didn't think Mr. Rushman understood her reasons for wanting to withdraw the book, because, if he had, he would have done something by now to try to change her mind—a gesture of goodwill, if you will. When Mr. Rushman said he was under the impression she had changed her mind about the book because she had, well, developed cold feet—which was understandable, he hastened to add, most authors felt that way about their autobiographies at some point, isn't that right Kate? Yes, Mr. Rushman, you're right, they do (the meeting was going just like their old meetings back in the days when Kate had been Golden Girl)—Lydia responded that cold feet was not the reason why she had withdrawn the book and that Andrew thought so only confirmed everything she had suspected.

"What do you mean?" he said.

"That you have no idea what's been going on here—who was responsible for making me withdraw my book from Bennett, Fitzallen & Coe," Lydia said.

Mr. Rushman got it in an instant. He nodded, saying, "I see. That's why you didn't want Rebecca present in this meeting—you feel that she has compromised your relationship with the house in some way."

"Destroyed it is more like it," Lydia said.

Well, there it was. Kate knew she would not be getting fired today. Rebecca would probably be demoted, certainly after corporate found out that it was she who had blown the only money-maker for the fall.

No, Kate realized in the next moment, she was wrong. Rebecca probably wouldn't be demoted—she'd probably get fired. Rushman was livid. "And if the person responsible for creating this misunderstanding were to be dismissed, Lydia," he said, "would you let us go ahead and publish your book?"

Lydia hesitated a split second and then answered, "Yes."

"Very good," Mr. Rushman said, smiling, "then consider it as good as done."

"No," Kate heard herself say.

Lydia and Rushman turned to look at her. "Mr. Rushman," Kate said. She paused, clearing her throat. "Mr. Rushman, there's been a very bad misunderstanding. I don't think Rebecca was really responsible. Lydia may think she is, but she wasn't." Pause. "In fact I know she wasn't."

"Oh, so now you're inside my head," Lydia said, sounding annoyed. "And how do you know what Rebecca said to me?"

"I have known every side of this book's development," Kate continued to Rushman, "and the plain truth of it is, the book the house wants to publish is no longer a book Lydia can write. I've known that for some time now and yet I've continued on with it, hoping that somehow the situation could resolve itself." Pause, swallow. "It can't resolve itself, Mr. Rushman."

Lydia was looking at Kate as though she was nuts.

Rushman was just staring at her.

"There is no publishable book to get out of Lydia. And it's nobody's fault." Pause. "Except mine. For not telling you earlier."

"What are you doing, Kate?" Lydia asked point-blank.

Kate didn't know what she was doing. All she knew was that she wouldn't let Lydia do this and that she hated lying and that she hated working at Bennett, Fitzallen & Coe now and that in all honesty, she had no desire to hurt Rebecca de Loup, she only wished to get the hell away from her. She didn't frankly care that much about Rebecca anymore. She didn't frankly care much about anything at B, F & C anymore except the newfound knowledge that she wanted out. She hated this place and would hate herself if she stayed here.

"What you don't know, Lydia," Kate said to her, "is the changing economic climate and the enormous pressure management has been under here. It's meant that Rebecca has had to act as the hatchet man for the guys upstairs—and that that reflects nothing about her or the house except their combined strength to make the house go on when so many others are going under. So whatever Rebecca said or did not say to you, you have to believe me, she is simply an integral part of the machine that would have made your book a blockbuster bestseller."

"I don't want to discuss it," Kate said to Lydia as they walked back to her office. "I just want to get you out of here." They turned into her office, where Kate gathered up Lydia's things and handed them to her. Then she stopped, looked at Lydia, and threw her arms around her. "I love you," she said.

"I love you too," Lydia said, hugging her back.

"Thank you for what you tried to do," she whispered.

"Thank you for not making me do it," Lydia whispered back.

"What happened?" Mark whispered from the door.

The women released each other and Lydia looked at Mark, rolling her eyes. "Walk me over to the Plaza and I'll tell you all about it. Miss Fireworks here says she has to stay for the post-explosion show."

"Wait," Kate said as they were leaving. She walked outside her office. "Catrell?" she said to the temp. "Would you be so kind as to make sure that Mrs. Southland gets out of the building safely?"

"Would I?" Catrell said, jumping up out of her chair, swinging her six-foot-long scarf back over her shoulder.

"Catrell's an actress too," Kate told Lydia.

Lydia smiled graciously. "Good for you. Supporting yourself while getting your first acting jobs."

"Right," Catrell said. "I have a callback today for a cat food commercial."

"Wonderful," Lydia said, moving down the hall with Mark and Catrell. "You know, I supported myself as a secretary too when I first came to New York."

"You did not!" Kate called down the hall.

"Oh, all right," Lydia said, "I *played* a secretary in a TV commercial when I first came to New York and that's how I got started in show business."

Kate laughed and she heard Lydia laugh too. Kate sighed then, smiling, crossing her arms and leaning against the doorway of her office. She felt enormously better. Relieved.

"Hi, Kate," Tad Haskins said, coming down the hall with Ruthie Renquist.

"Hi," Kate said. "Hi, Ruthie."

"Is it true?" Ruthie said, stopping. "Is she here?"

"She just left," Kate said.

"Phew," Ruthie said, wiping her brow. "How you ever worked with that bitch is beyond me, Kate."

Kate smiled and went back into her office.

She was fired shortly before noon.

— *67* —

Kate walked along Central Park South wishing that Lydia had chosen anywhere to stay but the Plaza.

The Plaza. *Harris,* she thought. *The Plaza will always be haunted by Harris.* But she had just been fired, right? So all of Central Park was haunted now anyway.

So there went the city. It was official now. Kate Weston had failed in every part of Manhattan; *all* of it was haunted.

Lydia had a suite, of course. *Twelve years in New York and I visit suites at the Plaza twice in three months,* Kate thought on her way up in the elevator. *I wonder what that's supposed to mean.*

As soon as Mark opened the door, Kate knew something was up. First of all, Mark appeared to be a bit tipsy.

"I'm so sorry," Mark said, giving her a hug, "but I can't help but be glad too."

Lydia, sitting in a chair in the living room of the suite, was toasting her with a champagne glass. "To freedom," she said.

"Would you like some champagne?" Mark said, walking back into the living room to the luncheon cart that was there.

"Please," Kate said, slipping off her coat and hanging it up in the closet. "So this is how the other half lives," she said, looking around. It was some suite. There was even a cage with canaries in it.

"Are you terribly upset?" Lydia said.

"I don't know what I feel," she said honestly. Mark brought over a glass to her. "Thanks," she said accepting it. She took a sip.

"What kind of severance?" he said. "Did you discuss it?"

She shook her head, swallowing. "He said six months plus six more if I didn't get a job—and I signed. Probably stupid of me," she sighed, "but I just wanted out of there."

"That's what Mark was afraid of," Lydia said, "that they'd slap papers in front of you while your head was still spinning."

"By the way," Kate said, sitting down on the couch and looking up at Mark, "when, may I ask, did you and Lydia become so chummy as to be discussing the state of my career behind my back?"

Lydia giggled. It was a very funny sound considering that Lydia, Kate was quite sure, had never in all her adult life ever willingly giggled before. But it was unmistakable—Lydia, feet curled up in the chair underneath her, champagne glass in hand, giggled and then said, "Champagne, please, more champagne, Mark."

He dutifully brought the bottle over and refilled her glass. Lydia peeked around him at Kate. "I'm going to the airport after this, so you two are going to have to fight it out in my absence."

"Fight what out?" Kate said.

"Whether or not you'll work for me," Lydia said.

Kate blinked. "What?"

"I want you to head up my new production company at Bestar."

Mark chuckled at Kate's expression and sat next to her on the couch.

"I'm going to produce at least two TV movies a year that I'll star in," Lydia continued. "And at least one more that I won't be in, but will serve as executive producer on."

Kate was frowning. "But I don't know anything about TV."

"You know story, you know character, you know what's commercial, what works with the public," Mark said. "You know how to run numbers, you know how to handle people, you know packaging—and, Kate, you know the people who would be producing the books Lydia would most likely want to option."

"And most importantly," Lydia added, "you know how to do something no one else at Bestar really knows how to do." She finished off her glass of champagne and set it down on the table. "You know how to handle me."

"That would be the biggest part of your job in the beginning," Mark said, "being the go-between between Lydia and Mortimer Pallsner while setting up the company. But you'll have a coexecutive; you won't be running it by yourself."

"Mortimer *Pallsner?*" Kate said. "Why on earth would I want to have anything to do with Mortimer Pallsner?"

"He doesn't seem any worse than those people you've been working for at Bennett, Fitzallen & Coe," Lydia said. "And at least Mort knows something about our business—and he, and Bestar, will be financing our films."

Kate blinked. "Wait a minute," she said. "Do you mean to tell me that you're going into partnership with the guy who tried to blackmail you?"

Lydia shook her head. "Not a partnership. Southland Productions is an independently owned operation that will be using the Bestar staff and studio facilities—that's all. Besides," she added with a smile, "for some reason Mort seems to think your father has something to do with the CIA. Gary doesn't expect you'll have much trouble with him."

Kate drank down her champagne.

"Seventy-five to start and a company car," Lydia said. "A convertible of some kind—of course."

Kate stared at her.

"It's not much by TV standards, but you'll do very well with me if it works, Kate, you can count on that," Lydia said. "We start with a two-year contract—percentage of gross profits and bonuses spelled out. You'll make no less than one hundred the first year and one twenty-five the next. And you'll have an office at the studio and a full-time assistant." Lydia paused to smile. "What's the matter?"

"Nothing," Kate said, "I'm just in a state of shock."

"I want Southland Productions to have the kind of credentials Bestar doesn't," Lydia said. "I want taste, style, and smarts—and I want it aboveboard—so I want a snazzy, sophisticated big New York editor to come out west and legitimize the joint." Pause. "I need you, Kate. I want you to be the front lady for Southland Productions. I want you out in the world representing my interests."

"And if things work out," Mark said, "and Lydia leaves the show in a couple years, the company will be in place for her to do more of the projects that interest her."

"The idea of my retirement was a bit premature, I'm afraid," Lydia said, "by about forty years, I think—but I still don't want to be just an actress forever. I'd like to produce some things for television, find and develop new talent." She smiled. "Do what you've always done as an editor, Kate—only now I want you to come do it with me in TV."

"I see," Kate said, leaning forward to put her glass down on the coffee table. She sat back in the couch, thinking. "But I'd have to live in Los Angeles," she said after a moment. "I couldn't be bicoastal."

"Not really, no," Lydia said. "Although you will be making trips back to New York—probably two or three times a year."

"And this would be starting when?" Kate said.

"As soon as you're ready," Lydia said. "September I hope."

Kate nodded. And then she excused herself to use the powder room. She closed the door behind her and washed her hands, looking at herself in the mirror for quite some time. She sighed then, dried her hands, and went back into the living room.

"It's an incredible opportunity, Lydia," she said, plunking herself down on the couch, "but I'm afraid the timing's not very good. I can't leave New York right now."

"Why not?" Lydia said.

"But you want to go, Kate, don't you?" Mark said, taking her hand. "You could see yourself happy in a job like this, couldn't you? In L.A.?"

She hesitated and then nodded. "Yes, I can. Easily. But—"

"Then take it," Mark said.

Pause. "But I can't leave you," she said. "Not now." She squeezed his hand. "Either I stay or you come with me."

He smiled. And then kissed her gently on the mouth. "I *am* coming with you," he said. "And we'll have side-by-side offices, just like always."

There was a loud sigh from Lydia and Kate turned around to look at her. She was a bit teary eyed. "It's so wonderful to see you two together," she said, blinking rapidly.

Kate whirled back around to Mark.

"Lydia offered me a job too," he explained. "As coexecutive of Southland Productions." Smile. "We'll be working together, just like always."

She sat there, stunned.

She didn't believe it. None of it.

And then she did believe it. All of it. Because all of it came together and made sense in some grand cosmic way that told Kate she couldn't have possibly made this one up—she couldn't have even dreamed it—and hence it was probably meant to happen.

Wow. So the Plaza wouldn't be haunted after all. Nor would New

York be anymore. To the contrary, from now on they'd always be the places where she had been given yet another chance at life—and this time she would have taken it.

"So the answer's yes?" Mark said, putting his arm around her.

Kate looked at him. "And this, you think, is appropriate office behavior?"

SEVEN

Chances Taken

— *68* —

By eastern standards, the hill was not a hill at all, but a very gentle slope. Still, it was lovely here, the highest land in the cemetery, and there was a tree just above the grave, a cypress, that at this moment was rustling in the September breezes, shading the grave from the sun.

ELIZABETH ANNE GATES WESTON
BELOVED DAUGHTER, BELOVED WIFE, BELOVED MOTHER
1933–1970

Tears were running down Kate's face, but she was smiling. She knelt down and placed the vase of roses at the foot of her mother's grave and then moved around to sit next to it. "Oh, Mom," she said aloud, "I'm sorry it took me so long to come."

She swallowed, her throat hurting, her heart hurting; she missed her mother as much as she ever did. Then she cleared her throat and turned around, reaching behind her to take his hand and bring him forward. Mark knelt down beside her.

"Mom," Kate said, "this is Mark. And you'll be glad to know he's not a bit like any of us." And then she laughed. And then Mark laughed.

And then Kate was pretty sure she heard her mother laugh, too.

— *69* —

When they arrived in Los Angeles from Dallas, Mark was the first to spot the driver in the baggage claim area. WESTON/FIDUCIA his sign said. It turned out, however, that the driver had not been sent by Lydia—as Kate said she bet he had been—but was, the driver said, sent courtesy of Mr. Mortimer Pallsner.

"Oh, great," Kate muttered, "he's probably going to drive us to South America."

"But we have a car we're supposed to pick up," Mark said to the driver.

"Two cars," the driver said. "And they are both parked at Mrs. Southland's. That is where I am to take you."

"Well, okay," Kate said, "but we'd like to stop at our hotel first and drop off our bags. We're staying over in Santa Monica."

"Mrs. Southland has you booked in the Beverly Hills Hotel," the driver reported. "After I take you to her house, I was told to deliver your luggage there." Pause. "I believe you are already checked into the Bestar suite."

Mark looked at Kate and smiled. "Lydia certainly seems determined to do things her way, doesn't she?"

Kate looked at the driver again. "We are going to Santa Monica," she said firmly.

The driver smiled, took an envelope out of the breast pocket of his jacket, and handed it to her. "Mrs. Southland said you would say that."

Kate,

We think we've found the ideal apartment in Santa Monica, but you can't get in for ten days. As you requested, it's a real apartment building, à la New York—but with views of the ocean from the living room and master bedroom, underground parking, and lots of privacy.

You can afford it, too—and Bestar will cosign mortgages if you choose to exercise the option to buy.

And so, dear Kate, I hope you will forgive me for insisting that you and Mark spend your first ten days near me. We have a ton of work to do and I'd rather not have you off in Santa Monica quite yet playing honeymoon hotel at the Shangri-La.

So now won't you come straight over for dinner with the gang? Everybody can't wait to see you.

Love,
Lydia

P.S. I have a surprise for you.

*

The gate.

The sight of it made Kate's throat tighten. Even from the backseat of this limousine—designed, surely, to make one feel as though nothing could touch those privileged to sit in it, nothing outside of it certainly—the sight of the gate was overwhelming to her, even more so when the driver pressed the intercom button.

So much had happened since that first day. So much.

"This is where the dogs tried to get you," Mark said, giving her hand a squeeze.

Oh—that's right, she thought, *I'm with a man who remembers every-thing I say.* "Yes," she said, kissing him softly on the cheek.

"Yes, hello?" they heard Gracia say through the intercom.

"I have Ms. Weston and Mr. Fiducia," the driver said.

There was a pause. And then Lydia's voice came over the intercom, saying, "If they're from that idiot studio, tell them not to bother—we're not buying any!" And then Kate rolled down her window, thinking she heard in the distance . . .

Yep. In a moment there were two loud *thunks* against the inside of the gate and the heads of Cookie and Cupcake appeared over the top, snarling and barking their heads off.

"Jesus," the driver said. He turned around. "I'm sorry, I'm not sure what's going on here—she told me to bring you here."

Kate was laughing and so was Mark. "It's okay, she's just playing around."

"Cookie! Cupcake!" they heard Lydia shout. The dogs disappeared and Gracia came back on the intercom.

"The señora is most glad to see Señorita Weston and Señor Faith and Trust. Please drive in."

The driver, shaking his head, inched the car ahead as the gate swung open. "Better close that window back there," he called to Kate. "You never know."

"Kate," Mark suddenly said to her.

She looked at him.

"I love you."

"I love you too," she said.

"We're doing the right thing, aren't we?" he said.

"I know we are," she said.

He kissed her. Hard. And then backed off as they came around the drive.

"There she is," Kate said, spotting Lydia out front and waving to her.

Before the car even stopped, her door was flung open and Lydia and Gary and Noël were pulling her out for hugs, hellos, and kisses. While Kate was busy laughing and talking a mile a minute, Gary started tugging at the sleeve of her blouse. "Kate, Kate," he said, "we have news."

Kate stopped talking and looked at him.

Gary looked at Lydia.

Kate looked at Lydia.

"We're engaged to be married," Lydia said, taking Gary's hand.

Kate's mouth fell open.

"Told you it'd blow her mind," Noél said.

Kate was hugging Lydia an instant later—and then Gary, too, congratulating them, and Mark was shaking hands, saying congratulations.

Gracia came rushing out of the house. "Señorita Weston!" she cried, giving her a big hug. "Welcome to California!" And then she went over to "Señor Faith and Trust!" and gave him a big hug too.

The group slowly made its way through the house and down to the living room where, strung across it, was a paper banner that said in big block computer printout letters:

KATE & MARK, WELCOME TO L.A.

Standing by the living room stairs as they came in, looking a bit shy, was Holly Montvale. Kate smiled and Holly came forward, offering her hand. "I'm Holly," she said.

"Yes, I know, we met once before," Kate said, shaking her hand.

Holly leaned forward and added, quietly, "But you didn't meet me as Noél's friend." Then she stepped back, waiting for Kate's reaction.

Kate smiled and tightened her grip. So she was to be considered a real friend of Noél's. Kate couldn't help it then—she threw her arms around Holly and gave her a hug.

"Come on," Lydia said, pulling at Kate's arm, "I have a surprise for you, but first you have to say hi to everybody and introduce Mark."

Outside on the terrace were helium balloons—pink and white with ribbons streaming—and party decorations (picked out by someone who was probably about seven years old, since they included hats and horns to blow) and there was Allyson, playing dolls with Gracia's granddaughter, Cathy; there was the nanny, Judith; Billy was out on the tennis court playing with a friend; Imelda came out to shake hands hello and then resume her serving duties; Mark was introduced to Max and his wife, Sally; Skip and his wife, Jill; Aaron and his girlfriend; Wesley Hart and his girlfriend (whom Kate presumed he was tying up at night); six writers of "Cassandra's World" and their spouses and lovers; and many other production people, but no Mortimer Pallsner

("Whose charmed acquaintance we'll save only for office hours, thank you," Lydia said, prompting people to laugh).

After the introductions were made, Lydia turned to Kate and said, "And now there is one other person I'd like you to meet, Kate. Your new assistant."

Kate tried not to frown. "You hired my assistant?" she said. "*For me?*"

If Lydia sensed any irritation on Kate's part, she seemed utterly delighted by it. "Yes, I did."

"Hi, Kate," a voice said.

Kate blinked. She knew that voice. She turned around.

It was Sarah Steadwell.

Kate couldn't believe it.

Sarah laughed, coming forward. "Hi," she said again.

"Sarah!" Mark cried, hugging her and lifting her up off the ground.

"Sarah?" Kate said cautiously, moving over to them. "I'm so scared this is a dream I don't dare—"

"It's true! It's true!" Sarah said, flinging her arms around her. "I just got in yesterday!"

"And you're going to work with us?" Kate said, looking at her, holding Sarah's arms, still not believing this.

"And work on my master's part-time at night," Sarah said.

"UCLA?"

Sarah nodded. "And Kate, you wouldn't believe what they're paying me."

"Everything's unionized out here," Gary said to Kate. "Except producers—which is what you are."

Sarah whispered her salary in Kate's ear, prompting Kate's eyes to get very big. "You're kidding," she said.

"No," Sarah said. "So my cousin's going to come out too. I'm going to get us an apartment in Westwood."

As Sarah went on and on about the studio and UCLA and how Lydia had called her in New York out of the blue and then arranged everything, and Gary explained more about their offices at Bestar, Kate looked around for Lydia and saw that she had slipped away to sit near where Allyson and Cathy were playing. When Sarah and Gary were finished with their stories, Kate excused herself and went over to her.

"Lydia," Kate said, "how can I ever thank you?"

Lydia looked up from the Barbie doll she was fussing with and smiled. "Being there is all the thanks I have ever needed from you," she said. She looked down then, seemingly a little embarrassed by what she had just said, and zipped up the prom dress on Barbie. "Ever have one of these?"

"Sure," Kate said. "And Ken. And a car."

"Is that how you came to love convertibles?" Lydia asked her, looking up.

Kate smiled. "I don't know, maybe."

"Aunt Lyddie?" Allyson said, coming over. "Cathy says there's a doll that looks like you. Is that true?"

Lydia rolled her eyes. "Oh, it was supposed to, sweetheart," she said, brushing a strand of hair back off of Allyson's face, "but it was awful and so I wouldn't let them make the doll."

"But Cathy says there *is* a doll," Allyson persisted. "She said she *saw* it."

"Oh, thanks a lot, Cathy," Lydia called. "You like to see your poor aunt Lydia looking like an old hag, don't you?"

Cathy giggled.

"No, you're beautiful!" Allyson suddenly said, throwing her arms around Lydia's neck.

Over Allyson's shoulder, Lydia was smiling. "Oh, little one," she sighed, gently patting her back, "don't you know? All people who love are beautiful."

And Kate Weston smiled, knowing for sure that this was absolutely true.

ABOUT THE AUTHOR

Laura Van Wormer grew up in Darien, Connecticut, and graduated from the S. I. Newhouse School of Public Communications at Syracuse University. She is the author of two previous novels, *Riverside Drive* and *West End*, and has also written books with the writers and creators of the television shows "Dynasty," "Dallas," and "Knots Landing." Prior to her writing career she was a book editor with a leading New York publisher. She lives on Riverside Drive in Manhattan, spends summers in the Hamptons of Long Island, and makes frequent trips to Los Angeles.